With big dreams of being a published author since she was an eleven-year-old girl writing *Beverly Hills 90210* fan fiction before fan fiction was even a thing, **SHANN MCPHERSON** has been writing angsty, contemporary romances for most of her thirty-something years.

Living in sunny Queensland, Australia, when she's not writing Shann enjoys making memories with her husband and cheeky toddler son, drinking wine, and singing completely off-key to One Direction's entire discography.

Also by Shann McPherson

Where We Belong
Sweet Home Montana

The Long Way Home

SHANN MCPHERSON

ONE PLACE. MANY STORIES

HQ
An imprint of HarperCollins*Publishers* Ltd
1 London Bridge Street
London SE1 9GF

www.harpercollins.co.uk

HarperCollins*Publishers*
1st Floor, Watermarque Building, Ringsend Road
Dublin 4, Ireland

This paperback edition 2021

1
First published in Great Britain by
HQ, an imprint of HarperCollins*Publishers* Ltd 2021

Copyright © Shann McPherson 2021

Shann McPherson asserts the moral right to be
identified as the author of this work.
A catalogue record for this book is
available from the British Library.

ISBN: 9780008471354

To those who have ever lost themselves

Chapter 1

The atmosphere at the field was electric. The baseball diamond was illuminated by the bright glow of floodlights, the giant bulbs humming loudly. The bleachers were packed to capacity with excited parents and overzealous fans waving clappers, blowing hooters, their horns ringing through the air. This was accompanied by the lingering smell of corn dogs and other deep-fried foods hanging heavily in the night air.

March had brought with it a newfound warmth after the shrill cold of the winter months, but a chill persisted, which caused Maggie to tuck her hands between her knees as she searched the crowded stands.

She checked her watch for the fifth time in as many minutes, shaking her head to herself. *Where is he?* He wasn't just late; he was half an hour late. She pulled her cell phone from her handbag, but it only added to her frustrations to find the screen void of contact from him. No call, no text, no email, and God knows that man couldn't tear himself away from his inbox for longer than a few minutes. Her jaw clenched with annoyance.

"Dad's gonna miss it!"

Maggie glanced down to where her son, TJ, was devouring his hot dog with gusto, ketchup smeared all over his chin. His big blue eyes met hers and when he offered a cheeky grin, she couldn't help but smile despite the anger roiling deep inside her.

"He'll be here," she managed with as much confidence as she could muster. But deep down, that confidence was waning. Tom had called her earlier to say he'd been caught up in an unexpected and last-minute meeting, and that he would come straight to the high school from his office. He'd also told her that he was on his way. But that was forty minutes ago.

Maggie's gaze shifted in the direction of the main entry gate, the view shrouded by people waiting in line at the concession stands. Her knees bounced up and down as anxiety stirred low in her belly.

Tom had been missing moments like these more and more lately. For the last six months, at least, his work had managed to take priority over his children. Sure, he was a big-shot lawyer at one of the most prestigious firms in the city, but he'd promised. He'd promised, no matter what, he would be here tonight. It was his son's very first varsity baseball game. He'd been selected from the junior varsity team due to an injury. If Tom missed Jack's varsity debut, she could only imagine how devastated her teenage son would be.

A sudden flurry of excitement followed a thunderous roar, pulling Maggie from her thoughts. TJ jumped up onto the metal bench, screaming his big brother's name as the team ran out from the dugout. Maggie zeroed in on number four—her handsome son—and a proud smile spread over her face as she stood up, clapping and cheering with vigor. But then she saw Jack turn, taking in the bleachers from the pitcher's mound, his gaze almost instinctively settling upon her, and she could pinpoint the very moment he realized his father hadn't shown. That heartbreaking look of disappointment on his face was painfully obvious, even from high up in the stands.

But Jack was strong. Resilient. He always had been. Stoic. So much like his father. And his despondency was replaced by a tight-lipped smile that he quickly hid by pulling the brim of his ball cap ever lower, shielding the sadness in his eyes before joining the rest of his team. But Maggie knew her son better than anyone, and she could see it in the way his shoulders remained slightly hunched in defeat, the way his cleats dragged ever so slightly over the grass. He was crushed.

Maggie could handle Tom's neglect, she'd been putting up with it for a little while, she was almost used to his work taking precedence over her. But she refused to sit by and watch her husband neglect their sons. She refused to watch either of her sons cry tears Tom had caused.

You'd better have a damn good excuse this time, she thought with gritted teeth.

*

"You were so good, Jack!" TJ jumped up and down, praising his brother as they walked through the dimly lit parking lot.

Maggie bit back her smile as she glanced sideways at Jack, but her smile fell the moment her gaze landed upon him. He didn't look like a fifteen-year-old who'd just won his very first varsity baseball game. His head was bowed, shoulders hunched like he had more than just the weight of his gym bag resting on them. He kicked at a loose pebble on the pavement before glancing up at his mother as they arrived at the car. "Have you heard from Dad?"

Pressing her lips together, Maggie shook her head. She tried calling Tom a few times, but each call went straight to voicemail. "He probably just got caught up at the office." She continued with a little more conviction, "He landed a big case at work."

Jack rolled his eyes and muttered something under his breath, which she couldn't quite hear, but she decided not to press him. He was upset. And he had every right to be. He had been so excited since being selected to start on third for the varsity team at only fifteen: the youngest player in the school's history. All he wanted was to show off a little in front of his father, make him proud. And yet Tom wasn't there to see him hit his very first home run, propelling the team to an unexpected victory at the bottom of the seventh.

Maggie sighed as Jack got into the front passenger seat without so much as another word, but she forced a smile onto her face as she waited for TJ to climb up into the back. He was ten with a solid build, but short for his age, like a little pit bull. While he insisted he no longer needed his mother's help getting into the car, she always stood guard, making sure he buckled up safely much to his dramatic dismay.

The mood in the car was low as Maggie settled into the driver's seat. With caution, she glanced at Jack, finding him staring out the window, his eyes empty, face long. When she checked the rear-view mirror, she saw TJ staring at her in the reflection, and she offered him a wink which made him smile, causing her heart to warm.

"Who wants to go home and make ice cream sundaes?" She knew her cheery tone sounded forced as it rang through the uncomfortable silence, but she had to try to lighten the mood somehow.

"I do! I do!" TJ hollered, his hand held in the air for effect.

Maggie flashed her youngest son a knowing smile. Of course he did, that much was a given. She turned to Jack. "Jack?"

"Whatever," he murmured without looking at her.

*

Belmont was a small hamlet in Middlesex County, twenty minutes outside of Boston. And the drive from the high school through the village to their home took all of about eight minutes. Maggie tapped her hand against the steering wheel to the tune of the song playing across the radio, temporarily lost in the moment. But when she made the turn onto the immaculate, tree-lined street, where nearly identical colonial homes sat atop manicured frontages, her brows knitted together at the glare of flashing lights illuminating the night's darkness.

"Is that the cops?" Jack shifted in his seat, leaning closer to the windshield.

Maggie's heart sank into the pit of her stomach and she didn't know why. She eased her foot off the gas, rolling to a stop when she noticed two police cruisers parked outside their home. She felt a painful pinch in her chest, but somehow managed to unfasten her seatbelt with shaking hands.

"You boys wait here," she whispered under a rushed breath.

The night air was cool, the breeze whipping against her heated cheeks as she walked past one of the police vehicles, eyeing it dubiously. She continued up the steep driveway to the front porch where two uniformed officers were standing in the shadows.

"Can I h-help you?" Her words wavered, caught in the back of her throat, and her voice trembled.

The officers turned, the older of the two speaking first. "Mrs. Morris?"

She nodded once, tentatively glancing between them. "Yes, I'm Maggie Morris."

When they stepped down off the porch, the glow of the curb-side lamppost illuminated their faces, highlighting the blatant look of sorrow in their eyes as they stopped just shy of her on the flagstone path.

"Ma'am, I'm afraid we have some bad news," the other officer began, his voice gruff and full of strained discomfort as if this were the last place he wanted to be on a Friday night. "Your . . . husband, Thomas?"

Maggie nodded again. "Tom." He always hated Thomas; it reminded him of his father.

"He's um . . . I'm afraid he's been involved in a car accident."

With her heart racing painfully in her chest, Maggie searched the man's face for something, anything, but she came up blank. "W-where is he? I-is he . . . is he *okay*?" Her voice was hoarse, suddenly incredulous and desperate. She'd spoken to Tom less than two hours ago. He was fine then. Of course he was okay. He had to be.

The officers glanced at one another, and she watched as they shared some kind of silent understanding. Why were they stalling? What were they not telling her? She clutched at her chest, and could feel her heart beating so hard, so fast she could barely breathe through the rapid thundering.

"No, ma'am." The first officer reluctantly shook his head, his eyes sincere when they met hers. "I'm afraid he's not okay."

Burning tears pricked Maggie's eyes. An overwhelming panic she could hardly contain consumed her from the inside. When her knees went weak, she almost fell to the ground, but one of the officers swooped in just in time, collecting her, holding her upright.

She turned, looking over her shoulder to find TJ and Jack being assisted out of the car by two other uniformed police officers. TJ was inconsolable, tears streamed down his beet-red cheeks. Jack was yelling out for her, *screaming* for her. She tried to call out to them, to tell them that everything was fine, that everything was going to be fine. She tried to scream but she had nothing. No voice, no air, no breath, nothing. She'd been rendered entirely useless and uncomfortably numb. And then, when it all became far too much, the world around her turned darker than it had ever been before as the blackness consumed her.

Chapter 2

Maggie had signed her name so many times over the last month, the signature she'd had since marrying Tom in the District Courthouse of Rhode Island sixteen years ago was now almost unrecognizable. Nothing more than an inconsistent scribble that would unlikely hold up in a court of law, if it ever got to that. But she continued signing, regardless. Paper after paper, desperate to get everything finalized in the hope that it might help her start to move on.

Her husband was dead. At thirty-six years old she was a widow. Even now, a whole month later, she couldn't believe he was gone.

She dropped the pen once she'd finished scrawling on the final form, giving her cramping wrist a vigorous shake. Sliding the stack of documents across the shiny walnut table, she met James's sad eyes, finding him smiling at her. He was just trying to be kind—she knew that—but that smile flared her anger and resentment.

She'd known James more than ten years. He and Tom had gone through law school together. They'd started as interns at the same questionable strip mall ambulance-chaser firm. They went on to top their class and then make junior associates at one of Boston's most prestigious law firms six months after one another.

But James was still here. Tom was not. And that smile James now wore, the one laced with pity and sadness, didn't help one bit despite whatever good intentions were behind it.

"How are you?"

Maggie heaved a sigh, her eyes flitting to the legal papers on the table. "I'm okay," she lied. It was a lie she'd perfected over the last few weeks.

"You should come over for dinner sometime. Bring the kids," James suggested with a shrug of one of his broad shoulders. "Marissa would love to see you."

She swallowed the lump that seemed to have permanently wedged itself at the back of her throat over the last month. With a noncommittal nod, she offered the sincerest smile she could manage as silence thick with tension settled in the air between them.

"It gets easier, Mags. I promise," James said after a few beats, his words tentative, like he wasn't sure he should say them.

Maggie almost laughed. She couldn't even begin to count the number of times she'd heard those exact words over the last month. If she had to hazard a guess, it would've been at least a thousand. Neighbors, parents she hardly knew and rarely talked to while waiting at school pick-up, people at the grocery store. It was ridiculous how many times she'd been forced to listen to that exact same shell of a promise from people who only said those words just to say them. Filling the uncomfortable void of silence that hung around her wherever she went.

"When?" Maggie asked.

Of course she didn't expect James to be able to give her an answer. God, she didn't *want* an answer. Frankly, she was terrified of whatever it might be. The truth was it hadn't gotten better yet. Not even a little bit. And it'd been a month. So, when was it supposed to get better? Tomorrow? A year from now? Ten years? When would she finally be able to wake up in the morning and not spend the first fifteen minutes of her day smothering herself with a pillow so her sons couldn't hear her cry?

8

James scrubbed a hand over his angled jaw, his shoulders falling as he glanced down at the fancy gold pen resting on the table between them, clearly avoiding Maggie's eyes.

That was something else she was becoming accustomed to: people's sudden inability to meet her gaze, as if looking into her eyes was too difficult for *them*.

"I should go." Maggie stood, hitching the strap of her handbag onto her shoulder. "TJ has a therapist appointment."

"Little guy's still not sleeping, huh?" James asked, buttoning his suit jacket as he rose to his feet.

"He sleeps," she muttered with a shrug. "He just wakes up screaming at least three times a night."

"Poor kid." James shook his head, joining Maggie at the end of the long board table. With a comforting hand placed upon her shoulder, he walked her out of the room. "You know, I can always stop by and pick him up. Maybe take him to get a bite to eat, or to a Sox game?"

With her lips pressed firmly together in the semblance of a smile, she nodded once. But she refused to commit to anything. TJ was far from fragile; at ten years old he was a stocky, slightly uncouth brute. But he was still her baby. And he was broken in the worst possible way. Four weeks ago, he would have jumped at the chance to go see a Red Sox game. Now, he could barely make it out of bed in the mornings, not even when the new little league season began. What was once an obsession with baseball, bordering on unhealthy, was suddenly no more than a dusty mitt and a grass-stained ball he used to throw around in the backyard with his dad; a ball and a mitt that now sat tucked away in a darkened corner of his bedroom.

James and Maggie stopped in the sleek foyer. She could feel the curious gaze of the blonde receptionist bore into the back of her head, but she managed to ignore her. She didn't like to be rude, but she couldn't handle yet another look of pity accompanied by a sad, contrite smile.

"I'll get everything filed by the end of the week." James looked down at Maggie, placing a hand on her arm. He squeezed gently, steadying her with an imploring gaze. "Please don't hesitate to call me if you need anything. Any time, day or night, I don't care."

When the threat of tears started to burn her eyes, Maggie averted her gaze, looking down at the shiny marble floor. She nodded, but then she felt a pair of strong arms come around her as James pulled her in close, embracing her unexpectedly. He was just doing what most friends would do in such a situation, she knew that, but she couldn't stop herself from recoiling, her arms lax at her sides, hands balling into fists. He needed this more than she did. So, she allowed it.

After an awkward moment, Maggie stepped out of the embrace. She forced her chin up, meeting his eyes, and she smiled tightly when he told her he'd be in touch. She responded that she'd give him a call. But the likelihood was that she wouldn't give him a call. James was Tom's friend, Tom's colleague. The sleek foyer in which they stood, in the sky-scraping building on the busy city street, was Tom's life.

Without Tom, Maggie didn't have any reason to exist in James's world. But she smiled anyway. And, with a slight wave, she turned and continued out through the glass doors to the elevator bank, desperate to be alone even if only for the twenty seconds it took to return to the ground floor.

Outside, Maggie was met with a dreary afternoon which matched her mood, the threat of rain looming heavily above in the low-hanging clouds—March weather at its finest.

She navigated the busy sidewalk, hurrying to catch the flashing walk signal to make it across the street to the parking garage. As she started down the concrete stairwell to the basement level where she'd parked, her cell started ringing from the bottom of her handbag. She struggled with the contents of her purse, finally retrieving the vibrating device just in time. But when she noticed the familiar number flashing on the screen, she stopped abruptly, cursing under her breath.

"Maggie speaking," she answered with a blunt, knowing tone.

"Maggie, it's me, Brian."

What now? Exhaling a heavy breath, she closed her eyes and counted to three before she allowed herself to speak.

"You're going to have to come pick him up," Brian continued over the phone. "Principal Hendry's suspended him for three days."

As anger caused her blood to boil just beneath the surface of her skin, she shook her head to herself. "What's he done *this* time?"

"Another fight, I'm afraid." Brian sighed heavily; he sounded almost as defeated as Maggie felt. "Broke a kid's nose."

"Jesus . . ." She closed her eyes a moment, pinching the bridge of her nose. "I'll be there as soon as I can."

*

Maggie's grip on the steering wheel was tight. So tight she could feel the dry skin around her knuckles stretch and strain, turning a stark shade of white. As she pulled up to a stop in the faculty parking lot of the high school, she forced herself to take a moment to compose what she could of her emotions. With a few deep breaths, she watched as the rain drops trickled haphazardly down the windshield in chaotic streaks, an accurate representation of her mind's state.

Out of the three of them, Tom's passing had affected Jack the most. Before, he was so kind and thoughtful, selfless and gentle. He was a great kid. Now, he was almost impossible. His mood swings were unpredictable and terrifying. He snapped at Maggie, at TJ. He'd quit the baseball team. He skipped school at least once a week and journeyed into the city to do God knows what with God knows whom. His grades had dropped significantly. All he did now was sit in his bedroom every night—and all day on the weekends—playing video games while listening to offensive heavy metal music. Lately, he'd been violently lashing out. Never at Maggie, and never at his little brother. But he'd been getting into fights at school with boys who used to be his best friends.

Maggie tried to get him to go to therapy, to talk about the warring emotions that were ravaging him from the inside, but he refused. Brian, the student counsellor, had been keeping an eye out for him at school, but now that Principal Hendry had stepped in and enforced a suspension that would likely remain on Jack's transcripts, Maggie was at a complete loss about what to do.

With a fortifying breath, she forced herself out of the car and hurried through the rain and up the front steps of the administration building.

*

After a long discussion with Brian and Principal Hendry, Maggie walked ahead with Jack trailing sheepishly behind her. He refused to look at her, and she chose not to look at him, not to say a word. She didn't know if she could trust herself to say anything. She needed to let the proverbial dust settle. She was far too angry right now, and ashamed. And she hated that; she'd never been ashamed of either of her kids before.

As she drove the short distance from Belmont High School to the elementary school, she could feel Jack's fleeting glances in her direction from across the silent car, but she refused to indulge him by meeting his eyes. She didn't give anything away as she concentrated on the wet roads ahead while her mind raced a million miles a minute, her jaw fixed tight.

She didn't really know what to do. She was at a loss. TJ was a shell of the vibrant boy he was. Jack was quickly beginning to lose his damn mind. Maggie was trying to keep it all together for the two of them, but deep down it really didn't feel like she had much left to give. She was terrified that her family—her whole life—was falling apart, and there was nothing she could do about it. And at that thought tears pricked her eyes, but she blinked them away, willing herself to stay strong. Just long enough to collect TJ from school, take him to his appointment, make it home, cook dinner, tidy up and drag herself upstairs to crawl into bed where she could finally cry the tears she so desperately needed to release.

"I'm sorry, Mom."

Maggie blinked once at the sound of Jack's timid, broken voice. She knew she shouldn't get into it right now but she also knew she couldn't ignore him.

"You *broke* a boy's *nose* . . ." was all she could manage, still shocked by what had happened at the school. She glanced briefly at him before turning back to the taillights of the car in front.

"Why?" She shook her head, exasperated, incredulous and everything in between because she couldn't for the life of her begin to understand. Violence had never been condoned in their household. TJ and Jack had been taught at a young age to use their words, that violence is wrong. This was so unlike him. It had to be some kind of dangerous combination of the unrelenting anger coursing through him and those damn video games he spent all his time playing.

Jack sighed loudly, and she could see him crack his knuckles from the corner of her eye.

"*Why*, Jack?" Maggie pressed, a little louder and slightly incensed as she grew increasingly impatient for an answer.

"He looked at me the wrong way."

She gaped at him, her eyes wide. "He *looked* at you the wrong way?" A humorless laugh slipped from her lips. "What does that even *mean*? How does somebody *look* at you the *wrong* way?"

She noticed his jaw tightening. He was clenching his teeth, staring straight ahead with a sullen look on his face, and she was taken aback by just how much he looked like his father right at that moment. He was the vision of Tom; just as stubborn, too.

"Do you think this is *fun* for me?" Maggie continued before

Jack could even attempt an answer. "Do you think I like having to come pick you up because you've been suspended for *fighting*? For breaking a kid's *nose*?" Her voice was shrill as it rang through the silence, cracking with emotion. "Do you think I like calling TJ's therapist and telling her we're running late, that I can't bring my ten-year-old son to his appointment on time because my other son, who's old enough to know better by the way, is getting into fights at school because some kid *looked* at him the wrong way?"

Jack turned away, staring out the window. "It's always about *TJ* . . ."

Maggie snapped her mouth shut at the sound of his murmured words. She doubted he had meant for her to hear him. But she did. Loud and heartbreakingly clear. She inhaled deeply, the breath shuddering through her as she stared out at the gray afternoon, the red stop light casting an ominous glow over the busy intersection.

She wanted to say something to him, but she didn't know what. She wanted to tell him that he was wrong. That it wasn't always about TJ. That it was about both of them. That they were her whole world equally. But the signal turned green and the traffic started creeping forward. So, without saying anything, she continued driving through town toward the elementary school, realizing now more than ever just how much her sons needed her.

Chapter 3

After an almost silent dinner with the boys, the air thick and weighty with palpable tension, Maggie found comfort in a glass of cabernet once they'd gone off to bed. She locked up downstairs and tiptoed back up with her wine, careful not to make a sound as she moved past TJ's room.

She continued into the master suite at the end of the hallway and closed the door quietly. With a sip of wine, she stood looking over the bedroom she'd once shared with her husband.

Not so long ago this was a space she had loved. One filled with so many beautiful memories. It was all theirs—their escape from the boys when they needed it. But now, without Tom to hide out with and watch movies or read books, or just lie together and talk about their day, the master suite suddenly felt far too big, too empty and cold. In fact, nowadays, the entire house felt empty and cold. It was no longer the home it once was.

Bed was calling Maggie's name, but after a day like today she knew the minute she crawled beneath the covers there was no way she would be able to sleep. She'd spent too many nights lying in that bed, staring up at the ceiling, and watching shadows cast from outside as they danced across the room. Mocking her with every minute she was left sleepless and wide awake. And with nothing but her own haunting thoughts to keep her company.

Tonight, she wanted to be close to Tom. She wanted to feel him, smell him, touch him one last time. She wasn't completely deranged and knew she couldn't. So, for the next best thing, she walked through to the closet and paused in the doorway, glancing at his clothes. Racks of impeccably tailored suits stared back at her. Rifling through the collection, she pulled a charcoal suit jacket from its hanger, catching a waft of that painfully familiar scent. Tom's scent. Painfully familiar because she missed it like crazy, and every time she caught a whiff of it in the house or on a random stranger passing her on the street, her traitorous mind would trick her into thinking that he was still there, that the last month had never happened.

Lifting the lapels of the jacket to her nose, she breathed in deep, closing her eyes as fond memories of her husband flooded through her. For as long as she could remember, since the day she'd first met Tom on that blustery fall day back in college, he'd smelled the same. Spicy with the slightest hint of cocoa. It was a scent she'd memorized, one she could smell from a mile away, even more so now that he was gone.

She looked down at the jacket, gently trailing a fingertip along the lapel, and she managed a sad smile. Thankfully, it hadn't been dry cleaned since he last wore it. Perhaps she could add this to her stash. The stash no one knew about which contained a few items like the T-shirt he'd last worn to bed that she kept tucked under her pillow, so she could hold on to it on the loneliest of nights. It had long lost his scent, but it felt like him; if a T-shirt could feel like another person. That T-shirt was also the last thing she'd seen Tom wearing before he died. He'd left so early that morning, before Maggie had woken up. She couldn't possibly bring herself to let go of it, whether it smelled of him or not. But now that she had this suit jacket, and it still held his comforting scent, perhaps she could cuddle it at night instead, so that when she closed her eyes and breathed in that intoxicating aroma, she could pretend Tom was still right there with her.

Basking in the scent it provided, her eyes fluttered closed as she imagined Tom's eyes, his beautiful smile. She cuddled it close. But then she felt something in the breast pocket. She reached inside, feeling something with her fingertips before pulling out what appeared to be a cocktail napkin. She checked it to make sure it wasn't anything important, noticing the familiar logo of the Empire, a boutique hotel downtown.

At first, she didn't think anything of it. The Empire had one of the best cocktail lounges in Boston. It wasn't unusual for Tom to catch up with clients and colleagues for drinks there after work every now and again. But when she turned the napkin over and caught sight of the unfamiliar handwriting on the back, instantly she felt her heart lodge itself at the back of her throat.

The Oakmont. Room 612. B xoxo

What the hell? Maggie stared at the napkin for an unreasonably long moment, trying to make sense of the words written in a neat, obviously feminine scrawl.

It had to be a mistake. Surely. Perhaps it was just trash, a discarded napkin he'd picked up by mistake. Maybe it was meant for someone else. She racked her brain as she continued staring down at the napkin, her hands trembling uncontrollably.

Who the hell is B? She frowned as her mind began to get carried away with itself.

Placing the jacket and the note aside, she pulled the matching slacks from the hanger, rifling through the pockets for something, anything, but she came out empty-handed. Nothing. Not even an errant ball of lint.

B xoxo. The delicate lettering glared back at her from the Empire napkin, goading her. And of course, she immediately thought the worst. What was she supposed to think?

Suddenly her heart was racing at a violent pace. She clutched the napkin in her hand and hurried out of the stifling closet to the sitting area by the bay window.

She fell to her knees beside the archive box of Tom's belongings that had been delivered to the house from the office a few days earlier. She hadn't gone through it yet. She assumed it contained no more than a few old picture frames he used to keep on his desk and maybe a planner. And when she lifted the lid, that's exactly what she found inside. But, beneath the photo of her and Tom on their shotgun wedding day, and another of her with the boys, and Tom's gilt-framed university degrees, at the very bottom of the box, Maggie found his personal laptop.

With a tremulous breath, she pulled the MacBook out and placed it onto the suede ottoman, staring at the device for an excruciatingly long beat. She knew she shouldn't think too much into it. Surely, it was nothing more than a misunderstanding. It was more than likely some random napkin left on the table. Probably left there by the person before Tom. Perhaps he didn't even know it had anything written on the back of it, and maybe he just tucked it into his pocket without thinking.

But Maggie couldn't ignore the dread dwelling in her chest. She felt sick. Like she might actually be sick. Panic coursed through her at warp speed, mixing uncomfortably low in her belly with anxiety and trepidation.

Was this actually happening? Was she really on her knees right now, with a racing heart trapped at the back of her throat? Staring at her dead husband's laptop while wondering if she could possibly hack into it and find out if this B person was of any relevance to him? And what if they were? What if she found what she was desperately hoping she wouldn't? What then?

With a hand pressed against her churning stomach, Maggie racked her brain, wondering if her inkling could in fact be real. Tom was the love of her life. He was her one and only true love. They had been meant to be together ever since they literally ran into one another all those years ago. She glanced down at the note in her hand. Had it all been a lie? Could Tom really have been doing something unimaginable, unforgivable, behind her back?

With a deep breath, Maggie opened the laptop and powered it up. The screen illuminated to a background shot of the turquoise ocean from their last family vacation in Puerto Vallarta over the New Year, a few months before Tom passed.

When his name appeared on the screen above the password box, she lifted a hand to her mouth and idly chewed on her pinkie fingernail while she considered every single possible password option. Who knew what she would find? If she'd even find anything. All she knew was that she had to know the truth, whether she liked it or not.

*

The sun was beginning to rise, painting the sky with its rays as they broke through the looming clouds smattered with mauve, pink and peach. And Maggie was still sitting on the floor, staring bleary-eyed at the laptop screen in front of her. Caught deep within the darkness of the rabbit hole that had consumed her for the last six hours. A rabbit hole which led to the heartbreaking confirmation of her husband's infidelity.

Months and months of messages and email correspondence between Tom and the firm's beautiful blonde receptionist, Rebecca Holmes—or Becca, as she seemed to be affectionately known to him—glared back at Maggie. Obscene text messages. Explicit picture messages. Flirty emails. It went back at least six months before Tom's death. Her husband had been cheating on her, living some sort of secret double life.

Becca,
I've booked a room at the Marmont on Sunday night. I
told Maggie I'm catching an early flight to Chicago so I can
get a start on the witness interviews on Monday morning.

I've asked the concierge to leave a key for you at the front desk. Room 704. Wear that sexy red dress that shows off those beautiful tits. You know what it does to me.
Tom

Maggie winced at the words glaring in front of her. They burned her skin like the residual sting from a slap to the face. What hurt the most was that he had lied to her about catching a plane halfway across the country. And now all she could think was what if something had happened to that flight? What if it had gone down, leaving her to imagine her husband, the father of her sons, had perished in a plane wreck? And yet, the whole time, he'd been holed up in a hotel room with his mistress instead? Anger flared in the pit of her belly.

Tom,
Thank you for the necklace. I've never been given real diamonds before. I love it. You're so good to me. I can still feel you inside me. Do you think we could sneak into the bathroom after your partner meeting without being noticed?
Becca xoxo

Of course he bought her diamonds, Maggie sneered in disgust. Bile began climbing up the back of her throat as hot tears of rage burned her eyes.

But she couldn't stop reading. In fact, the farther she delved the more she discovered how deep her husband had been embroiled in a tawdry, illicit affair with a twenty-four-year-old woman. He'd taken her on weekends away when he'd told Maggie he was off working. He even had keys to her apartment. The nights Maggie had spent alone in bed, thinking Tom was busy working, when all along he'd been with this woman.

Slamming the laptop closed, Maggie released a shaky breath. Sitting back against the armchair behind her, she hugged her knees to her chest, staring out the window. Suddenly captivated by the breaking dawn, she watched as the sun illuminated the morning with an eerily foreboding glow.

So many scenarios played in her head. So many questions that would likely forever go unanswered. But one thing was certain: the man she called her husband and her best friend, the man she loved more than any man, the man she'd spent the last month mourning, was no more than a liar and a cheat.

Maggie's already broken heart was now shattered and she didn't believe it could ever be repaired. She wanted to scream. She wanted to throw something, anything. As she took a look around the bedroom she'd once shared with Tom, her skin pricked painfully. It was all a lie. Everything. His love, his words, the way he would look at her as if she were the only woman in the entire world, it had been nothing but a goddamn lie.

Chapter 4

Maggie had been on autopilot all morning. She'd washed her face, brushed her teeth, changed from one pair of jeans and a sweatshirt to another pair of jeans and a different sweatshirt. She'd then proceeded downstairs in a total daze, trying so hard to act like nothing was wrong. She'd cooked the boys breakfast like she did every day, dropped them at school, and then afterwards, she went off to the grocery store like she did every Wednesday morning.

But today was different. As she ambled aimlessly up and down every aisle she was almost catatonic, like a zombie, staring straight ahead at nothing in front of her while filling the cart with items she didn't need, to the tune of some generic pop song playing through the muffled speakers in the ceiling.

The monotony of the grocery store afforded her time to think. Time to try and come to terms with the gravity of the situation she was forced to deal with. Her husband had been cheating on her. Her husband, whom she had loved more than life itself, had been having a sordid affair with another woman. Her husband, the father of her children, had betrayed her in the worst possible way.

If Tom were still here, Maggie would have tossed his clothes out onto the lawn with dramatic flair. Kicked his sorry ass to the proverbial curb and made a big scene of it for all the nosy neighbors to pretend not to watch and then gossip about afterwards. But Tom wasn't here. He was gone. And less than twenty-four hours ago she'd been mourning him, wondering if and when things might get easier, wondering when her broken heart might finally begin to start healing. Now, she didn't quite know what to think, how to act, what to do or say.

It'd always been just the two of them. Tom and Maggie. Now it was just her, and the memories of her husband and the love they shared were suddenly tainted. She didn't have any friends of her own. She'd moved to Rhode Island from Michigan so she could attend art school. But then she got pregnant and went on to become a young wife and a mother at nineteen. When they moved from Rhode Island to Boston, so Tom could attend law school, Maggie was a stay-at-home mom to a toddler with no time to make friends. As the years went on, all her so-called girlfriends were just wives of Tom's friends or colleagues.

Maggie's mother had passed away from lung cancer not long after Jack had been born, and Maggie had never known her father. She had no real family, only Tom's sister who she'd never gotten along with, and his father, a wealthy lawyer who'd retired to Boca Raton and only bothered to see them once a year, sometimes every other year. He was the kind of man who believed a trust fund in his grandsons' names for when they reached twenty-one, and a card with some money in it every Christmas and birthday, helped to cross off his obligatory grandparent duties. Needless to say, he never had much to do with his own son, either. Tom and his father's relationship was strained to say the least. They rarely saw him when Tom was alive, and it was unlikely they would see him now that Tom was gone.

Maggie had no one. No family. No friends. Her whole life had been her husband and her kids. They were all she ever needed or wanted. Sure, she had acquaintances, women she would catch up with every now and again for lunch, but no solid relationships outside of the four walls of her home. It suddenly felt as if a big part of her life had been a lie. Since Tom's death, she'd felt like a shadow of her former self. But now that she knew the truth, after a month of unrelenting tears and insufferable heartache, not only did she feel depleted, she felt like a damn fool.

"Maggie?"

Maggie stopped. She knew that voice all too well. In fact, it almost caused a shiver to run down her spine. Reluctantly, she glanced over her shoulder. When she saw the familiar redhead approach from the deli, she felt her entire body tense, her grip on the shopping cart tightened to the point where her nails were digging painfully into the heels of her palms.

Catherine Dewitt was certainly not the kind of woman Maggie felt like dealing with today, or any other day for that matter.

"Hi, Catherine . . ." Maggie muttered through gritted teeth, forcing a smile she knew didn't look genuine at all.

Catherine stopped in front of her, her head cocked to the side, that same condescending look in her green eyes which only accentuated the pitiful smile pulling at her cosmetically plumped lips. "Sweetheart, what are you doing *here*?"

"Groceries," Maggie answered, glancing at her cart full of items, as if it were obvious. Smoothing her hair back from her face, she looked Catherine up and down.

In comparison to Catherine, Maggie was a total mess. Where Catherine was preened to perfection, dressed head to toe in designer workout wear straight from the country club Pilates studio, Maggie looked like death warmed up twice in the micro-wave: unkempt hair twisted into a knot on top of her head, scuffed Converse, faded jeans and an old gray sweatshirt with the *Jurassic Park* logo printed on the front which, now that she looked at it, she was almost certain was TJ's. She sighed. Who was she kidding? Even on her most glamorous day, Maggie would pale against a woman like Catherine.

"Darling, should you really be out and about?" Catherine reached out a perfectly manicured hand, touching Maggie's arm.

What am I? Maggie thought derisively. *A goddamn invalid?*

"You know the girls and I are only a phone call away," Catherine continued. "I can do your groceries for you."

The girls? Maggie was forced to suppress an eyeroll. Catherine used the term as if they were her closest friends when, in fact, the *girls* were nothing more than a group of wives and girlfriends of Belmont's most successful men, most of whom Maggie couldn't stand.

Tom had been one of those successful men. It had been his goal since graduating law school. To own the big house. To drive the expensive car. To be invited to all the exclusive events. And, for all intents and purposes, he'd made it. Ironically, he was a carbon copy of his father, the one man he loathed the most.

But Maggie had been right there by his side—the perfect little trophy wife. She had hated every minute of it, of course. Associating with entitled, self-important women such as Catherine Dewitt was never high on her list of priorities, but she had felt obligated to conform because she loved her husband, and he would have been disappointed otherwise.

As Catherine's concern dissipated and she began talking animatedly about something she'd heard on the proverbial grapevine of Belmont gossip, Maggie tuned out completely. She watched how the woman's pupils dilated with unbridled excitement with each word. She lowered her voice every so often, leaning in close so the sordid details of her gossip wouldn't be overheard by the other shoppers in the store. Belmont was a thriving community, but the elite inner circle was small.

And at that thought, Maggie's heart came to a crashing halt in her chest.

What if the details of Tom's affair somehow managed to get out?

Her mind flashed with an image of Catherine whispering about Maggie's business to someone else in the aisles of this very grocery store, or the nail salon, or one of the many designer clothing boutiques that dotted the main promenade. And it suddenly felt as if she couldn't breathe.

What if her boys found out?

TJ and Jack loved and idolized their father. Tom had been—and still was—their hero. And despite his flaws and what he'd done to Maggie, he'd worked so hard to have the kind of relationship with his sons that he never got to experience with his own father. Jack and TJ couldn't find out the truth. It would kill them.

Panic settled low in Maggie's stomach as she began to imagine the worst.

"Are you okay, sweetie?"

Blinking a few times, Maggie shook her head in the hope that it might snap her out of the unwelcome reverie. Her gaze zeroed in on Catherine to find a genuine look of concern in her eyes.

Clearing the bubble of emotion from her throat, she forced a wavering smile. "Yeah . . . sorry." She looked around, for what she didn't know, her cheeks heating, the skin at the back of her neck prickling. She glanced at her shopping cart loaded with food, and her heart raced. "Actually . . . I'm n-not feeling very well."

"You're white as a ghost!" Catherine shrieked incredulously before calling for assistance.

A stock boy came running from somewhere, a concerned look on his face as he glanced from Catherine to Maggie and back again. Maggie couldn't hear their exchange through the loud whooshing of her pulse in her ears. Catherine said something to the college-aged boy and he nodded with an understanding smile, taking the shopping cart from Maggie's death-like grip. Before she was able to say or do anything, Catherine helped Maggie out of the store with an arm secured around her waist.

Outside, the rain was coming down hard, puddles pooling in the parking lot. But Maggie could breathe again. She placed a hand over her chest, feeling every erratic beat of her heart beneath her palm as she glanced sideways at Catherine. The woman still had a hold of her, a stark look of worry marring her otherwise flawless face.

"I'm fine," Maggie managed through the lump in her throat. "Just a little dizzy is all, sorry."

"Please don't apologize. You *poor* thing," Catherine said with an overly condescending smile. "You've had a difficult few weeks." Her eyes trailed Maggie up and down before she added, "And goodness, it looks like you've lost at least ten pounds!"

Maggie nodded as Catherine's words grated on her. She was so sick of the pity, the sympathy. It was no longer warranted. Now, she just wanted it all to stop, to go away. To end.

"I've asked the store to deliver your groceries to the house." Catherine pointed back through the glass windows before giving Maggie another close look. "Are you *sure* you're going to be okay?"

She wanted to say no. That she wouldn't be okay. That she would never be okay ever again. But she didn't. Instead, she said, "I'm fine" because that was easier.

Avoiding Catherine's scrupulous stare, Maggie focused on the parking lot. All she wanted was to get the hell out of there, away from the likes of Catherine Dewitt. Gossip was that woman's forte and she was almost certain the self-professed Queen Bee of Belmont would be able to see straight through Maggie's thinly veiled melancholy sooner or later. She simply couldn't risk lingering any longer.

"Thanks, Catherine." Maggie reached into her purse, pulling out her keys.

"Are you okay to drive?" Catherine asked, eyeing her warily.

"I'm fine." Placating the woman's concerns with a tight-lipped smile, Maggie turned away before any more could be said. With her head down in the rain, she hurried through the lot to her car, desperate to get away from Catherine's prying eyes.

*

27

She should have gone home. Straight home. She needed to calm down. She needed to be alone to cry, or scream, or punch something. Anything to release the pent-up aggression of the chaotic emotions creating havoc deep down inside. But Maggie didn't go home. Instead, she found herself parked in the loading zone right out the front of the building that had been, until not so long ago, home to her husband's office.

Her heart raced. Her stomach twisted. Her palms, gripping the steering wheel, were clammy as she stared out through the windshield, the rain pelting hard against the glass.

She took a moment to consider her options.

Sure, she could've burned the Empire napkin, deleted the emails and the text messages. She could have continued living a lie as the once doting wife and now widow of the late Tom Morris. But the problem was she knew the truth, and it was gnawing at her like a rabid dog out for blood.

Maggie knew she was teetering on the verge of dangerous territory, but, for some reason, she just had to do this. She needed that confirmation, and she needed to see it in the eyes of the only surviving offender. So, she forced herself out of the car and, without another moment's hesitation, she marched right up to that building with every last sliver of determination she could summon.

Chapter 5

All eyes were fixed on Maggie. Of course she looked out of place, surrounded by corporate types eyeing her curiously, no doubt wondering what the frazzled, slightly unhinged-looking woman wearing a ten-year-old's *Jurassic Park* sweatshirt was doing in their elevator. But she didn't care. And when the robotic voice cut through the awkward silence to announce the twenty-first floor, she proceeded off the elevator with her chin held high in a show of confidence she didn't really feel before she came to an abrupt stop in the lobby.

Peering in through the glass doors brandishing the firm's logo, Maggie saw her.

She was perched at the sleek reception desk. Perfectly styled blonde hair. Flawlessly made-up. Rebecca Holmes looked as if she didn't have a single care in the world as she typed something into her computer, laughing with whoever was on the receiving end of the dainty headset she was talking into. Her carefree smile caused Maggie's hands to ball into trembling fists at her sides, but she managed to maintain what little composure she had left as she continued through the doors with unyielding defiance in every one of her strides.

Rebecca glanced up mid-conversation and Maggie met her curious gaze as she approached the desk. All she could think about was how this woman had been in her house. Memories of a brief encounter they'd shared at the wake of Tom's funeral flashed through her mind. Rebecca had been in Maggie's house with tears in her eyes, supporting her like she gave a damn.

In the flash of an instant, so fleeting Maggie almost missed it, Rebecca's face fell, her cheeks paled ever so slightly. But she was quick to recover, plastering that same well-rehearsed smile onto her face. She flashed a set of straight, gleaming white teeth that Maggie suddenly wanted to punch right out of her mouth. And it was that unexpected yearning to physically hurt this woman that terrified Maggie the most; she had never been a violent person.

"Can you please hold for a moment?" Rebecca asked the person on the line in a saccharine voice that dripped with insincerity. "Thank you."

Maggie waited, looking down at the beautiful blonde as her gaze lifted to set on her, fake lashes fluttering innocently. "Mrs. Morris." She smiled. "How can I help you?"

The greeting hung awkwardly in the air as Maggie stared at the woman. A million thoughts swirled around in her dangerously conflicted head, her heart hammered painfully in the cavity of her chest.

Rebecca's dark blonde eyebrows pinched together in confusion. "Mrs. Morris . . .?"

Maggie released a shaky breath. "It's *Ms.* Morris. I'm a widow. My husband died . . . remember?" She arched a brow, staring directly into the doe eyes of her husband's mistress, watching as all the blood seemed to drain from her pretty face.

What felt like an eternity passed as the two women stared silently at one another, the reception switchboard lighting up like a Christmas tree, its calls going unanswered. Then Rebecca cleared her throat, forcing an uncertain smile that didn't meet her eyes.

"Yes, sorry. Of course, *Ms.* Morris." She shook her head with a light, humorless laugh. "I-I didn't know you were coming in this morning," she stammered, giving away her nerves. Averting her eyes to her computer monitor, she frantically clicked her mouse while focusing intently on the screen. "Who are you here to see? James? He's just—"

"I'm here to see *you*, as a matter of fact," Maggie interjected, her voice cold and void of any emotion whatsoever.

Her gaze trailed down in time to see Rebecca's throat bob with a hard swallow, which drew her attention to the iridescent sparkle of diamonds reflecting the downlights, shining from the base of her slender neck. "That's a beautiful necklace you're wearing."

As if without thinking, Rebecca lifted a hand, her delicate fingers idly tracing the precious stones of the necklace while her eyes glazed over. But she quickly composed herself. Shaking her head again, she pushed up from her chair, standing to a height that, even from behind the desk, towered over Maggie's five feet four inches.

Rebecca looked down her perfect nose at Maggie. With a condescending smile, and a patronizing tone in her voice she said, "Why don't you take a seat, and I'll let one of the partners know you're here."

While Maggie had never been one to cause a scene—she'd always loathed unwanted attention—on this occasion she swallowed the trepidation that lingered at the back of her throat, silencing the voice in her head that was pleading for her to walk away. *Walk away, Maggie. Be the bigger person.* No. Not today. She was so sick and tired of doing what she was told; all that ever had awarded her was a cheating, dead husband. So, steadying Rebecca with a steely regard, she leaned in as close as the desk would allow, staring directly into the woman's azure eyes. And, with a low, gravelly voice that cut through the thick silence like a serrated butcher's knife, she whispered, "You fucking *whore*."

Rebecca gasped, looking down to see the crumpled-up Empire napkin as it fell from Maggie's trembling fingers and landed on her desk, her eyes widening with horror as realization came crashing over her.

"How long?"

With eyes full of tears, Rebecca looked up from the discarded napkin, meeting Maggie's beseeching gaze. Her nostrils flared as she raked her teeth over her painted-pink lips, obviously stalling, obviously thinking of some kind of excuse. But there was no excuse; the proof was right there in front of her in black and white.

"*How long?*" Maggie asked again, her voice louder, more demanding.

"I-I don't . . . I'm not . . ." Rebecca stumbled over her words, panicking. She glanced furtively around the foyer as if searching for a lifeline, her hands shaking as she smoothed down the front of her prim silk blouse. "It's not what you think . . . I was—"

"Don't you *dare* lie to me!" Maggie hissed. And, unable to keep her emotions in check a moment longer, she reached for the only thing she could get her hands on. The glass jar full of individually wrapped candies that sat on the front desk never stood a chance. With every last ounce of strength she could muster, she picked it up and threw the jar across the space, causing it to shatter against the marble floor with an almighty crash.

Taking an unsteady step backward, Rebecca's face was stark with fear and horror. Hurried footfalls sounded from the hallway behind the frosted glass wall of the reception area, and a man came running into the foyer, his eyes bulging with concern.

"How *long?*" Maggie screamed, her painfully raw voice cracking as hot tears hit her cheeks.

"What is going on?" the man asked, moving in front of Rebecca as if to shield her from the unpredictable danger of the crazy woman throwing glass jars.

"Maggie?" A familiar voice sounded from close by.

Maggie blinked hard, turning as James tentatively stepped into the foyer, his eyes full of alarm as they flitted from her to Rebecca to the smashed glass on the floor. His brows knitted together as he asked, "What's wrong?"

"Did you know?" Maggie cried in response, searching his face. His eyes bored into hers as he held his hands up in defense, shaking his head slowly. "I have *no* idea what's going on . . ." He spoke so calmly, so steadily, taking a careful step forward. "Talk to me." He glanced briefly in Rebecca's direction, taking another step closer to Maggie. "Tell me what's going on."

A sob bubbled up the back of Maggie's throat, one she was unable to contain. She pointed an accusatory finger at the blonde who was now an inconsolable mess, crying on the shoulder of the hero who had come to her rescue. "Her and T-Tom! He was . . . he was having an a-affair with *her*!" she stammered through her emotion before breaking down completely.

"Hey, come here." James quickly swooped in, collecting her in his arms before she could crumble to the floor, which was smattered with shards of broken glass and wayward candies. He pulled her against his chest, his hand rubbing soothing circles over her back as she heaved with every uncontrollable sob that racked through her.

"He was *lying* to me," Maggie cried, her tears staining James's white Oxford shirt. "He was . . . They were . . ." She couldn't finish her words, they hurt too much.

"Come on." James tucked her closer into his side, walking her toward the door while spearing Rebecca with a withering glare. "Let's get out of here," he whispered.

Maggie glanced back over her shoulder, finding Rebecca watching on with mascara-stained tear tracks covering her cheeks, her eyes red rimmed, the whites bloodshot.

"I hope you're happy now!"

Rebecca covered her face with her hands, her shoulders trembling through her sobs.

Maggie allowed James to assist her out of the lobby and into a waiting elevator, and once they were safely inside, the metal doors shutting out the rest of the world, she allowed herself to break down right there, James's strong arms the only thing keeping her from falling in a heap on the floor.

*

The flow of downtown traffic was at a standstill on Congress Street, impatient drivers beeping their horns to the tune of the construction work going on all around. The rain had eased some but the thick gray clouds up above warned that another torrential downpour wasn't too far away. The unpredictable Boston weather was a constant reminder of Maggie's inner melancholy as she stared unseeingly out at the city street. Blissfully ignorant people walked by, completely unaware of the unbearable agony plaguing her. The painful assault of her own emotions was unrelenting. She envied the strangers who walked past. She wished she could be one of them.

Naively, she'd thought it would be different after confronting Rebecca. Easier. Now that she knew the truth. That Tom was a cheating bastard. Like ripping off a Band-Aid, she'd thought she'd be able to move on from her dead husband and finally start to rebuild her life. But it wasn't different. It wasn't easier. And she doubted she could ever repair her heart after such an unforgivable act, an act she now couldn't deal with because Tom was dead. She had no choice but to just learn to, somehow, live with it without any semblance of explanation or apology because he wasn't here to give her one. No closure whatsoever.

James reappeared, placing a to-go cup of coffee down in front of Maggie before taking the chair next to her. He sipped his coffee, watching her closely, the weight of his stare almost stifling. She avoided his gaze, continuing to stare out at the bustling city street, her cold hands wrapped around her coffee cup which helped to warm the iciness that had settled inside her.

"So, you really didn't know?" Maggie asked after a beat, still unable to look at him. She noticed him shift in his seat from her periphery, and when he released a heavy sigh, she knew immediately that he was biding his time. She finally offered him a sideways glance, meeting his eyes.

"I mean—I had my suspicions." James shook his head. "They were always . . . *friendly* with one another. A little too friendly if you ask me. Sometimes they'd go to lunch together, and if I said I'd join them, he'd stop me, tell me he was getting her to take notes on a new case over a sandwich. Said he was helping her out because she was planning on studying to be a paralegal." He shrugged. "But . . . there was just something about the little jokes they'd share. It was borderline inappropriate. So, I came right out and asked him to his face."

Maggie's eyes widened with surprise. "What did he say?"

He pressed his lips together, shaking his head, his gaze drifting through the window to the dreary day outside. "Called me crazy. Said he loved you and the boys, that he would never do such a thing." He met her eyes as he continued, "He was my best friend. Of course I believed him. And I knew how much he loved you."

She sighed, her shoulders falling. "Yeah, evidently not enough to stop from screwing his receptionist. It's an actual cliché . . ." she scoffed, glancing down at her coffee. "I've been racking my brain trying to think of the catalyst of our downfall, where it all went so wrong that he felt forced to seek comfort with another woman, that an *affair* was his only option, but I can't." She offered James a hopeless look. "Our marriage was *almost* perfect. Well, it was until about six months ago. Then he started to pull away. Now I know why. But it still doesn't explain why he did what he did. He loved me and I loved him. We were best friends *and* lovers, and partners. I just—I don't get it." She shook her head. "God, I almost feel sorry for her."

"Who? Rebecca?" James guffawed.

She shrugged again. "Yeah, I mean . . . I know better than anyone what it's like to fall in love with Tom Morris. And, as messed up as it is . . ." She paused, a derisive, humorless laugh slipping from her lips. "As messed up as it is, she lost him too."

*

Maggie kept herself busy when she returned home from her meltdown in the city. She put away the groceries that had been delivered from the store, she did laundry, cleaned the house from

35

top to bottom. But even those arduous tasks only helped to take her mind off things for so long. When she was finished, the place was spotless, everything put in its rightful spot, the scent of a vanilla and rhubarb candle lingering low in the air. But as she stood at the island counter, staring at the breakfast table, at the vase of calla lilies that sat in its center, their delicate petals beginning to wilt and fall to the glass tabletop, the silence was almost too much to bear.

Never before had the place she'd called home for the last ten years of her life felt so empty. Never before had she felt so alone in all her thirty-six years.

She thought back to how many laughs she'd shared with Tom and the boys at that very kitchen table. The Saturday mornings when TJ was a chubby toddler making a mess of his Cheerios while Jack sat dressed in his little league uniform, bouncing up and down excitedly, ready to play his very best while his daddy watched on from the stands.

She remembered the nights she would be in this kitchen tidying up after a casual family dinner while Tom tucked the boys into bed. He'd stroll in after getting them to sleep, smiling at Maggie in that way that was so him, watching as she wiped down the table. The look in his eyes was one of both adoration and mischief, desire and lust. Sometimes, he would come right up behind her, his hands gripping her hips, lips attaching to the base of her neck. She would turn in his arms and their kiss would turn fervent and needy. Sometimes, they would make love right there on the kitchen table, because even after so much time together they were still so undeniably in love with one another in every single way.

Maggie tried to swallow the lump of emotion which dwelled painfully at the back of her throat, but as tears burned her eyes that lump was well and truly stuck there. Blinking hot tears onto her cheeks, she glanced down at the countertop, sniffling quietly. How was it that in a place full of so many beautiful memories, in the house she'd made a home with her family, the past was suddenly and without warning nothing more than a bad case of a broken heart? This was her home. A place of love. Now, she felt uncomfortable and unwelcomed, surrounded by lies, deceit and betrayal. It was almost like she didn't belong there anymore.

How could he do this to her? To their children? Why would he do such a thing? They were meant to be for forever.

Slapping a hand over her mouth to stifle the sob bubbling out of her, Maggie closed her eyes tight. But when the weight of everything became too much, she turned and slid down the cabinet doors, crumbling to a heap. She hugged her knees to her chest and she cried. She cried for Tom. She cried for TJ and Jack. She cried for all that she'd loved, and everything she'd lost. Hell, she even cried for Rebecca Holmes. Right there, on the hardwood floor, Maggie cried like she'd never cried before.

Chapter 6

A few weeks had passed since discovering the awful truth of her husband's secret, double life. April had turned into May. Spring had officially sprung. The dreary rain made way for the sunshine. But Maggie was still a mess on the inside, despite how together she'd been trying to appear on the outside. She went about her days like she always had. She'd wake up, shower. She took the boys to school, ran errands, but then she'd come straight back home and cry all alone until it was time to go and collect TJ and Jack.

She spent her days trying so hard to keep her mind busy and void of the heartbreaking truth she was forced to keep buried. The truth she needed to pretend didn't really exist. The truth she couldn't risk her boys finding out. But nothing worked. And whenever she found herself idle, her traitorous mind taunted her with images of her husband with another woman. Images that would likely remain there forever.

She'd been taking each day at a time, each hour, each agonizing second, merely surviving until she could go to bed at night and try to forget it all. But that's when the harrowing thoughts of what could have been would torment her, leaving her sleepless and mentally exhausted and drained. Now, her life was nothing more than one big, never-ending bad dream she couldn't seem to wake up from.

It was Friday night and Jack was at his friend's house playing some new video game that had just been released. So, it was only Maggie and TJ. They sat together on the sofa in the den, eating popcorn and watching a movie from TJ's favorite superhero franchise. But TJ was tired, and just twenty minutes into the film, Maggie felt his head bobbing against her arm. He finally gave up his fight and fell asleep, and she'd been forced to watch *Thor* for an hour and a half. Not that *Thor*, or Chris Hemsworth, was anything to complain about.

When the movie finally finished, Maggie took the moment to really look at her baby. His dark hair was overgrown, flopping down over his forehead. Thick lashes fanned over his pale cheeks. His hand clutched the afghan so close to his chin as if it was a shield from all that was bad in the world. He looked so small, so innocent, so vulnerable. She wanted to wrap her arms around him, hold him tight and never let him go. But he was sleeping and she didn't dare wake him.

Shifting carefully, she reached for the remote, turning off the television. Casting a wary glance at her son, she held her breath as she pushed up from the sofa, slowly so as not to wake him. TJ sighed heavily but then nestled down into the plush couch cushion, curling up soundly. Maggie briefly considered carrying him up to his room, but she wasn't nearly strong enough. She was only five feet four, and although he was only ten years old, he was a solid unit. She didn't want to wake him. He needed his sleep. So, with a gentle kiss to the top of his head, she pulled the cover up and tip toed out of the room, dimming the lights on her way.

With a list of to-do items she hadn't gotten around to over the last couple months, Maggie made herself a cup of herbal tea and decided to get a start on the things she'd been putting off. Updating the insurance, paying the electric and all the other mundane tasks she was now responsible for. Tom had always been the one in charge of the finances. She was never good with money. She could spend it, but keep track of it? Not so much. Now, clueless, she was left to her own devices to muddle through the confusing spreadsheet he'd created over the years.

Ambling into the small office, Maggie flicked the light switch with her elbow while looking down at the handful of window-faced envelopes. She made herself comfortable in the cushy leather desk chair as she turned on the computer.

A photo of her, Tom and the boys from a few years back when they'd vacationed on Nantucket, caught her eye. She reached for the frame, looking closer at the picture. Sadness washed over her, but so did a smile. TJ was holding a big shell he'd found on the beach, smiling, so proud of himself. Jack had his arm around his little brother's shoulders, offering a thumbs-up to the camera. Her gaze zeroed in on Tom and she studied him closely. Dressed in a crisp linen shirt, unbuttoned to his sternum which hinted at his strong chest and tanned skin. His dark hair was untamed and unruly in stark contrast to the slicked-back style he wore to the office every day. He looked striking, effortlessly cool. And with a carefree Maggie by his side wearing no more than a bikini top and a pair of jean shorts, the four of them gave off the illusion of the picture-perfect happy family.

Maggie's eyes narrowed instinctively as her probing subconscious began to wonder whether he was cheating on her back then. Shaking her head, she dismissed those same dark thoughts that had taken up permanent residence in her mind. It was beginning to get the better of her, but she couldn't let it. She wouldn't. Placing the frame back where it had been sitting, she chose instead to focus on the task at hand as the computer came to life through the dim light of the room.

With the bills taken care of, Maggie was about to shut down when a notification alert chimed, indicating a new email. Curiosity got the better of her, and when she clicked on the pop-up she was immediately captivated by the digital real estate brochure radiating back at her from the screen.

A photograph of a picturesque lake framed by lush green spruce trees and striking red maples appeared before her. The inky water looked like glass, reflecting the fluffy white clouds sitting high up in a cerulean sky. And there in the middle of it all sat a rustic colonial home surrounded by nothing but an idyllic New England backdrop.

A few years earlier, Tom and Maggie had entertained the idea of purchasing a holiday house. A way to get out of the city, far from the pressures of their day-to-day lives. A place to spend long weekends and summers with the boys, to watch them thrive and grow and appreciate the beauty of nature. Maggie, ever the dreamer, signed up to myriad newsletters with estate agencies in the northern New England region so she could be notified of any new listings when they became available. But sadly, their dream never came to fruition as life always managed to get in the way. But now life was at a standstill, and she couldn't stop herself from reading the digital listing presented before her.

Charming fixer-upper on two acres
overlooking Diamond Lake

Built in 1860, and listed for the first time in over fifty years, this stately lake house boasts three levels, all with uninterrupted views of Diamond Lake.

This secluded piece of prime property is only a five-minute drive to the heart of Jewel Harbor, a quaint seaside village on the beautiful New England coast and only two hours' drive north of Boston.

This is a must-see for investors, holidaymakers, or those seeking a sea change from the hustle and bustle of city life.

This priceless piece of history will not last long. Be quick!

Maggie scoured each photo one by one. Sure, it needed a coat of paint and a little TLC, but it was a steal and it had character. You couldn't even consider buying something like that anywhere near Boston without spending a fortune.

The more closely she inspected the pictures the more her wistful smile grew. From the thicket of trees lining the boundary of the property to the blue shutters on the windows, to the two Adirondack chairs painted fire engine red and perched at the end of the small floating dock overlooking the water beneath a dusty mauve sky.

She had always wanted that. She wanted it with Tom. She wanted a place where the family could make memories. She wanted a place where she and Tom could continue visiting even after their boys had grown up and moved on. A place the boys could eventually bring their own families for the holidays. Maggie wanted somewhere she and Tom could grow old, a safe haven they could call their own until the end. But now things were catastrophically different. Tom was gone. And everything she once knew, once wanted, had all changed.

She stared at the illuminated screen, considering her limited options. Maybe she could still have it. Maybe she, TJ and Jack could create a safe haven, just the three of them. Their own private piece of heaven. Sure, Maggie would need to get a job. She hadn't had one since she served coffee to kids in college. She had her high school diploma, but that was it. With two children and a husband going through law school, she'd never managed to go back and get her degree.

Stupidly, neither she nor Tom had a life insurance plan because it wasn't something they'd thought would ever happen to them. Ignorance and naivety at its finest. Sure, they had savings, but not enough to spend on a holiday house they didn't need, no matter how heavily discounted it was. With a resigned sigh she shook her head. It was all a dream then, and it would forever be a dream. Unattainable, but a nice dream to allow her a mental escape when she needed it.

Logging off, Maggie collected her empty mug and the discarded envelopes. As she continued out of the office, she was stopped in her tracks by a sudden and unexpected knock on the front door. She checked her watch. It was almost midnight.

Who in the hell? She hurried to the entrance as quick as her sock-covered feet could carry her over the polished hardwood, careful not to slip in her haste. When she pulled the heavy door open, her shoulders fell at the sight before her. There, held up by the scruff of his sweater by a very unimpressed looking Mr. Wilcox, Jack swayed unsteadily, pissed drunk.

"I believe *this* belongs to you." Mr. Wilcox deadpanned.

"What have you *done*?" Maggie gasped, her eyes wide as she took in her son's state. She looked at his best friend's father and back again at Jack as he failed to find his balance.

"It seems Bill and Jack decided to take it upon themselves to consume half a bottle of Scotch." Mr. Wilcox held up a near-empty bottle of liquor.

As she looked closer at the bottle, Maggie realized it was the same kind of expensive Scotch Tom had been collecting for the last few years. A rare bottle she was almost certain had been locked away securely in the cellar in their basement. She reached out, grasping the front of her son's sweater. "Jack Morris!"

Jack simply muttered a few incomprehensible syllables, stumbling into her, his sheer size almost knocking her to the floor in the process. She struggled to hold herself upright, her imploring eyes begging Mr. Wilcox for assistance.

"I'll get him upstairs, shall I?" he said before grabbing Jack and heaving him up, practically carrying her son's uncoordinated body.

Maggie stood frozen at the threshold, watching idle as Jack's semiconscious form flopped about as Billy Wilcox's dad helped him upstairs.

Closing her eyes a moment, she took a few deep breaths in through her nose, desperate for a reprieve from the overwhelming anxiety that had suddenly started eating at her from inside.

All thoughts of hundred-year-old lake houses, and beautiful red maples were suddenly drowned out by the reality of the nightmare that was her life.

*

With the cordless Dyson in her hands, Maggie waited a few moments, watching the seconds count down on her watch. TJ stood across the landing, leaning back against the balustrade, watching on with a hint of curiosity in his eyes. She hadn't planned on him being awake yet. She really didn't want to do this in front of her ten-year-old son, but she supposed it was good for him to see it now so that he would be less likely to consider getting obliterated drunk at the age of fifteen.

When the clock struck 7 a.m., without hesitation, she barged into Jack's bedroom, pushing the door open with such gusto it crashed loudly into the wall, causing the lifeless body wrapped in blankets on the bed to sit bolt upright. But she didn't stop with that. Switching the Dyson on to max power, she began vacuuming the floor, collecting anything and everything in her path. She knocked into the desk, the chair, anything she could as long as it made as much noise as it possibly could.

Over the loud whir of the vacuum she could hear Jack's groans, but she ignored his objections, continuing. Her gaze flitted to her son, finding him hunched over, his head in his hands, quilt pulled over his head like the Grim Reaper's cloak.

She'd been there, herself, many moons ago when she was an insolent teenager, but she chose to show no mercy because she also went on to fall pregnant and drop out of college. She intended on making an example out of Jack, regardless of his blatant pain and suffering. She could keep this up all morning. And if the vacuum wasn't enough to break him, she would start hammering unnecessary holes into the walls. But thankfully, for the sake of the drywall, Jack broke first.

"I'm sorry!" he yelled, his voice raw and croaky over the Dyson's motor.

Maggie ignored him at first, watching from the corner of her eyes as he shifted, tossing the bedsheets off his body and scrambling to the foot of the bed.

"I said I'm *sorry*!"

Switching off the vacuum, Maggie fixed Jack with a pointed look, her eyes blazing with anger that seemed to make him instinctively cower.

She released her hold of the Dyson, allowing it to fall to the floor with a hard thud. She stared down at him, racking her brain to think of what she might possibly say to try and get through to him. Not even a school suspension was enough to force him to wake up to himself. What hope did she have?

Jack's bloodshot eyes searched hers, his gaze one of obvious pleading. "I didn't mean to."

"You didn't *mean* to?" she repeated his words with stark exasperation. "So, you didn't *mean* to sneak downstairs to the basement without me knowing?"

He pressed his lips together, swallowing hard.

"You didn't *mean* to steal a bottle of Scotch from the cellar?"

He avoided her accusatory eyes, choosing instead to look down at his hands.

"You didn't *mean* to hide the liquor . . . that you *stole* . . . in your backpack to take to Billy's house?"

Jack blinked hard, his jaw clenching when he lifted his gaze to meet hers once again.

She continued, "I think you absolutely *meant* to do all that, Jack." She shook her head. "And the worst part of all is that you only care *now* because you got *caught*."

All he managed was a slight nod, his shoulders falling.

Maggie glanced over her shoulder to find TJ's small frame in the open doorway, his face pale and eyes wide with worry. She sighed. Although she knew she could scream bloody murder and yell until she had no voice left, she also knew there wasn't much point. The damage was already done. All she could hope was that the pain Jack was currently feeling—both emotional and physical—would be enough to scare him away from hard liquor, at least for the time being.

"You're grounded."

Jack gaped at her; his eyes wide with incredulity. "For how long?"

His tone made something inside of her snap. "For as *long* as it takes for you to realize you can't just go around punching people who look at you the *wrong* way," she yelled, her hands thrown in the air in frustration. "For as *long* as it takes you to realize you can't drink alcohol at *fifteen* years old!" Her voice was steely, scarily so as she leaned in closer, adding through gritted teeth, "For as long as it takes for you to stop being a selfish, unconscionable little brat!"

Jack stared at her, and she witnessed a flash of something in his eyes; recognition, perhaps.

Turning away from him, she collected TJ on her way out. "Come on, Teej. Let's go make pancakes." She threw a withering glare over her shoulder at her eldest son. "This room had better be cleaned up before you even so much as *think* of showing your face downstairs."

Chapter 7

Maggie tucked her hair behind her ear for the tenth time before placing her fidgeting hands on her lap. Nerves pecked like starving scavengers at her insides. When she'd received the call from Mr. Wylie, the bank manager who had looked after her and Tom for the last ten or so years, confusion flooded through her. She wasn't sure if it was normal protocol for bank managers to personally phone customers on the weekend and ask them to come in first thing on a Monday morning. Ever since Mr. Wylie's call, her stomach had been knotted painfully and she'd been on edge. Something was wrong. It had to be.

"Maggie?"

Looking up from her hands, Maggie spotted the rotund man dressed in a suit a size too small, smiling kindly, his eyes watching her over the top of his wireframe glasses. He waved her into his office and she stood, gripping her handbag tight as she crossed toward him.

"How are you?"

"I'm okay," she managed in a slightly higher pitch than normal. The truth was she wasn't okay. She was nervous, and she didn't know why. The only time she'd even been to the bank in person was when she and Tom initially applied for a mortgage

47

on their house. And again with Jack and TJ when they wanted to open a junior savings account with their birthday money a few years back.

The inside of the office was cluttered and old, and minimal daylight broke in through the timber shutters. The occasional ray of sun highlighted the dust particles floating aimlessly through the stale air. Maggie sat on the chair opposite Mr. Wylie as he took his place behind the desk. Squaring her shoulders, she smiled when he glanced up from the haphazard stack of papers in front of him.

"Thank you for coming in at such short notice." He shifted a little awkwardly, averting his gaze, looking anywhere but at her.

"It sounded quite urgent over the phone," she noted, her eyes wandering to the documents in his hand. She assumed whatever was on them was the reason she was there. "What seems to be the problem, Mr. Wylie?"

The man removed his glasses, and, with his stubby thumb and forefinger, he pinched the bridge of his nose, his eyes shut tight as if he had a headache. Then, those weary yet kind eyes landed on her and immediately, with just one look, her suspicions were confirmed. This was not good news.

"I don't know an easier way to say this," he began through a resigned sigh, dropping the papers onto the desk. "So, I'm just going to have to come out and say it." He speared her with a serious look, folding his hands together. "The last four mortgage payments have bounced."

Maggie quirked a brow. She hadn't been expecting that.

"Due to the nature of your . . . *delicate* situation and the fact that you and Tom have been long-standing clients of my bank, I managed to pull some strings with corporate and have had the payments paused. But, unfortunately . . ." He trailed off with a pained expression. "They're unwilling to continue with any further grace periods."

Maggie stared at him.

"So, I took it upon myself to investigate what the issue was,

48

and . . ." He stalled, unable to continue for some reason, his discomfort glaringly obvious.

Maggie blinked, shaking her head. "I'm sorry, I have no idea what you're talking about. We don't have a mortgage. We paid it out three years ago. I remember. Tom stuck the final closing statement to the fridge."

The man's face fell, his shoulders sagging, and he rubbed his hands together, clearing his throat. "Tom took a . . . a mortgage out on the property a little over a year ago."

"He what?" she guffawed. "What for? H-how much? Why didn't I know anything about this?" Panic was coursing through her.

Mr. Wylie looked down at a piece of paper in his hand, and read aloud, "Two hundred and fifty thousand. It says here it was to put in a swimming pool and to purchase stocks and bonds."

"A swimming pool?" She snorted.

His gaze lifted over his glasses, settling on her. "You didn't know about this? Is that, there, not your signature?" He held the document up so she could see.

"Yes it is, but I . . ." She shook her head, racking her brain to try and remember what had happened a year ago. Surely, she would remember something as serious as taking out a quarter of a million dollar mortgage on their home for stocks and a goddamn swimming pool.

Had she signed something without realizing what it was? Tom wouldn't do that to her. There was no way. He was a lawyer. He wouldn't . . . Well, at least she'd like to *think* he wouldn't have done that to her, but she never would have thought he'd cheat on her either.

"Two hundred and fifty grand," she whispered with a sigh, watching helplessly as Mr. Wylie began shuffling through the papers in front of him, turning them over one by one, scanning each document. And then, glancing up at her, he hesitated before reluctantly sliding one over.

She pulled it closer, looking down at it. It was an annual

statement. Their savings account which was linked to their checking account. The opening balance looked about right. Most of what they had managed to save over the years since Tom had finished his internship and had started as a junior associate. It wasn't a lot, given the cost of living, but a decent chunk nonetheless. Her gaze zeroed in on the closing balance and she couldn't contain a gasp. "What the hell?"

They rarely accessed the savings account. It was for emergencies only. At least, that's what she'd thought. Scanning each and every line item on the linked checking account statement, it went back to well before Tom died, and all she could see were debits of ludicrous amounts glaring back at her. Jewelers. Hotels. Lingerie stores. Cash. American Express? They didn't even have an American Express . . . Thousands and thousands of dollars at a time, all gone. With the lavish outgoings, and little to no deposits, the bottom line—the balance on both accounts, and every last cent Maggie now had left to her name—was less than a few thousand dollars.

"But this . . . it doesn't make sense." She glanced up at Mr. Wylie, meeting his sympathetic gaze from across the desk. "Where did the settlement of that so-called mortgage go? And where are Tom's salary deposits?"

The man cleared his throat, shifting again before pulling another document from the stack of papers. He hesitated before handing it to Maggie, pity evident in his eyes. "I'm afraid it looks like he had a separate account for his salary, but . . . well, it's all gone, too. On the same type of frivolous spending, I'm afraid."

Maggie glanced down at the second statement, and her throat started to close up on itself as the conclusion settled in her belly like lead. Tom had been siphoning money from her, from their *children*, for the last twelve months before his death. He'd pissed it all away on his lavish, secret life with his mistress, taking her to five-star hotels, buying her lingerie and Chanel handbags, all while paying her credit cards and her goddamn rent. Now, it made sense why he had a key to her apartment; he was paying for it.

She felt sick. She couldn't breathe. She was so stupid. Tom had managed their finances and she'd let him, she hadn't thought anything of it. She'd trusted him and he'd fleeced her for all they had. Ignorance at its finest; she only had herself to blame.

Maggie looked around for something, anything, she didn't even know what. But, thankfully, Mr. Wylie did know, and within seconds he was standing by her side holding out a chilled bottle of water.

"I can't—" She stopped herself to consider her words. She searched for something to say but she had nothing. Literally no words. She looked at the man, her voice trembling with fear, "I don't know what to do. There's no life insurance. We have nothing. The bills and living expenses . . . the boys' college fund . . . *and* this mortgage." Her hands shook as she glanced down at the statements. "I can't afford—" A sob bubbled up the back of her throat, causing her voice to crack. "What am I going to do?"

Mr. Wylie frowned. He reached for the box of Kleenex on his desk, plucking a few and handing them to her. She took them from him, tearing anxiously at the delicate paper as she stared straight ahead at nothing, dread settling low in her stomach.

"Look, I hope you don't mind me saying so, but . . ." He crouched down, placing a kind hand on Maggie's forearm. "Might I suggest you consider selling the house? The market is strong at the moment. At least you'd walk away with enough to pay out the mortgage, and have a decent amount left over for a sizeable down payment on another property."

"There's no way I'll get approved for a bank loan. Not on my own!" Tears stung her eyes when she met his kind gaze. "Besides, that's our home. My boys' *home*. I can't—" She snapped her mouth shut, placing a trembling hand over it. She couldn't even bring herself to say the words. There was no way she could move her kids out of their home. Not now. Not after everything they'd already been through.

"I'm so sorry, Maggie." He patted her arm in a show of support. "If there was anything more I could do, you know I would in a heartbeat, but I—"

"No. Please," she interjected, managing a smile through her tears. "Please don't apologize. I should thank you for letting me know before the bank came knocking." She sniffled, sitting up a little straighter. Squaring her shoulders, she collected herself as best as she could because now was not the time to cry, no matter how justified her tears were. "H-how long do I have?"

"Thirty days." Mr. Wylie walked back around to his side of the desk, stacking all the documents together and placing them into a folder. "If the mortgage isn't brought back into line by day thirty, a foreclosure notice will be issued."

Maggie nodded. "Okay. I'll make a few calls, talk to my solicitor." Her brain ran through a long list of things she was going to have to urgently get on to. "How much . . . how much is owed to pay the mortgage out?"

She watched as he tapped something into his computer, his gaze narrowed as he scanned the illuminated screen before twisting the monitor in her direction. With interest and fees, it was an obscene amount of money with a lot of zeroes, but she nodded regardless, taking a deep breath in an attempt to contain her emotions.

*

Less than forty-eight hours later, Maggie was sitting out on the patio, overlooking the yard, a cardigan covering her shoulders. She took a sip of her wine and smiled. The night air was cool against her skin, helping to provide a clarity she hadn't felt in a long time. She'd just made a huge decision. A life-altering decision that would change everything. But she also knew, regardless of the consequences, it was for the best. Her life, and her sons' lives, would eventually start to unravel the longer they stayed in Boston. Tom's choices and the selfish, unthinkable things he'd done would come back to haunt not only herself, but TJ and Jack. She had to do something to try and fix things. So, she did. It might be considered running away, but she was a mother and it was her job to do whatever she had to do to protect her boys. They might hate her. But that didn't matter. A mother's priority, above all else, is to protect a child at any cost.

The French doors from the house opened and Maggie knew without even glancing over her shoulder that it was Jack.

"Mom, can I talk to you?"

The break in his voice struck right to her heart. He sounded so despondent, so fragile. All she wanted was for him to talk to her. She longed to hold him. *Really* hold him. Her arms yearned to feel her son wrapped safe and warm and protected in the embrace only she as his mother could provide. But, instead, without giving herself away, she simply nodded once, not obliging him with even so much as a sideways glance. They hadn't spoken more than a few words since his drunken escapade, and it'd been a living hell.

The metal legs of the patio chair scraped across the flagstone, and suddenly he was right there, sitting in front of her, and she was forced to look into his eyes, which were so sad, and so full of heartbreaking hopelessness. It was a look that tore her up inside.

Jack clamped his bottom lip between his teeth, a crease of contemplation appeared between his brows. "You were right," he said finally, his voice nothing more than a whispered hush. "I knew what I was doing with that liquor. I did it intentionally."

Maggie allowed herself to meet his eyes, but she said nothing as she waited for him to continue.

"I just . . ." He shook his head, dropping it into his hands, his fingers tearing at the lengths of his hair as he released a shuddering breath. "I thought if I could forget about everything, even if only for one night, then maybe when I finally remembered it wouldn't . . . it wouldn't hurt so much."

She quirked a brow. "How'd that work out for ya?"

He glanced up from his hands, and when he noticed the wry smile ghosting over her lips he chuckled humorlessly. "Made everything hurt a million times more."

She nodded.

"I just miss him so much. I miss how everything was." A lone tear trailed down his cheek catching the glow of the garden lights, glistening almost beautifully. He made no effort to wipe it away as he continued, "I wish things could go back to how they were. But I know they never will and that's what sucks the most. That this is it."

Maggie nodded. "This is our life now, Jack. We need to adjust, to make a new kind of normal. Without your father."

He buried his face in his hands and she watched on as his shoulders trembled with every silent cry he tried so hard to conceal. Seeing him so broken, so defeated, so utterly distraught, it broke her too. She hadn't seen him so sad since the family dog, Buster, passed away. Of course, the gravity of losing a father was a lot heavier than losing a dog, but the sadness was comparable in a way. Jack had lost his first best friend, and now, seven years later, he'd lost his hero. For the second time in his fifteen years, he'd been left heartbroken. It was too much loss for a kid his age to have to deal with. It wasn't fair.

Maggie watched her son a little longer, raking her teeth over her bottom lip as she contemplated her words. With a deep breath, she reached out and placed a hand on his shoulder, gently squeezing in a show of support. "Jack, I want to talk to you about something."

He sniffled, finally looking up. He wiped his nose with the back of his hand, his eyes glassy and red rimmed and rife with anguish.

She searched his face, thinking of the right words to say. She knew she needed to tell him, she just didn't know how. Shifting in her chair, she cleared the ball of nerves from the back of her throat with a sip of wine.

"What is it?" Jack asked, his brow furrowing with a combination of confusion and concern.

"Well, I spoke with TJ today," Maggie began, moving her gaze to the glass in her hand. With a hard blink she reminded herself, once again, that she was the authority figure in this situation. Lifting her chin a little higher, she fixed Jack with an unwavering look. "I-I think it's best . . . for *all* of us . . . if we . . . if we move."

He stared at her for a long moment, his eyes flitting between hers, his expression unreadable. "Move?"

She nodded. "Make a fresh start. Away from this house, this . . . this *place*." She waved a hand in the air, indicating their surroundings.

"Move from *Belmont*?" He gaped at her. "Would we stay in *Boston*?"

Swallowing hard, she studied the fraught look of panic in his blue eyes. "I've found a place by the ocean. In New Hampshire. It's only—"

"You wanna move out of the state?" His voice was pitchy and uneven as he stood to his feet so abruptly his chair toppled backward, tumbling onto the flagstone with a loud clatter.

"It's not even two hours away, Jack. You can still come and visit Billy and all your other friends. You'll have your driver's license at the end of the year. We can get you your own car. You can—"

"No!" He folded his arms defiantly across his broad chest, glowering down at her. "I'm *not* moving."

With a heavy sigh, Maggie glanced up at the inky night sky in the hope that it might help her to collect her thoughts. She stood to her feet and, although Jack still towered over her, she asserted herself as best as she could. "I've already submitted an offer on a house, and . . . it was accepted this afternoon." She snapped her mouth shut, holding her breath while waiting for his reaction.

Jack's eyes widened with incredulity.

"Your dad always wanted a place by the water for you boys, and—"

"Don't you *dare* bring my father into this." His words were icy as they cut straight through her attempt at an explanation. "This has *nothing* to do with him. This is you!"

She stared at him for a few beats, witnessing something in his eyes that she hadn't been prepared to see. Pure, unadulterated hatred stared back at her. "Jack." Her voice wavered. "If you can just hear me out, you'll realize I—"

"Why bother, Mom?" He threw his hands up at his sides. "You've obviously already made your decision. What say do I have?" And, with that, he turned and stormed back inside the house, the door slamming shut violently behind him.

Releasing the breath she'd been holding Maggie slumped back in her chair. Her shoulders sagged with the heavy weight of resignation. She finished the rest of her wine. Despite Jack's reaction, this was a time for celebration. She'd made the first big financial decision of her life, and she had done it all on her own for her *and* her boys.

One day, Jack would understand that—moving away from this place, away from this chapter in their lives, away from what would eventually keep them from moving on—it was all for the best. It was time to start a new life where no one knew them or what they'd been through, where they could move on together and be happy. Yes, this was for the best. For all of them. Sooner or later, Jack would see that. At least, that's what she hoped.

Chapter 8

The sun managed to break its way through the thick cover of gray cloud, shining a dull glow upon the house Maggie and the boys had called their home for the last ten years.

"Will Daddy know where we've gone?" TJ asked, looking up at the house. The three of them stood on the driveway next to the car Maggie had spent all morning packing up with the personal belongings they didn't want to put in the moving truck.

She crouched down beside her youngest son, snaking an arm around his slight shoulders. "Of course he will. Daddy will always know where you are because he's in here." She placed her hand over his chest, right where his heart was.

"Oh, brother," Jack scoffed, looking down at the ground, his hands shoved deep into his pockets.

Maggie rolled her eyes at Jack before managing another smile at TJ. She stood, brushing her hands over the back of her jeans. "Okay. Are we ready?"

"Yeah." TJ shrugged, big eyes looking up at her as he added with uncertainty, "I guess."

"No," Jack muttered, pouting dramatically.

"Well, on that *enthusiastic* note . . ." With a wry smile, she clapped her hands together, pointing to the car. "Let's go!"

*

They'd stopped for an early lunch at a truck stop on the Interstate, and they'd been driving for just over an hour since their break. TJ had been sleeping for a good twenty minutes, so it was just Maggie and Jack accompanied by an uncomfortable awkwardness overwrought with tension. She'd tried to indulge in casual conversation, but her son would offer no more than a scowl while tapping his headphones, flashing her a death-like glare from across the center console every time she said a single word. She chose, instead, to listen to the music playing over the radio. She didn't stop herself from getting carried away with Tom Petty as he crooned through the speakers.

"God, can you *stop!*" Jack suddenly said, ripping the headphones off his head. "I can hear you over my podcast!"

Maggie ignored him, smiling to herself as she sang to the chorus completely off-key with likely a few wrong words here and there, her hand tapping against the steering wheel in time with the beat.

"This song sucks." Jack lurched forward with a huff and switched off the radio. A heavy silence fell around them.

Maggie watched from the corner of her eye as he sagged back in his seat, glaring out the window. "Do you want to listen to something? You can put on whatever—"

"No!" he snapped back, silencing her. "I just want to sit here and not listen to you singing your pathetic old-people music."

Old people? She wanted to laugh. She was yet to turn thirty-seven, but *okay, Jack*. She rolled her eyes with a quiet sigh, gripping the steering wheel as she concentrated on the road ahead. The scenery changed before her eyes, the Interstate lined with lush spruce trees and sky-high firs and she couldn't contain her smile.

"Where the hell, even, are we?"

Maggie blinked, choosing to ignore his tone and profanity. He was angry. And she would accept it for now. But if he thought he was going to make a habit out of maintaining that attitude, then he had another think coming. She wouldn't hesitate in shipping him down to Boca to live with the grandfather he hardly knew.

"We crossed over the border just after lunch." She managed a tight smile, continuing with enthusiasm, "We're officially in New Hampshire."

Another silence settled between then, but the pressure was palpable. She could feel the anger emitting from almost every one of his pores as he shifted in his seat. He obviously had more to say; she was just waiting for it.

"You know, Dad wouldn't like this."

And there it was. Maggie tried to act unaffected by his words, casting a fleeting, casual glance across the center console. "Wouldn't like what?"

He speared her with a hard glare she pretended not to notice. "Pulling us out of our schools. Moving us out of our home. Taking us across state lines. We're minors; I'm sure there's some kind of law against that."

"I'm your *mother*!" she guffawed, trying to conceal her exasperated laughter.

"Yeah, well, Dad wouldn't like it," he sassed, folding his arms across his chest with stubborn finality.

Maggie pressed her lips together, and although she knew she shouldn't antagonize him when he was in such a riled-up state, she just couldn't help herself. "Well, Dad isn't here anymore, is he?" *And he didn't leave us with much choice*, she wanted to add, but chose to bite down on the inside of her cheek instead.

She felt Jack's gaze flare with anger, and she knew if looks could kill she'd be the one who was currently buried six feet under in the cold hard ground, not Tom.

Jack scoffed, shaking his head and staring out through the windshield. "You might be able to fool TJ and tell him this is what our father always wanted, but I know the truth. This is *you* being *selfish*."

"Selfish?" She entertained his accusatory presumption, arching a brow.

"Yeah. I think *you* miss him, and it was too hard for *you* to be in that house all by *yourself. You're* running away from *your* sadness, and you couldn't care less about *ours.*"

His words hurt, and she was forced to bite her tongue. *Oh, Jack, if only you knew.*

"God, I wish he was still here," he muttered, adding under his breath, "I wish it'd been you . . ."

And Maggie wished like hell she hadn't just heard that. But she did hear it. To be fair, she was almost certain he hadn't meant for her to hear it. But she did. Loud and clear. And it cut right through her, jagged and painful, leaving a wound that hurt unbearably. She swallowed hard, her grip on the steering wheel tightening to the point of pain.

Sure, she could let it go. Allow his brutally painful words to slide. Brush them beneath the proverbial rug. But the tears pricking her eyes were making it almost impossible to act as if she wasn't the slightest bit hurt. She couldn't let this go. She couldn't, not even if she wanted to. So, she didn't. This time, he needed to be held accountable.

She cleared her throat. "You know . . . I hope you mean that, Jack."

He turned at her words. She could feel his eyes settle upon her. But he didn't say anything.

"One day I'm not going to be here," she continued, still fixed straight ahead on the road. "I'm going to be gone. And you're going to be left with nothing but the memory of every horrible, unimaginably mean thing you ever said to me, just to hurt me. You're going to spend your days wishing you could take those words back, and beg for my forgiveness. But I won't be here to forgive you. And moments like this will live on with you forever, eating you up on the inside." She offered him a quick glance, meeting his wide, slightly fearful eyes. "Words might just be words, but once you've said them you can never take them back. Sorry doesn't always cut it. So make sure you *mean* what you *say.*"

His throat bobbed with a hard swallow, jaw ticking, and she

could feel him watching her long after she'd turned back to the road, his gaze weighty and hard. But he said nothing, turning to stare out his window, a contemplative silence hanging in the wake of Maggie's words, shrouding them both.

Maggie turned the radio back on, and they continued the rest of the way as her *old-people music* played throughout the otherwise silent car.

*

"I think it's just after this bridge." Maggie peered out through the windshield as she navigated the car through a narrow, covered bridge, turning left straight after. The property sat off the main road and down a rocky trail. Looming trees lined the track, their branches entwining overhead to create a canopy that allowed for the occasional ray of sunlight to crack through, lighting the way.

"We're literally in the *boonies*." Jack huffed, skeptically taking in their surroundings.

"This is where Jason lives!" TJ cried, and Maggie silently chastised Jack for letting his little brother watch *Friday the 13th* with him a few months back.

"No, honey." She shook her head. "Remember, Jason isn't real."

"Oh . . . my God." Jack sighed heavily, his face screwed up with disgust. "Is that it?"

Maggie continued rolling the car down to the end of the rocky drive, clearing the trees to an open patch of overgrown grass and a somewhat familiar looking three-story structure which was nothing like the advertisement.

Oh no . . .

"What a freakin' *dump*!" Jack hissed.

Pulling up to a stop, Maggie shut off the engine and silence hung in the air as they all stared out at the dilapidated building before them.

The place needed a hell of a lot more than just a coat of paint like she'd originally anticipated. The front steps were uneven, the wood buckled. The downstairs windows were boarded up. The porch screening was torn into shreds as if some rabid wild animal had tried to claw its way in. She warily looked around, for what, she didn't even know, as regret settled like lead in her belly.

"Oh, look, there's a tire swing!" She pointed to the big oak tree that sat rooted by the lake's edge, its branches hanging over the water. "I bet that's fun." She glanced hopefully in the mirror, watching TJ crane his neck to see the swing. "Looks like a good climbing tree," she added, hopefully.

"We're actually going to *live* here?" Jack eyed her dubiously.

Maggie rolled her eyes. "It's not so bad. I mean, sure it needs a bit of work. But the land is great." She looked out over the picturesque vista; the lake's calm water was like glass reflecting the lush trees surrounding it, and the peaks of the mountains poked up through the sky-scraping canopy of pines. "And it's got a beautiful view."

"Is it even *safe*?" he asked, adding, "It looks like a damn crack house."

"What's a damn crack house?" TJ enquired innocently.

"Jack!" Maggie chided, her eyes widening as she glowered at him. He ignored her, of course, so she unfastened her seatbelt and changed the topic. "Let's go have a look. The realtor said the keys will be in the mailbox at the front door."

Jack muttered something under his breath but she chose to ignore him, focusing on getting out of the car and helping TJ before leading the way up to the house. There was a path hidden somewhere beneath the knee-high weeds and she made a mental note to add lawnmower to her growing list of things to purchase. They'd always had someone come and take care of the yard back in Belmont. If she bought a lawnmower, she would do it herself or bribe Jack to do it.

The porch steps were lopsided. A rusty nail was poking up in the corner of the first one and Maggie made sure TJ stood back with his brother as she tentatively checked each timber plank for rotting wood. They would need to be replaced.

Sighing, she pushed open the rickety screen door which wobbled on only one rusted hinge. Inside, cobwebs hung from up above, dried leaves were scattered across the decking, and the windows were so thick with dust and grime she couldn't even see into the house.

With a deep breath, Maggie lifted the top off the mailbox and reluctantly reached inside, feeling around with caution. She was almost certain she was going to touch something that moved, and she had no idea what she'd do if she did. Thankfully, all she felt was an envelope and she pulled it out to see her name written across the front with a smiley face. She couldn't help but wonder if it was the realtor being facetious.

Did she actually think I'd be happy? She rolled her eyes.

Fixer-upper was the understatement of the century; the place should've been condemned. But Maggie refused to let the boys witness her defeat. This was their new life. And, after a little work, she was sure this place would be great for them. She forced a smile.

"Come on up," she called over her shoulder as she took the two silver keys out of the envelope. "Don't step on that nail!"

Wrestling with the rusted lock, she muttered a few choice words under her breath before finally jimmying the front door open while holding her breath.

Surprisingly, inside wasn't too bad. Dust floated through the air. Cobwebs hung from the ceiling. Drop sheets covered old furniture left by the previous owner. But as she took it all in, it was actually quite impressive. She smiled. It was places like this that reminded her how important it was to never judge a book by its cover. While the outside of the home didn't do this place justice, the moment she stepped over the threshold and into the entry she couldn't help but release a long sigh of relief. Intricate moldings and exposed beams greeted her. Original hardwood floors, a stone fireplace, picture windows which, when the boards were removed, would provide a beautiful view of the lake. It was definitely in need of some updates but it was cozy and it automatically felt like a place Maggie and the boys might be able to call their home.

She turned to gauge TJ and Jack's reactions, opening her arms out wide as she took a step backward into the den. "Well . . . what do you guys think?"

TJ stepped inside, glancing up at the beams, his eyes wide with surprise, mouth forming a perfect O. Jack, however, was a little less impressed, frantically brushing a cobweb from his arm. He liked to act all tough but spiders were his greatest fear.

"It needs some work." Maggie nodded, gauging their expressions. "But we can do it. Together." She smiled at both of them, watching as TJ took a tentative step further inside to explore.

Walking through to the kitchen, Maggie was pleasantly surprised to find natural light flooding in from the conservatory-style breakfast nook. Gingerly, she opened a few of the cabinet doors to make sure there was nothing lurking inside before running a hand over the countertops, dust covering her palm which she was quick to wipe away on the back of her old jeans.

She inspected everything. Tucked under the stairs were two doors; one opened to a half-bathroom, and the other opened to a narrow set of stairs which led down to the basement where the furnace was hidden away. A mudroom sat off the kitchen and opened onto a small back deck that looked out onto a thicket of trees. It was so private, so quiet. So unlike anything she was used to.

"Shall we go explore upstairs?" She glanced at Jack and TJ.

"You first." Jack shrugged, adding, "*I* don't wanna fall through the floor."

"Oh, how chivalrous of you," Maggie muttered under her breath, rolling her eyes before moving back through the den. But her son had a point. The place was old. And clearly hadn't been lived in for some time. She timidly touched each step, pressing her foot upon it before deeming it safe enough to support their weight, the boys staying close behind.

Upstairs, a small landing led to a corridor with three doors on one side, two on the other, and one at the end which Maggie assumed led to the third-floor attic. The first door opened to a full bathroom. A shower head hung over an antique claw-foot bath that looked almost as old as the house. It was perched in front of a big window looking out over the sprawling lake and the mountains in the distance. She couldn't wait to have a soak in the tub while staring out at that awe-inspiring view.

The next door opened to the master. A small fireplace sat on the far wall, and another impressive view across the water to the forest of lush red maples was on display through the windows. There was a small closet. Tiny, compared to the one she had back in Belmont, but she had to keep reminding herself that it was just her, so it would suffice. There was no en suite bathroom and she knew one bathroom with two boys would likely pose a challenge, but she was sure they could manage.

Before closing the door, Maggie glanced dubiously at the closet once more. She doubted her shoes alone would fit in that thing.

Across the hall was a small room that would work as an office or a study for the boys, and two slightly bigger identical bedrooms. On this side of the house, the roof was pitched, and the windows were gabled adding a charming character to each of the rooms.

"I like this one," TJ said, stepping into the last bedroom and doing a little spin.

"Yeah?" Maggie smiled, thankful that at least one of her boys was showing a little more zest toward the house. "What color would you like to paint the walls?"

"Hmmm . . ." He tapped a finger against his chin, assessing the space around him as if in serious deliberation. "Maybe . . . yellow?"

She nodded in agreement, looking around at the space. "Yellow could work."

"Can we go to the hotel now?" Jack asked, a bored tone in his voice. "I really wanna catch the start of the game. If they even have ESPN in this hillbilly—"

Maggie speared him with a warning look. "Yes. We'll go now. I have to make it to the Piggly Wiggly to pick up some cleaning supplies." She had to come back to the house so she could give it a thorough clean before the movers arrived in the morning with the furniture. She was exhausted, and hadn't anticipated spending her evening cleaning, but as it was it had to be done. There was no way she was moving her things into a filthy house.

Jack turned around quicker than the Flash himself, clearly desperate to get out of there, but when he turned, he let out a piercing shriek, his voice cracking with fear as he jumped almost a foot off the floor.

"What is it?" Maggie rushed toward him, her heart hammering.

"Huge *spider*!" He flapped his hands in the air like a madman.

She peered over his shoulder to see the offending arachnid. "Jack . . . it's a daddy-longlegs."

TJ giggled from behind her, and it was a glorious sound she hadn't heard in what felt like forever. Jack shrieked again, ducking underneath the innocently dangling spider before bolting out of the room, his footfalls echoing loudly on the hardwood.

Maggie shook her head, glancing back at TJ. He grinned up at her, and taking her proffered hand they followed in Jack's wake, although she was almost certain he was halfway to the car already.

Chapter 9

Jewel Harbor was the quintessential New England port village. Just driving through the main street, which slanted down toward the harbor at the very end, put a smile on Maggie's face as she took it all in.

Flowering trees lined the sidewalks, gas lantern lampposts peppered between them. Quaint *Hansel and Gretel* store fronts with major street appeal showcased picturesque window presentations to attract the most discerning shopper. An old-time movie theater sat next to an old-time ice cream parlor. A bakery sat next to a bookshop next to a candle store next to Barb's Beauty Salon. Across the road was a quaint Old English pub aptly named The Crown Jewel. Next door was Mick's Hardware Store, a pet shop named Woof's, and Jane's Café was beside Miller's Family Department Store *for all your apparel needs*, or so the sign promised.

If a place could be this beautiful in the spring, Maggie could only imagine how breathtaking it would be come winter. She couldn't wait to see the illuminated store windows lighting up a snowy afternoon. The naked branches of the trees twinkling with fairy lights and lush green garlands wrapped around the lampposts.

"What do you boys think of the place?" Maggie asked, glancing sideways to find Jack taking in the sights as they drove through the main street.

"There's a movie theater," TJ noted, staring longingly at the marquee as they continued past.

Maggie smiled at her youngest son.

"Snoresville," Jack said derisively.

She rolled her eyes at her teenager.

"Why don't we stop and get an early bite before we head to the hotel?" She turned into a parking spot outside Jane's Café. It was almost five o'clock. An early dinner while the sun was still shining, and an even earlier night was exactly what the boys needed after their long day.

"But the game?" Jack held up his cell phone, showing Maggie the small screen displaying what looked to be a baseball game.

"Jack, it's baseball." She deadpanned. "That game will go on long into the night. You'll be fine."

He muttered something as he huffed and puffed his way out of the car. Maggie ignored him and hopped out to open the back door for TJ, noticing the slight pep in his step as he jumped down to the pavement. This place was going to be good for him, she could already tell; his eyes hadn't been so bright in a long time. And that thought alone made her realize this had been the right decision, despite her lingering doubts.

The little bell over the door to the café jingled as the three entered. Inside was cozy and homely. Music played from a vintage radio that sat on the sill of the wall cutout to the kitchen. In the corner, two cushy armchairs were set up next to a bookshelf loaded with paperbacks; an antique-looking floor lamp was casting a soft glow. Empty tables set for two and four were strategically placed throughout, complete with tiny glass mason jars full of delicate roses and peonies adding to the shabby chic aesthetic. A few booths bordered the dining room, looking out onto the street and across the road to the harbor. Running along the dining area, lined with stools, was a big service counter on which were displayed glass dome cake stands full of delicious looking muffins, decadent cupcakes and homemade slices. It was cute and quaint, but, above all else, it was welcoming.

The café was almost empty, save for a man perched at the counter sipping from a mug of coffee while reading a newspaper.

"Well, hi, hello there." A musical voice rang through the air, and Maggie turned to find a petite blonde woman standing at the end booth, dirty dishes stacked carefully upon the tray she was holding.

"Hello." TJ waved at the lady while instinctively stepping closer to his mom.

Jack ignored the woman and everyone else as he moved to the very first booth, sliding into the banquette while staring vacantly at his phone.

"Hi." Maggie smiled, ushering TJ to the table to join his brother.

"I'm Jane." The woman beamed on her approach.

Maggie sat down next to TJ as Jane stopped by their table.

"Welcome to my humble little abode." Placing her tray down on the table behind her, Jane pulled a notepad from the pocket in her apron and plucked a pen from somewhere in the mess of blonde curls piled high on top of her head. "What can I get you all?"

TJ glanced up from the menu in his hands, his brow furrowed in thought. "Do you have fries?" he asked, his voice quiet and meek.

Jane placed a hand on her curvy hip, cocking her head to the side. "Do I have *fries*? Why of course I do! I've got bacon-loaded fries, disco fries, cheesy fries, sweet chili fries, sweet potato fries, zucchini fries, fries with brown gravy, you name it."

TJ's eyes widened, overwhelmed by choice. He glanced curiously at Maggie before settling his gaze back on the friendly lady. "Um, can I please have normal fries with some ketchup on the side?"

"Of course you can, sweetheart." Jane made a note of his order, jotting it down on her pad.

"And can I please have a Dr Pepper? With a straw, please. Paper not plastic, because of the turtles, ma'am."

"Well, aren't you just adorable. And such wonderful manners," she gushed as she finished writing, flashing a wink at Maggie. Then, glancing in Jack's direction, Jane's smile faltered momentarily when he didn't bother looking up from his cell. "And for you, young man?" she prompted.

"A burger. No pickles," Jack murmured.

"Jack Morris." Maggie warned, glowering at him from across the table.

Slowly he looked up, meeting his mother's glower with one of his own as he said through gritted teeth, "And a Coke." He flashed the innocent woman an insincere and downright deplorable smile as he added with an icy, sarcastic tone, "*Please.*"

Maggie offered the kind woman a rueful look on behalf of her horrible son, but Jane dismissed her silent apology with a casual wave of her hand and another dimpled smile. "And for you?"

Maggie pointed to the counter before sliding out of the booth. "I'll come up."

Following Jane to the counter, she watched the woman as she began pouring the boys' sodas. She was around Maggie's age, maybe a little older, curvy with a pretty face and big blue eyes that were smiling when she turned back, carefully placing the two fountain glasses on top of the counter. She added a red and white paper straw to the Dr Pepper, offering Maggie a wink. Maggie smiled tightly in return.

"You okay, hun?" Jane asked, her eyes kind and sincere.

"Yeah." Maggie shrugged, realizing she'd been caught faking a smile, something she'd grown accustomed to over the last month and a half.

"Oh, and I'm sorry about *him*," she said, nodding back toward the booth to where Jack was still focused on his cell phone. "Baseball season's in full swing. He'll be oblivious to everything for the next few months, at least."

Jane laughed. "And then football season begins, basketball, and it starts all over again. My husband's the same. *Boys*," she harrumphed with jest. "And I've got a girl about his age, so I know *all* about the perils of parenting a teenager."

Managing another smile, Maggie nodded, introducing herself, "I'm Maggie."

"You're the new family moving into the old Diamond Lake house." Jane narrowed one eye as if in serious thought. "Boston, right?"

"Yeah . . .?" Maggie's brows knitted together, assessing her with questioning curiosity. "How do you know that?" She added a light laugh to try and conceal her suspicion, but her anxiety was peaking. She didn't want the people in town to know her just yet. She was looking forward to being a stranger for a while, a nobody.

"Small town, honey." Jane waved a hand in the air. "Not a lot happens around here. In fact, you're the biggest news since Cindy Simmons was caught with Vice Principal Cullen in the locker room at the high school during the Columbus Day dance. He had his pants down around his damn ankles, and she was supposed to be chaperoning." She shook her head, rolling her eyes with dramatic flair before changing the subject. "We've all been real excited to meet you."

Her smile was genuine and it beamed. And it seemed infectious. Maggie couldn't help but smile her first real honest to God smile in what felt like forever.

"Now, you go sit," Jane ordered with another brush of her hand. "I'm going to make you up a bowl of my famous chowder, and get you a sneaky glass of pinot grigio." She winked.

"Um, okay . . . thank you." Maggie laughed once under her breath as she turned back to the booth to find Jack still enamored of his baseball game and TJ staring aimlessly out at the afternoon as the sun began to head toward the horizon.

As she took her seat, handing Jack his Coke and placing TJ's Dr Pepper in front of him, she glanced back to find Jane humming along to the song playing on the radio, and her smile lingered. She couldn't remember a time she'd ever felt so welcomed by a complete stranger.

While she knew it was only a matter of time before the small town caught wind of her tragic past—a matter of time before the pity smiles and whispering behind her back started up again—it was refreshing being in a place where no one knew who she was or what had happened. Here, she wasn't Maggie, the widowed wife of Tom Morris. She was just Maggie. And never before had being herself felt so right. This place was going to be good for her, *and* her boys. She could tell.

Chapter 10

In all her thirty-six years, Maggie couldn't remember a time she'd ever felt so physically exhausted. Not even after twenty-eight hours of labor with Jack had she felt as truly spent as she did right now. Pushing up from her knees, hands on hips, she arched her back to crack out her spinal kinks, taking a long hard look at the bathroom floor she'd just spent the best part of two hours scrubbing. She released a heavy sigh, allowing her tight shoulders to sag as she moved her head side to side in an attempt to ease the painful knot in her neck.

Last night, she'd left the boys at the hotel and had come back to the house with the trunk of her car loaded with the cleaning supplies she'd picked up from the Piggly Wiggly. Through the silence of night she dusted, disinfected, mopped and vacuumed until two o'clock in the morning. Then she went back to the hotel, caught up on a few hours of sleep, and then took the boys to the bakery for breakfast before dropping them back at the hotel and returned to the house to meet the movers.

Exhausted was an understatement. She hadn't showered in the last twenty-four hours. Her hair, a nested mess on top of her head, needed to be washed, and she had dirt caked beneath her nails. But she was a determined woman. She wasn't planning on stopping until every piece of furniture was in its rightful place, and every last cobweb and dust particle had been swept out of sight.

Wiping the sweat from her brow with the back of her hand, Maggie's ears pricked at the sound of an engine disrupting the quiet morning and of gravel crunching beneath tires. She moved to the big window in the bathroom, and looked down to see an old pickup truck pull up next to her car. A man dressed in coveralls hopped out, looking up at the house.

"The contractor," she hissed, cursing under her breath when she realized the time, and the horrible state she was in.

Nobody outside of her sons and Tom had ever seen her so disheveled. In fact, she'd rarely even let her husband see her in such a state. Tom would have made some comment, passing it off as a half-hearted joke, but his words would have cut her deep down. It was usually best for Maggie's self-confidence if she looked as put together as she could at all times for her husband.

Shaking her head, Maggie snapped herself out from that unexpected thought and remembered the situation she was currently dealing with. How she looked was the last thing that mattered. Smoothing down her T-shirt, she brushed errant strands of hair from her face as she hurried out of the bathroom and down the stairs, dodging the two burly movers as they carried a mattress past her on her way out the front door.

Outside, the morning was beautiful and sunny, and Maggie was forced to lift a hand up to shield her eyes from the glare as she continued down the porch steps, crossing the yard to meet the man who was currently staring up at the house, scratching his head.

"Hello." Maggie waved as she approached him.

"Mrs. Morris?" The man held his hand out and she shook it. "I'm Ned."

"Please, call me Maggie. Thank you for coming at such short notice." She pointed back at the house with her thumb. "Would you like me to show you through?"

Ned nodded, taking a small notepad and a pencil from the chest pocket of his coveralls, pausing a moment to take down some notes. This caused her anxiety to spike. She was dreading this quote.

*

"Okay," Ned began, flicking through the notes he'd taken throughout his thorough forty-minute inspection of the house.

Maggie watched him with bated breath, desperate to know the extent of the damage but dreading it also. Her hands trembled as she wrapped them around her coffee mug.

"Porch steps need a full reconstruction." He glanced up at her before continuing, "The deck needs to be replaced, too. Wet rot."

"Oh, really?" Maggie glanced at the deck on the front porch. It looked fine to her. She hadn't been expecting that. She sighed heavily, knowing this was not going to be good.

"New screening. Obviously." Ned pointed to the torn and tattered porch screening, and Maggie nodded because that much was a given. But when he went to continue, she could sense his reluctance, and her stomach dropped. "The furnace needs to be replaced. That can probably wait now a few months, given we're coming into summer. But you're gonna wanna get it fixed no later than September. You won't survive the winter, otherwise." He grimaced at the sheer mention of winter before adding through gritted teeth, "That's gonna be expensive . . . a grand, at least."

Maggie closed her eyes, exhaling a ragged sigh as he went on and on with everything he'd marked down in his notebook.

"And last but definitely not least, because . . . well, this is the *real* kick in the teeth . . ." Ned paused, gauging her reaction.

"What?" she asked impatiently, because seriously what else could possibly have been wrong with the place?

"You got three major leaks in your roof." He shook his head, glancing down at his notepad before tentatively meeting her eyes again. "The whole dang thing needs replacing."

Maggie gaped at him. "I need a new *roof*?"

He nodded, pursing his lips.

"Oh my God . . ." Scrubbing a hand over her face, she glanced up at the house—or money pit—and she wondered momentarily if she should just hire a bulldozer and plow the whole thing down. Maybe she could claim insurance.

"I'll prepare an itemized quote listing everything in order of urgent repairs and get it back to you this afternoon. But, Maggie, I need to warn you . . . it ain't gonna be cheap."

Maggie winced. "How *not cheap* are we talking?"

With a contemplative sigh Ned looked down at his notepad, scanning through the pages. His lips moved as he silently calculated in his head. Narrowing an eye, he glanced up toward the sky before fixing her with a look full of trepidation. "I mean, the roof alone, you're looking at around twelve, thirteen at least."

Maggie sighed, her shoulders sagging with relief. "Oh, thank goodness. Thirteen hundred I can handle. I was scared you were going to say . . ." She trailed off when she noticed the confusion in Ned's eyes.

He blinked at her once, twice, his brows climbing up high beneath the peak of his faded old ball cap. "Uh, no, ma'am. Sorry, I meant thirteen *thousand*."

"Wait. Did you say thirteen *thousand*?" she exclaimed. "As in . . . *dollars*?"

He stared at her for a moment before nodding.

She almost dropped dead right there in the overgrown weeds.

"And then, of course, the furnace and the . . ." His voice petered out when he looked up again, clearly concerned by her reaction.

Instinctively, she placed a hand on her chest in the hope that it might help to soothe her racing heart.

Thirteen thousand dollars for the roof, alone. Plus everything else. And the other bits and pieces she'd been planning to do to redecorate inside and make the place look nice. After the sale of the house in Belmont and finalizing everything . . . she simply couldn't afford a new damn roof.

Maggie had never hated anyone in her life—hate was an ugly emotion—but right at that moment, she really hated her late husband for what he'd done to her and the boys, for the position he'd put them in.

"Are you okay?" Ned asked, cutting into her overwhelming thoughts. She looked up to see his kind brown eyes flicker with sympathy. "You look a little pale."

"Yeah, I just . . ." She shook her head. "I didn't think it would all be so much, I . . ." She had no words. She looked up at the three-story house that could have been a beautiful place to call home, but, now, all she could see was every last cent she had left to her name. She couldn't help but glare at the structure, silently wishing Mother Nature might do her a solid and strike the house with a giant crack of lightning from up above and burn it to the ground.

"Can I ask why you didn't get a pre-sale survey done of the property?" Ned asked after a beat. He removed his sweat-stained ball cap to scratch the back of his head. "All this would've been picked up on inspection," he said, as if it were obvious.

Maggie looked up at him and sighed heavily with a shrug. "I was trying to save money." She almost laughed, it was so ironic. Shaking her head, she muttered, "And because I'm a clueless half-wit."

"Look, we don't have to do everything all at once." Ned held a hand in the air as if in surrender. "We can start with the urgent repairs. We can replace the shingles and patch the holes in the roof. That might buy us another couple more years." He shrugged a shoulder. "Why don't I head back to my office, write up the quote. I'll send it through to you and you can take a few days to decide."

"Is this place safe?" she asked, quirking a brow. "I'm moving my sons in tonight."

He nodded. "This old girl's been around for a hundred and fifty years and she'll last a few hundred more. But we gotta take good care of her. She's been a little neglected."

Maggie had never related to a house more.

"But you and your boys'll be safe." Ned smiled reassuringly.

"Thank you." She tried for a smile of her own but it was just about impossible. She thought she'd made the right decision moving out here. She really thought it was the best for everyone, that this was the way they could all get back on their feet. And yet, here she was, day two, already in way over her head.

*

Maggie had been in this godforsaken hardware store for over an hour. The only other person was a pink-haired teenage girl perched behind the counter, chewing gum while staring vacuously at her cell phone. She was wearing an apron with the store's logo emblazoned across the front of it, but she looked as if she'd have less of an idea than Maggie. So, she let the girl continue watching whatever it was that enthralled her so deeply, and carried on. She was a grown woman, after all.

After Ned left the house, she'd had a mini meltdown. In fact, there had been nothing *mini* about it. She even took to the buckled porch steps with one of the boys' old baseball bats. Not that her slight frame and limited strength did much damage, but it was good to let out the aggression that had been roiling inside of her. The movers had witnessed her momentary snap but, thankfully, they said nothing. They'd likely seen it all before. The stress of moving, and all. But just in case, Maggie gave them a generous tip. Her way of thanking them for allowing her to lose her shit in peace.

There was a lot that needed to be fixed at the house, and it was going to cost a ton of money. Money Maggie didn't have. She wasn't certified to do the repairs herself, neither was she even close to capable, but there were a few things she could do to save herself some money and maybe bide some time. She could replace the kitchen cabinet handles, and remove the boards from the windows. She was even confident she could fix the buckled porch steps. There was a wealth of knowledge on the internet for a novice like her. She had spent the last few hours watching YouTube videos, and it didn't look too difficult, she just needed the right equipment. But as she searched the wall of hand tools, reading each label closely, confusion overwhelmed her as she took it all in. Who'd have thought there were so many different kinds of Phillips head screwdrivers?

Maggie's newfound confidence in home renovations was vanishing with every second she stood there wondering what the hell she was doing. As she reached for a packet of screws on the top shelf, she knocked the shelf below with her breast, causing three tins of nails to go tumbling to the ground with a loud clatter, one coming open, its contents scattering all over the floor.

"Crap!" she hissed, looking around to check no one had witnessed her mishap.

Dropping to her knees, she gathered as many of the wayward nails as she could, bending down to try and see beneath the shelving rack. Some were well beyond her reach, and she shrugged in defeat as she pushed up to her knees.

"You missed a few."

Startling from the deep, slightly humored voice behind her, Maggie turned, looking up from her position on the sawdust-covered floor to see a bearded man wearing a backwards ball cap, watching her with one raised brow and the hint of a lopsided grin.

Her eyes betrayed her, trailing down of their own accord. An old flannel shirt stretched over a pair of broad shoulders, unbuttoned and left open over a white T-shirt which skimmed a strong, defined chest. Well-worn blue jeans smeared with dirt and grease looked as if they'd been made to fit only his thighs. Scuffed work boots completed his blue-collar ensemble.

Realizing she was still on the floor, Maggie collected what she could of her wits. As she rose up from her knees, a big hand with grease-covered fingers appeared in front of her face. Reluctantly, she accepted the offer of help, and the man lifted her effortlessly to her feet with one swift tug of his arm.

"Thanks," she muttered, brushing her hands over her already filthy gray cotton T-shirt.

"No problem." His voice was laced with humor.

She didn't need to look up to know that he was smiling at her. But she did anyway. And damn. That hint of a grin had turned into a million-watt smile, and she was left a little breathless by the glint of mischief flashing from deep within a cerulean gaze.

Clearing the sudden bubble from the back of her throat, Maggie turned back to the shelf, replacing the tins of nails with shaky hands, fully aware of his presence still lingering closely. His eyes were fixed on her with such an intensity that she could feel the sensitive skin at her nape burn.

"Need a hand?" he asked wryly after a few beats.

His offer to help immediately got her defenses up. He wasn't being rude, as such. But it was as if he doubted she had any idea what she was doing. While that were mostly true, she refused to be *that* woman: timid, meek, and incapable of picking out a box of damn screws. She schooled her expression, throwing a curt "I can manage" over her shoulder.

The man continued lingering for a moment longer, but she made a point of ignoring him as best as she could.

"Suit yourself," he murmured with a low chuckle, his steady footfalls moving away.

Maggie released the breath she'd been holding and her shoulders fell when she realized she still had no idea what she was looking for. If she kept up this defiant attitude, she really could be stuck in this store all afternoon. And she needed to get back to the hotel to pick up the boys and check out before they charged her for another night.

"Actually—" She spun around, finding the man only a few feet away, his broad back to her as he stared up at the wall of power tools. He turned slowly, a curious smile in his eyes despite his stoic facade.

She sighed heavily, her face scrunching up with confusion. "I need a Phillips head screwdriver and some bugle head screws. Do you know where I might find them?"

His brows drew together with a deep furrow, but that grin was back, ghosting at the corners of his mouth. He walked back to her, glancing up at the boxes of nails and screws. Maggie watched him from the corner of her eye. He was tall. Not quite as tall as Tom, but a good six feet. Short lengths of chestnut hair poked out from beneath his cap, and his beard was kept short. Not completely lumberjack-like; but long enough that maybe he just hadn't shaved in a week or so.

"What size?"

"Huh?" She was pulled from her reverie by his unexpected question.

The man flashed her a sideways glance, as he repeated with another chuckle, "What size?"

She gaped at him incredulously. "There are different *sizes*?"

Biting back his smile, he scoffed, "Most screws come in different sizes, yeah."

Maggie threw her head back with a groan.

"What do you need them for?"

She composed herself enough to look him straight in the eye. "I need to fix my porch steps."

He balked. "With a screwdriver?"

Maggie blinked. "Yeah . . .?"

Slowly, his lips curled upwards, but then suddenly he was laughing. Out loud. Really loud. Obnoxiously so. She stared at him before looking around, wondering what the big damn deal was, her brows drawn together in annoyance.

Thankfully, he picked up on her frustration and forced himself to stop laughing, coughing a few times to conceal the last couple of chuckles. "Okay, you can't replace porch steps with a screwdriver. You're gonna need an impact driver . . ." He stopped, obviously noticing her blank expression. With a knowing smirk, he turned, pointing to a power tool displayed on the wall behind him. "One of *these*."

"Three hundred *dollars*?" Maggie gasped, taking in the price tag dangling from the shiny red device. She glanced at him and sighed. "Maybe I should just pay the contractor . . ."

"Contractor?"

Maggie nodded. "Yeah . . . I mean, if I'm being honest, I need to fix a little more than just a few porch steps. New decking. New screening. A whole new roof! Around every corner I discover another hidden death-trap just waiting to claim its next victim," she said with a derisive snort.

"Ah, so you bought the old house over on Diamond Lake, huh?"

"Yeah. How did you guess?" She gauged his reaction curiously.

He shrugged. "Two and two. You're new around here and I heard that place finally sold to an out-of-towner."

"You mean an out-of-town *sucker*, right?"

He bit back a smile. "Mr. McDaniel stayed there a few years too long. His family had to get a court order to get his stubborn ass into the retirement home down in Manchester," he explained. "Almost burned the joint down twice in the last few months he was there. That place has been empty now for a few years, at least."

"Well, I guess that explains a lot." She shrugged.

He peered over her shoulder to her buggy which was full with planks of timber, a roll of screening, two one-gallon drums of paint. He seemed to hesitate, clamping his bottom lip between his teeth before tentatively meeting her eyes. "You know, if you want, I could stop by and help you fix up a few things. I've got my own tools. Might even save you a few bucks with your contractor." He lifted his ball cap to ruffle a hand through his short hair before replacing it again, his gaze flickering momentarily to the gold ring on Maggie's finger that she was subconsciously twisting around and around. "Unless, of course, your . . . husband is gonna—"

"No husband," Maggie snapped, her tone sharp and uncharacteristically terse. Moving her hands out of sight by stuffing them into the back pockets of her jeans, she managed a tight-lipped smile, her gaze narrowed dubiously. "Why would you want to help me? You don't even know me."

"I'm Evan," he said with a casual smile. "I fix boats down at the wharf." He pointed to his shirt and she narrowed her eyes to make out the faded wording, *Hannigan's Boat Repairs*. She quirked a brow, staring down at his proffered hand as it hung awkwardly in the air between them, calloused fingers smeared with grease.

"And . . . this is usually the point in a conversation where you offer your name in exchange." Evan laughed under his breath. "Or even just a *hey, Evan, nice to meet you*, would do," he added, a high pitch timbre in his voice as he tried to sound like a woman.

Maggie finally shook his hand, meeting his smiling eyes. She didn't know this man, this *Evan*, if that was his real name. For all she knew, he was just some creep who hung out at the hardware store waiting for an unsuspecting woman like her to take advantage of. Or, maybe her mind was getting a little carried away with itself.

"Maggie. Maggie Morris."

"See? Now I know you," Evan retorted with a smug smile, continuing, "This is a small town, Maggie. We help each other out when we can . . . it's just what we do around here."

Maggie assessed him. She concluded that this man probably was just trying to be friendly and, from the few interactions she'd had with the locals so far, it seemed this was what people were like in Jewel Harbor. But this was supposed to be her new life as a strong, independent woman; she couldn't accept help from the first man to offer, no matter how handsome he was.

"Thanks for the offer, Evan, but I can manage." She pressed her lips together in the semblance of a smile. "I'm sure these will be fine," she said, taking the box of bugle screws from him and tossing them into her buggy with the rest of her items. She turned and began wheeling the cart toward the counter, leaving him standing there alone in the aisle.

"Don't forget this!"

Maggie stopped, turning to find him holding a shiny screwdriver in his hand, the metal reflecting the fluorescent lights above, every shimmering glint mocking her. She groaned internally. With a forced smile that concealed her gritted teeth, she took it from him with a muttered thanks, and turned away, noticing the slightly trite smile lingering on his lips.

"Bye, Maggie," he said with a soft chuckle.

She threw a quick wave over her shoulder, hurrying as fast as she could, unable to risk another glance back at him.

Chapter 11

On her way back from picking the boys up at the hotel, Maggie received the itemized quote from Ned. For everything from the new roof to the furnace replacement, the porch deck and stairs, and all the little jobs she'd mentioned she wanted to do to improve the inside, the total price came to . . . a lot. Too much. Way more than she had. She'd stupidly looked at the email while stopped at the traffic lights in the center of town. Then she'd ended up getting honked by the car behind, and had dropped her cell in the process. She felt sick the entire way home.

There was no way she could afford to fork out that amount of money. Doing so would leave her with less than nothing in their rainy day fund. And she couldn't do that. It was too much of a risk. She was all the boys had left. All she kept thinking was, what if something happened to her? TJ and Jack would have no one and nothing. It was unlikely Tom's father would help out; not that she would accept help from him, even if he did. Maggie refused to put them in that situation, but they also needed a roof over their head which didn't leak.

By the time they pulled up to the house, Maggie was a mess, but, thankfully, the movers were gone and everything was in its rightful place, which helped to ease her anxiety some. There were a lot of boxes lying around to unpack, but the old house was starting to look and feel a lot more like a home. It just needed repairs costing a whole heap of money she didn't have. Maggie rolled her eyes at that taunting thought as she placed her purse and keys on the console table by the front door.

"Boys, can you please help me unload the things from the car?"

TJ paused halfway up the stairs before stomping back down the steps like the baby elephant he was. He stood in front of Maggie as if he was reporting for duty, and she couldn't help but smile, ruffling a hand through his thick mane of chocolate brown hair. Then she glanced over to find Jack flopping down onto the couch, kicking his feet up to rest his sneakers on the cushion, completely ignoring her.

She sighed. "Jack?"

He didn't bother looking up from his cell.

"Jack!" She raised her voice, placing a hand on her hip. When he finally obliged her with a perfunctory glance, she said, "I need your help."

"Later," he muttered.

Now, normally, Maggie might've let that slide. She could admit, shamefully so, that she'd never really been the parent to make the demands. It had always been Tom's role. And she was beginning to realize she'd done herself an injustice with Jack because he didn't seem to respect her the way a child should respect a parent. Things had to change, and quick.

Maggie glanced sideways to find TJ watching on. She swallowed her hesitation, and moved to stand over him. "No, Jack." Her steely tone captured his attention, and when he met her eyes, she offered her most serious look. "*Now.*"

He stared at her for a long moment, his face otherwise impassive save for the look of disdain flaring in his gaze. But, after a few beats, he sighed heavily, tossing his phone onto the couch cushion before heaving himself up. With a few incomprehensible words murmured under his breath, he stormed his way out the door.

Maggie mentally high-fived herself because, regardless of his attitude and sass, she considered that a win.

*

Jack made the decision that, instead of sleeping on the same floor as the rest of his family, he wanted to turn the attic into his bedroom and sleep up there. He'd been traipsing up and down the stairs all afternoon, huffing and puffing, removing load after load of dusty old boxes, discarded furniture and whatever else the prior homeowners, the McDaniels, had stored up there over the fifty years they'd occupied the residence. Maggie had been helping TJ unpack his boxes in his bedroom. They heard the occasional, and often hilarious, high-pitched shriek followed by an excessively long hiss of the can of bug spray Jack had taken up to the attic with him. The both of them giggling quietly each time.

"Mom?"

Maggie looked up from where she was storing away some of TJ's winter clothes in the bottom drawer of his dresser, turning to find him watching her from his place on the rug. That was when she noticed his old baseball glove and ball in his hands, and instinctively her chest tightened. With a soft sigh, she crossed the room, moving to sit on the floor beside him.

"What is it, honey?" she asked, gently placing a hand on his shoulder. She glanced down to where he was absentmindedly tossing the ball into the mitt.

"Do you think . . ." He stopped himself, lifting his chin and meeting her eyes, his teeth clamping down on his bottom lip as he seemed to contemplate his words. "Do you think it would be okay if I went back to little league?"

Her brows climbed high, her eyes widening. She definitely hadn't been expecting that. She wanted to smile, desperately, because she never thought she'd hear him mutter those words ever again. And yet, there he was, ball in hand, a hopeful look of trepidation in his eyes as if he wasn't sure he should be asking such a thing.

She cleared her throat, schooling her expression. "Do you . . . do you *want* to go back to little league?"

TJ released a heavy sigh, his slight shoulders falling as he stared longingly at the ball in his hand. He nodded, but then he looked at Maggie once more, his gaze full of apprehension. "I do. But it . . . it feels wrong."

She gauged his reaction a moment, frowning with confusion. "Why does it feel wrong?"

"Because I really love playing baseball, but Daddy's . . . in heaven." He looked away to the far corner of the room, focusing on nothing, his eyes glazing over for a moment. He shrugged one of his slight shoulders, continuing, "I feel like I should be sad, not playing baseball."

Maggie was taken aback by that statement. It sent a chill down her spine. "TJ, you can feel whichever way you want to feel. Sad, angry, happy . . ." She shook her head when he looked at her. "There's no certain way anyone should feel right now. And, if you *want* to go back to little league, then you absolutely should. And I bet Daddy would want that because he knew how much you love baseball, and he'd want nothing more than for you to be happy again." She hated that those last few words tasted like poison on her tongue. She wanted so much to wish it were true, that Tom had wanted nothing more than for his sons to be happy, but, now, she simply didn't know if that was true or if it was just part of the lie Tom had lived.

"Remember when he used to stand with Coach? And Coach would go mad at him for yelling too loud." TJ smiled wistfully. "Coach banned him from coming anywhere near the diamond during play time."

Maggie found herself smiling, her mind wandering back to a

couple of years ago. She'd been at home in the backyard tending to the rose garden she'd been trying to get to flower all season. Tom came huffing out through the French doors and she looked over her shoulder to see his face set so angry, hands on his hips as he paced back and forth along the patio, taking a few deep breaths.

"What's wrong?" she asked, standing up, her heart suddenly at the back of her throat. "Is TJ okay?"

Tom paused, glancing at her. He waved a hand in the air. "Yeah, he's fine." He continued pacing. "But that asshole, Todd Derry." He sneered at the mention of TJ's little league coach. Shaking his head, he muttered something under his breath before continuing, "Can you believe he actually had me *banned* from the diamond?"

Maggie's eyed widened. "Tom, what'd you do?"

"Me?" He was incredulous, pointing at himself like he couldn't possibly believe she would immediately assume he did anything to get himself banned from a little league diamond. "I was simply standing there by the dugout, telling TJ how to—"

"Tom!" Maggie interjected. "You're *not* the coach. Todd is."

Tom gaped at her. "That's *my* kid!" He threw his hand back in the direction of the house. "I'm his *father*. I have every right to tell him how I think he should hit a goddamn ball. I know a hell of a lot more about baseball than *Todd Derry*!" He exclaimed his name with a derisive snort, ever the mature adult.

Maggie rolled her eyes behind the tint of her sunglasses but she remained silent. If there was one thing she knew, it was when to let her husband go off on one of his self-righteous tangents.

"I'm going to write a letter to the League." And with that he'd turned and stormed back inside, leaving her alone with the rose bushes.

Maggie couldn't help but laugh at the memory now. "Oh, I remember. He came home in a real huff. He was going to write a letter of complaint to the League!" She smiled. "I talked him out of it once he managed to calm down."

TJ giggled but then he pressed his lips together, swallowing hard. "I kind of . . . am." He chanced a glance at her before continuing, "Starting to feel happy again, I mean."

Her heart swelled in her chest and tears pricked her eyes.

He went on, "I mean, I'm still sad that he's gone. And I miss him so much. I'll always miss him. But . . . I'm also happy. You know?" He took a look around his room, adding, "And I like it here. This house, the trees, the lake . . . You can smell the ocean in the breeze when the windows are open. It makes me happy. And I think Daddy would have liked it here, too."

Swallowing her emotion, Maggie managed a nod. Thinking of Tom being there with them in their new life, it spoiled it somehow. She hated how, now she knew the truth, all thoughts of Tom were tainted. If she were being honest with herself, if he were still around, she wouldn't want him here after what he'd done. But she smiled, pushing those thoughts aside.

"You should play little league again." She wiped at her tears with the back of her hand, laughing once to cover the sob bubbling out of her. "In fact, why don't I make a few calls tomorrow to find out where we can sign up. Does that sound okay?"

With a small smile, TJ nodded, looking from Maggie to his ball and back again. And she couldn't hold it any longer. She wrapped her arms around him so tight she wasn't even sure he'd be able to breathe. Closing her eyes, she basked in the feeling of her son safe in her embrace. She smiled despite those pesky tears. But this time, they were happy tears.

Chapter 12

Given the fact they had little food in the house, Maggie decided to treat the boys to dinner at the pub. After scrubbing away the dirt and grime she had collected throughout the day, she actually made somewhat of an effort for the first time in a long while. She blow-dried her hair, applied some mascara and a little blush. She chose a nice pair of jeans with a cute satin camisole beneath a pretty cashmere cardigan. This was their first official night out as a family of three in their new home; it was worth the effort.

After parking the car, her muscles were stiff and achy as she followed Jack and TJ down the sidewalk to the bustling Crown Jewel. The sound of music, and the jovial voices accompanying it, spilled out into the night air through the open doors and windows lining the patio, floating through Main Street and mixing with the low-lying scent of the ocean.

They paused awkwardly in the doorway, waiting with uncertainty. Maggie wasn't sure if they should wait to be shown to a table or not. The only places they used to go out to dinner as a family back in Boston were the places Tom chose: the country club, fancy restaurants, venues with hosts and hostesses who would lead them to the table they'd had to book weeks in advance.

Tom would walk through the maze of tables, nodding to those

he passed as if he were some kind of local celebrity, and Maggie would trail behind like a loyal puppy with the boys dragging their feet. Half the time, TJ wouldn't eat anything on the menu, and Maggie would make him a grilled cheese sandwich when they got home. Tom would admonish her, saying that if TJ refused to eat anything then she should force him to go without, that he would never eat when they went out for dinner if he knew there would be an option for common food when he returned home.

But they never went anywhere the boys wanted to go. In fact, they never really went anywhere Maggie wanted to go. It was always about Tom, and his constant need to mingle with the elite and climb the proverbial social ladder.

Searching the dimly lit space, Maggie scanned the tables of people eating together in the restaurant, friends enjoying a drink at the bar, others playing pool or watching the ball game on the multiple flat screen televisions on the wall. Everyone seemed to know everyone else and it was intimidating—like arriving at a party you weren't invited to.

"There's a spot!" TJ pointed to a table for four situated off to the side by the empty stone fireplace.

"Okay, I guess we'll grab that one," Maggie said with a shrug, glancing around before leading the way inside. When no one shouted out for them to stop, she carried on while managing a small smile to those she passed before reaching the lone out-of-the-way table.

Jack was uncertain as he took in the environment around them. "Everyone's *staring* at us," he said under his breath, his face twisted with uncertainty.

"No, they're not," Maggie lied with the most convincing smile she could fake. Everyone was absolutely staring at them; their gazes obvious and piqued with thinly veiled curiosity.

Removing her cross-body purse and placing it onto the table, she took a seat. Jack rolled his eyes, throwing a surly glower at the people around them before slumping into a chair. TJ, oblivious as always, made quick work of plucking a menu from the center of the table, inspecting each item as if he were a connoisseur of fine pub fare.

"I think I'm going to get the lobster bisque . . ." Maggie pondered out loud, glancing at the specials board, which was precisely when her gaze settled upon a somewhat familiar set of blue eyes watching her from across the bar, the same knowing smirk playing on his lips when her eyes met his.

Evan . . .

Like Maggie, Evan had cleaned himself up, changing from his ball cap and grease-covered clothes into a smart black button-down, the collar left open, showing off a light smattering of chest hair, sleeves rolled up, exposing those strong, ropey forearms. His hair was styled in that messy way many men deem acceptable; as if he'd showered, dipped his fingers into a tub of drugstore wax product and raked it through the longer layers on top before walking out the door.

Her mind wandered back to Tom at that moment. No matter where he was going—golf, dinner, work or a gala event—he made every effort to look as put together as he could. Not a single hair out of place, slicked back with the expensive pomade he'd buy online from Italy. Men like Evan were the polar opposite of those like Tom Morris.

She noticed Evan's eyes sparkle from across the way, his lips curling upwards, hinting at a smile as he lifted a little higher the huge glass of beer he was holding in the air, adding a nod of recognition. In return, Maggie pressed her lips together in the hint of a fleeting smile before returning her focus to the menu in front of her, trying desperately to ignore the unfamiliar feeling in her stomach.

"Mom?"

Startling, Maggie looked up to find Jack staring at her expectantly. "Yes? What? Sorry. What is it, honey?"

He jutted his chin over her shoulder and she turned to see

a pretty brunette wearing a yellow T-shirt with the pub's logo printed on it, prepped with a pencil and notepad in her hands.

"Oh, I'm so sorry." Maggie managed a light laugh, tucking her hair behind my ear.

"My name's Fiona, and I'll be your server this evening." The woman introduced herself with a well-versed lilt. "Would you like me to go over the specials, or do we know what we're having tonight?"

"I would like the pizza please." TJ took the lead. "Could I please have pepperoni on one half and three cheese on the other, with stuffed crust and ranch on the side?"

The server offered an impressed smile, winking at him. "I like a man who knows what he wants."

TJ's cheeks flushed.

"I'll have the grilled chicken sandwich with bacon." Jack nodded with a tight smile that looked as if it almost pained him, then returned his attention to one of the flat screens, focusing intently on the ball game.

Maggie cleared her throat. "I'll have the bisque special, please." She smiled as she handed their discarded menus to the woman, her eyes furtively glancing over toward the bar. She was only half surprised to see that Evan was now occupied with a heavily made-up woman who, leaning on the counter beside him, fluffed her blonde hair while openly flirting with him.

"Okay . . ." The waitress repeated their order back, smiling sweetly. "I'll be back soon with your basket of complimentary mozzarella sticks."

TJ's eyes lit up at the mention of free cheese.

"Oh, excuse me?" Maggie reached a hand out to stop her and, with a friendly smile, asked, "Can we order drinks?"

"There's a self-service soda fountain over by the condiment station for the kids." The lady pointed to the area which was currently crowded with children. "And you can order adult beverages directly from the bar." With another smile she indicated the bar with a jut of her chin before walking off in the direction of the kitchen.

The bar? Maggie cringed at the thought while staring longingly at the bottles of liquor lined upon the shelves behind the counter, sparkling temptingly beneath the shine of the down lights. She'd never needed a glass of sauvignon blanc more than right at that moment, but she really didn't feel like encountering Evan again. She didn't know what it was about him but there was just something that made her nervous.

She began idly twisting the gold band on her ring finger, considering her options. When her need for a glass of wine won the internal debate she stood, albeit reluctantly, and grabbed her purse. He was still there, head thrown back in laughter, completely engrossed by his female companion. He probably wouldn't even notice Maggie. She rolled her eyes at her own ridiculous deliberations. This was absurd. She was a thirty-six-year-old woman, for goodness' sake. She was entitled to a glass of wine.

"You okay, Mom?" TJ asked, glancing up at Maggie with a curious look.

She forced a smile, nodding at him as she clutched her purse a little tighter. "I'm just going to grab a drink from the bar. I'll be right back."

With a deep breath, she began toward the bar, to where a young man, who looked to be in his mid-twenties, moved fluidly, smiling to himself as he sang along to the song playing from the Wurlitzer jukebox, which stood pride of place between the two pool tables. From the way he mixed drinks with the ease of Tom Cruise in *Cocktail* to the way he flashed the occasional dimpled, cocky smile, she could tell he must be the town flirt. Which was precisely when he set his sights on her. With a definite swagger to his hips, he approached from the opposite end of the counter.

"You're new." He arched a brow, one hand placed upon the bar as he looked at Maggie with a curious smile. It was *almost* a greeting.

She cleared her throat. "Yes. Yes, I am." She tried to smile but the bartender had attracted the attention of the others standing around the bar, and when she felt Evan's smiling gaze land on her, her cheeks burned with an involuntary blush. She hated the attention.

"I'm Liam." The bartender held out a hand. Maggie glanced down at it briefly before forcing herself to shake it. "And you are . . .?" he asked after a silent beat with a friendly laugh.

"This is Maggie."

Both Maggie and Liam turned to see Evan watching on from his perch at the end of the bar, his blonde lady friend practically hanging off him while eyeing Maggie suspiciously.

"I can introduce myself, thank you very much," Maggie said matter-of-factly.

"Oh really?" Evan chuckled. "You weren't so forthcoming with introducing yourself earlier today. So, I thought I'd save you the hassle and do the honors." He shrugged nonchalantly, flashing Maggie a wicked grin before turning back to Liam. "Maggie's new in town, from Boston. Just moved into the old place over on Diamond Lake."

"Nice." Liam nodded, regarding Maggie with silent approval.

Maggie guffawed. It was like she wasn't even there. She butted in, "Excuse me, Liam? I hate to interrupt but . . ." She threw Evan a pointed look before continuing to the young man behind the counter. "Could I bother you for a glass of sauvignon blanc? Anything from New Zealand, if you have it."

"Sure thing, Miss Maggie." Liam nodded with a devilish grin, turning away to pour her drink.

She waited patiently, tapping her fingers against the bar while staring straight ahead at nothing in front of her. She was fully aware of Evan's weighty gaze still fixed on her from the other end of the bar, but she pretended not to notice. Once again, she began twisting the wedding band around her slender finger, something she knew full well she was doing, yet couldn't seem to stop herself. It was almost like a tic. Anxious more than nervous. That wedding ring had been like a shield for her over the years; she wasn't sure she could step out from behind it.

"Nice to see you again."

Startling from the overwhelming warmth brushing against her, Maggie pulled back just enough to see Evan sidle in beside her, his strong chest grazing her shoulder. He casually rested his elbows on the countertop, the same glass of beer still clasped between his big hands as he stared straight ahead.

"Are you *stalking* me?" she asked, only half-joking.

He simply chuckled, shaking his head, and she rolled her eyes.

"So, how'd you go with those porch steps?" he asked with a knowing side smirk.

She looked down at her hands, at her wedding ring glistening beneath the lights hanging down over the counter. "I didn't get around to it. But I will. Tomorrow," she said with forced confidence.

"My offer to help still stands, you know."

She glanced sideways from the corner of her eye to find him staring straight ahead, lips smiling over his glass as he took a big swig, Adam's apple bobbing in his throat with a hard swallow.

"Thank you." She nodded when he looked at her. "But, as I said today, I can manage. I don't mean to be rude, but this is just . . ." She paused, contemplating herself a moment, her newfound independence wavering with every single sliver of relentless self-doubt. Suspiciously, that taunting self-doubt began to sound more and more like Tom's voice the longer she listened to it.

Swallowing her nerves, Maggie looked into Evan's eyes, a little more vulnerable than she'd intended as she admitted, "This is just something I have to do."

Evan nodded slowly, his gaze flitting down to her wedding ring before focusing over her head. "They your boys?"

Maggie glanced over her shoulder finding TJ and Jack seated at the table. TJ was innocently sipping from a glass of soda, taking everything in with wide eyes full of intrigue. Jack was still totally transfixed by the baseball game playing on the television. Her heart tugged in her chest at the sight of them, and she smiled.

"Yeah. Jack's fifteen, and a total pain in my butt at the moment," she explained with a humorless laugh. "And TJ is ten. He's my baby." She turned back to Evan just in time to see a flicker of emotion glaze over his eyes, an emotion she couldn't quite place. But it was gone almost instantly, replaced by that same cocky smirk.

Liam returned, drawing her attention to him and the glass of wine in his hand.

The charming bartender placed the wine glass on the counter, and Maggie reached into her purse for her wallet but he waved a hand at her. "First drink's on the house." He half bowed with a little dramatic flair, adding, "My welcome gift to you, Miss Maggie."

Evan sniggered and Maggie caught him shaking his head, hiding his smirk behind his beer glass. She ignored him, accepting the wine from Liam with a smile and a thank you.

She turned away but then stopped. Meeting Evan's eyes once more, she jutted her chin in the direction of his female friend who was now glowering at him for being left to wait so long. "I think your date's waiting on you."

He followed her gaze, glancing casually over his shoulder and Maggie watched on as the blonde woman tried so hard to play it cool, like she hadn't just been shooting daggers into the back of his head.

"Oh, umm . . . absolutely *not* my date," Evan said out of the corner of his mouth before forcing a small smile and waving at the woman. She flushed profusely, waving back with a coy smile before taking a sip of her sickly-sweet looking cocktail.

"Well, then . . . enjoy your *not*-date." Maggie smirked at him when he looked back at her, and with her glass held aloft in silent cheers, she nodded once at Liam before turning and heading back to the table, feeling both men watching her as she walked away.

Chapter 13

Maggie woke early—before the sun—and, unable to go back to sleep, she decided to get a start on a few of the tasks from her seemingly never-ending to-do list.

Before coffee, she'd removed the remaining boards from the downstairs windows and scrubbed years' worth of grime and dirt off every pane of glass; the natural light now allowed in was ethereal and made a huge difference to the inside of the house.

After coffee, she drove TJ and Jack into town to see the early session of some new action hero movie that was playing at the cinema. She came home and got straight back to work, tearing down the tattered porch screening ready for Ned to come and replace it with the screening she'd purchased from the hardware store. Although, she still wasn't completely convinced she wanted screening at all. It was an ugly green color and hindered the spectacular view, so that was a maybe.

Annoyingly, Evan had been right. YouTube had failed her. It was impossible to replace the porch steps with a Phillips head screwdriver. She had tried and failed, and received multiple blisters in the process. Another job she would need to forfeit to Ned. But she was able to replace out all the kitchen cabinet handles with newer, sleeker styles, which she'd done using the Phillips head screwdriver; so at least it hadn't been a completely wasted purchase.

It was while she was unfastening the screws on the only hinge that was holding the porch screen door in place that she heard the murmur of an approaching engine. Craning her neck, she noticed a white SUV break through the trees that lined the property. She watched on as the vehicle came to a rolling stop, her brow furrowing when a blonde head of hair hopped out from the driver's side.

"Hi, hello!" Jane, the friendly lady from the café, walked around the car holding a huge basket in her arms as she navigated the unsteady ground, lifting her sunglasses to rest upon her head. She smiled warily as she made her way up the wonky steps.

"Oh, hi," Maggie said, trying to conceal her confusion. She had no idea why the woman was at her house, but she wasn't mad about it.

"I hope you don't mind me dropping by. I wanted to bring you this." Jane's smile beamed when she made it onto the porch. She huffed breathlessly, holding out the basket which was laden with items like breads, cakes, homemade jams, boxed chocolates, soaps, wine. "It's just a little pack a few of us local business owners put together to welcome you to town."

"Oh wow! Thank you." A little overwhelmed by such generosity, Maggie accepted the basket which was almost as big as she was, and struggled as she carried it through the open front door. "Come on in."

"This place looks *incredible*," Jane chimed as she stepped over the threshold, following closely.

Maggie smiled, following the direction of Jane's gaze to the front sitting nook which was almost finished. "Yeah. It looks a lot better *now*, but there's still a *long* way to go."

"I *love* that!" Jane pointed to the statement fuchsia wingback armchair with its contrasting turquoise ottoman. The seat was surrounded by shelves of books, their spines organized by color to display a rainbow. Something Maggie had kept herself busy with late last night when she couldn't sleep.

"You have a gift," Jane added with a slight air of awe.

Maggie laughed as she felt her cheeks heating at the compliment. "I love decorating. It's something I've always enjoyed. In fact," she continued with shy uncertainty, "I was featured in *House and Home* magazine a few years ago. They did a spread on the redecorating I did at our old house." She wanted to add that it was the only thing she'd ever been good at, that it was what she'd initially been studying in college before falling pregnant with Jack, but she didn't. Because regardless how genuinely kind Jane seemed to be, she was still a stranger she needed to keep at arm's length until she knew she could trust her. So, instead, she offered a nonchalant shrug, continuing through to the kitchen.

Placing the big basket of goods onto the counter, Maggie pointed to the coffee machine in the corner. "Can I get you a coffee?"

"You won't ever hear me say no to a cup of Joe." Jane laughed, watching Maggie as she grabbed two mugs from the overhead cabinet. "Cream, no sugar."

"Same as me." Maggie smiled as she went to work, making their coffees.

*

Maggie and Jane sat out on the Adirondack chairs at the end of the floating dock overlooking the lake. The sun was warm as it shone down from the blue sky that was smattered with fluffy white clouds. Birds were chirping high above in the canopy of trees. Gulls squawked noisily overhead. Somewhere in the distance a boat's horn honked through the harbor. It really was a beautiful setting. Maggie couldn't help but bask in the serenity. It was still so hard to believe that this was all hers.

Jane blathered on between sips of her coffee, "I was born

and raised here. Met my husband, Brad, in high school. He's fire chief at the county station. We were married at twenty-three. We had Katie not long after. She's fifteen. And then Sam came a few years later. He's twelve. Ben's seven; my baby." She gushed at the mention of her three children. "I took over the café from my mother. Back then it was Viv's Café. When my father passed, Mom decided to sell up and she moved to South Carolina to be closer to her sister. These northern winters were wreaking havoc on her arthritis." Taking a sip of her coffee, Jane glanced at Maggie. "Well, look at me talking your ear off. You haven't managed to get a word in edgewise. I have a bit of a habit of talking too much. Brad's always giving me grief for it. Sometimes, he'll time me on how long I can stay quiet. I swear, I never even make it to a minute and a half." She laughed. "So, tell me about you, hun."

Trepidation flooded through Maggie. She swallowed hard, clearing her throat and offering a casual shrug. "Well, there's not really a lot to tell."

"Sure there is." Jane giggled. "Did you grow up in Boston?"

Maggie shook her head. "No. Michigan, just outside of Grand Rapids. I moved to Rhode Island to go to art school, which is when I met Tom, my . . . my husband." Instinctively, her fingers moved to her wedding band, toying with it subconsciously. "I fell pregnant at nineteen. Tom and I got married. Then we moved to Boston a few years later so he could attend law school."

Jane nodded, but she remained silent, her gaze flitting down to the gold band Maggie was currently twisting around her finger.

Maggie knew what she was thinking, what she so desperately wanted to ask but had the good grace not to. But she also knew that it was only a matter of time before it would get out. So, with a deep breath, she managed a small smile. "Tom passed away a couple of months ago."

"Oh my *goodness*." Jane gasped, placing a hand against her chest. "I'm *so* sorry. I noticed your ring yesterday, but I didn't . . .

Well, I assumed he wasn't in the picture but I didn't know he—"
She stopped herself, shaking her head. "I'm sorry."

"Thank you. But it's okay," Maggie assured her. "This is our
new start. Well, at least, that's what I was hoping for, but this
damn house . . ." She scoffed, glancing back at the house with a
look of disdain. "It needs a lot of repairs done. Almost twenty
thousand dollars' worth and I don't—" This time, it was Maggie
who stopped herself when Jane's jaw dropped in pure shock.
Suddenly, she regretted admitting that piece of information. The
last thing she wanted was a pity party; a dead husband was bad
enough. But the house repairs, too? She'd never been one to open
up to people about her problems. And she'd always been told
not to talk about money in front of people; it was considered
rude and tacky.

Maggie smiled, offering a casual shrug. "I guess I just didn't
realize it was going to be this difficult." She decided on another
route to steer the conversation, one she already knew Jane could
relate to. "Jack is just . . . *horrible* at the moment. He's been an
unstable nightmare since the accident. He resents me for taking
him away from Boston. He even told me the other day that he
wished—" A sudden lump formed in her throat at the memory of
what Jack had said to her in the car. They hadn't spoken about it
since, and it was weighing heavily on her. She cleared her throat
and rolled her eyes as if it wasn't a big deal, continuing, "That
he wished it'd been me instead of his father."

"Oh, Maggie, he didn't mean that!" Jane reached out, touching
Maggie's arm. "If there's one thing I know, it's teenagers. And
they're horrible at the best of times."

Maggie laughed, nodding in agreement.

"How's your youngest doing?"

Maggie sighed. "Poor TJ. He's just now starting to come back
to me. He told me yesterday that he's finally ready to go back to
little league. TJ was *obsessed* with baseball, but after Tom died
he couldn't even look at a ball. And it's a huge deal now that he

wants to play again, but I don't even know where to take him to sign up. That was always Tom's job. The doting dad standing on the sidelines on Saturday mornings, cheering on his kids." She threw a hand in the air in frustration. "I searched the internet, but couldn't find anything. I don't even know if they have a league here."

"No league?" Jane shrieked. "Honey, let me tell you, baseball is bigger than Jesus in this town. And it's something I *can* help with." She smiled reassuringly. "My Sam used to play, but now he prefers basketball. If you head down to Bolson's Field, on the other side of the river across from the Piggly Wiggly, you can sign up there."

"Oh, good. I'll take him down tomorrow. Thank you." Maggie smiled.

"I suppose I should be heading off." Jane stood from the deck chair, huffing out a tired sigh and Maggie followed suit, taking the empty mug from her and walking her up the embankment.

"I need to get to the café to relieve my morning girl. We're running on just the two of us at the moment. Apparently, I use my daughter, Katie, for *child labor* on Saturdays." She laughed, shaking her head. "I need a vacation. Or at least another server to replace Maxine. She retired a month ago and I still haven't been able to fill her spot. I was going to hire one of the local high schoolers but they're limited with hours and, well, half of them are just little . . . *assholes*." She whispered the last word with a sardonic roll of her eyes and Maggie couldn't help but laugh out loud.

As the two women continued to Jane's SUV, Maggie looked down at the empty coffee mug in her hands, contemplating herself in that moment. She needed a job, needed some money coming in, and she could serve coffee. Maybe she could work at the café. But she barely knew Jane, and she didn't want to be presumptuous and just straight out ask her for a job. She didn't like to put her on the spot like that, but maybe that's what she had to do. Ask. But, before she could do or say anything, Jane spoke again.

"Why don't you come over tomorrow afternoon?"

Maggie snapped out of her thoughts, realizing Jane was talking to her. Inviting her where? To her house?

Jane continued, "We're having a cookout. You can bring those handsome boys of yours, they can meet my terrors and a few of the other kids. I'll introduce you to some of the locals as well. It'll be great."

Oh God. Maggie grimaced a little on the inside. This was not at all what she wanted. She hated attention, and she wanted to keep a low profile for a while. She was sure dinner with Jane and her family and friends would be the exact opposite of low profile. But this woman was just so genuinely nice and kind, Maggie felt obligated. And who knew, maybe this was precisely what she and the boys needed.

"What should I bring?" Maggie asked with a wavering smile.

"You just bring your sweet self, honey." Jane waved off her offer as she hopped up into her SUV. "Leave everything to me. See you tomorrow. Any time after four." She winked before pulling her door closed, and then she was gone, hidden behind the dark tint of the window.

Maggie stood holding the two empty coffee mugs in her hand, watching as the white Jeep Cherokee rumbled over the rocky drive before disappearing into the thicket, and she smiled to herself realizing she was pretty sure she'd just found a friend.

Chapter 14

Maggie had been trying to get Jack out of bed for more than an hour on Saturday morning, with no success. She threatened to drag his butt out, but that was an empty threat if ever there was one; he was at least fifty pounds heavier than her. She threatened to fill a bucket with icy water and dump it over him. She even threatened to take his beloved video game console and toss it into the lake. But nothing worked. So, she and TJ left without him. And although she hated to admit it, the drive into town was obviously lighter without Jack's sullen energy hanging heavily in the air.

"Mom? Is Jack ever going to be nice again?"

Maggie glanced in the rear-view mirror, her brows knitting together at TJ's unexpected question. She met his eyes, finding nothing but innocence within his gaze, and it hurt her heart a little to think that her ten-year-old son had such concerns.

"Jack is just . . ." She was at a loss for words because, frankly, she didn't know quite how to explain it when she had no idea what was going on with her eldest son. "He's just sad at the moment."

"About Daddy?" TJ's brows climbed higher.

She nodded.

He continued with a shrug, "I'm sad, too. But I'm not *mean* about it."

"No, you're not." She smiled ruefully. "But Jack's a teenager. And teenagers have a lot of different emotions. Emotions that you don't feel at your age. He'll be okay. It's just going to take him a little while."

TJ seemed to think about that for a few moments as he looked out the window, watching the side of the road whizz by in a blur. After a beat, he spoke again, his voice small as he said, "I'm sorry if I'm mean when I'm a teenager, Mom."

Emotion pricked Maggie right in the heart, tears burning her eyes at his sweet words. She didn't know how to respond. She had no words. Even if she did have the words, she wouldn't have been able to say them through the lump caught at the back of her throat.

TJ was suddenly preoccupied, busy with tightening the string on his baseball glove. So, she decided to say nothing at all and allow herself to treasure the moment, to engrain his words into her memory so that when he was a teenager, and most likely being a little asshole, she'd remember this moment and his heartfelt and sincere pre-apology.

*

Bolson's Field sat overlooking the harbor and town square. And Saturday morning at the baseball diamonds proved to be the most popular spot in town. The sun was shining, the gulls were flapping overhead, parents crowded the diamonds, filling the stands. Boys and girls ran about, dressed in their team colors, excited to play.

Maggie glanced down at TJ to see him smiling in a way she hadn't seen him smile in a long time. This was his happy place. He was home.

Field Four was where they needed to be, according to the man at the registration desk set up by the parking lot. TJ was a few weeks late for this season's sign-up, but he was given a place in Coach Boyd's team, The Badgers, much to his relief.

The stands surrounding Field Four were crowded, more so

than the others, and as they approached, Maggie's brow quirked to see a confusingly high number of women filling the stands, only a few men scattered here and there.

"I need to find Coach Boyd," TJ said, changing his beloved Red Sox cap for the Badgers cap provided to him at sign-up on receipt of the registration fee.

Maggie scanned the area, and assumed the men standing by the left side dugout were members of the coaching staff. She turned to the nearest woman seated on the first bench of the stands. A bleached blonde who wore a little more make-up than most moms might for Saturday morning little league.

"Excuse me?"

The woman looked up at her, smiling curiously.

"We're looking for Coach Boyd?"

The blonde's hazel eyes lit up, and she stood quickly, smoothing down her short jean skirt, which was when Maggie noticed just how revealing her tank top was; full cleavage on display. She tried not to stare, but she sure did have the girls out to play early on a Saturday.

"I can take you over." The lady placed a hand against the small of Maggie's back and, with a little too much pep in her step, she ushered them through the gate, past the opposing team's dugout and to the far side.

"Coach Boyd?" The blonde waved a hand in the air, her glitter-painted nails glistening beneath the sun as she continued toward three men with their backs to them. "Excuse me, *Coach*?"

"Yes, Cindy?" A deep voice replied with a flat, irked tone.

Maggie looked up from TJ in time to see Coach Boyd turn around, and a pair of familiar striking blue eyes met hers right at that moment.

Oh no . . . She closed her eyes momentarily, cursing herself.

She opened her eyes in time to catch the briefest of smiles ghost Evan's lips before a stoic expression came over him like a mask. He wore a bottle-green polo shirt with the team's logo embroidered on the chest pocket. The shirt pulled across his broad chest and the sleeves were tight around his bulging biceps. A Badgers ball cap sat on his head, the peak pulled low over his eyes, and he held a clipboard in his hand looking every bit the legitimate baseball coach.

"Maggie." He nodded, glancing furtively to TJ by her side and offering a tight-lipped smile at the boy.

Cindy looked between the two of them, edging a little closer to Evan or *Coach Boyd* as he was affectionately known. "Oh . . . you two know each other?"

Evan ignored the woman, his gaze fixed on Maggie.

"Hi." Maggie shifted from foot to foot, her hand placed on TJ's shoulder. "This is my son, Thomas Junior." She smiled down at him. "TJ."

"Hi, Coach." TJ lifted the peak of his ball cap in greeting.

"You ready to play today, buddy?" Evan asked, his voice laced with authority as he looked down at TJ with a small smile.

"Yes, Coach." TJ nodded, standing up a little taller, shoulders squared.

"What's your position?"

"Short stop, Coach."

"Well, head on over to the team," Evan said, clapping TJ on his shoulder as he hurried past, positively sprinting toward the other boys who were already watching on with piqued interest over who the new kid was.

Reluctantly, Maggie met Evan's gaze before he glanced sideways at Cindy who was still lingering, maybe even thrusting her breasts out a little more than she had been moments ago. He nodded at her. "Thank you, Cindy."

Cindy smiled at him, lashes fluttering. She glanced briefly at Maggie before turning on her heels and heading back toward the stands where every other woman was watching on with wide eyes. Maggie almost laughed; now she knew the reason for the numerous number of females perched eagerly in the bleachers surrounding Field Four.

Evan rolled his eyes to himself, sighing heavily as the woman retreated. But the smile quickly returned to his gaze when it settled on Maggie, a knowing grin pulling at his lips. "So, are you *stalking* me?"

Maggie deadpanned, feeling her cheeks heat up as he used her line from the other night at the pub. "No!" she scoffed as she continued, "Besides, it looks like you already have more than your fair share of stalkers." She nodded her head back toward the stands.

Evan leaned in closer, lowering his voice. "Half those women don't even have kids on my team."

She couldn't help but laugh at the seriousness in his eyes, but then he smiled, and she was momentarily taken aback by just how handsome he was. The women crowding the stands suddenly made sense; she forced herself to avert her gaze. "I suppose I'll go . . . join the groupies."

"Bye, Maggie." Evan chuckled lowly from behind her as if he could read her mind, and she felt her face flame beneath the warmth of the morning sun.

Making her way back to the other side of the chain-link fence, the bleachers were full, so Maggie chose to stand on her own, away from the bevy of women who were all watching her with intense curiosity.

"How do you know Evan?"

Glancing over her shoulder, she found Cindy watching her, one of her perfect brows arched dubiously. The other women watched on with seemingly bated breath, waiting eagerly for Maggie's response.

"Oh, I don't *know* him." Maggie shook her head, adding a shrug. "I just—I met him the other day in the hardware store."

Cindy, suddenly no longer as outgoing and friendly as she had been, whispered something to the just as heavily made-up woman beside her. They both shot fleeting yet judgmental glances in Maggie's direction, eyes trailing her from her flip flops to the old Levi's and plain white T-shirt she was wearing. Unlike them, Maggie wore no make-up and her long hair had been left to air dry after her shower, leaving it wavy and a little frizzy. She suddenly felt like she was back in high school, paling in comparison to the beautiful yet mean girls in the popular crowd, and instinctively she cowered, feeling her shoulders shrink.

"Oh, don't worry about them."

Maggie turned to see a woman move in to stand next to her. Unlike Cindy, this lady seemed kind, a small, friendly smile playing on her lips as she stared out at the baseball game that was just beginning to get underway.

"Evan Boyd is a popular man among the single females in this town." The woman cast Maggie a wry glance. "Saturday morning baseball has turned into a weekly episode of the damn *Bachelor* since he's been back," she scoffed.

"Back?" Maggie questioned, looking to the lady for more information.

"Born and raised here. Good family." She nodded, continuing, "Moved away for college. Played in the Minors in Oklahoma for a few years. He could've gone pro but something happened . . . many have assumed, but no one really knows the truth. He gave it all up and came home about five years ago." She flashed a withering glance over her shoulder at the women lining the bleachers. "Those *ladies* have been after him ever since his return."

Maggie's gaze settled across the field to where Evan stood with another man, both of them looking down at the clipboard in his hand. And something came over her as she remembered back to the look of sadness she'd seen flash in his eyes the other night at the pub. It had been fleeting and she'd almost missed it, but it was there. Something he so clearly tried to conceal with that cocky, slightly smug persona. She wondered if that sadness he worked so hard to hide had something to do with the reason he gave up on professional baseball and came back to Jewel Harbor.

"I'm Barb, by the way." The woman turned, cutting through Maggie's thoughts with a friendly smile. "I own the salon in town."

"Hi." Maggie managed a smile, taking in the woman in all her pouffed, slightly over-bleached glory—from the way her eyebrows

111

had been powdered on so expertly to the way her lipstick cracked into the wrinkles around her mouth. She was obviously older, the well-concealed smile lines gave that away, but she looked good for her age. And, unlike the other preened women perched up in the bleachers watching Evan like birds of prey ready to attack at any moment, Barb was friendly and welcoming.

Maggie indicated to the field of boys. "Which one's yours?"

Barb laughed. "Oh, honey. I'm sixty-eight. My youngest is twenty-five and lives in Keene." She thumbed back in the direction of the parking lot. "I've been happily married to that grumpy old bastard at the registration desk for near forty years. I bring him his coffee every Saturday morning on my way to the salon, and . . ." She paused, offering a conspiratorial wink, jutting her chin in Evan's direction. "Well, there's no harm in stopping by famous Field Four for a look, right?"

Maggie's jaw dropped slightly, a light laugh slipped out as she looked from Barb over in Evan's direction and back again.

Barb smiled suggestively, touching Maggie's arm as she turned. "You ever want a pamper sesh and a chin wag? You stop by the salon any time you want, sweetie."

"Uh . . . thanks." Maggie nodded, biting back her own smile. "I'll definitely do that."

"Bye, Evan honey," Barb called out with a saccharine voice, waggling her perfectly manicured fingers with a flirty wave.

Evan glanced over then, craning his neck. He offered a tight-lipped smile at Barb and a wave of his own before turning back to the game.

Barb threw another wink at Maggie before strutting away, nodding to the women in the bleachers on her way past with a curt, "Ladies."

Releasing a breath, Maggie laughed to herself, shaking her head. But when she turned back to the field, her breath was stolen when she found Evan watching her from beneath the peak of his ball cap, the hint of a smile tugging at his lips before he slowly turned back to the game.

Chapter 15

With the game over, Maggie waited around for TJ. When he came running back toward her with a mile-wide smile, she considered thanking Evan. She also wanted to find out where to get the uniform from, she hadn't wanted to ask the other unwelcoming mothers. But when she noticed all the women hanging around unnecessarily, she reconsidered, deciding against waiting to speak to him like a pathetic schoolgirl with a crush. Instead, she and TJ headed across to the Piggly Wiggly to pick up some groceries and a few extra items to make an iceberg salad to take to Jane's cookout.

After returning home from little league, TJ was in the best mood he'd been in since, well, before Tom's passing. He was running around outside, tossing the ball in the air and racing to catch it, practicing his body slides. He was covered in dirt by the time he ambled back inside, but he was happy. He'd told Maggie that he liked his teammates, most of whom would be in his class at school, and he liked his coach. It was a relief for her to hear. She knew TJ was going to be okay. Now, she just had to work on Jack.

*

Maggie studied herself in the reflection of the free-standing mirror that leaned against her bedroom wall. Although she hated attention and didn't want anyone to make a fuss, she wanted to make a good first impression.

Dressed in a nice pair of skinny jeans, a loose white button-down and with a pair of espadrilles, Maggie left her hair in the same natural state it had been all day and she added a little bronzer and some mascara. She looked nice, but for the first time in a long while, maybe even well before Tom's death, she looked happy.

Staring at her reflection, she toyed nervously with the gold wedding band on her ring finger. It was almost funny; after the accident, she thought she'd never be able to stop wearing it. Now, she'd considered taking it off at least a thousand times since finding out the truth of his affair. But there was something stopping her. And suddenly, she found herself remembering back to the shotgun shambles that had been their wedding.

She was only nineteen and she was fourteen weeks pregnant when Tom proposed to her in his college dorm room during the last few weeks of her freshman year. Tom was a junior, but they were both so young and terrified; they hadn't been dating more than six months.

Maggie's mother had been upset when she'd found out her daughter was pregnant. She'd told her to come back to Michigan, that she would help her raise the baby. Tom's father had told him to "take care of it", that law school would be impossible to manage with a toddler running around. But Tom and Maggie were in love and they knew, no matter what, theirs was the kind of love that could make it through anything.

So, while they were lying together on Tom's king single, Maggie crying on his chest when she realized they were officially on their own, he'd grabbed her left hand, entwined his fingers through hers and, without a ring, he'd asked her to marry him. It wasn't just the baby. He told her he loved her, and that they were going to be married sooner or later, so why not now? In retrospect, it was catastrophically unromantic. There had been an episode of *Friends* on the television in the background. But, at the time, Maggie fell even more in love with Tom that night, and, of course, she said yes.

That summer, Maggie and Tom tied the knot at the District Courthouse, before a stern judge and a kind registrar. Maggie in a white dress which, by some miracle, still fit her and her burgeoning bump, and Tom in a smart button-down and slacks. There had been no engagement ring. While Tom was from an obscenely wealthy family, after vetoing his father's recommendation to schlep his girlfriend to an abortion clinic, he'd been subsequently cut off from the multi-million-dollar Morris fund. But he didn't care. And, with what he'd managed to save over the years, he paid for a pair of simple nine-carat gold wedding bands.

Theirs was an unconventional start that had been doomed to wind up as another sad statistic. But they had a surprisingly perfect marriage. Sure, they had their issues. What married couple didn't? But they were in love and their love seemed to conquer almost everything.

Now, as Maggie looked down at the slightly tarnished wedding band Tom had bought as a two-for-one deal from a small pawn shop—the symbol of their humble beginning and the anchor that had kept them together through the most difficult of beginnings—the ring and the promise it held was tainted in more ways than one. But every time she went to remove it, she could feel a part of her, somewhere deep down inside, ache with a pain she hadn't been prepared to deal with. The pain of his death, the pain of his betrayal, the pain of knowing that, whether he'd died or not, she had no longer been what he'd wanted. Removing that ring would be closure, and although she wanted nothing more than to be able to move on, to close that chapter of her life and start afresh, she couldn't. She might never be able to. So, she left it on. For now, the ring would stay. But she knew it couldn't last forever. In time, she would have to deal with it, for her own sake, at least.

Tucking her hair behind her ears, Maggie released the breath she'd been holding, making a move to collect her handbag. It was almost four, and although Jane had said any time after four, she didn't want to be rude and show up too late.

Hurrying out of her bedroom, she continued downstairs to find TJ dressed in his finest; a neat button-down and a pair of cargo shorts, his hair styled to the side with what looked like gel. She smiled at him, but her smile fell quickly when she noticed Jack lounging back on the sofa dressed in sweatpants and an old T-shirt, bare feet kicked up on the cushion, cell phone in hand.

"Jack?"

He glanced sideways at her from his cell.

She shook her head incredulously. "Why aren't you ready?"

"I'm not going," he scoffed, as if that much were a given.

"Yes, you are." Maggie huffed a sigh, moving through to the kitchen. "Jane is expecting all three of us to be there. Now, hurry up and get ready," she yelled back through the doorway, busying herself with taking the salad out of the fridge.

"No!"

Gripping the edge of the countertop, she closed her eyes a moment, taking in a deep breath and counting to three before storming back into the den. She stopped behind the back of the sofa, glaring down at her insolent son.

"Jack. You are getting on my last nerve," she warned through gritted teeth. "You're coming. Now, you have five minutes to get your butt upstairs and get ready. Or else . . ."

He offered her a mocking glance, sniggering. "Or else *what*? What are *you* gonna do about it?"

Thinking for a moment, Maggie did something she'd never done before. Before Jack knew what was even happening, she launched forward, snatching his cell phone right from his hands, and grabbing the television remote from the couch cushion at the same time.

He gaped at her, his eyes wide.

"Or else . . . no phone, no TV, no video games. Nothing!" She blinked at him, her stern glare unwavering.

"Jack, just come," TJ spoke up from the armchair across the coffee table. Both Maggie and Jack glanced at him to see his brows raised in hope as he added, "It'll be fun." He shrugged, slinking down a little beneath the weight of his big brother's glower.

Maggie flashed TJ a reassuring smile before glaring at the back of Jack's head. "Four minutes, Jack." She made a point of checking her watch. "The clock's ticking. It's up to you. You either come with us or you stay here all night, staring at the walls, which is precisely what you'll be doing for the next month without these." She held his phone and the remote up in the air to further emphasize her intended punishment.

Jack sat there for a moment longer, looking down at his clasped hands. Just as she was about to give him another warning, she stopped herself when he made a move to stand. Without a word, he walked out of the room and up the stairs, the floorboards creaking beneath his weight.

Another win. She smiled victoriously to herself, turning back into the kitchen.

*

Maggie walked with TJ down the rocky drive that led from the road to Jane's home tucked away in the woods. A sprawling colonial, it had soft gray cladding with crisp white shutters, and was surrounded by lush green trees. Jack followed behind, dragging his feet.

Music and voices were coming from the back, so instead of knocking at the front door, Maggie led the way around the side, coming to a stop when she saw a group of people standing around two picnic tables situated on the neatly mowed lawn. She felt awkward as hell, suddenly wishing she'd knocked on the front door.

"Oh, great, you're here!"

Jumping a little, she turned to see Jane walking down from the back deck carrying a tray of glasses, and of course her excited announcement caused all heads to turn, eyes focused intently on Maggie and her boys.

Gripping her salad bowl as if her life depended on it, Maggie forced a smile. "Yeah, hi . . . Sorry, I didn't know if I should knock."

"Ha! Knock!" A tall, brawny man with wide shoulders wearing a bright Hawaiian print shirt and holding a beer in his hand, snorted with a loud laugh. "We wouldn't have heard you over Jane's jabbering." He stepped forward, holding out his free hand. "I'm Brad, Jane's husband. You must be Maggie."

"Hi." Maggie smiled up at the handsome man.

Jane placed the tray of drinks onto one of the picnic tables, smiling as she joined her husband.

Maggie held out her salad as an offering. "It's just an iceberg salad with a blue cheese vinaigrette . . . store bought," she added sheepishly. "Oh, and I brought wine." She held up the bottle cooler bag in her hand which contained her own wine to drink, and another as a gift. Tom had always insisted they take a gift when invited to someone's home. Only Tom's idea of a gift was a two-hundred-dollar bottle of Scotch; Maggie imagined him rolling in his grave at the sixteen-dollar bottle of chardonnay she'd purchased from the Piggly Wiggly.

"Oh, Maggie, thank you. You didn't have to bring anything."

Maggie blushed, waving off Jane's gratitude.

"And who do we have here?" Brad asked, looking down at TJ with a broad smile.

"I'm TJ." He craned his neck, looking up at the towering man with a shy smile. "And this is my brother, Jack. He's annoyed because he didn't wanna come."

"Teej!" Jack hissed angrily, nudging his little brother in the back.

"Didn't want to come, huh?" Brad guffawed, eyeing Jack dubiously. "You like baseball?"

Jack nodded with a noncommittal shrug.

"Jack got picked to play on the varsity team. He was the youngest ever varsity player in the school's history," TJ spoke up, still so proud of his big brother, in spite of all that had happened.

"Wow!" Brad exclaimed, continuing, "Well, Jack, if you're interested, we're going to play a game of ball after dinner in the lot next door. Maybe you can be a team captain."

Jack looked down to the ground, and Maggie could tell he hated the attention. In that way he was a lot like her.

"Dad, where do you want the burger buns?" An angelic voice asked from somewhere behind Brad's looming figure, causing everyone to turn.

A cute blonde around Jack's age, with a heart-shaped face and crystal-blue eyes stood there holding a bag of burger buns, smiling innocently while fluttering her thick lashes.

"Oh, Maggie," Jane said, glancing at the boys. "TJ. Jack. This is my daughter, Katie." She wrapped an arm around the beautiful girl, squeezing her close.

Maggie chanced a sideways glance in time to see Jack immediately perk up. He squared his shoulders, puffed out his chest a little, and raked a hand through his thick mane of unmanageable hair.

Jane said, "Actually, Jack, Katie's your age. She'll be in a few of your classes at school."

Katie smiled bashfully at Jack, the hint of metal braces flashing which she quickly hid by pressing her lips together, cheeks flushing. She tucked her silky blonde hair behind her ear, glancing down at the ground a moment.

"Katie, why don't you take Jack and TJ around to meet Sam and Ben and the other kids?" Jane suggested.

Katie handed her father the bag of buns and smiled again, looking from Maggie to Jack, and then TJ. "Come on." She waved them over. "The boys are shooting hoops." She glanced at Jack. "Do you play basketball?"

Jack smiled smugly. "Yeah, but I'm *way* better at baseball."

Maggie watched her two boys follow Katie around the side of the house. She smiled to herself, feeling a wave of relief wash over her. Finding Jane and Brad watching her, she shook her head dismissively, explaining briefly, "It's been a long time since I've seen them like that."

Jane beamed, and then she threw an arm around Maggie's shoulders. "Come on. Let's get you a wine and I'll introduce you to everyone."

Maggie nodded and she quashed every last sliver of doubt that had been plaguing her. Wrapping her arm around Jane's waist, she went willingly.

Chapter 16

"Maggie, TJ is adorable and Jack is *so* handsome!" exclaimed Heather, one of Jane's friends, from across the island counter, positively gushing as she glanced out the window to where all the kids were playing a game of HORSE.

While the men all stood around the grill outside, drinking beer and laughing as Brad regaled them with a story that was obviously hilarious and likely quite crude, the women were in the kitchen, gossiping, drinking cocktails and helping to prepare the rest of the food. Much to Maggie's relief, Jane's friends seemed as nice as Jane was.

"They take after their father. Identical. TJ's a little bit of me mixed in, but Jack is almost Tom's doppelgänger." Maggie smiled to herself as she peeled a few hard-boiled eggs, but then an obvious silence fell throughout the kitchen and she looked up in time to see Heather and the other woman, Julie, glance awkwardly at one another. Jane speared them each with a warning glare.

"What's wrong?" Maggie asked, her brows drawn together in confusion.

Jane forced a smile, moving to Maggie and placing a hand tentatively on her arm. "I-I hope you don't mind, but I told the girls about your . . . your husband." She offered a rueful smile, adding quickly, "When I told everyone you were coming, they all asked if . . . if he would be joining you and I didn't really know what—"

"It's fine." Maggie placated Jane's ramblings, holding a hand up with a smile. "It's okay." She then glanced at Heather and Julie who were all looking on with contrite smiles. "My husband was in a car accident in March. He passed away. Now . . . here we are." She smiled again, despite the awkward tension which loomed heavily in the wake of her words.

Thankfully, the moment was interrupted by Brad entering the kitchen to collect his pork ribs that had been marinating in the fridge. He paused, glancing at everyone, his brow furrowed.

"Everything okay?" he asked before a slow smirk pulled at his lips, his gaze landing on his wife. "Jane's not talking. That means there's gotta be something wrong." He laughed at his own joke, which, despite it not being at all funny, did help lighten the mood.

"Oh, Brad." Jane rolled her eyes, swatting her husband away with the dish towel. "You should do stand-up at the Improv. You're *hilarious.*" She snorted derisively, but when everyone went back to their business, she quickly glanced at Maggie and winked, the two women sharing a moment.

*

After washing her hands and freshening up in Jane's downstairs guest bathroom, which was unusually clean for a home with three children, Maggie collected herself enough to rejoin everyone outside.

She'd needed a moment. Telling the women about Tom had been difficult, but not for the reasons she had thought it would be. She didn't mind people knowing that her husband was dead—it was silly to think they wouldn't find out eventually—but she hated seeing the pity and the sympathy in their eyes. She wanted to tell them the truth: that he was a cheating son of a bitch and she was better off without him. But she couldn't say that. She couldn't risk people knowing the truth because then TJ and Jack would know, and she'd promised herself she'd do all she could to keep it from her boys for as long as she could. When they were old enough to understand, she might tell them. But for now, she would sacrifice whatever she had to, to keep that piece of information under lock and key. Maybe that meant she would forever be forced to continue living her lie, but she'd do what she had to do. The whole truth wasn't possible at the moment. And that was like a big black cloud coming over her, a cloud she thought she'd left back in Boston.

With a fortifying breath, she raked her fingers through her wavy hair, smoothed a hand down the front of her shirt and forced another smile on her way out to join the party; she was the guest of honor, after all.

Outside, dusk was beginning to settle. The setting sun had turned the sky from blue to yellow to orange and red, to the beautiful inky mauve with pink swirls it was now. Garden lights illuminated the boundary and lanterns hanging from the branches in the trees overhead lit up the space as everyone enjoyed one another's company, laughing and talking.

Maggie paused on the step down from the back deck, finding Jack seated at one of the picnic tables, laughing with Katie as she showed him something on her phone, his eyes shining brightly. She could tell he was quickly becoming besotted by the pretty blonde. She couldn't blame him; Katie was gorgeous, and as sweet as her mom. *Maybe he won't hate life so much in the sticks, after all*, she thought hopefully.

"Mom?"

As she turned, Maggie's smiling eyes found TJ standing by the fire pit roasting marshmallows with Sam and Ben, and Heather's son, Chase. And Evan. *Wait, what?* She did an almost comical double take, gasping quietly as her gaze settled upon the man smirking back at her with a knowing glint in his shining eyes.

123

"Well, now I *know* you're stalking me," Evan said with a chuckle, folding his muscular arms over his broad chest.

He was dressed in jeans which pulled in all the right places, Chuck Taylors and a vintage Guns N' Roses T-shirt, his hair left messy. He looked good. Maggie had to force herself to look away. She hated how he made her feel. It wasn't right. She swallowed hard, focusing intently on the ground as she walked toward him, racking her brain as to why the hell he was even there.

"Mom?" TJ waved her over excitedly. "Coach is here!"

"I see that." Maggie nodded with a small smile, moving beside her son while dubiously eyeing Evan.

"Coach is Sam and Ben's uncle." TJ smiled, glancing fondly up at Evan. "How cool is that?"

Maggie's brows knitted together in confusion, but before she could say anything they were interrupted by Jane as she sidled up next to Evan, wrapping an arm around his waist, beaming up at him like a proud . . . what? Sister? Now that they were together side by side, despite the fact that he towered over Jane's petite frame, the resemblance was almost uncanny—same eyes, exact same smile.

"Maggie, this is Evan . . . my brother," Jane said.

"We've already met," Evan said with a smirk, his playful gaze fixed on Maggie.

A curious glint flashed in Jane's eyes as she studied them both, her smile faltering momentarily before it returned. "Oh, of course! Little league."

Maggie stared at Evan, feeling her cheeks flush beneath his penetrative stare.

"Yeah." Evan nodded, focus still set intently on Maggie. "Little league."

Sure, Maggie could have corrected him. Could have told Jane that she'd met Evan a few days ago at the hardware store, and that they'd later run into one another at the pub. But, for some reason, perhaps it was the look of mischievous secrecy in Evan's gaze, she didn't correct him. And she didn't even know why. All she could manage was a shy smile, glancing casually at Jane who was watching her with one eye slightly narrowed with thinly veiled suspicion.

"Soup's on!" Brad's booming voice echoed throughout the yard, interrupting the moment. And Maggie had to hand it to the man; his timing was impeccable. *Saved by the Brad.* She breathed a sigh of relief, quick to turn away from Evan's smiling eyes and Jane's piqued curiosity.

*

Evan hadn't wanted to come tonight. Sure, he loved seeing his niece and nephews, loved being invited to his sister's perfect house to have dinner with her perfect family, and talk about their lives like they were perfect. But once or twice a week was more than enough. Anything more than that just made him feel like an imposition, or a charity case.

Poor, lonely Evan, they all thought. Little did big sis know that most nights he was far from lonely.

When Janie had called him the night before to invite him to the cookout, he'd almost said no. He'd planned on heading out to the pub so he could get drunk like he did most Saturday nights; well, drunk enough to forget, but not so drunk that the people in this small town would start talking about him, like his life was any business of theirs. But when Janie had mentioned the cookout was to welcome Maggie, the nice new woman from Boston, of course he had to say yes.

There was just something about Maggie, something he'd noticed within the first few seconds of meeting her, something he couldn't quite put his finger on. Of course, she was gorgeous, but it was more than that. Behind that dimpled smile she tried so hard to downplay, deep within those green eyes that sparkled with flecks of gold and silver, there was a sadness. It wasn't

125

obvious, but it was there. And Evan knew there was a lot more to it than just that wedding ring she wore on her finger. He'd heard the news. Her husband had died. News like that traveled like wildfire through a town like Jewel Harbor, especially when Jane was involved. But he knew there was more to it; her kind of sadness was more than just a dead husband. There was something else, something raw, something that was eating at her. And he wanted to find out—*needed* to find out—because, well, frankly, he'd never met anyone he could relate to more, even from that first fleeting glance they'd shared at the hardware store. Perhaps, in some totally screwed up way, they were kindred spirits.

Standing around while everyone took their seats, Evan watched on, waiting. He was so used to being on his own at parties and dinners and social gatherings, waiting to take the last single chair, it all came as second nature to him. But, tonight, he wasn't the only one alone. He looked up beneath his brows, watching as Maggie stood awkwardly, waiting to find a place at the table for herself. Everyone else sat together—Jane and Brad, Heather and Chris, Julie and Travis. The kids all crowded on the other table, giggling and laughing mischievously. It was literally just Evan and Maggie left standing once everyone else had taken their seats. And in that anxiety-inducing moment, their eyes met from opposite ends of the picnic table.

"Maggie, honey? Come sit here, sweetie," Jane sang out, hand in the air, waving her over like a damn dog.

With another quick glance at Evan, followed by a tight-lipped smile, Maggie hurried over and squeezed in between Jane and Julie. Evan glanced at the kids' table. There was ample space for him there, and, honestly, that's where he'd be most comfortable. But he was a thirty-five-year-old man, surely he could act like an adult for at least a couple of hours. So, flashing Heather, Jane's oldest friend who'd had a crush on him since he was fifteen, even after she married Chris, his trademark, panty-dropping smile, he perched himself at the very end of the table, next to Travis as the amiable dinner chat got underway.

"So, Maggie?" Heather began with a smile. Across the table, Maggie had paused as she reached for the potato salad. "Tell us a bit about yourself."

Evan watched as Maggie's cheeks turned pink; even beneath the muted light of the lanterns hanging overhead, her blush was obvious. Her shoulders seemed to cower almost instinctively as all eyes settled on her. He could tell straight away that she wasn't one for attention.

"Well, there's not a lot to tell, really . . ." she said with a gentle laugh. "Born in Michigan. I moved to Rhode Island for college, met my husband, and we moved to Boston where we lived for the last twelve or so years." She dished herself out some salad, and it was obvious, even from where Evan sat at the other end of the table, that she wanted the conversation about her and her past to end.

"What did you study in college?" Julie asked with keen interest.

"Oh, um . . ." Maggie thought for a moment, fingers instinctively going to her wedding ring in a move Evan had come to realize was something she did when she was nervous, maybe even without knowing she was doing it. "I was studying design. Interior." She glanced over her shoulder to the kids' table, her gaze momentarily checking for her boys before she looked back and added quietly, "But I fell pregnant. So, I only completed my first year."

"Oh, she's a wonderful designer," Jane interrupted, smiling at everyone around the table. "I saw some of the work she's done so far at the lake house. The attention to detail is just remarkable. If I hadn't just had the whole house redone, I'd get you in to redecorate our den." She nodded at Maggie.

Maggie blushed again, and when it seemed as if everyone was choosing to eat instead of toss questions at her, she relaxed enough to start picking at her plate of food with her fork.

"What field of law did your husband practice, Maggie?" Heather asked after a few beats.

Maggie dropped her fork, the silver clanging loudly against her plate, and in the flash of an instant, Evan watched her face fall before she quickly recovered with that same smile she wore only to be polite.

"Criminal," she answered with a nod. "Defense."

Heather gasped, her eyes widening excitedly. "Did he defend any real bad—"

"What is this?" Evan suddenly butted in with a humored tone that didn't match the warning look in his eyes as he glanced at both Heather and Julie. "The Spanish Inquisition?"

An awkward silence ensued, and Jane shot him a look that fell from his eyes to the beer bottle in his hand and back again. She arched a brow. But he didn't care. Maggie was obviously uncomfortable and he was sure she hadn't agreed to come to dinner just so she could be interrogated by two of Jewel Harbor's biggest gossips. He rolled his eyes, taking a drink from his beer to wash down his mouthful of chewy steak. Brad was the world's worst cook; his apron—*BBQ King*—was a blatant lie.

"So, Maggie?" Brad broke the awkward silence. "How's the new place going?"

With a sigh, she took a sip from her glass of wine, eyes flickering to Evan before returning to Brad with a smile. "It's old. And it's been a little neglected. So, there's a bit of work that needs to be done, but I can—"

"A *bit* of work?" Jane shrieked incredulously, glancing at everyone around the table as she added, "Try twenty thousand dollars' worth of work."

A collective gasp filled the void.

"What on earth needs to be done that's gonna cost twenty grand?" Brad asked with complete indignation.

Maggie shook her head. "Just a couple of things that cost a lot of money," she said with a dismissive wave of her hand. "The

128

furnace needs replacing, leaks in the roof, that kind of thing." She shrugged a shoulder nonchalantly like it was no big deal.

Brad looked at Travis questioningly. "Who do we know in roofing?"

Travis glanced up to the sky a moment as if in thought. "Isn't Munroe's brother in Manchester a roofing guy?"

Maggie's eyes moved furtively between the two men, and Evan could see she was beginning to panic.

"I'll speak to him at the station on Tuesday." Brad nodded. "See if he can make a call and get you a good quote."

"Oh, it's fine, really, I . . ." Maggie stopped herself when she realized Brad and Travis had moved on to a discussion between themselves about the electricians they knew who could replace her furnace.

Evan shook his head to himself, taking another sip of his beer before announcing unnecessarily loudly, "Who caught the end of that Orioles game?"

All eyes turned to him, most full of confusion at his abrupt interruption.

He took another big swig from his beer bottle, finishing it with a few more mouthfuls. Slapping a hand on the table with gusto, he continued, "God, that kid from Syracuse, huh? What a *slugger!*"

Suddenly, the men around the table seemed to perk up in unison, each of them chiming in animatedly about the nail-biting game, and all talk of furnaces and qualified journeymen was soon forgotten.

From the corner of his eye, Evan noticed Maggie visibly relax, her shoulders dropping with the big breath she'd been able to finally release. She glanced up at him, and when their eyes met, she mouthed a *thank you*. With a small smile, Evan nodded in her direction before obliging in ball talk with the men.

Chapter 17

Maggie carried her mug of steaming hot tea out onto the dock, taking a seat in one of the Adirondack chairs and smiling as she looked over the still water. She released a long breath, stretching her legs out, taking in the darkness of the woods on the other side of the lake. There was no moon tonight, just myriad stars shining bright above in the inky midnight sky. A light salty breeze blew through the leaves of the big tree that sat on the bank, but apart from the occasional rustle, the night was silent and still. Eerie, yet calmingly so.

TJ had fallen asleep in the car on the way back from the cookout. She had to wake him when they pulled up at the house. She'd been worried she was going to have to help him up the stairs by herself. But, much to her surprise, Jack hadn't immediately disappeared inside the house and up to his room like he normally would have. Instead, he'd stayed and helped his little brother out of the car, and walked with him upstairs. She hadn't heard a peep out of either of them since.

Dinner had gone smoothly. After Evan had successfully steered the conversation away from Maggie and her dead husband, and the thousands of dollars' worth of repairs that needed doing to the house, the rest of the night had gone by without issue. In fact, it had been nice. It'd been a long time since she'd actually had fun at something like that. Tom would have spent the night off with the men, smoking cigars or doing God only knows what. But tonight, everyone had sat together; the only time the group had parted was when they'd separated into two teams and played a game of softball. Everyone. Maggie hadn't realized how unfit she was until she'd actually hit the ball and had to run to first base. Sadly, she hadn't made it, and had been caught out by a victorious Ben who sure knew how to rub it in. She gave up after one bat and walked off the makeshift diamond with a stitch.

What she couldn't seem to shake after tonight, however, were the occasional glances she'd been receiving from Jane any time Evan had tried making conversation with her. It wasn't that she was being nasty, as such, but it was obvious, the look in her eyes laced with a touch of unease, in spite of the woman's friendly smile. She hoped Jane wasn't getting the wrong impression; that Maggie was trying something on with her brother, because that absolutely wasn't happening. Yes, she considered Evan handsome, and, in any other situation, he would be the kind of man she would be attracted to. But it couldn't happen. Tom's body was barely cold, and she was still trying to get over the fact that her dead husband had managed to break her heart after his death.

Maggie could tell Jane was protective of Evan. She'd mothered him throughout the night and would keep asking if he was okay every time she walked by. Her questions were quietly murmured but Maggie was able to hear, and she could see the frustration flicker in Evan's gaze every time, which he would quickly cover with a smile that shone in his eyes. Maggie didn't know what their exchanges were about, and, frankly, it was none of her business, but there was definitely some kind of underlying tension between the brother and sister.

"Hey, Mom."

Startling from her thoughts, Maggie turned to see Jack coming down from the house, tentatively stepping onto the rickety dock. His hair was damp, and he was dressed in sweatpants and a T-shirt, ready for bed.

"Hi, honey." She smiled at him, watching as he took a seat in the chair next to her.

With a tight smile and a heavy exhale, he looked out over the water, and in the moments that followed, a companionable silence fell between them.

As she glanced sideways at her son, Maggie realized it had been a long time since they'd sat together, just the two of them, without it coming to blows. She was on tenterhooks, waiting for him to start yet another fight. When he spoke, however, it wasn't at all what she was expecting. "Do you need me to get a job?"

"What?" She gaped at him.

He shifted a little awkwardly, clearing his throat, not meeting her eyes and he continued while staring at the water, "I overheard you tonight talking about the house and how much it's gonna cost to fix everything." He flashed her a furtive glance, looking away just as quickly. "I thought, maybe, w-we're having, like, money trouble or something." He shrugged again.

"Oh . . ." Maggie looked down a moment, staring at the mug in her hands. Briefly, she considered telling him the truth. That his beloved father had left them with nothing, that this whole move had been her attempt at saving their hides, that *she* was the hero, not Tom. But she shook her head at the thought. She knew the truth would only hurt Jack, and he was already hurting enough. One day he would know the truth. She'd be sure to tell him. She owed it to him; he deserved to know. But not now.

"Jack, it's fine." She shook her head. "I mean, of course, with your father gone we no longer have his salary as a safety net, but don't worry." She offered a droll smile when he met her eyes, continuing wryly, "We're hardly *destitute*."

Jack nodded once. He glanced up at the starry sky and another silence fell between them. But this silence wasn't quite as easy as it had been before his question. This one was rife with trepidation and apprehension.

"I . . . I'm sorry," he said after a few beats, his words hushed and murmured under his breath.

Confused, Maggie turned to look at him fully. She watched as he seemed to struggle with his words. He glanced down, his hands twisting together in his lap. When he lifted his head, fixing her with an earnest look, his eyes were glassy, reflecting the muted light of the night.

"Honey, what is it?" Maggie pressed.

He raked his teeth over his bottom lip, nostrils flaring as he tried so obviously to keep his emotions in check. Sniffling, he looked over her shoulder, off into the distance behind her, like he couldn't possibly bear to meet her eyes.

"What I said to you . . . the other day in the car—" A sob bubbled up the back of his throat, cutting his words short with a hiccup and tears spilled out. He closed his eyes tight before he buried his face in his hands. "I didn't mean it," he cried, shaking his head. "And I really need you to believe me when I say that."

For a moment, Maggie just sat there, watching him cry into his hands. She wanted so badly to go to him, to hug him, to tell him it was okay, that he was forgiven. But she knew he needed this. He needed to talk through his feelings. It was almost as if he needed to break in order to truly be able to start to heal. So, she waited, watched him break.

Jack scrubbed his hands over his face, wiping away what he could of his tears, and with another sniffle, he looked at her with all sincerity. "I love you, Mom. And I *hate* what I said, because I didn't mean it. And it's been eating at me ever since. And I need you to know that I am so sorry that I said it, that I even *thought* to say it. I love you and I'm so thankful to have you. Without you, I don't know what . . ." He trailed off, closing his eyes at whatever it was he was about to say. When he opened them again, he looked harrowed at the thoughts plaguing his mind.

Maggie placed her mug of tea onto the arm of her chair before pushing up slowly. She went to Jack, crouching down in front of him, placing a hand on his knee. He met her gaze and she smiled at him. Without the need for words, she reached out, pulling him in, and she wrapped her arms around his shoulders in a hug so tight, so desperate, she wasn't sure how she was ever going to be able to let him go. She breathed him in, smiling through her tears. She finally had her boy back.

*

That night, when the house was still and silent, and darkness had settled outside along with what sounded like one lonely cricket, Maggie couldn't sleep. It was after two and she was still perched up against the headboard, the laptop on her knees, illuminating the room as she idly surfed the internet.

She started researching budget-saving roof restorations and DIY leak repairs, and that developed into looking at affordable ways to create more closet space without the cost of a contractor. Since Jack was inhabiting the attic, she could transform the spare bedroom into her own personal dressing room. It wasn't as if they needed a guest bedroom. It wasn't like she had anyone to invite to stay with them, unless, of course, Tom's sister ever stopped being a total witch.

But from there, her mind seemed to wander without any clear intention or reason to a certain blue-eyed man, and she suddenly found herself typing 'Evan Boyd' into the search engine.

There were quite a few results. Most were just Evan's name listed in long registers of baseball game fixtures and stats. According to one website, he played for Georgia Tech after which he was drafted to a Triple-A Minor League team in Oklahoma. But then nothing. It seemed he just stopped playing after a few years and there was no apparent explanation or reason why.

She wondered what had happened. Why did he quit? Why did

he move back to Jewel Harbor? What happened for him to give up on something he was obviously very good at, something he was passionate about, to come back to his tiny hometown and coach little league and fix boats?

She clicked on the photographs. Most were action shots of Evan which came up in the images tab. She allowed her gaze to drift over his form. He was good-looking. Obviously. Cocky. That much she'd witnessed firsthand. And he was clearly a ladies' man about town. But there was something else about Evan Boyd, something about him that intrigued her. Despite his strong exterior and the perma-smirk that played on his lips, there was a lingering sadness that seemed to loom heavily over him. She'd seen it the night at the pub, when he'd glanced at TJ and Jack, and she'd seen it tonight at the cookout, when Jane had walked past him, stopping momentarily and placing a hand on his shoulder, offering a quick squeeze. Each instance had been fleeting, but it was definitely there; an emptiness in those blue eyes that were otherwise so happy and effortlessly carefree. She hoped it wasn't anything too serious, but deep down she had a feeling it was. And, given the glimpse into his past that she'd received from Barb, the flirty salon owner, Maggie couldn't help but wonder if, maybe, she and Evan had a few things in common.

Chapter 18

The thunderous rumbling of an engine broke through the peaceful sleep Maggie had managed to fall into sometime well after three o'clock. As she opened her gritty eyes, she was met with the hazy glow of morning breaking through the cracks in the curtains. The sound of crunching gravel accompanied the revs of the engine. Then there were voices. Male voices. Multiple.

Immediately, her eyes flew wide open and she sat bolt upright, flinging off the covers. Dressed in her pajamas, she crawled off the foot of the bed, hurrying to the window. She peeled the curtain aside just enough to see outside and, sure enough, she found two pickup trucks parked right outside her house. Her eyes grew wide at the sight of Jane's husband, Brad, and his buddy, Travis, climbing out of a rusted old Chevy, followed by Evan jumping down from a shiny black Dodge.

"What the hell?" she shrieked.

Panicking, she paced her bedroom, looking down at herself dressed only in sleep shorts and a T-shirt. She cursed under her breath and ran to her dresser to find some jean shorts and a bra. She did all she could to make herself decent enough to face a group of random men first thing in the morning. Hurrying downstairs, she tried to catch her breath.

The front door was open, and Maggie ran out to find TJ, dressed in his *Iron Man* pajamas, talking with Evan. Evan's gaze lifted to look at Maggie, his eyes telling when they met hers. He immediately held his hands up in surrender as he approached, glancing back at Brad before looking at her again.

"I told him not to, but . . ." He shrugged.

Maggie sighed in frustration, taking in the power tools and the equipment being loaded out of the back of the trucks. She shook her head, raking her fingers through her messy hair, at a total loss.

"Look," Evan started, taking a step forward. He steadied her with a reassuring once-over. "Just let them have a look at the roof. It'll make them feel better. And then, I promise, they'll be out of your hair."

Maggie raised a brow dubiously, looking up at him. "Really?"

"Scout's honor." He chuckled, holding up three fingers.

Twisting her lips to the side, she allowed her shoulders to fall with an exhale. She hated feeling like a charity case, but she also didn't want to be rude. It was kind of them to help, and it seemed that was the way the people in Jewel Harbor operated: on kindness and handshakes.

"Fine." She rolled her eyes. "I'll make coffee."

"No need." Evan shook his head.

She sighed. "It's the least I can do for all—" Her mouth snapped shut as another car pulled up. A white SUV. One she'd seen before. Maggie watched Jane and Julie hop out, carrying trays of coffees and paper bags with Jane's Café logo over them.

"Well . . ." Maggie shrugged. "You guys really did think of everything."

Evan flashed her a wry grin.

"I'll go change into my work clothes," she said with a resigned sigh, turning and hurrying back inside to brush her teeth and change into her overalls and work boots so she could at least help with whatever they had planned behind her back.

*

137

It was after four by the time everyone finally left. Well, everyone except Evan.

Maggie stretched her stiff body, listening to the satisfying cracks as she arched her back. She was sore. More than sore. Exhausted. But as she looked up at the house from where she stood on the embankment, that exhaustion made way for a smile. Her current state of fatigue was well worth it.

The porch screening was completely gone. In fact, the entire porch was gone. All that was left were the newly constructed steps and the deck frame which Evan was still working on, securing each plank of timber with the utmost precision. He said he wasn't going anywhere until the porch was done, said he didn't want Maggie or one of the boys to forget it was missing and walk out in the middle of the night only to fall straight through the frame.

The house looked good. Different and so much better. Travis had power soaked the cladding and it was now refreshed, glowing bright white. Ryan, a fellow firefighter Brad had corralled to help, had re-painted the window shutters, the blue popping against the refreshed white. Brad had harnessed up and climbed onto the roof. He replaced every cracked shingle, which he guaranteed would stop the leaks until Maggie could afford to get the whole thing replaced. Inside, Jane and Julie had helped Maggie finish painting the rest of the downstairs in the same light gray Maggie had committed to. Everything was slowly starting to come together, piece by piece.

"Would you like a beer?" Maggie asked, walking back up to the house.

Travis had gone on a beer run into town earlier to grab a couple cases from the pub. It was the only time Maggie had ever had beer in the house. Tom was a Scotch drinker. She was strictly wine, sometimes hard liquor if the occasion called for it. But today she'd consumed her first beer since high school, and she had to admit, after a hard day's work, it sure did quench her thirst more than any wine ever could.

Evan sat back on his haunches, glancing over his shoulder. He had a screw clamped between his lips, his ball cap sat backwards on his head, a smear of dirt lined his cheek. He looked almost as tired as she felt.

Checking the time on his watch, he considered something a moment, removing the screw from his mouth to ask, "You having one?"

She nodded.

"Sure." He shrugged. "I think we've earned it."

Smiling, Maggie walked around to the rear of the house to enter via the back deck. Inside was quiet. Jack was up in the attic. He was really starting to turn it into his own retreat now that they knew the leaks had been fixed. TJ was in Maggie's room, watching a movie on her laptop.

Opening the refrigerator, Maggie pulled out two bottles of the beer Travis had bought, hurrying back out to find Evan sitting on one of the newly erected porch steps. He rested his elbows on his knees, ducking his head to lift his cap off, ruffling a hand through his hair. She sat next to him, handing him a beer, and he thanked her with a lopsided smile, twisting the top off easily. She watched from the corner of her eye as he tipped his head back, his Adam's apple bobbing in his throat with a few hearty swallows. When he came up for a breath he groaned with a combination of relief and satisfaction, a sound Maggie found her body reacting to of its own accord. She quickly averted her gaze, looking down at her own beer.

"Cheers," Evan said, holding his bottle out.

She managed a smile, tapping the neck of her bottle with his. "Cheers."

Taking a sip of beer, she looked back at the deck to find all the planks in place, and she smiled.

"I don't know if I want to put the screening back up," she pondered out loud, glancing back to the lake, to the peach-streaked sky illuminated behind the silhouette of mile-high pines. "It's such a beautiful view."

"Bad idea." Evan shook his head vehemently. "You'll get eaten alive by mosquitoes come July. Won't even be able to sit out here and enjoy that there view."

"Oh . . ." She sighed. "I guess that makes sense."

"Yeah, but you can get this really great screening now. It's practically invisible. Can't even see it's there until you're right up close to it."

"That sounds way better than the stuff I got from the hardware store!" Maggie cringed at the thought of putting up the ugly green screening only to ruin the aesthetic of the house and the view that had sold this place to her in the first place.

"If you want, I'm heading down to Manchester this week. I can pick you up some from Home Depot. Maybe stop by and hang it up for you?" He shrugged a shoulder before finishing his beer.

"Oh, you don't have to do—" She snapped her mouth shut when he threw her a knowing look, the smirk lingering on his lips. "What?" she asked after a beat, her brows knitted together at the look in his eyes.

"You really need to work on accepting help." He looked out over the water as he continued, "It doesn't make you a charity case. It's just what friends do."

Maggie cowered a little, hugging her knees as she focused intently on the ground. "Sorry. I guess I'm just not used to it." She risked a sideways glance to find him watching her curiously. She laughed, shrugging her shoulders in defeat. "I guess I've never really had that many friends who would voluntarily come and fix my entire porch on a Sunday."

"It's nothing. I like to keep busy," Evan said with another casual shrug.

And it was right at that moment that she witnessed it again. That look in his eye. It was more than sadness; it was pure melancholy and it was gone in less than a second. But she'd seen it. There was something wrong. Something deep down that he tried to hide, and he did it so well. She was sure only she could see it; maybe because she was hiding her own demons, too. She wanted to ask him if he was okay, but she hardly knew the man. So, she stayed silent, choosing instead to scratch at the label on her beer bottle.

"How long were you and your husband married before he passed away?" Evan asked out of the blue.

Maggie looked up at him, finding him staring out over the spectacular vista, unperturbed by his own question, seemingly unaware of her surprise.

She cleared her throat, shifting a little before answering reluctantly, "Sixteen years." And for some reason she added, "I was pregnant when we got married."

"What was he like?"

"Who? Tom?" She looked at him and he nodded. "Um, he was tall and handsome. And he—"

Evan interjected with mocking laughter. "I don't care what he *looked* like." He smirked at her. "What was he *like*?"

Maggie contemplated his question. She wanted to tell him the truth, but she knew she couldn't. So, she decided on the answer she had well versed and saved in the back of her mind like a pre-recording. "He was a great father. He and I met in college. I was working at the coffee house between our neighboring campuses and one day he literally ran right into me. Spilled iced latte all down the front of me. He felt so bad, he demanded I allow him to take me out for dinner to apologize. I did. And . . . that was that." Maggie smiled at the memory. Despite everything that had happened, their meet cute was still smile-worthy. "He worked a lot. He was always a hard worker. Nights, weekends." *Because he was busy screwing his side piece*, she wanted to add but didn't. "But he always made time for . . ." She stopped when she noticed the dubious look in Evan's eyes. It was almost as if he didn't believe a word she was saying, and it was that correct assumption that took her breath away, her throat suddenly dry.

They shared a moment, one where Evan stared so deep into

141

her eyes it was like he could see straight through her facade and deep down into the murky depths of her anguished soul. He managed a small smile, void of its usual cocky smugness. "You know you can be honest with me, right?"

Forcing herself to look away, Maggie guffawed, shaking her head. "What are you talking about? I *am* being honest. You asked me what my dead husband was like and I'm telling you. He was a good father, a hard worker, and a *wonderful* husband." She couldn't even begin to hide the disdain in her voice as she said those last words. She shrugged, lifting the bottle of beer to her lips and taking a big, unladylike gulp, fully aware of his gaze set intently on her.

He so obviously wanted to say something but, thankfully, he kept his lips set in a firm line as if to stop himself.

Maggie softened a little, her false bravado dissolving with every second they stared at one another. She looked down at the bottle in her hand with a heavy sigh. "He *was* all those things," she said softly, adding with a whisper, "At least that's what I thought."

Evan said nothing. He just watched her, waiting.

Maggie's gaze flitted between his eyes, seeing an earnest sincerity within them. But there was something else. Something real. Something that made her feel completely at ease in his presence, and so, despite the walls she tried so hard to keep up, she continued, "He really *was* a good father." She nodded. "The boys idolized him, and he loved TJ and Jack more than anything in the whole world." At that, she stopped, her brows knitting together with a frown as she contemplated her words.

Did he though? She found herself wondering this more than she'd have liked. Ultimately, Tom chose his life with his mistress over Maggie, but he also chose that life over his sons, too. He took money from his family, and he spent it on his whore. Maybe—and she hated thinking this when he wasn't around to defend himself—but maybe Tom wasn't the world's best father like she'd been led to believe over the years. Maybe Tom had been a liar and a cheat and a phony all along; she was just too stupid and in love with him to realize it.

"We fell in love, young. And fast," Maggie continued, staring down at the overgrown grass. She didn't know why, but she felt like she had to talk. It was not just Evan's question. She needed this. She needed to confide in someone. She needed to let it out to someone and, for some reason, she felt like she could trust this man. "But then life happened. Next thing you know, it's sixteen years later."

She saw Evan nod from her periphery, and she swallowed the trepidation that had been lingering at the back of her throat. Taking another pull from her beer, she prepared herself to say the words out loud. She needed to say it out loud, to tell him, to tell anybody. With a deep fortifying breath, she closed her eyes. "My husband was cheating on me when he died." She took a shaky breath and continued, "I didn't find out until after he was gone."

Evan didn't say anything for a long moment. Nothing but the sound of a few gulls off in the distance accompanied the tension that had settled between them.

Maggie glanced nervously at him to see his face seemingly impassive, and she wondered for a moment if she'd even said the words out loud. Perhaps he hadn't heard her. She went to say something, but he turned to her, his eyes full of understanding, with a hint of the same sadness she'd witnessed glimpses of during their few brief encounters.

"Your boys don't know?"

She shook her head quickly.

"You're not gonna tell them?"

"I don't want them to know. They don't deserve that," Maggie replied.

"Neither do you," he said without missing a beat.

She said nothing, staring down at her hands, at that ring shining on her finger in the muted light of night falling overhead.

"You don't," Evan repeated with a little more conviction, his deep voice steely. "You know that, right?"

She shrugged with a heavy sigh.

"Any time you need to talk to someone, you can talk to me." Evan continued, "I know what it's like, having to keep secrets." At the hushed sound of his gruff words, Maggie looked at him, his face set in a hard scowl as he stared straight ahead, teeth raking painfully over his bottom lip as he said with a whisper, "It'll drive ya crazy."

She wanted to ask him what he was talking about. What was he keeping bottled up? What secrets was he hiding that were driving him crazy? Was this the reason behind the jaded sadness that flashed in his eyes? Was it the reason he moved back to Jewel Harbor? But before she could say anything, press him for answers, they were interrupted.

"Mom?" Jack's booming voice came from inside the house.

Jumping, Maggie cleared her throat and turned. "I'm out here, honey."

Jack soon appeared in the open front door, looking from his mother to Evan and back again, a small crease of confusion appearing between his brows. "What's for dinner?"

"Oh, um . . ." Suddenly flustered over what she'd just disclosed about her cheating husband with her children right inside and within earshot, Maggie tucked the loose strands of her hair behind her ear, flashing Evan a fleeting glance before getting to her feet. "Um, I was just going to fry up some salmon."

Jack nodded, his curious gaze landing on Evan once more.

Evan looked awkward all of a sudden, and he stood, smoothing a hand down the front of his filthy T-shirt. "I'm just gonna finish securing these planks and then I'll be out of your hair."

Maggie watched as he went back to work, drilling a screw into the timber. "Would you like to stay for dinner?" she asked. "It's the least I can do to thank you for all your—"

He waved a hand in the air, refusing her offer. "I sure do appreciate that, but I've got some things I need to get done tonight."

On a Sunday? Maggie watched him. *Probably another hot*

not-date. She almost rolled her eyes but then she found herself wondering where the jealous voice inside her head had appeared from. Instead, she forced a smile and nodded, picking up his empty beer bottle from the step.

"Mom?" TJ appeared beside Jack, sticking his head out through the gap between his brother and the doorjamb. "Can I have a Pop-Tart?"

"No, Teej, it's almost time for dinner."

"Balls to that."

Jack laughed out loud at his little brother's unexpected response. Evan chuckled.

"TJ!" Maggie chastised, throwing her hands in the air and shaking her head. "Come on, you two. You can help me with dinner."

She flashed another furtive glance at Evan, one which he met with a tight-lipped smile, and she carefully stepped over the unsecured planks of timber, ushering her sons inside.

Feeling a little heavier in the chest, a little knotted in the stomach, Maggie ignored it as best as she could. She wasn't ready to explore these confusing feelings. Not just yet.

Chapter 19

Maggie thought telling her secret would have been like a weight lifting off her shoulders. A release. But it didn't have such an effect. And ever since she'd confessed the truth to Evan, she'd felt uneasy and anxious. She'd hardly slept a wink and now, running on coffee and not much else, she was on edge, gripping the steering wheel so tight her knuckles were white as she pulled up to the curb outside Jewel Harbor High.

It might have seemed pointless to have TJ and Jack start at their new schools with only a few weeks left in the school year, but she wanted them to get to know their way around campus for when classes resumed in the fall, and to hopefully make a few friends before summer vacation.

"Oh, Jack, there's your *girlfriend*," TJ teased from the backseat.

Maggie snapped out of her daze, looking to find Katie waiting on the grassy knoll. She waved at the cute blonde who offered a shy smile in return.

"Mom!" Jack hissed. "Do you have to be so *embarrassing*?"

"For waving?" Maggie laughed, turning to see him shrink down into his seat, his cheeks flushed crimson.

He'd dressed in his finest khaki shorts and button-down, his hair styled neatly. He might have gone a little overboard with the

Old Spice, but he looked handsome, and Maggie couldn't help but bite back her smile at the realization that his effort to look good had little to do with his first day at a new school and everything to do with a certain blonde who was currently watching their car with what appeared to be bated breath.

"Better hurry up for your *girlfriend*." TJ giggled, his head poking in through the middle of the two front seats.

"Shut up!" Jack snapped back, but his abrupt words were said with laughter he tried to conceal.

"Hey!" Maggie turned, pointing at TJ. "Back in your seat, Mister." She rolled her eyes at her youngest before focusing on Jack. "Do you have everything? Lunch money? Registration form?"

He nodded with an exaggerated sigh. "Yes, Mom."

"Okay." She gripped the steering wheel again, looking straight ahead at all the teenagers milling about, enjoying the morning sunshine in those final few moments before the first warning bell. She didn't know why, but she was suddenly overcome with emotion; tears burned her eyes. "Well, have fun."

"Wait. Are you *crying*?"

She could feel Jack lean in, studying her closely, but she brushed him off with a wave of her hand and scoffed, "No. Of course I'm not *crying*." But she totally was. There were definite tears. Today was a big day. It wasn't just the first day at their new schools, it was the first page of their new chapter, the first day of the rest of their lives. She didn't want to make it a big deal, but it was.

Much to her utter shock, Jack leaned in and placed a chaste kiss on her cheek, leaving her completely speechless. She couldn't even respond when he murmured goodbye. All she could do was sit there with a gaping mouth, watching as he grabbed his backpack from the floor and hurried out of the car. She continued watching as he jogged up the hill to meet Katie, the two sharing shy, awkward waves before Katie turned and led him off into the school building.

While sitting there, a little shell shocked, Maggie couldn't for the life of her remember the last time Jack had actually kissed her. A hug here and there, yes. But never a kiss. She could still feel her son's lips lingering on her cheek, and it was a feeling she hoped she could treasure for the rest of her life, because who knew when she might get her next kiss from him.

"Mom?"

Waking up from that reverie, Maggie glanced in the rear-view mirror to find TJ watching her expectantly.

"I'm gonna be late," he sang with a knowing tone.

Maggie regained what she could of her composure and, winking at him in the reflection, she shifted the car into drive and pulled away from the curb. And, despite the conflicting emotions warring deep down on the inside, she smiled the whole way from the high school across town to the elementary school.

*

By the time Maggie had returned to the house after dropping the boys at school, she found a somewhat familiar shiny black pickup parked by the house. Her brows knitted together in confusion as she hopped out of her car. When she rounded the house, her feet faltered as she stopped dead in her tracks. There, with his back to her, wearing only a pair of seriously worn-out Levi's and not a stitch more, was Evan.

She was immediately transfixed. Unable to look away. Hypnotized by the way the muscles pulled beneath taut skin with every movement of the paint roller in his hand as he lathered each plank of timber. His jeans hung low—impossibly so—showing off a glimpse of the elastic waistband of his underwear. He had earbuds in, and his head bobbed to whatever beat was playing, otherwise oblivious to Maggie as she stood there watching him, gaping at him, biting down on her lip like a goddamn pervert. She knew she should avert her eyes—she was being a literal creep—but she simply couldn't. Her body wasn't cooperating with her brain.

When Evan turned to dip the roller into the paint tray, his eyes widened when he caught her standing there. He was startled, jumping so high he almost tripped over his own booted foot, the paint roller falling to the timber decking with a loud clatter.

"Jesus Christ, you scared the shit out of me!" he yelled, quickly tearing the buds from his ears.

Maggie still stood there. Just staring. This time her eyes trailed down over his strong chest smattered with hair to the pack of six defined abdominal muscles, and the outline of a V-shaped pelvis that dipped down into those jeans he wore dangerously well.

It was the sound of stifled laughter that finally forced Maggie from her daze. She came to and saw Evan was smirking at her. She'd been caught staring. Outright *ogling* him. She wanted to die. But damn, what a way to go.

Shaking her head and with a suddenly dry throat, she found herself asking, "W-what are you doing here?" Much to her frustration the question came out hoarse and raspy and shamefully stammered.

Evan bit back his smug smile, looking away. He bent over to pick up the roller, grasping the long metal handle. "Looks like rain for the rest of the week." He pointed to the sky which was a contradictory shade of blue, continuing, "Thought I'd pop over and give the deck a quick coat of sealant. It should dry in a few hours."

"Oh, okay." Maggie successfully averted her eyes, looking down to the ground while tucking her hair behind her ear. She suddenly wished she'd dressed more appropriately for school drop-off; flip flops, faded leggings and an old Backstreet Boys tour T-shirt was the farthest thing from attractive. She was the definition of a not-so-hot mess right now.

Flashing him a tight-lipped smile, she muttered a thank you before turning to head toward the back entrance to escape into the house and hide out until he left.

"Hey, I was thinking of driving down to Manchester after I'm done here," Evan said, effectively stopping her mid-step. She glanced over her shoulder, meeting his eyes. "I gotta grab some things from my parts dealer. You wanna come? We can stop in at the Home Depot and check out that screening I was telling you about." He lifted his ball cap and raked his fingers through his mussed hair before pulling the peak down low, that same lingering smile playing on his lips.

"Um, yeah." Maggie shrugged. "Sure. I'll just grab a shower." She cringed at her choice of words. He really didn't need to know that she was about to hop in a shower after gawking inappropriately at his naked torso.

Pointing to the house as if to further justify herself, she continued, "Just come and grab me. I-I mean *get* me . . . when you're r-ready to go."

Evan quirked a brow, flashing a mischievous grin as he said, "Come grab you in the shower?"

Oh God. She grimaced. "No. I mean . . . I . . . I, umm, said I—"

Her useless stammering was interrupted by Evan's barking laughter, effectively shutting her up. And, with flaming hot cheeks, she ignored his eyes that were positively dancing with delight.

Hating herself, and him right now, she turned and scurried around back and inside the house, desperate to get the hell away from him before she made an even bigger idiot of herself.

Upstairs, Maggie locked the bathroom door and checked the window to make sure Evan wouldn't be able to see her from downstairs. She highly doubted he was the kind to try and cop a sneaky perv—unlike her, apparently—but she didn't want to risk accidentally flashing him. Not after their awkward exchange.

Stripping off, she turned the tap for the hot water, the pipes screeching to life behind the wall. When steam began to rise up into the air, she stepped into the tub. As the steady stream hit her head and shoulders, she closed her eyes and sagged with relief. It had been a long time since she'd been able to luxuriate in a hot shower. Well before Tom's death. Now, with the boys at school and no one to rush her, she intended on taking her sweet time.

But then, as she lathered her hair with vanilla-mango shampoo, images of a half-naked Evan entered her mind causing her to startle, and it was suddenly impossible to focus on anything other than the fact that he was right downstairs while she was up here, wet and naked.

God, get a grip, Maggie. She shook her head at her train of thought, almost laughing at herself.

But it wasn't surprising that this was where her mind was wandering at the first sight of a half-naked man. It'd been a while. Sure, Tom had passed away less than a few months ago, but it'd been longer than that.

She thought back to exactly how long it had been. Mexico, January. It had been a beautiful week of sun, sand and swimsuits. But on their last night, after being intimate together twice in the shower, Maggie had come out of the bathroom dressed only in a towel and Tom had glanced up at her from where he'd been lounging on the bed dressed in a fluffy hotel robe. His hair was still damp, his gaze slow and assessing as it raked over her from head to toe. She'd flushed, thinking he was going somewhere else with his thoughts, especially considering the explicit things they'd just done to one another in that shower. She definitely hadn't anticipated his words.

"You've packed on a few, huh?"

Maggie had paused while rifling through the closet, her search to find a dress to wear for dinner effectively halted. She'd turned to find him staring down at his cell again, the screen illuminating his face, highlighting the small smile which tugged at his lips. He'd obviously meant his words to come off as light, like some half-hearted joke. And while Maggie had tried to play it off with a roll of her eyes, his words stuck with her.

She'd always been conscious of her body, and Tom knew that. He'd said those words to hurt her, whether they were true or not. So, after that one careless, throwaway comment, she never let him see her naked again. It was only now, after the fact, that she was beginning to realize how unbothered he was by their lack of intimacy after that night. And now she knew why. He was getting it somewhere else, from a woman much more perfect than her.

Pulling herself from those thoughts, Maggie continued washing her hair. But suddenly, without warning, the hot water turned icy cold before a shuddering, almighty shriek came through the wall, the shower pressure dwindling to nothing but a dribble.

With soap in her eyes, Maggie glanced up at the shower head, her brows pinched together. She tested the taps, turning them one way and the other, but nothing.

"Are you serious, right now?" she hissed under her breath, looking down at her wet, naked body, shampoo bubbles sliding down her face, hindering her vision.

She cursed under her breath and ripped the shower curtain aside, carefully stepping out of the tub and grabbing a towel to cover herself. She checked the faucet on the bathroom sink, turning the brass taps but she was greeted with nothing more than a hiss and groan of objection coming through the pipes.

"What the hell?" She glanced around, for what she didn't know, as she tried to figure things out. She had shampoo in her hair and it was starting to sting her eyes, and she had no damn water to wash it out.

She gave a big sigh of resignation. She really didn't want to but she knew she didn't have any other choice. So, clutching her towel as if it were a lifeline, she walked out of the steamy bathroom and stopped at the top of the stairs.

"Evan!"

Nothing.

"Evan?" she yelled again, slightly louder.

Still nothing.

Oh, for God's sake! Rolling her eyes at her own predicament, she couldn't help but laugh as she glanced down at herself again. Dressed only in a towel, her wet hair clinging to her shoulders, she decided this had to be some sort of karma.

*

Evan hummed along to the Counting Crows as they played through his earbuds. He was just finishing up the last coat of sealant, satisfied with his meticulous attention to detail with every smooth stroke of the paint roller. Stretching, he craned his neck to take in the sky. The rain clouds were beginning to roll in from the Atlantic, and the threat of a potential storm lingered in the thick, soupy air.

He glanced back at the house, and suddenly his mind wandered to Maggie.

How could a man ever, in a million years, cheat on a woman like her?

He shook his head at the question that had been plaguing him all night, racking his brain over what she had confessed to him yesterday. Not only had he been having an affair, but she'd had to find out after the fact, after his death, that the husband she'd loved for half her life had been cheating on her. And now she was forced to carry that around with her. How the hell could any woman move past a betrayal like that? God, it made him sick to his stomach. And after her admission, he felt this sudden yearning need to protect her, protect a woman he hardly even knew.

His eyes moved up to the window where he knew the bathroom was. She was up there right now, in that shower. He swallowed hard as he remembered back to that look in her eye moments ago, when she'd been openly staring at him, eyes raking over his bare chest.

He hated to seem cocky but he was used to it. He'd been appreciated and downright objectified by most women and many men ever since he'd hit the peak of puberty at thirteen. He was an attractive guy. That much he knew. But there was something about Maggie. Her attention didn't automatically make him recoil and inwardly roll his eyes. Being looked at wantonly by a woman like her, who was otherwise so reserved and wary, it made his heart surge in a way he hadn't felt in a long, long time.

Stepping off the deck, Evan walked to the back of his truck and pulled himself up to sit on the tailgate. He grabbed his thermos from the icebox and took a few long swigs from the bottle, eyes closed. But he kept picturing her up there. Naked. Wet. Soapy.

Jesus Christ, man, get it together, he thought with a scoff, splashing some of the icy water over his face. He removed his ball cap to douse his hair, but just as he wiped the droplets from his eyes, he heard something over the music playing through his earbuds.

Turning, his brows drew together as he pulled out an earbud. And then his heart lurched into the back of his throat at the sound of his name being called from inside the house. Maggie. She was calling out to him. Screaming. She was in trouble.

He jumped down from his truck, racing around the side of the house and in through the back door. His long legs made quick work of the stairs, taking three at a time before crossing the landing and continuing toward the sound of her voice. He pushed his way through the slightly ajar door before coming to a skidding halt on the wet bathroom tile, his eyes growing wide.

Holy shit . . . There she was, standing in just a towel that she was clutching to her naked body as if her life depended on it, her hair wet, and clinging to her damn skin. Her cheeks were rosy and an adorable little line was etched between her eyebrows as she looked from him to the shower and back again.

"What's wrong?" he asked, his voice coming out gruff and a little hoarse thanks to the current state of her almost naked form.

"The water stopped." She pointed an accusatory finger at the tub. "And I have shampoo in my hair!"

Evan balked. Was she serious right now? Shampoo? He thought she'd been up here getting hacked apart by a psychopath with a machete. He shook his head to himself, scrubbing a hand over his face, stifling his own laughter.

"And just what is so *funny*?"

Her dubious tone caused him to glance at her over his shoulder. She had a hand placed on her hip in an attempt to look authoritative, but it wasn't working while she was dressed only in a towel, looking like an adorable drowned raccoon.

He laughed under his breath as he looked back at the taps. "I thought you were up here getting stabbed to death."

"I'm about to stab someone if I can't get this damn shampoo out of my hair."

Evan smirked to himself, twisting the taps to no avail. He turned, wiping his hands on the backs of his jeans, which was when he realized they were both half-naked in the center of a steamy bathroom.

He cleared the sudden bubble from the back of his throat, averting his eyes to the doorway. "I'll just, um . . . grab some tools from my, um, my truck. Hold tight."

Chapter 20

An hour later, Maggie was perched in the cab of Evan's truck as they continued on the road out of town, the highway sign indicating it was forty-five miles to Manchester. She drummed her fingers against her jean-clad thighs, suddenly feeling very awkward being in such a confined space with a man who, not so long ago, helped her wash shampoo out of her hair in the backyard, using what was left of the icy cold water in his thermos.

The Foo Fighters played over the car stereo and Evan hummed along to the song, tapping his hand against the steering wheel. Maggie snuck a sideways glance at him, assessing him silently. He was dressed—thank goodness—having pulled on a plain white T-shirt over his head before hopping into his truck. But now that she knew what was under that thin cotton, it was impossible to focus on anything else.

"What are you thinking about over there?"

Pulling herself from her inappropriate thoughts, she caught Evan watching her before he focused back on the highway ahead. He looked effortlessly casual in his jeans and T-shirt. His beard was extra scruffy, hair messy after being contained by his ball cap all morning, one elbow rested on the doorjamb, his thumb and forefinger steering the wheel.

"Nothing . . ." Maggie shrugged, looking down at her handbag in her lap.

"Can I ask you something?" Evan's tone was cautionary, tentative, suddenly void of its usual cocky timbre, and that made her head snap up.

"Me?"

He chuckled under his breath. "No. The other person in the truck."

She deadpanned which only made him laugh out loud.

"Sorry," he apologized half-heartedly, clearing his throat, and that smile made way for a slight crease to pull between his brows, his jaw fixed tight as he watched the empty road straight ahead. "Yesterday," he started, but didn't continue.

She noticed his grip on the steering wheel turn a little tighter and immediately she knew exactly what he wanted to ask. With dread settling low in her belly, she closed her eyes. "Yeah?"

He hesitated before finally saying, "If you ever need to talk, you can trust me. You know?"

Even with her eyes closed, she could feel him watching her. Slowly, she forced her lids open, and looked at him, meeting that weighty blue gaze.

"Thanks," she said softly, clearing the lump from the back of her throat. "I've been going through so many confusing emotions this morning."

"Like what?"

She turned, looking out the window as the side of the road whizzed past, the pine trees blurring into a dark green haze. "I thought telling someone would make it easier, somehow. Would make me feel like I'm not suffocating anymore. But . . . it hasn't."

"Why?" Evan asked.

She shook her head. "I don't know. It's like I'm trapped by my past. And I *want* to move on. Hell, I moved my kids across state line to try to get away from it, but it's like it's followed me here. I feel like I'll never get away from it. Tom will always have one up on me. It's almost like . . . almost like he planned this. Which I know sounds ridiculous and jaded, but . . . I don't know." With a hard sigh, she glared out at the horizon, knowing her words were ridiculous but standing by every one of them regardless. The truth was she did feel trapped. Trapped by the thoughtless, unspeakable actions of her dead husband.

"I wish I'd never found out," she admitted so softly she wasn't sure Evan would hear her. But he did. She could feel his gaze settle on her again. "I'd rather the pain of missing him than this-this hollow, empty feeling in the pit of my stomach. I could have eventually learned to live without him. To move on from that pain. But this betrayal, it's just . . ." She shook her head again as infuriating tears burned her eyes. Tears of anger. And that only frustrated her even more, swiping, almost violently, at the solitary tear that had broken free.

Suddenly they stopped. Confused, Maggie looked up to see they were pulled over on the shoulder of the highway, a big road train sped past them; dust and dirt swirled up into the air as it thundered past causing Evan's truck to tremble.

Maggie glanced across the cab, finding him sitting there staring straight ahead, hands casually resting on the steering wheel, an impassive, unreadable expression masking his face.

"W-what are we doing?" she asked while furtively looking around. It was dangerous to be parked in such a way; she was worried another big rig might speed past and crash into them.

Evan shifted in his seat, turning to her. But his eyes avoided hers, his stare empty and hollow, looking over her shoulder and focusing out the passenger window as he scrubbed a hand over his face.

"My fiancée left me," he finally said, and his voice was raw and gruff, like the words hurt to say them out loud.

Maggie started at him, shocked by his confession. Fiancée? Evan was engaged? Wow. She pretended not to notice the brief twinge of what she could only describe as jealousy fluttering in her belly. She was being absurd. Evan had been engaged. So what? His fiancée left him. He wasn't engaged anymore. Was that it? Was that the secret he'd been hiding that had been driving him crazy?

"She left me . . . at my worst." He swallowed hard, his Adam's apple bobbing in his throat. Then he looked at Maggie, and she witnessed that same flash of heart-wrenching sadness in his eyes, a sadness she was familiar with. "Don't let him win, Maggie." He shook his head, his eyes hauntingly sincere. "Don't let him win because if you do, *you'll* be the one paying for the rest of your life. Trust me."

Evan turned away, and with a hard sigh he shifted the truck into gear and pulled back out onto the highway. Maggie watched him, studied how his overwhelming sadness and anger, which so obviously tormented him, radiated from him.

His fiancée left him. At his worst? She wondered what that meant. His worst. Was that the reason he quit his career in baseball and returned to Jewel Harbor? Was that the reason behind his sadness? Perhaps they had a little more in common than she'd first anticipated. She wanted to ask him more. She wanted to know more because she had a feeling he was battling with more than just being left by his fiancée. But she didn't want to pry. So, she remained quiet. And together they continued along the highway in silence, with nothing but the sound of the Foo Fighters playing through the cab of the truck.

*

Maggie had never been into a Home Depot before. Walking through the automated doors, she stopped in the entry, taking in the ginormous shelves stacked way up high, full of items she didn't need yet which automatically captured her attention. She continued into the sprawling store in a wistful daze, like a kid in a candy store.

"Anything else you need while we're here?" Evan asked.

The moment between them in the truck was quickly forgotten by the time they began navigating their way through the busy streets of Manchester. Evan had suddenly broken the overwrought silence by yelling at a driver who had pulled out in front of him without any indication, and Maggie couldn't stop herself from laughing as his fist waved in the air. It was her laughter that made Evan crack a smile. They'd continued through the small city, Evan pointing out all the main attractions. Maggie stared longingly at the big-name chain stores she hadn't realized, until now, she'd missed in the little time she'd been away from the city.

"I was hoping to grab some paint for my bedroom." She looked up at him, her brows raised in hope, like he might possibly tell her no. "But if you don't have time, I can just—"

Evan cut her off, pointing straight ahead and, following the direction of his forefinger, Maggie's eyes lit up at the huge wall of paint swatches, her jaw dropping at the display.

"Wow . . ." She sighed, staring up at the myriad colors and shades, completely spoiled for choice. She'd heard all about this place, but she never knew it was the stuff dreams were made of.

Picking up two swatches of the colors she'd been deliberating for days online, she stared at them closely, studying them with pure determination.

"What do you think?" She turned to Evan who was busy sneakily taking the color samples and swapping the names around while chuckling to himself. "Evan!" she chided, trying not to laugh herself. "You can't do *that*!" She looked around to make sure management weren't coming to kick them out.

Evan flashed her a wicked smirk, then stood back and folded his arms over his chest while he glanced innocently up toward the metal beams hanging high overhead.

Maggie rolled her eyes at him, holding the two samples up. "Pale Mist?" She indicated the card in her left hand. "Or Endless Dusk?" She held the card in her right hand slightly higher.

With a pensive look in his eyes and a deep crease etched

between his brows, Evan looked from Maggie to the swatches and back again, meeting her eyes with a wry expression. "Maggie, both these colors are *exactly* the same."

Maggie looked down at the cards in her hands, shaking her head. "No. No they're not." She moved next to him, holding up the Endless Dusk. "There's more of a blue undertone to this. See how when the light hits it at just the right angle it's almost as if it shimmers like a d—" She looked up and paused. A glaze had fallen over his eyes as he stared at her, and she knew immediately she'd lost him.

Shaking her head again, she placed the Endless Dusk back into its holder. "Never mind. I'll go for the Pale Mist. It'll look better against the Casper White and the Mocha Latte."

Evan snorted with laughter but she ignored him. She clutched the card tight as she headed toward the paint counter to get a tin made up. On the way, she noticed rows and rows of wallpaper and made a beeline for the display. Evan chuckled to himself as he followed closely behind.

"Sorry, I'm in my element, here." Maggie laughed over her shoulder, moving to a black and white striped paper she could envision lining the bottom half of the wall in her front sitting nook. She continued, rifling through the paper samples. "I redecorated our whole house a few years back. It featured in a magazine. But I never actually got to come to a place like this. And, despite having little to no interest in it whatsoever, Tom had the final say over everything I did. I never had full rein." She felt her shoulders fall at that admission, something she'd never confessed to anyone before.

"He sounds like a bit of dick, if you ask me," Evan said before quickly adding, "No offense."

Maggie looked back at him. "You know, I'm only now starting to see him for what he truly was." She shrugged a shoulder. "Don't get me wrong, I loved him. But the lanky, slightly awkward boy I fell in love with in college was a far different person from the man he ended up becoming. And now that I know the truth, it's like the smoke screen is finally lifting." She turned and continued down the aisle, glancing blankly at the shelves. "Before I discovered he was cheating, I thought our marriage was perfect, but now . . ." She shrugged again, flashing Evan a sardonic smile. "Well, they say hindsight's twenty-twenty, right?"

Evan nodded with a noncommittal shrug. "Sometimes."

Maggie glanced at him, finding something there behind his murmured response, but before she could question him, they were interrupted by a Home Depot worker, asking if she could be of any service.

"Yeah, we need a couple gallons of this gray paint," Evan said, taking the card from Maggie and handing it to the woman.

"It's Pale Mist," Maggie corrected him, pointing to the name on the back of the card the woman was now holding.

"Light gray." Evan retorted with a smug smile.

Maggie balked, narrowing her eyes at him and laughing once under her breath. "It's *so* not light gray."

The woman looked between the two of them with a knowing smile before turning and heading off toward the paint counter. Maggie and Evan glanced at one another and suddenly started laughing at the same time before following the lady.

*

Bucky, an old school friend of Evan's and a plumber from a few towns over, had been and gone. And a few hundred dollars down—a quarter of the cost she would have paid anyone else—Maggie had running water again, just in time for the boys' showers before bed.

After their trip to the Home Depot, Evan and Maggie had stopped for lunch at a small diner about halfway back to Jewel Harbor, in a tiny town of two hundred people. There, they'd talked more over burgers and sneaky lunchtime lagers.

Maggie asked Evan about his baseball career. He was humble, but uncharacteristically curt at the same time. She could tell he didn't really like talking about himself. Or perhaps it was his past he didn't like talking about. He told her he'd studied business in college while playing ball, and that he'd always dreamed of playing in the Majors but, in his words, it just *hadn't worked out*. When she asked what happened, he swiftly and seamlessly steered the topic of conversation back to Maggie and her love of interior design.

"Have you ever considered going back to school?" he asked. "You know it's never too late."

She laughed it off, but of course she had considered going back to school. Every day for the past sixteen years. She'd even looked into online courses a couple years back when TJ had started school and she found herself with several hours free each day. But Tom had somehow managed to convince her, over the years, that interior design wasn't a real career. It was a hobby. And it was more important for her to stay at home and raise their sons than worry about some fickle little hobby.

"You obviously love it," Evan said, adding with a teasing smile, "I ain't ever seen anyone look at a wall of paint samples the way you did back at the Home Depot. Serious heart-eyes."

Maggie could feel her cheeks flush.

"You should do what you love." Evan nodded, finishing his beer, but then he fixed her with a look she hadn't been expecting, one that felt as if he knew exactly what she was thinking. In a whispered voice, he said, "He can't stand in your way anymore."

*

Hours later, a storm raged outside. Save for the thunder, rain and the incessant cracks of lightning, the house was silent. Both boys were in bed after their successful first days at school, and Maggie moved to the couch and settled with a mug of hot tea. Pulling her laptop onto the pillow on her lap, she began searching courses.

The community college offered a degree in interior design, and she would be able to use the credits she'd earned from her freshman year at Rhode Island as recognized prior learning on her admissions application. That would take the three-year course down to a year and a half. She read the information thoroughly, studying all the photographs. They offered workshops and online courses. They even had a staging studio; it was all very legitimate. She smiled, and, for the first time in a long time, her heart raced with healthy anticipation.

She hesitated as her mouse hovered over the submit button. What was the harm in having an application pack sent out to her in the post? But then, as a loud crack of thunder boomed right over the house, reality reared its ugly head. And that smile faded, as did the racing of her heart.

Who was she kidding? She was a thirty-six-year-old with two kids. She couldn't go back to college with a bunch of high school graduates. She had to focus on her boys and *their* college educations. She had to earn money to put food on the table. Going back to school was a dream she gave up years ago, one that was unrealistic and a little selfish, given their current predicament. She appreciated Evan's enthusiasm and encouragement, but it was time to get real.

Maggie shut the laptop and placed it onto the couch cushion beside her. Taking a sip from her tea, she closed her eyes and exhaled a heavy breath, hoping the sound of the pouring rain might lull her into a false sense of assurance. This was her life now. They had a roof over their head. Her boys were safe. She was taking care of business. That was all that mattered now.

Chapter 21

The following few days went by in a blur. The weather was temperamental, alternating between sunshine and rain; there was no in between. Maggie's days played out on repeat. One after the other. She woke up, cooked breakfast, took the boys to school. She came home, did as much of the house repairs and works as she could in the hours between nine and three-thirty. She showered, collected the boys from school, came home, cooked dinner, and then she spent her nights either relaxing in front of the television with TJ, or nestled in bed with a good book after the boys had gone off to sleep. Until the house was exactly how she wanted it to be, those were her days. If it took her forever, she didn't mind.

Evan didn't stop by on Tuesday. Maggie had assumed it was because of the inclement weather; there wouldn't be a lot for him to do at the house in the pouring rain. Or perhaps he'd been too busy with work. On Wednesday, when the sun was shining, she wondered if he might stop by to put up the screening she'd bought at Home Depot. But he didn't. She hadn't heard from him. By the time Thursday rolled around, and the rain had settled in once again, she found herself wondering if she was ever going to hear from him again. She spent every free moment going over their day together in her head, wondering if she had said or done something that might make him not want to see her again. She hoped not. Not only had he been a huge help to her with all that he'd done around the house, if she was being honest, she kind of liked just having him around.

On Friday morning, Maggie decided to stop by Jane's Café after dropping the boys at school so she could grab a coffee on her way back to the house to continue painting her bedroom.

The bell above the door jingled as she stepped inside. It was a lot busier than she'd seen it in the few times she'd stopped by. Two men, fishermen by their appearance, were perched at the counter drinking coffee and talking between themselves. A man dressed in a suit was sitting in a booth reading a newspaper while talking on his cell phone. Two women were sitting by the far window, gossiping over cake.

Maggie smiled as she continued to the counter, pulling out a stool at the far end. Moments later, Jane came out through the swinging doors from the kitchen, carrying a plate of waffles, a cordless phone perched between her ear and her shoulder. She looked flushed and breathless, and run off her feet. Maggie felt bad for her as she watched her place the waffles in front of one of the men at the counter.

"Excuse me, Miss?" The man in the suit called out with an abrupt tone that caused Maggie to look at him.

"Sorry, just a moment." Jane held up a finger, going back to her phone call.

The man in the suit huffed, dramatically flicking through the pages of his newspaper.

"Janie?" One of the older fishermen held his hand in the air, waving at Jane as she hurried past. She made an exasperated face, as if something had just dawned on her, and she returned with a knife and fork wrapped in a paper napkin, handing it to him with an apologetic smile.

"What do you mean you *forgot* to process the order?" Jane released a heavy sigh before disappearing into the kitchen. She returned moments later with a plate of scrambled eggs and bacon, placing it in front of the other fisherman at the counter.

166

"*Excuse* me?" Suit-man called out again, this time his voice was laced with condescension and he stood to his feet. "I drove all the way from Concord for a meeting. I don't have *all* morning."

Maggie's brows knitted together. *How rude.*

"I'm so sorry, sir," Jane apologized, placing a hand over the phone's receiver. "What would you like?"

"I want some *damn* service!"

Jane's cheeks flushed pink, and with one hand she fumbled around in her apron pocket, likely for her notepad and pen, her eyes welling with the obvious sheen of tears.

Without considering her actions, Maggie stood and turned. Moving between the empty tables, she stopped at the abhorrently rude man. She wanted to tell him to calm down, to act like a decent human being or do everyone a favor and leave. But this was Jane's business; she had no right running her customers out. So, she did the next best thing.

"What can I get you, sir?"

The man looked Maggie up and down, a deep crease etching between his brows. And she couldn't blame him. She was dressed in paint-splattered overalls over an Adele concert T-shirt from when she had seen her perform at Radio City in New York. But she held her chin defiantly high and pressed her lips together in the semblance of a smile, waiting for the man's order.

"A coffee. Black," he said with a resigned sigh. "And the French toast with fresh berries, hold the syrup." His lack of manners was appalling, and the fact that he didn't seem to care was even worse. He sat back down in the booth and went back to his newspaper, without so much as a care in the world.

Maggie's hands balled into fists as she looked at him a moment longer. It was almost confronting; he was Tom if Tom had survived to be fifty-something and lost some of the hair on top of his head. It seemed the more expensive the suit, the more arrogant the man. She rolled her eyes and turned, heading back to the counter to find Jane smiling at her with a touch of awe.

"Sorry," Maggie whispered.

Jane shook her head, waving her over to the other side of the counter. Maggie looked around curiously before making her way to her.

"Can you make coffee?" Jane asked over her phone call.

Maggie offered a reluctant nod.

"Can you give Joe in the kitchen that man's order and make his coffee?"

"O-kay . . ." Maggie pulled her bottom lip between her teeth wondering what exactly she'd just gotten herself into.

"You're a *lifesaver*!" Jane whisper-yelled, moving around her and heading through the swinging doors.

Maggie stood there a moment, looking out over the café. It sure did look different from the other side of the counter. Bigger, more intimidating. She tapped a finger against her chin as she searched the countertops before locating the coffee pot. She made quick work of getting down to business. The last thing she wanted was for Mr. Suit to get his tighty-whities in another wad.

*

Forty minutes later, Maggie was standing behind the cash register, processing her third sale for the morning, an apron tied around her waist like she belonged there.

When there was a break in customers and the café was empty save for Joe in the kitchen, Jane released a groan, slumping forward against the counter with a harrumph. Maggie felt terrible. The poor woman looked exhausted.

"Let me make me you a coffee," Maggie said, moving quickly to the big espresso machine.

"Oh, honey, you are an *angel*!" Jane sighed. "I've been on my feet since four o'clock baking muffins for the morning tea at the nursing home. I normally whip them up the day before, but I was in Manchester yesterday with Katie getting her braces off."

"Sit down." Maggie smiled, moving around the coffee machine with expert ease. "Relax and put your feet up."

"You're a natural," Jane said with a small laugh as she took a seat on a stool on the other side of the counter. "I can't believe you got that horrible man to leave a tip!"

Maggie smiled to herself, remembering the man in the suit and his contrite smile as he paid his bill, thanking her with a murmur before hurrying out as if he was the busiest person in the entire state of New Hampshire. He'd left a five-dollar tip—so not a total monster.

"You want a job?"

From where she was frothing the creamer, Maggie glanced over at Jane, finding her watching on with a wry smile. She wasn't sure if she was being serious or not, but it was the opening she'd been hoping for.

"Well, actually . . ." Maggie laughed nervously, pouring the creamer and foam into the two mugs of espresso. She carried them both back to the counter, placing one in front of Jane before taking a sip from the other. "I kind of do . . . Want a job, I mean."

Jane gaped at her. "Really?" She made a point of looking around the quiet café with the slightest hint of derision. She snorted. "*Here?*"

Maggie shrugged. "Anywhere, really. I'm not picky. I was thinking of filling out an application at the Piggly Wiggly." She took another sip of her coffee. "I don't have a lot of experience doing much else. And I could do with the money now that . . . now that the boys and I are on our own." She wanted to add *since my husband spent all our savings on his whore* but she swallowed those words before she had a chance.

Jane's eyes grew. "When would you want to start?"

Maggie chuckled, looking down at the apron she was wearing. "Well, no time like the present, right?"

Jane released an almighty sigh, her shoulders sagging. "If I weren't so dang tired I'd climb right over this counter and kiss you, Maggie!"

Laughing into her cappuccino, Maggie's gaze lifted in time to see a shadowy figure walk through the door, the bell chiming musically. Involuntarily, her eyes widened at the sight of Evan, and she felt her body react, her shoulders straightening a little as she tried so hard to play it cool.

Evan's gaze landed on Maggie first. A sliver of something came over him but he recovered so smoothly she wasn't sure if she'd imagined it. A grin tugged at his lips as he stopped by Jane, leaning down to press a kiss to the top of his sister's head, his gaze still firmly planted on Maggie.

"Oh, hi, honey." Jane looked up at him with a tired smile.

"What's goin' on here?" he asked, jutting his chin to Maggie standing on the other side of the counter, his eyes taking in the apron wrapped around her slender waist.

Maggie went to say something, but Jane spoke first. "Maggie's going to work here!" she exclaimed excitedly. "Can you believe that?"

"No, I can't." Evan's smiling eyes met Maggie's, one brow quirked in confusion, and she knew exactly what he was thinking.

Their last conversation had been about her looking into design courses, not becoming a server at his sister's café. At a loss for words, she simply shrugged one shoulder and smiled, taking another sip from her coffee.

"Larry brought by a fresh batch of lobster tails. I made you a sandwich," Jane said to her brother. "It's out back."

Evan groaned before kissing the top of her head again. "What would I do without you?"

Jane rolled her eyes at him, flashing Maggie a droll look, but Maggie wasn't really paying attention. She was too busy staring at Evan, eyeing him appreciatively. He was dressed in what she'd come to realize were his work clothes. Jeans, boots, a slim fitting T-shirt bearing the logo of his boat repair business, the sleeves stretching tight around his muscular shoulders. His hair was mussed, his beard scruffy, eyes bright blue beneath the drop lights in the café. She pulled her bottom lip between her teeth, staring at him over the top of her coffee mug.

"You okay, hun?"

Maggie snapped out of her inappropriate daze, finding Jane watching her with a curious smile.

"Yes. Sorry. What?" She could feel a heated flush creep up from the base of her throat, spreading to her cheeks at the sight of Evan's growing smirk.

Thankfully, before Jane could say anything further, Evan spoke, the lingering hint of his knowing smile playing on his lips which he was at least kind enough to attempt to hide. "I'm almost finished at work," he said, thumbing over his shoulder in the direction of the docks across the street. "I was thinking about stopping by your place afterwards. Put up that screening?"

Maggie pressed her lips together, trying for a smile which she knew looked awkward as hell. But she nodded regardless, finishing what was left of her coffee.

Jane looked from Maggie to Evan and back again, her brow furrowed, but before she could say anything, Evan walked around the counter and disappeared into the kitchen before returning quickly with the sandwich his sister had made for him.

"Thanks for this, sis." He held the sandwich wrapped in brown paper in the air on his way to leave, glancing at Maggie with a small smile. "See you back at your place."

And then he was gone, leaving an obvious silence in his wake.

Maggie quickly turned away, busying herself with opening the dishwasher and placing her empty coffee mug onto the top rack. She could feel the weight of Jane's curious and assessing gaze on her, but she did all she could to ignore it, chewing nervously on the inside of her cheek. She didn't know why, but she felt as if she'd been caught out in some tawdry, clandestine secret. Evan was simply helping her at the house. It wasn't as if she was paying him with lewd, sexual favors.

Thankfully, Jane said nothing. She remained silent, contemplative as she watched Maggie move to the place where she'd left her keys and her purse earlier.

With a casual smile, Maggie untied her apron and placed it

171

onto the counter, collecting her things. "So, when would you like me back for my first *official* shift?"

"How's Monday?" Jane said, still watching her with an uncertain look in her eyes. "Same time?"

Maggie nodded with a tight smile, looking away before heading for the door. The atmosphere between them had quickly shifted. It was thick with palpable tension, and she needed to get the hell out of there in case Jane had a change of heart on the job offer.

"Maggie, sweetheart?"

Pausing at the door, her hand poised at the handle, Maggie closed her eyes momentarily, her shoulders falling as she released the breath she'd been holding. *Oh no.* This was it. She'd had a feeling Jane was the overprotective big sister type, but would she really go back on her offer of employment?

"Yeah?" Turning with a hopeful smile in her eyes, Maggie looked at her, waiting.

Jane stood, looking at her from across the dining area. "Evan's been coming to your house?"

Maggie nodded after a beat. "Yeah." She shrugged her shoulders. "Just helping out with a few things. He's been a *huge* help," she answered as lightly as she possibly could. But despite the fact that it had been nothing but innocent, she couldn't help but feel guilty.

Jane seemed to contemplate something, glancing down to the hardwood floor before meeting Maggie's eyes with a tentative smile that looked forced.

She went to speak but stopped herself, then finally said, "Just . . . be careful."

It was almost as if her own words had pained her. Like she didn't want to say them, but had to.

Maggie watched her struggle for a moment, before she finally managed a smile that met her eyes and, without saying anything further, without any semblance of elaboration, she turned and headed into the kitchen.

Chapter 22

Evan pulled up outside Maggie's house just as the thick gray cloud cover was beginning to clear and roll out to the ocean. He stayed put for a moment, hands gripping the steering wheel, surrounded by nothing but silence, the ticking of the engine accompanying the sound of his ragged, heavy breaths.

He'd planned on stopping by on Tuesday, but it had been raining. Then on Wednesday he was in no fit state after the night before. Drunk was an understatement. He'd gone home with Cindy. Again. He had to sneak out of her house before sunrise, careful not to wake her so she didn't cause a damn scene like he knew she would. *Why are you leaving? Stay. Be with me. Why do you use me like this? How dare you, Evan Boyd!* He couldn't risk that. So, he'd snuck out while still drunk as sin, had gone straight home and crawled into bed, feeling disgusted with himself. He'd only managed to get out of bed this morning, two days later.

He really needed to cut the crap and get his life in order, especially now with Maggie around. She relied on him and he felt bad, like he'd somehow abandoned her during her time of need. Then when he'd seen her at the café, standing there behind the counter wearing a goddamn apron, he knew he had to make an effort. And find out what the hell she was doing working for his sister.

Forcing himself out of his truck, he collected his toolbox from the back and walked around the side of the house, noticing the front door was wide open, the familiar tune of a Fleetwood Mac song spilling out into the afternoon accompanied by a terribly off-key voice. Smirking to himself, he placed his toolbox onto the porch, and crept over the decking, sneaking inside.

It took a moment for his eyes to adjust to the muted light inside the house, but when they did, he came to a sudden stop. There, standing on the kitchen countertop, oblivious to everything but the music, was Maggie. Dancing. Her hips swaying to the beat of the music. She sung unapologetically loud and out of tune, getting nearly every second word wrong. Evan relaxed against the door frame, folding his arms over his chest, watching the show with a wicked grin.

It wasn't until halfway through the second verse of 'Dreams' that he finally came to, jumping when Maggie reached up to the light that hung over the countertop, a spare bulb in one hand. It was almost as if it was happening in slow motion. He sucked in a deep gasp, glancing furtively to the switch on the wall, his heart jumping up into the back of his throat as he lurched forward with a roaring "Stop!"

Terrified, Maggie turned so fast, a shrill blood-curdling scream exploding from her. Her bare foot slipped off the side of the butcher block countertop, and she went tumbling toward the floor.

Evan kicked into gear, closing the distance and catching her in his arms in the nick of time; a split second later and she'd have landed on the hardwood and potentially done some serious damage to herself.

"What the *hell* are you doing? You scared the crap out of me!" Maggie shrieked, face stark and eyes wide as she gaped up at him. She struggled out of his awkward embrace, finding her feet after a few unsteady moments.

"You could've electrocuted your-*damn*-self!" Evan yelled just as indignantly, his abrupt words hoarse and raw. He knew his neck veins were likely popping, but he was incredulous. Raking his fingers through his hair, he tore at the ends as he tried to calm himself.

"What are you talking about?" Maggie asked with a huff, clutching at her heaving chest while trying to catch her breath.

Evan stormed across the kitchen, stopping at the wall. With dramatic flair, he indicated the light switch like it was a prize and he was one of those showcase girls on *The Price is Right*. "This is a light switch! An electrical current flows through this to that!" He pointed at the light hanging above the counter.

Maggie shook her head, her brows drawn together in confusion. "Yeah. The bulb blew," she said, holding up the spare light bulb in her hand. "I'm changing it."

Evan stared at her long and hard, wondering if she was actually that clueless. Then it dawned on him. She was that clueless, and by no fault of her own. He softened a little, asking, "Have you changed a light bulb before?"

She looked down at the new bulb. "No. But . . ." She met his eyes again as she continued, "I mean, it's hardly rocket science, right?"

Evan muttered a curse under his breath. He took a moment to calm his frustration, pinching the bridge of his nose before offering her an exasperated look. "Maggie, the switch is on." He pointed to the light switch again. "When a light bulb blows, the first thing you need to do is turn the switch off. There's electricity running through the wires. One wrong move and that bulb bursts, you could've . . ." He stopped himself, scrubbing a hand over his weary face with a murmured, "Jesus Christ."

Shaking his head to himself, Evan flicked the switch into the off position and went back to her, holding his hand out.

She looked up at him with rueful eyes and a sheepish smile. And an unfamiliar emotion tugged in his chest, right there in the big gaping void where his heart once sat. He cleared his throat, managing a contrite smile as he took the bulb from her dainty hand.

175

"Here." He nodded to the kitchen counter, slapping a hand upon the surface. "Hop up. I'll show you."

Folding her arms over her chest, Maggie shot him a steely look. "I'm not some damsel in distress, Evan. I can change a damn light bulb."

He steadied her with a doubtful once-over. "If I'd been five minutes later, you'd be frying on the damn floor."

Maggie rolled her eyes, but thankfully relented. She moved around him, pulling herself back up onto the wooden countertop, the new bulb held carefully in her hand.

"Okay, so, you always want to check the switch is off," he began, "especially when a bulb blows. So many people forget."

Maggie shifted from foot to foot, and he could see she was a lot less confident than she had been only moments before, dancing to Fleetwood Mac like she was at her own private concert. He gave her ankle a reassuring squeeze.

"So, reach up and you wanna gently unscrew the old bulb." He watched as she did as instructed, her hand gentle as she twisted the glass, a small gasp escaping her when the bulb popped off. He smiled to himself. "Okay. Now you need to carefully twist the new bulb in. Not too tight, though."

She did just that, slowly moving her hand away as if at any moment the new bulb was going to spontaneously combust.

Evan stepped back to the wall, flicking the switch again, and the kitchen was illuminated with a soft white glow. Maggie looked down at him, her eyes wide and a victorious smile curling at her lips. Pure pride. He couldn't help but chuckle at just how adorable she was.

"Voilà." He waved a hand in the air, smiling smugly when she met his eyes.

"Thanks," Maggie muttered and, with a derisive snort, she wiped her hands over the back of her overalls before moving to climb back down.

Before he even knew what he was doing, Evan swooped in,

his large hands securing around her waist before easing her back down to the safety of the floor. With a gasp, she turned in his arms, looking up at him with wide eyes, her breath seemingly caught at the back of her throat.

There was suddenly no space between them, and the air shifted as they stared at one another for mere moments that felt more like an eternity. He glanced from her eyes, shining so bright, full of piqued curiosity and thinly veiled trepidation, maybe even the slightest hint of desire, dipping down to her full lips parted just enough for him to hear her labored breaths.

Unexpectedly, Evan felt something deep inside, something he hadn't felt for a long time. So long, in fact, he'd thought it was dead and gone. So long, it almost felt foreign.

"Thanks." Maggie bowed her head, the first to break their intense moment.

Evan took that as his cue to step away, and he did, as far as the limited space in the kitchen would allow. He turned quickly, heading for the door.

"I'm j-just gonna go . . . get a start on the, umm . . . the screening," he stammered without another glance over his shoulder.

He couldn't look at her. Not after that. He couldn't trust himself to look at her again. He couldn't trust himself to look at her and not kiss her. He didn't know what the hell that was all about and he sure as shit couldn't risk finding out, either.

*

Maggie paced back and forth in her bedroom as she tried so hard to wrap her brain around what on earth had just happened between her and Evan downstairs in the kitchen. Not only had he snuck into her house, he'd stood there watching her make a damn fool of herself on the kitchen counter before she'd almost gone and killed herself. Then, he'd touched her, his hands holding her in a way she hadn't been held in so long. She'd felt his breaths hasten. She'd seen his Adam's apple bob in his throat with a hard swallow. She was almost certain she'd seen lust in his eyes as he stared down at her. He'd licked his goddamn lips when he'd looked at her mouth, for Christ's sake.

She kept thinking back to Jane and the warning she'd given her back at the café. *Be careful.* Be careful? Be careful of what? What did that even mean? What did she need to be careful of?

"Oh my God." Maggie shook her head as an overwhelming feeling of dread settled deep in her belly.

This couldn't be good. Evan had looked as if he was about to kiss her. And the confusing truth was, if he had tried to kiss her, she would have let him. She would have let him kiss her, and she would have kissed him right back. What the hell? She hardly even knew this man. She was a widow. Tom was barely even dead. This was not okay. It couldn't be. Could it? She shook her head again at that thought, raking her hands through her hair as she took a few deep breaths in through her nose to try to calm her frantically racing heart.

Stopping at the windows, she looked out over the lake, up to the sky at a flock of gulls flying out toward the ocean. Her thoughts immediately drifted to her late husband, and, without even realizing, her fingers moved to the wedding ring on her left hand, twisting it around and around. She closed her eyes, silently chastising herself. Here she was, feeling guilty for even thinking of kissing another man two and a half months after Tom's death. And yet, he'd been living some messed-up secret life with another woman, behind Maggie's back, for more than a year. But even though she knew how ridiculous it was, she still couldn't shake that feeling of betrayal. Like she was doing something wrong.

She glanced down at the wedding ring on her finger. After she had said "I do" to Tom, she'd never imagined looking at another man in such a way again. Now her heart was racing, fluttering, skipping mandatory beats at the sheer thought of Evan's lips having been so close to her own. It wasn't right. It couldn't be. But maybe it could . . .

"Get it together," she hissed to herself, looking up to find her reflection in the mirror leaning against the wall.

Blowing a breath out between her lips, she shook her head at her own confusing deliberations. Whatever it was that had almost happened between them, she couldn't hide away upstairs. She was a grown woman.

Pulling her long hair up into an unkempt knot on top of her head, she smoothed down the front of her paint-splattered overalls and took a long, hard look at herself. She almost laughed at the sight. Shapeless overalls over a concert T-shirt a size too big because that's all they had left at the merchandise stand. Messy hair. Not an ounce of make-up.

She was starting to think the moment between her and Evan had been her imagination playing tricks on her. He'd almost kissed her? Yeah, right. The pure notion itself was utterly ridiculous. Evan was a handsome, single man with what appeared to be his own fan base of beautiful women who wanted him. And here Maggie was, looking like a thirteen-year-old tomboy. She scoffed at her reflection and turned to head back downstairs, her chin held high in a show of self-confidence she didn't really feel on the inside.

Maggie walked outside in time to see Evan standing on the porch steps, taking the mail from the UPS lady. He stopped when he saw Maggie walk out of the door, dropping his eyes to the envelopes in his hands before crossing the deck and handing them to her.

"Thanks." She smiled when he met her eyes, their fingers touching at that moment.

Evan turned quickly to get back to the task at hand, otherwise ignoring her. And with a heavy sigh, Maggie took a seat on the top porch step, trying not to think too much into his evasion of her as she opened the mail. Nothing but bills, which wasn't really a huge surprise. But then she came to the big white envelope, the one stamped with the *Manchester College—School of Design* seal, and her brows pulled together as she dragged her index nail under the tab, tearing it open.

Brochures and pamphlets fell out of the envelope as well as a letter.

> *Dear Ms. Morris,*
> *We are delighted that you have shown interest in enrolling in the Interior Design course offered by our School of Design. Please find enclosed an information pack, containing everything you should need to know, and an application . . .*

Maggie looked up in thought, staring out over the water, racking her brain.

"Everything okay?"

She startled, glancing over her shoulder to find Evan watching her, a roll of screening under his arm. She managed a light laugh, and a dismissive shrug.

"What is it?" he asked, craning his neck to get a better look at the letter in her hand.

"It's an information pack from the college in Manchester," she explained, looking back down at the glossy fold-outs on her lap. She shook her head. "But I didn't . . . Well, I mean I *did* look online, but I didn't request anything to be sent." She thought back to a few nights ago, to when she'd been so close to submitting her request for more information, but her self-doubt had managed to get the better of her. "So weird . . ."

"You gonna apply?"

Maggie looked back over her shoulder, watching as he got on with his work. "I don't know. I mean . . . I *want* to. I'd *love* to. But . . . with the boys, and now that I have a job, I don't—"

"What's with that, by the way?" Evan interrupted.

"What?"

He cast her a wry glance, and a dubious smirk tugging at his lips. "Working at the café."

She shrugged. "I need a job. And Jane needs the help."

He seemed to consider her response momentarily, but then he stopped what he was doing, placing the screening down and walked over, taking a seat on the step beside her. He looked at her, one scrutinizing eye narrowing like he was suddenly able to see straight through her casual, nonchalant facade. She swallowed hard, trying to remain indifferent.

"What about what *you* want, though?" He pointed to the brochures in her lap. "Interior design."

She looked down at the information pack. "I don't need some fancy degree. It's not brain surgery. I can redecorate a room without a framed certificate of authentication. Besides, I need to focus on my boys. What I want doesn't really matter anymore."

Evan nodded slowly, as if he couldn't really believe a word she was saying. Then he looked down at the letter in her hand, pointing to it and meeting her eyes. "Well, *someone* submitted your details online. Maybe they think what you want *does* matter." And, with that, he stood and went back to the screening, leaving her to contemplate his words.

Maggie glanced at Evan once more, watching as he started stapling the screening in place, his brow furrowed with determination. And with a smile, she couldn't help but wonder . . . Perhaps it had been him who had submitted her details online.

Chapter 23

Later that night after TJ had gone to bed, and while Jack was busy in the attic hanging up all his posters, Maggie walked out to her newly screened porch with a glass of wine in one hand and the college brochures in the other.

She took a seat on the porch swing the boys had helped her secure before dinner, and momentarily she was captivated by the clear, calm night. Evan had been right, the new screening was so fine, so sheer, it was almost non-existent and provided an uninterrupted view of the river, the trees, the starlit sky—pure tranquility laid out before her like a picture.

She smiled to herself, releasing a long sigh before going back to the brochures she'd only managed to skim so far.

"Hey, Mom?"

Looking up from her reading, she found Jack's head poking out through the front door. "Yeah, honey?"

"Do we have any of those sticky wall hook thingies?"

"I think there's a whole new packet of small hooks in the top drawer in the mud room." She narrowed her eyes dubiously when she realized what he was asking. "Why? What are you doing?"

He rolled his eyes. "I just want to hang a few things on my walls."

"Oh. Okay." She nodded slowly. "Do you need help?"

He shook his head, and then his gaze flitted down to the brochure in her hand, his brows knitting together. "What's that?"

Maggie looked down at the information fold-out and suddenly felt silly. She didn't know why, but she was worried Jack might get upset at her if he found out she was considering going back to school. Sheepishly, she held the brochure up in the air. "Oh. Nothing really. Just an information pack on a design course—"

"It arrived already?" he asked, cutting her off.

She snapped her mouth shut, blinking as it suddenly dawned on her. "Wait. *You* submitted my information?"

"Yeah," he said with a casual shrug. "I saw the page open on your laptop when I was looking at the baseball scores on Tuesday morning."

"But . . . w-why?" she stammered, unable to find the words.

"Because it's what you love." He shrugged again. "You should do it, Mom."

Maggie, looking down at the brochure in her hands, had been rendered speechless.

"I'm gonna head up to bed," Jack announced, clearly oblivious to the shock his mother was currently experiencing. "Goodnight."

She looked up, but he'd already disappeared back inside before she could say or do anything. And, with tears in her eyes and a smile ghosting over her lips, she managed a quiet "Goodnight" in his wake, her heart so full right at that moment.

*

Evan finished what was left of his beer, bobbing his head to the beat of the Red Hot Chili Peppers song as it blared through his boat shed. He'd been tinkering with Bob Sheffield's trawler motor for a few hours. Anything to take his mind off Maggie and the fact that he'd been almost stupid enough to kiss her.

Not even four beers had managed to blur the image of Maggie's lips, or the scent of her hair which had lingered with him all afternoon. He was hoping to lose himself in his work in an attempt to take his conflicted mind off the woman who had occupied almost every one of his waking moments since he'd first set eyes on her. It'd been a long time since a woman had turned him into such a pussy. He hated it. He knew he wasn't good enough for her. She deserved a man who would treat her right, not a washed-up has-been with serious commitment issues like him.

"Hello?"

Startling at the sound of the familiar voice coming through the open shed door, Evan turned, his eyes narrowing to make out her silhouette as she stepped tentatively over the machinery and the crates strewn over the floor. When she came into the glow of the fluorescent light, he could see the look in her eyes and he knew exactly why she was there.

"I brought you over some leftovers." Jane smiled, holding up a glass dish of what appeared to be vegetable lasagna. Her eyes glanced furtively over his shoulder, and he could see a small crease appear between her brows when her gaze landed upon the collection of empty beer bottles lined on top of his workbench.

"Thanks," Evan muttered, taking the dish from her and placing it onto his tool trolley. He wiped his grease-covered hands on one of the old flannel shirts he'd torn into rags, and turned back to his sister to find her standing there looking awkward, hands wringing together in front of her. He knew she had something she was dying to say. He was just waiting for it.

"Are you okay?" she finally asked.

He nodded, adding a casual shrug. "Yeah. I'm fine."

She jutted her chin toward the near-empty bottle of beer in his hand. Meeting his eyes again, she raised an eyebrow. "You sure?"

He fixed his jaw hard, his teeth gritting together. "Yeah. I'm sure. Just a long day, that's all."

She stared at him for a moment longer, studying him. And then, smoothing a hand down over the pretty floral dress she was wearing, she came right out and asked, "What's going on with you and Maggie?"

Evan frowned. "Nothing."

It was only a half-lie. Technically, there was nothing going on. But that didn't mean he wasn't hoping like hell to get another shot at kissing her. Especially now, four beers in. If he could go back a few hours with the kind of Dutch courage he was feeling now, he'd have wrapped his hand around the back of her neck and crushed his lips to hers with such force, she'd have been seeing stars for a week. Sure, he knew he was no good for her; didn't make him want her any less.

Jane looked away, moving to one of the crates in the corner and taking a seat. "You've been spending time with her."

It wasn't a question, but he knew she wanted answers. "I've been helping her with her house." He shrugged.

"I saw it in your eyes at the cookout, and I saw it again today in the café." She shook her head to herself.

"You saw *what*?" Evan scoffed once more. "What are you talking about, Janie?"

Jane stood to her feet and stepped right up to him, even though she only came up to his chest. "The way you look at her. It's like the old Evan. Like you're not that hollow shell you've been for the last five years. Like my brother is right back here with me."

Evan glanced down at the old wrench in his hand. "I don't know what the hell you're talking about. But . . ." He met her eyes with a raised brow. "Isn't that a good thing?"

Jane cocked her head to the side, hesitating before continuing softly, "She's a widow, Evan. She's broken. Her husband died just a few months ago." She admitted tentatively, "I don't want you to get hurt. Not again."

"I'm not gonna get hurt." He shook his head.

"You might think that, but if you start falling for her, you will. I don't want to lose you again. She's mourning her husband. She's emotionally unavailable. She's—"

185

"He was cheating on her!" Evan said the words without even thinking, snapping his mouth shut, knowing he had no right to tell her that information.

He suddenly hated himself. Maggie had opened up to him, confided in him. She'd trusted him with that confession. And he'd just gone and told the biggest gossip in all of Jewel Harbor who just so happened to be the sister he loved with all his heart.

Jane's eyes went wide as she processed his words. "What?"

"Yeah." He nodded with a sardonic laugh, unable to stop himself from continuing, "Yeah, she *was* mourning him. But then she found out, in the worst possible way, that she was mourning a man who had been seeing another woman for at least a year before he died."

He knew it wasn't his business to tell anyone. But he had to. In a way, it helped him to justify his own confusing feelings toward Maggie. He continued, "She's been living this lie ever since she found out. She can't tell anyone. No one. She doesn't want her boys to know. So, she confided in *me*!" He pointed to himself. "Because, as messed up as it is, I'm all she's got."

Jane shook her head again, clearly battling with her words. "You're not . . ." She stopped herself again, raking her teeth over her bottom lip. "It's not your—"

"We almost kissed today."

Jane's eyes nearly bugged right out of her head. "You *what*?"

He nodded. He could tell she was pissed, but he didn't care. Sometimes he liked to rile her up. Served her right for butting into his business.

"Evan, you can't—"

"Calm down, *Mom*." He chuckled with a roll of his eyes before turning back to his work. "I said we *almost* kissed. I wanted to. And I'm pretty sure she wanted to, as well." He smiled to himself at the memory. "But we didn't." He wanted to add that it was only a matter of time, but didn't. It was though, he could feel it. Soon enough, Maggie would see he was right for her. First, he just needed to make sure he was strong enough not to screw it up. He couldn't risk hurting her. She'd been hurt enough.

Evan could feel his sister watching him, her eyes boring into the back of his shoulders. He knew she was just looking out for him—she'd seen him at his worst, and he knew she never wanted to witness his downfall again—but he was also a thirty-five-year-old man. He didn't want to push her away, but it was time she let him go. She had three kids of her own; she didn't need to mother him too.

"I'm worried about you." Jane's voice was soft and tentative, and wavered with the hint of fear.

As much as he tried to act unaffected, it broke him on the inside. He didn't want to scare her. He'd already put her through enough. Turning, he forced a smile. The kind of smile he'd used ever since he was old enough to realize that when he smiled like that, women fell for it. Not even his big sister was immune to the *Evan Boyd* charm.

As he crossed back to her, he held his hands up in surrender. "It's okay, Janie. You've got nothing to worry about. I promise." He crossed an X over his chest, and held up three fingers. "Scout's honor."

"You were never a Scout," Jane scoffed, rolling her eyes with a smile. She reached up, and her hands clasped his strong arms. She stared at him, imploring eyes still rife with fear, despite her smile. "You need to look after yourself." She steadied him with a serious look, one full of pleading as her grip on his arms tightened to the point that her nails almost pinched his skin. "Promise me?"

He nodded. "Okay, I will. I promise."

"I love you." Her voice cracked with emotion, tears shimmering in her eyes, reflecting the fluorescent overhead lights.

Evan pulled her in, wrapping his arms around her, but he said no more. He simply kissed the top of her head and embraced her. It was the only thing he knew to do, and it was what she needed.

*

Evan removed his ball cap to run his fingers through his hair. His head was killing him after one too many beers the night before. The Saturday morning sun was like needles in his eyes, the dark tint of his sunglasses doing nothing to help his cause. He wanted to crawl into a hole and die for a few hours. But little league was important to his boys and his boys were important to him. His hangover could wait.

This afternoon he was headed up to White Lake for an old high school friend's birthday camping trip. He didn't want to back up his efforts of last night, but it was a birthday; he couldn't really say no. Well, he could. He just didn't want to. Who wouldn't want to sit around a campfire drinking beer and talking shit like they did when they were nineteen and home from freshman year in college?

Taking a big drink from his thermos of water, he looked up in time to see Cindy walking toward him, her sky-high wedge shoes unsteady over the divots in the grass. She almost lost her balance twice, but she was quick to brush it off with a casual fluff of her pouffed hair. He inwardly cringed. He still hated himself for going there with her, and on more than one infuriating occasion. She was like a dog with a damn bone; she wouldn't leave him alone. Cindy's kid wasn't even on Evan's team. She was five and played T-ball, two fields over.

"Good morning, *handsome*," Cindy said with a purring lilt.

"Mornin'." Evan stepped away to grab his clipboard in an effort to put as much distance as possible between the two of them without being too obvious.

"I missed you at the pub last night." Her lashes fluttered as she looked up at him with doe eyes, pouting her glossy lips.

"I was working," he muttered, going over the roster in his hands.

"Care for a drink tonight?" Cindy asked with a shrug of her shoulder.

"Can't." He looked up this time, thankful he had an honest excuse. "Camping trip."

188

She stuck her bottom lip out and sulked. And he took the opportunity to look down at her through the shield of his tinted sunglasses.

He couldn't deny she was sexy, and she sure knew how to show off that sex appeal. But now things were different. The other night was a poorly timed mistake. Now, he had Maggie taking up permanent residence in his mind—Maggie and the memory of their almost-kiss. He didn't know what that meant, but he couldn't let his history with Cindy and every other woman he's been with in this town get in the way. Despite her curves, the cleavage spilling out of her tight top, and her long legs reaching up high into those short jean cut-offs, she no longer stood a chance with Maggie in the ranks. Neither did the women who sat in the stands every Saturday morning, obviously gawping at him. Only one woman had managed to occupy every one of his waking thoughts.

Speak of the devil.

"Hey, Coach!"

TJ ran around Cindy, dressed head to toe in a brand-spanking-new Badgers uniform.

"Hey, man." Evan held up his hand for the boy to high-five. When his gaze lifted to see *her* walk through the gates, he felt his shoulders involuntarily square, felt his chest puff out of its own accord, felt a somewhat familiar tug in his chest.

He smiled down at TJ. "Why don't you head over to the other guys and get warmed up. You're starting."

TJ cheered, punching the air before sprinting over to the dugout to join the few other boys who had arrived early.

Evan cleared his throat, looking at Maggie as she stopped in front of him. He lifted the peak of his cap in greeting, adding a small smile. "Morning, Maggie." He didn't want to give too much away, not with Cindy hanging around.

"Hi." Maggie smiled, despite the slight furrow between her brows.

189

He couldn't see her eyes through the tint of her sunglasses but he was almost certain she'd just cast a derisive glance in Cindy's direction.

God, she looked good. Cindy was an attractive woman, but Maggie was effortlessly beautiful. Dressed in skinny jeans, a black tank top and flip flops, her long hair was tied up in a twisted knot on top of her head and her tanned skin seemed to glow beneath the morning sun. The two women were in stark contrast to one another; there really was no competition Evan could kick his own ass for missing out on the chance to kiss her.

"Well . . ." Maggie finally broke the awkward silence, shrugging her shoulders before tucking her hands into the back pockets of her jeans. "Have fun." And with that she turned and walked back toward the stands, taking a seat on the bottom bench at the very end, as far away from Evan's unofficial cheer squad as she could.

"Aw, Ev," Cindy cooed, a wry smile tugging at her glossed lips.

Evan's brows knitted together at her use of the nickname she'd given him. He glanced down at her hand gripping his arm, her long nails digging into his skin.

"I think she has a little crush on you." Cindy giggled softly.

He looked at her from over the top of his sunglasses, meeting her eyes and steadying her with a stern glare that caused her smug smile to fade and her hand fall from his arm as he said, "Goodbye, Cindy."

Cindy huffed and turned on her wedges, strutting out of the field and through the gate.

Evan shook his head and turned to join his team, but his mind sure as hell wasn't on any baseball game, that was for damn sure.

Chapter 24

Maggie was nervous. She assumed it was just first-day jitters. Everyone got nerves on their first day of work, but Maggie's jitters were more than butterflies. They were like rabid dogs gnawing at her insides. The boys had wished her good luck when she'd dropped them off at school, but their well wishes had worn off by the time she walked into the café.

She looked around, taking it all in. She knew this place, but it suddenly looked different. She wasn't there to pull up a chair at the counter and enjoy a coffee, she was there to work, and with that came the potential to make a fool of herself or worse, destroy Jane's business with one wrong order. What if she served something with peanuts or eggs to a customer with an allergy?

"Oh, hey!" Jane held a hand up in a wave as she stepped through the swinging doors that led from the kitchen. She held a big container of what looked like cupcakes and, with a huff, she placed it onto the counter.

"Come on in," she said with a smile which seemed a little forced and wavered ever so slightly at the corners.

Maggie hesitated. Memories of the other day when Jane had warned her to be careful of Evan, came flashing back through her mind. And since then she'd almost kissed the guy. She'd gone over Jane's words at least a hundred times. And yet she was still unable to make any sense of them. Jane hadn't been mean or stern with her warning; it was as if she'd been afraid, and the look of sheer trepidation in her eyes had stuck with Maggie ever since, especially after her and Evan's moment together in the kitchen.

After their almost-kiss, she'd seen Evan at little league, but they'd stayed away from one another until after the game when he'd pulled her aside, much to the shock and disdain of his fan girls watching on like hawks. He'd just wanted to tell her that he was heading away with a few of his old high school friends on a camping trip, and that he would stop by the house in a few days to take a look at the floating dock that had a few loose planks.

Maggie had begged Evan to take at least a little money in return for all the work he'd done, but he flat out refused. She thought if she could pay him, maybe it would make the awkwardness that had settled between them after their almost-kiss disappear. But he was stubborn, that much was certain.

"Okay, I have your apron," Jane said, pulling out a floral apron from under the service counter. It was identical to the one she was wearing, and when Maggie unfolded it she noticed her name embroidered over the side pocket. She couldn't help but beam. She'd never had anything so official before. Her very first uniform.

"All right." Jane clapped her hands together excitedly. "I'll show you where you can hang your handbag out the back, and then we can get started."

Maggie nodded, quickly tying the apron around her waist before following Jane through the kitchen doors with a deep, fortifying breath. She was unable to shake the unease that lingered obviously and heavily in the air between them, no matter how hard she tried to ignore it. But this was her first day, and she desperately wanted to make a good impression.

*

By the time the lunch rush had ended, Maggie was an old hand at the café, moving fluidly behind the counter as if she'd been doing the job her whole life. Throughout the day, Jane had been quiet. Not rude. Just quiet, like her mind was off elsewhere. So, Maggie struck up a newfound friendship with Harold, the cook. He and Joe, the other cook, alternated their shifts in the kitchen.

Harold was six foot six, at least. Stoic and stocky. But he was a gentle giant of few words, smiling thankfully with every new order Maggie gave him, as if cooking food for other people was the sole reason he'd been put on this earth. He'd even surprised Maggie with one of his famous BLT sandwiches at lunch. Apparently, the secret was in the bread and toasting it after a light layer of mayonnaise. Whatever his secret, it had been delicious. She knew she was at risk of stacking on a few pounds while working at the café, but she didn't care. And after the last few months, she could afford to put on a little weight.

"Okay. I'm off." Jane stopped by the counter where Maggie was refilling the sugar dispensers between a break in customers.

Untying her apron, Jane offered a hopeful once-over. "You sure you're going to be okay until Cathy gets here for the afternoon shift?"

Maggie smiled. "I'll be fine."

"Call me if you need *anything*. And Harold knows his way around the point-of-sale terminal if you get stuck." She placed her things into her handbag, doing a double take of the countertops as if to make sure she hadn't left anything behind. She sighed with the first real genuine smile that had touched her lips all day. "God, this is my first full afternoon off in *forever*!"

"Go. Get a manicure or something. Everything will be fine." Maggie assured her with a casual brush of her hand.

"Ugh. You're a godsend, Maggie. Honestly." With a wave, Jane turned and headed for the door.

Watching her leave, Maggie could feel the question climbing up the back of her throat, on the tip of her tongue like word vomit. She wished she could swallow it, but she couldn't, and it was out of her mouth before she even had a chance to consider it, "Actually, Jane, can I ask you something?"

Jane paused, turning with a quirked brow and a curious smile. "Of course, honey. Go ahead."

Glancing down at the sugar bag in her hand, Maggie chewed nervously on the inside of her cheek. Unsure how to approach the topic and fully aware that she didn't really have a choice with Jane waiting, she looked up and saw the woman's kind yet tentative gaze fixed on her, and she released the breath she'd been holding.

"The other day when you told me to be careful with Ev . . . your brother," she began, her words cautious and quiet. "What did you mean?"

Jane looked at her for a long moment. She glanced over her shoulder, looking at the lone man seated at one of the booths reading a book and, with a heavy exhalation, she walked back, closing the distance and stopping at the counter. She averted her eyes, looking anywhere but at Maggie as she seemed to contemplate her words.

"Nothing's happening between us," Maggie felt the need to say, adding a light laugh to ease the tension. "If that's what you're worried about? Evan's just helping me around the house." She gave a casual shrug and an innocent smile, but the smile fell when she saw the seriousness in Jane's eyes.

"Look, Maggie. My brother, he . . ." She trailed off, as if she didn't quite know how to continue, looking around again to make sure no one was listening even though there was no one there who would care to listen. And her secretiveness only caused Maggie's concern to intensify.

Jane continued, "He's going through some stuff. I just . . . I've seen the way he looks at you. The way he . . . the way he wants to help you. In any other situation I'd say the two of you would be perfect for one another. Hell, I'd be the one doing the matchmaking!" She shook her head at herself. "But he's not . . .

he's not himself. He hasn't been for quite a while. And I don't want *either* of you getting hurt."

"But we're not . . ." Maggie laughed incredulously, searching for the words. She threw her hands in the air in frustration. "We're not *doing* anything!"

Jane cocked her head to the side, gauging her with a conspiratorial once-over. "So, you mean to tell me the two of you didn't almost kiss on Friday at your house?"

Maggie blinked at her, shocked by the question. She'd thought that moment with Evan had all been in her head. Now he was telling his sister about it? She didn't quite know what to think.

Jane softened. "I'm sorry, Maggie." She reached out, touching her arm. "I'm just, I'm really protective of him. He's my little brother." She smiled sadly. "I can't see him get hurt again. And I'm not saying *you'll* hurt him, but . . . well, Evan has this—this *tendency* to go all in and it often means he loses himself. His past is . . . well, he's been broken. And I don't want to see him break again. I can't."

Maggie witnessed a sadness in Jane's eyes, something which felt painfully familiar. A sadness which reflected an almost mirror image of the pain and suffering she had seen in Evan's eyes more than a few times. It caused her stomach to knot. She tried so hard to make sense of Jane's words, but her attempts were futile. She was so lost, confused, and concerned. Something was wrong with Evan. And she knew it had to do with a lot more than just his fiancée leaving him. While it was none of her business, she had an overwhelming feeling that maybe she could help him. But she knew she should let it go; how was she supposed to help someone when she didn't even know what was wrong?

Forcing a smile which she knew lacked sincerity, Maggie managed a nod. And then, with another wave, Jane turned and walked out, leaving her feeling the most deflated she'd felt since moving to town.

Chapter 25

Days passed, and again it seemed as if Evan had disappeared into thin air. Maggie hadn't seen or heard from him since their brief encounter at little league.

He'd told her he was heading off camping with his friends, but he'd also told her he would be back Monday morning and that he'd stop by. It was now Thursday, and she hadn't seen or heard from him. Actually, that wasn't quite true. She had seen him. She'd seen him on Tuesday, crossing the street from the wharf coming toward the café. Head bowed, ball cap peak covering his face, shoulders hunched, hands shoved into the pockets of his jeans. But then, and perhaps most confusing of all, he'd stopped, looked up and, after a moment's deliberation, he'd turned and walked back toward the docks.

Maggie had assumed he'd forgotten something back at the boat shed. His wallet or phone perhaps. But when he didn't return, she'd assumed there had been something else that had stopped him, and that thought made her feel sick to her stomach. Was he avoiding her? She'd spent all of Tuesday trying to rack her brain over what she could have possibly said or done for him to want to avoid her. But she couldn't think of anything, and that only made her feel so much worse.

By Thursday night, Maggie's mind was infuriatingly consumed by Evan and his reasons for avoiding her. But she tried to not let it affect her as she stood in the kitchen chopping up vegetables for dinner while TJ sat at the counter opposite her, finishing the first draft of his book report.

Jack walked into the kitchen, sweat dripping down his face, music blasting from the earbuds that hung around his neck. He walked directly to the refrigerator and pulled out an electric blue sports drink, standing with the fridge door open as he gulped a few big mouthfuls. He was training for the upcoming summer tryouts for the school's varsity baseball team and, despite his lack of manners and inability to close the fridge door, Maggie couldn't help but smile at just how far he'd come in such a short amount of time. She knew she had a certain little blonde to thank for her son's shift in attitude.

"How was your run?" she asked, turning back to her vegetables.

"It was okay." He shrugged. "I ran down by the harbor. Evan jogged with me up to the bluff and back."

Maggie dropped her knife with a loud clatter against the cutting board. "Evan?" She glanced at Jack, her brows knitted together. "Boyd?"

Jack nodded like it was no big deal. "Yeah. He runs every afternoon. Said for me to stop by the wharf if I ever want someone to run with. He also said he has a small gym set up in the back of his boatshed. Free weights and stuff. Said I can use it whenever I want." He shrugged a shoulder before finishing the remainder of his drink. "Did you know he played minor league and almost got called up into the MLB?"

"Everyone knows that, Jack," TJ sassed.

Still reeling over the fact that Jack had just been running with Evan, Maggie looked down at the carrots in front of her, her mind wandering off. Evan was avoiding her but then going running with her son? Now she was only more confused.

She managed a smile at Jack. "Well, it does look like he knows what he's talking about when it comes to fitness." She snapped her mouth shut immediately when she realized what she'd just said.

"Why, Mom?" Jack asked, a teasing cadence in his voice. "Because he's *so* buff and *dreamy*?" He chuckled, moving in next to her, fluttering his thick black lashes dramatically.

Maggie deadpanned at her son.

"Um, hello?" TJ waved his pen in the air, and Maggie looked at him to see his face scrunched up in disgust. "This is my baseball coach, remember?"

Jack chuckled. Maggie bit her smile, focusing back on her youngest son's paper. "Where are you up to?"

"Last paragraph." TJ looked down at his report and started scribbling down a few thoughts.

Maggie could feel Jack's eyes on her, and she turned to him, her brows raised questioningly knowing he had more to say. "Yes?"

"He asked me if you'd submitted your college application yet," Jack said quietly, one of his brows quirked, a smile still lingering. "How does *he* know about that?"

She stared at him for a long moment feeling caught out, and she hated it. She was the adult. "Because . . . he was here when the UPS lady delivered the information pack," she answered matter-of-factly with a breath of relief that she had an answer. "He was hanging up the porch screening."

Jack nodded slowly, his eyes boring into hers. "And . . . why does he care so much?"

She shook her head, shrugging. *You tell me, Jack*, she thought. *Why does he care so much when he can't even look at me?*

"Mom, please don't bang my baseball coach," TJ suddenly said with a resigned sigh, head buried between the pages of his notebook.

"Teej!?" Maggie shrieked, gaping at him.

Jack dropped his head back, barking out a loud laugh.

TJ glanced up, his eyes wide with innocence as he looked from his mom to his big brother, and back again. "What?"

Maggie reached for the closest thing she could, grabbing the dish towel. She whacked Jack's arm, glowering at him while trying not to laugh herself. "He gets these words from you!"

Jack laughed again. And before she could give him another dish towel lashing, he turned and ran out of the kitchen, yelling over his shoulder, "I'm having a shower!"

Shaking her head, she rolled her eyes before looking down to see TJ watching her with a stark curiousness in his big blue eyes.

"What does *bang* mean?" he asked, his brows drawing together.

"Nothing, sweetie." She shook her head, pressing her lips together in an attempt to stifle her smirk. "Hurry up and finish your report so you can wash up for dinner." And she quickly turned back to the vegetables chopped and prepped for the stir-fry. Her heart raced a million miles a minute, not only at her sons, but at the fact that, although he may have been avoiding her, it seemed not all was lost when it came to Evan.

*

Maggie sat in bed staring down at the laptop, entering all her details into the online application form on the college website.

After hours of research and planning and going over and over every single possibility, she'd realized going back to finish her degree was doable. She was only required to be on campus one day a week, which she was sure could be arranged with Jane. All other classes were held online, and she could do most of them at night after TJ had gone to bed. The cost of the course was a little more than she'd expected, but with all the money she'd been able to save from Evan's and Brad's and everyone else's help with the house repairs so far, it was affordable enough to manage without jeopardizing her boys' futures.

"Passport number," she read aloud.

With a groan, she tossed the covers off and padded out of the bedroom, across to the room she was planning on turning into the office. She hadn't done much yet, just set up the computer. Unpacked boxes full of documents and paperwork still lined the walls. Maggie had yet to go through them, she'd put it off until she had the mental capacity to deal with the task.

The family passports, birth certificates, social security details and other important information were all kept in the locked top drawer of the desk. Sure, the key was sitting in the lock, and it wasn't completely secure. Tom had been meaning to get a safe over the years, but it was something he'd not managed to get around to doing.

Unlocking the drawer, Maggie began rifling through the contents, pulling out a few sheets of random notebook paper with scribbles on them, which is when she came across something that attracted her curiosity: an unsealed envelope. Her heart jumped up into the back of her throat when she noticed her name scribbled across the front in Tom's messy handwriting, and her brows knitted together as she pulled it out.

The envelope trembled unsteadily in her suddenly shaking hand. She'd never seen it before. She hadn't looked in the drawer in a while; it wasn't often she needed passports or birth certificates. How long had this envelope been in there? She looked at the drawer and back again at the envelope, her skin prickling as she slumped down into the leather desk chair. Before she could overthink anything, she pulled out what appeared to be a handwritten letter. Her heart hammered in her chest. When had he written this? When had he planned to give it to her? She was so confused, terrified and conflicted. She didn't know if she even wanted to read it. The lump in her throat was making it difficult to breathe as myriad emotions swirled around her belly. Clutching the letter with both hands to keep the paper steady, she started at the beginning . . .

Maggie,
I've tried for so long to tell you the truth. But my own words keep failing me. Sure, I could say I've never found the

right time. Or, it never came up. But that would be bullshit. The truth is, I haven't told you this because I've been too scared. And you know me. I'm not scared of anything. But I'm terrified of witnessing the devastating look of heartbreak in your eyes when you discover the truth.

I love you, Maggie. I have always loved you, and always will because you're the mother of my sons. But now, that's it. There's nothing more, nothing deeper. I've fallen out of love with you. Somewhere along the way the love I felt for you changed. It's nothing you did. It's all me. Maybe my love for you hasn't changed at all. Maybe it's just me. Maybe I've changed. I've become a different person. And I can't apologize for that.

For the last year, I've been having an affair with another woman, Rebecca, and I'm in love with her. I love her in a way I've never been in love before.

It's more than just sex. I mean, yes, at first, maybe it was. In the beginning, she was giving me what you couldn't, or wouldn't. But now, what Rebecca and I have is so much more. At first, I thought—I hoped—it was just a fling, that it would end as abruptly as it began. She was young and beautiful and different, and she wanted me. How could I say no? But then I started to develop these feelings. Confusing feelings I haven't felt in a long time. And I knew my heart had shifted.

I've been avoiding making this choice because I hated the thought of losing my boys, but I can't keep hurting Rebecca. She wants me to choose, or else she's going to find someone else. I can't lose her. She means the world to me.

I'm sorry, Maggie, but I can't be with you anymore. It's time to end what will never be, for your sake as well as mine. And I know this is going to hurt you. I know you're going to hate me, but what's done is done, and now it's time to move forward with our lives. I want a divorce, and I'll be having the papers drawn up over the coming weeks. I want to be with Rebecca. I know this hurts, and I'm sorry. I wish I could've been the husband you deserve, and I wish you could be the woman I could love forever, but everything happens for a reason.

I'll be moving out of the house, and I think it's best we sell everything and divide our assets.

The letter ended there. There was no more. No sign off, nothing. Was that it? He was just going to move out and expect her to accept to just divide everything as if their life together had meant nothing?

Suddenly the silence felt heavy around Maggie. Heavy and dark, fueled by her own anger. She couldn't breathe. She clutched a hand to her chest, feeling for her heartbeat just to make sure she was still there, that the letter was real, that this wasn't some messed-up nightmare she was trapped within.

After a few moments, Maggie managed a breath which was more like a gasp. She trembled from the emotion that was beginning to crash over her, consume her. As she stared down at the letter, at Tom's messy scrawl, she felt tears burn the backs of her eyes. He'd ended it so abruptly. No sign off, nothing. She stared at the last few scribbled words wondering if he'd been interrupted while writing it and had quickly tucked it away for safe keeping until he'd grown the balls to give it to her. But perhaps he never got the chance.

All this time, all she'd wanted was an explanation, and now she had it. He'd fallen out of love with her, and fallen in love with someone else, as easy as that. Simple. Like deciding you no longer like a particular sweater before tossing it into a Goodwill box. He was planning on leaving her for his mistress. God, he hadn't even planned on *telling* her the truth; he'd written it in a goddamn letter.

Looking up through angry tears, she met her blurry reflection in the mirror in the corner of the room as realization came over her; Tom Morris was a heartless prick.

Chapter 26

Just as she had done after originally stumbling upon Tom's infidelity, Maggie acted as if everything was fine. After a night of no sleep, she showered, dressed, made the boys breakfast and dropped them at school. All the while, the truth of Tom's unapologetic and downright narcissistic confession played over and over again in her mind. Now, sitting in her car with silence surrounding her, Maggie gripped the steering wheel as she stared through the windshield at the café.

She glanced at the clock in the dash. She was late. She had to get in there. She had to put on a smiling face and get on with life. But she knew she wouldn't be able to pretend everything was okay until she'd gotten the closure she so desperately needed. Tom was a cheater. He had been planning on leaving her. If he hadn't died, she probably would have unexpectedly received divorce papers and that poor excuse for a letter. But she could have fought him, demanded an explanation, or an apology at least.

She startled at the sudden tapping on her car window. She turned to see Jane looking in through the tint, a concerned look on her face. Cursing under her breath, Maggie pressed the button, the window gliding down.

"I saw you sitting out here." Jane looked closer, her brows knitting together with obvious worry. "Are you okay, sweetie?"

Swallowing the lump in her throat, Maggie forced what she could of a smile. She shook her head. "No, I'm not." She reached up and touched the back of her hand to her forehead. "Actually, I'm not feeling very well. It just came on all of a sudden."

"You're white as a ghost!" Jane exclaimed, her blue eyes searching Maggie's face. "Do you want me to call someone?"

Someone? Maggie almost rolled her eyes. Who would she call? Her fifteen-year-old son? Her ten-year-old son? Besides her boys, she literally had no one. No one to call. And that thought alone brought tears to sting her eyes.

Shaking her head, she pressed her lips together in a smile. "No, I'm sure I just need to go home and rest."

Jane nodded, an unconvinced look on her face as she continued studying her. "I don't like that. You shouldn't be driving in your state." She looked back at the café, to the three people waiting at the counter inside.

"I only have Joe in there," Jane said, more to herself than anyone else. Glancing back at Maggie, she paused and then proceeded to pull her cell phone from the pocket in her apron. And without saying a word, she pressed the screen and held the device to her ear. "Hey. Can you come here? I need your help . . ." She paused, her eyes meeting Maggie's curious gaze. "It's Maggie. She's not well. I need you to drive her home."

"Who was that?" Maggie asked. But her question was in vain because suddenly, from her periphery, she caught a glimpse of a fast-moving figure. Turning, she made out Evan jogging out from the wharves, crossing the road and continuing up the sidewalk.

"What's wrong?" he asked out of breath, his eyes flitting from his sister, to the car, to Maggie through the windshield, his brow furrowed.

Jane pulled him off to the side, out of earshot, talking to him in a loud whisper. Evan's gaze fixed on Maggie and he nodded slowly. Turning back to his sister, he nodded again and stepped around her, moving to the driver's door.

"Hop out." He made a motion with his index finger. "I'm driving."

Maggie rolled her eyes. "I really am okay."

He leaned down, resting his forearms on the window jamb, his eyes serious. "Look, you seem to underestimate my sister. Either I drive you home, or she'll call Brad who will phone Sheriff Mason, and have *him* drive you home in his patrol car."

Without muttering another word, Maggie handed him the keys. He opened the door for her and stepped out of the way so she could get out. She offered him a tight-lipped smile before walking around the back of the vehicle and hopping into the passenger seat.

"Honey, I'll check in on you a little later. See how you're doing." Jane smiled, waving from the sidewalk.

Maggie waved back, managing a smile she knew didn't reach her eyes as Evan pulled out of the parking spot and continued on the way out of the village center.

*

Evan's jaw ticked as he clenched his teeth, gripping the leather steering wheel of Maggie's luxurious Audi. When he'd received the call from Jane, immediately he knew something was up. His sister never called him through the day. The occasional check-in text, yes. But never a phone call. Only if there was a problem. When she'd told him that Maggie was unwell and she needed him to drive her home, he'd dropped his tools onto the deck of the boat he'd been working on, and he ran, faster than he'd run in a long time.

They drove back to the house in complete silence. Not even the radio was playing to stifle the awkwardness. He glanced casually out the corner of his eye at her a few times. Maggie sat straight up, her hands wringing together in her lap as she stared out the windshield. She said nothing. Apart from her pale face and blank stare, she didn't look sick. He doubted she was. But there was something else. Something was wrong, and he was determined to find out.

As he navigated the car down the rocky drive, pulling up to a stop beside the house, he turned off the ignition. He remained seated and so did Maggie, the two of them looking out over the lake, watching the water glisten beneath the morning sun. Finally, Evan shifted, turning to face her, finding her staring unseeingly straight ahead.

"So, what's up?" he asked with a smile, hoping to maintain some semblance of casualness to his question. The last thing he wanted to do was interrogate her. "You okay?"

Slowly, she turned, blinking once, her gaze focusing on him. But still, she remained silent, eyes raking over his face.

Evan's brows pulled together. "Are you sick?"

With a swallow so hard he could see her throat bob, she finally shook her head, looking down to her hands. "I feel terrible. Your poor sister."

"Forget about Jane," he scoffed, shaking his head, and then he reached out a hand, placing it on her arm. "Maggie, what's wrong? Tell me."

When her gaze lifted again, he felt his breath catch in the back of his throat at the glimmer of tears in her eyes, shining brightly as they reflected the bright light of day. He felt his chest pull tight and he shifted again in his seat, snaking his hand down her arm, tentatively touching her hand. He didn't want to move too quickly, act too forward, but he needed her to know that he was there for her. And he almost sighed with relief when, instead of flinching or pulling away, she actually turned her hand in his, palm to palm, her fingers linking with his in a move he hadn't been expecting. She was holding his hand. Tight. Like she was afraid to let go.

"Talk to me, Maggie." He encouraged her with a nod, needing her to tell him what was wrong. Maybe he could help. Maybe he could fix whatever it was. Maybe he couldn't do either, but he needed to know so he could at least try.

She swallowed again, but this time she spoke. "I found a letter . . ."

He watched her, waiting, but she didn't continue. "A letter?"

She sniffled, and that was the only sign that her tears were winning the battle of emotion warring inside of her. With a shaking hand, she wiped at her cheeks quickly and then, removing her hand from his, she reached into her purse and pulled out a crumpled white envelope. She hesitated momentarily, staring down at it, her gaze flitting to Evan. With a tremulous breath, she handed it to him.

Evan took the envelope and made quick work of opening it, pulling out a neatly folded piece of paper. Glancing curiously at Maggie, he found her eyes fixed on the paper in his hands, her teeth raking so hard over her bottom lip it had to be painful. She was nervous. Or scared. And he hated that. He took her hand in his again, holding it tight as he read the scribbled words on the page before him, his stomach in knots after the very first line.

Shit . . .

*

Holding the coffees he'd made using the fancy espresso machine in Maggie's kitchen, Evan walked out of the house, stopping mid-step at the sight of the heartbreaking image before him.

Maggie sat hunched in one of the Adirondack chairs on the rickety old dock, her shoulders cowered and small as she stared out at the water. With a fortifying breath, he continued, stopping beside her on the weathered old dock he'd been meaning to come fix over the last few days.

At that thought, he suddenly felt as if he'd deserted her. He was supposed to come back. Yet, he hadn't been back and his reasons for staying away were piss-poor at best. And he hated it.

She needed him. She might not ever have admitted it. She might not have even realized it. And maybe he was a fool for thinking it. But she did. She needed him. And he hadn't been here when she'd needed him the most.

That letter. That damn letter. He shook his head at the memory of the words he'd read. He'd known there was more to her heartbreak. He even knew there was more to her husband cheating on her. But he never knew her husband could have been so cold, so heartless. And to think he hadn't been here because he was too damn selfish and stubborn. It caused something deep down inside of him—something he hadn't felt in a long time—to ache in a way he'd never felt it ache before.

"Here you go." Evan handed Maggie one of the mugs before taking a seat in the chair next to her. "I can't guarantee it's any good." He chuckled. "I'm an instant coffee kinda guy."

Maggie managed a smile, most likely at his pathetic effort to cheer her up, but a smile was a smile regardless, and he'd claim it as a slight victory.

He watched closely as she took a sip, humming in appreciation. "It's good. Thank you."

Evan felt his shoulders sag with relief, taking a sip from his own cup. To be honest, he wasn't much of a coffee guy, at all. He only drank the stuff in the morning after a big night. But today he would drink all the coffee he had to, because he wanted her to open up to him. To tell him the real truth.

"If I'm being honest, I suppose I knew something was going on before he died," she said after a few beats, her focus on a bird flying overhead. She sighed heavily. "He was always working. Like, more than any one person should work. His excuses were credible—I didn't know *not* to believe him. He was this big-shot lawyer, so of course I assumed they worked weekends and nights."

She glanced at Evan, her gaze imploring, as if she were waiting for a response from him. But he remained silent, watching her, waiting for her to talk. Because right now, what she needed to do was talk, and he needed to be the one to listen to her. She had no one else.

"When I found out he was having an affair, I didn't think it would be . . ." Trailing off, she shook her head at a loss for words. "I didn't think it was to such an extent. I mean, a divorce? It's just so . . . so final. He really didn't love me anymore. But I never would have thought . . ." Maggie sighed again, not finishing her sentence. Resting her elbows on her knees, she clasped her mug between her hands as she stared straight ahead. "How do you just end something? Just like that?"

Evan sighed, looking down at his barely touched mug of coffee. He was wrong; he couldn't drink it. Hell, he doubted he'd even be able to stomach a beer right now. He felt sick at the look of sheer despondency and rejection in Maggie's beautiful green eyes.

"You know what I think?"

She glanced at him, waiting.

He continued, "I think he did you a favor with that letter."

She stared at him.

"Don't you get it, Maggie?" He shook his head. "You don't have to be that grieving, faltering widow anymore. You're so much more than that. You're a strong, powerful, independent woman. You're a mom, for Christ's sake. You're worth so much more than to be just some dead asshole's wife. This is your chance to move on and leave it all behind." He didn't know if he'd said too much. Dead asshole might have been crossing some line, but he had to say it. And, thankfully, Maggie didn't look hurt or offended by his words—in fact, she looked empowered.

"I say, you and me, we drive down to Boston, and you end it once and for all."

She looked slightly confused, and he made a point of jutting his chin at the gold ring that still adorned her finger like a shackle. He knew better than anyone that Maggie needed to get rid of that ring in order to free herself.

Maggie glanced at her watch, her brow furrowed with thought. "We can't just go to Boston."

"Yes we can." Evan shifted in his chair, nodding. "I can get you there and back before school gets out. Scout's honor." He held his hand up in emphasis.

"You were never a Boy Scout, were you?" She narrowed one eye, a dubious smile pulling at her lips.

"Nah." He shrugged, grinning deviously.

With a deep breath, Maggie looked back at the water, biting her bottom lip in contemplation. "You're right. I need to end this."

He watched as she looked down at the gold wedding band. Then her eyes met his, her gaze wary and full of apprehension. "I need to finally move past Tom, once and for all."

Evan smiled, and, without hesitating, he reached out and took her hand in his.

Chapter 27

Evan and Maggie made it to Boston in record time. The mid-morning flow of traffic on the Interstate had been surprisingly quiet, and they made it in just over an hour.

"You all right?" Evan asked as they took the exit off the freeway.

Maggie toyed with her wedding ring, twisting it around and around. "Yeah." She looked out at the Boston cityscape as it flew by in a haze. A million conflicting thoughts raced through her head. "I'm just nervous."

She felt his hand touch her knee. Normally, that might have been an intimate gesture, a hand on her knee. But from Evan, right at that moment, his touch helped to ease the trepidation roiling low in her gut. It was his show of support. Thank God he was there with her; without him she didn't know what she'd be doing right now. She knew for sure she wouldn't have been in Boston, that much was true.

Taking a deep breath, Maggie closed her eyes a moment. This was it. This was what she needed to do. This was how she finally allowed herself the chance to move on, once and for all.

*

Fifteen minutes later, Evan was navigating the Audi beneath the lush canopy of sycamore trees lined on either side of the narrow road. Through the thicket, he witnessed flashes of headstones as far as the eye could see. Despite the bright sunshine and blue sky up above, the atmosphere in the cemetery was morbid and foreboding with sadness.

He glanced at Maggie as she stared out through the window, silent as she continued twisting the gold ring around her finger. She looked so small, so uncertain, so scared. He wanted to reach out and touch her hand, pull it into his. But he didn't. She didn't need him right now. She needed whatever it was she was about to do. And he was going to be right there with her.

"Stop here," Maggie said, her voice hoarse and soft.

Evan pulled over to the side of the cemetery road, putting the car in park and shutting off the engine. Silence ensued. Rubbing his palms up and down his jean-clad thighs, he glanced sideways at Maggie, following her gaze up the grassy knoll to the looming sycamore that hung over a marble headstone which looked a lot newer than many of the others surrounding it.

Maggie made a move to get out of the car, but Evan wasn't sure if he should follow or wait. When she looked back at him, he could see the pleading in her green eyes. She wanted him to go with her. Maybe she even needed him to go with her. He made quick work of unfastening his belt and hopping out of the car, hurrying to meet her on the other side of the vehicle. Without saying anything, Maggie began up the hill and he walked beside her toward the grave at the very top where they came to a stop. Evan read the inscription on the shiny Calacatta marble.

Thomas James Morris. Son. Husband. Father.

Cheater, he thought derisively.

In the center of the headstone was a picture of the man himself. Dark hair, chiseled jaw, handsome face. He looked a lot like Jack. Not someone Evan could imagine a vibrant, free spirit like Maggie to be married to. Far too clean cut and smarmy looking; a typical lawyer, really. But attractive nonetheless. It was easy to see why a woman might fall for his charms.

"You selfish, unimaginable bastard."

Surprised, Evan glanced at Maggie to find her glaring down at the grave.

"You cheat on me for a year and a half and don't even have the damn guts to tell me to my face. You write a poorly penned letter and expect that I'm just going to accept that?" she scoffed. "Well, no, Tom. No, I don't accept it. I did everything for you, everything you wanted, everything you ever needed, and you couldn't even find the decency deep within your black soul to be honest with me? Sixteen years, and for what? You end it with a fucking letter you weren't even sorry to write?" A sob broke through her words, and she wiped at the tears trailing down her cheeks.

Evan wanted to reach out, to place a hand on her trembling shoulder, just to let her know that he was there. But he didn't. He would be there if she fell or if she broke, but he knew right now, all she needed was to get her words out. This was her closure.

"I hate what you did, Tom. You broke my heart. You broke me." Maggie shook her head. "And I wish I could hate *you*, but the truth is, even after everything, I can't. I can't hate you because you gave me those two beautiful boys, and I love them so much that it *kills* me to think what would happen to them if they ever found out the truth. One day they'll know. I'll tell them the truth of what you did, but not now. Not for you, or for me, but for them. They don't deserve that." She sniffled, exhaling a ragged breath, glaring at Tom's picture as if it were him right there in front of her. "I can't keep carrying the weight of this. I'm better than this. I deserve better than this. I deserve to be able to move on, and I know that I can be happy again. Happy without you. So, this is it. I'm done."

Evan watched as she struggled momentarily, twisting her wedding ring off her finger. She looked down at it for a few moments, staring at the gold as it reflected the sun rays breaking through the canopy of the branches overhead. And then, with another heavy exhalation, she reached forward and placed the ring on top of the marble.

"This ends here," she whispered, adding with the faintest smile, "I'm going to be okay. Our boys are going to be okay. I promise, I won't let anything or anyone hurt them." She crouched down, and gingerly placed a shaking hand over Tom's photo. Bowing her head, she closed her eyes, her shoulders trembling with emotion. "Goodbye, Tom," she managed in a voice so soft it was almost lost in the afternoon breeze as it rustled through the leaves of the cemetery trees.

After a few silent moments, Evan watched Maggie force herself up onto unsteady legs. With a heavy sigh she scrubbed her hands over her face, sniffling again. Finally, she braved a look at Evan and he gave her a small encouraging smile. She walked to him, her hands shoved deep into the pockets of her jeans.

"You good?" he asked, reaching out and squeezing her shoulder gently.

"Yeah." She nodded, glancing back at the headstone once more before meeting his eyes again with a smile that momentarily took his breath away. "Actually, I've never felt better."

With another smile, and a moment's contemplation, Evan threw caution to the wind. Wrapping his arms around Maggie's slight shoulders, he pulled her against his chest, holding her so tight. With a soft kiss to the top of her head, he felt her relax against him, her arms moving around his waist. And there, by her late husband's grave, beneath the shade of a sycamore tree, he felt her let go.

*

The drive from Boston had been quiet and contemplative, but companionable between Evan and Maggie. The radio played Flashback Friday hits and the occasional song caused them to either cringe simultaneously, or laugh out loud. But, otherwise, not a lot had been spoken between the two. There was an obvious tension hanging between them, but it wasn't uncomfortable or uneasy, it was just there in the words neither of them said.

By the time they returned to Jewel Harbor, Maggie was due to collect TJ from school. As Evan pulled up to the wharf to head back to his boat shed, there was so much she wanted, *needed*, to say to him to thank him. He'd helped her today in a way she'd never imagined another person could help her. Driving her to Boston, to Tom. Being right there by her side the whole time. Giving her the nudge she knew she needed but, for some reason, couldn't seem to push herself. But how could she possibly thank him for everything in the thirty seconds before she had to leave.

"I'll see you tomorrow?" Evan glanced at Maggie, adding, "At little league?"

"Oh, yeah." She nodded, suddenly feeling so stupid for thinking he'd meant something else. Little league, of course. She almost rolled her eyes at herself. "See you tomorrow."

They both got out of the car, Maggie moving around the hood to the driver's door Evan was holding open for her. When she hopped in, he flashed her another smile and closed the door for her, waving once before turning and walking down the steps to the docks.

Maggie gripped the steering wheel tight, collecting what she could of her wayward thoughts. Sighing heavily at herself, she pulled out onto the road and headed in the direction of the elementary school. Her gaze momentarily flitted down to her naked ring finger, causing her to smile.

Chapter 28

Maggie picked the boys up from school, and the relief that she'd felt at finally letting Tom go was doubled when she saw the smiles on her sons' faces. They were happy. And their happiness was all she needed. She didn't need Tom's money or the status it provided. She didn't need the big house, or the vintage Porsche. She didn't need the affluence. Neither she nor her sons needed the kind of life Tom seemed to believe they were required to live. He was unhealthily obsessed with that first-class lifestyle—the kind he was born into and the kind he believed everyone aspired to. Maggie had gone along with it because he was her husband and, in a way, she felt almost trapped. But now that he was gone, she was strong enough to admit she didn't need or want it. All she wanted was for her sons to be safe and happy and healthy. And that admission was like a weight off her shoulders. She wished she'd been strong enough to admit it years ago. If she had, things would have no doubt turned out so differently.

"Jack's got a girlfriend! Jack's got a girlfriend! Jack's got a girl—Argghhh!"

Maggie was dragged from her thoughts by the shrill sound of agony resonating from the living room. Wiping her hands on the

216

dish towel, she ran to the door that led from the kitchen, poking her head out to see Jack pinning TJ on the rug in the center of the room. The two boys were wrestling as if they were the main event in some Las Vegas Ultimate Fighting Championship title bout.

"Stop it!" she yelled with a warning tone.

"He's being annoying!" Jack yelled while trying to get his little brother into some kind of chokehold.

"But . . . you've . . . got . . . a-a girlfriend!" TJ continued breathlessly, his teasing grin remaining in place despite his big brother's wrath.

"Stop it!" Maggie repeated, pointing at TJ. "Or no little league tomorrow."

"Ha!" Jack laughed, pushing TJ away. He was twice his size, but, thankfully, he knew to use minimal force. "Mom yelled at you."

"No, she didn't, she was yelling at both of us. Weren't ya, Mom?" TJ adjusted the skewwhiff neck of his T-shirt, following her back into the kitchen. "Mom? Did you know *Jack* is taking *Katie* to the *movies* tomorrow night?" he asked in that teasing tone, no doubt only to get a rise out of his big brother.

Maggie rolled her eyes.

"Keep it up, Teej, I dare ya!" Jack yelled from where he'd settled back onto the sofa in front of the television.

"I do know that, yes." She speared TJ with a pointed look as he pulled out one of the stools, perching himself at the breakfast counter to watch her continue making her famous lasagna. "And you should leave him alone. Maybe one day you'll want to take a girl to the movies. Would *you* want to be teased about it?" She raised a brow.

TJ made a mock gagging sound. "Ew, yuck. I'm *never* going to date."

"You're going to stay Mama's boy forever?"

"Nah, I'm gonna be a ladies' man." He flashed a mischievous grin, reaching forward to steal some of the grated cheddar from the glass bowl on the counter before shoving it into his mouth.

She blinked at him, wondering where her ten-year-old had gone.

Suddenly, Maggie's cell phone started ringing from the countertop where she'd placed it right next to her glass of wine. She glanced down to find Jane's name flashing on the screen, and she didn't know why, but nerves fluttered deep in her belly. Had she realized Maggie wasn't really sick today? Was she calling to tell her not to bother coming back to work on Monday? To tell her to return her personalized apron? Her heart hammered as she reluctantly reached for the device. She answered with a hopeful smile.

"Oh hi, honey," Jane's cheerful voice announced through the phone. "I was just calling to see how you're feeling?"

"A lot better," Maggie answered truthfully, conscious of TJ still sitting at the counter, careful not to say too much. "Thank you."

"Oh, I'm so glad." Jane continued, "I was also calling because Sam and Ben have asked if TJ can come sleep over tomorrow night."

"I'm sure he would love that. Just let me ask him." She pulled her cell away from her ear, TJ looked up with a questioning glance. "Would you like to stay over at Sam and Ben's house tomorrow night?"

His blue eyes lit up. "Yeah!"

Maggie laughed at his reaction, going back to the phone call. "Did you hear that?"

Jane chuckled. "I sure did. The boys will be so happy. Brad's going to set the tent up in the backyard so they can have a camp out. S'mores and everything."

"TJ will *love* that," Maggie said, smiling at her excited son. "Thank you for the invitation."

"Are you dropping Jack at the movie theater tomorrow night?" Jane's question sounded tentative, almost as if she was just as nervous as Maggie was at the prospect of her eldest child's first proper date. She admitted sheepishly, "I don't know how this is supposed to work. I'm sure times have changed since we were teenagers."

Maggie laughed. "I was going to drop him off and then pick him up at eleven. I told him to make sure he takes Katie for ice cream after the movie. And to be a gentleman, or else he'll have Brad to answer to."

"Oh, honey. Don't scare the poor boy." Jane laughed, adding, "This is so weird. Isn't it?"

"Yes!" Maggie exclaimed, turning to the stove to stir the ground beef and red sauce she had on simmer. "I suddenly feel very old."

"Oh, honey. Katie got her period at eleven! I've felt old for the last four *long* years."

Maggie laughed again and the two women said goodbye before ending the call.

TJ raced up to his bedroom to start packing his duffle bag in preparation for his sleepover adventure with Sam and Ben. Maggie was left alone with her thoughts. She couldn't help but smile at the prospect of having a night all to herself. Maybe she would take herself out to dinner. Maybe she would come home, order a pizza and put on a romantic comedy. So many options. She couldn't wait.

*

"Hey, Coach!" TJ yelled, running through the gates of Field Four. He high-fived Evan on his way, sprinting toward the rest of his team like a moth to a flame.

Evan chuckled on his way over to the fence. He removed his sunglasses and smiled at Maggie through the chain link as she stopped on the other side.

"How you feeling today?" he asked quietly, his voice low like he didn't want to allow the plethora of women hanging around nearby to overhear.

"I'm feeling a lot better." Maggie looked at her ring finger. There was a faded tan mark where her ring had sat for sixteen years, but she felt lighter without it. Free. "I didn't get to say thank you yesterday." She met Evan's striking blue eyes with a shy smile. "Thank you. Really. There's no way I would have been able to do that on my own."

He shook his head dismissively, before a whistle blew in the distance, causing him to look over his shoulder. "I should get back to the game." He thumbed back in the direction of the diamond where the boys were all taking their places. But then he paused, looking at her with an uncertain expression she couldn't quite place.

Was he nervous?

"Hey, what are you doing tonight?"

She felt all the air escape her lungs, unable to stop the curious smile from curling her lips. "Me?"

He chuckled. "Yeah, *you*."

She swallowed her nerves. "Um, TJ's staying at Jane's house with Ben and Sam. Jack has a . . . date." God, it was difficult for her to even say the word out loud; her first born was going on a date.

Evan arched a brow. "With my niece?"

Maggie smirked. "Yep."

"He better not get all handsy, or he'll have *me* to answer to."

"My son is nothing if not a gentleman," she replied with mock indignation, causing him to laugh.

Evan's smile waned, his eyes serious again. "I was wondering if maybe you'd like to grab a bite to eat. Maybe have a drink . . ." He clamped his mouth shut. "Oh God, this totally sounds like I'm asking you out on a date. I didn't mean . . . I mean . . . I don't . . . it's not—"

"Evan, it's fine." She flashed him a wry smile. "I know how you are with your not-dates."

He bit back his grin and she was almost certain she could see a tinge of pink flush his cheeks; uncharacteristic for a cocky, self-assured man such as him.

"Why don't you come over and I'll cook." She shrugged. "My way of saying thank you for yesterday?"

He stared deep into her eyes for a long moment, the hint of his smile still lingering despite his sudden seriousness. "You know you don't have to thank me, right?"

She nodded, her heart racing with anticipation. "I know. But I want to thank you. And it'd be nice to have some grown-up conversation over a meal and a glass of wine. It's . . . been a while."

"I'd like that." Evan winked at her. He actually winked. His smile, both adorable and devastatingly handsome, effortlessly stole her breath away.

Schooling his expression, he turned and jogged off to the team's dugout. All the while Maggie could feel the glaring eyes of Evan Boyd's fan club from behind her. But she didn't care. She smiled to herself. Tonight, she had a not-date with the most eligible bachelor in Jewel Harbor himself.

*

On her way through town, after dropping TJ off at Jane's house for his sleepover with Sam and Ben, Maggie glanced sideways as she waited at the stop light, her gaze landing upon the neon pink sign hanging above Barb's Beauty Salon. She looked at herself in the rear-view mirror, zeroing in on her wayward, flyaway hair and the drab color of her split ends. It had been forever since she'd had her hair done. And she remembered meeting the kind woman, Barb, at little league a few weeks back. She'd told Maggie to stop by any time. And what better time than now? She hoped.

On the green light, Maggie continued ahead instead of turning left, and she pulled into a parking spot outside the salon. She noticed the familiar blonde woman through the window, sitting on one of the station chairs, flicking through a magazine, dressed head to toe in leopard print. Maggie smiled to herself; she didn't know Barb, but she liked what she'd seen so far. She had a feeling the woman could be a friend.

Walking into the small salon, Maggie paused in the doorway,

taking in the somewhat familiar scent of toner and bleach, and the unexpected sound of a Shawn Mendes song playing.

"Oh hi, hun!" Barb glanced up from the magazine in her hands, a smile of recognition curling her painted-pink lips. "Maggie, right?"

Maggie nodded. "Yeah. You told me to pop in any time I was after a pamper sesh and a chin wag?" She shrugged her shoulders, nervously continuing, "Well, I was hoping you might be able to fit me in?"

"What're you after?" The woman stood, crossing the small salon, her gaze narrowed as she inspected Maggie's hair.

Releasing a big breath, Maggie swallowed her trepidation. "I feel like a change. Something a little . . . different?"

"Hmmm." Barb picked up a section of Maggie's long tawny brown hair, looking closely as she twisted the wavy lengths between her fingers. "Do you *trust* me?"

Maggie examined the woman's over-bleached hair, the dark roots poking through, the way it was teased a little to create volume she didn't necessarily need. Did she trust her? She didn't even know her. She lied, "Um, I . . . I guess."

Barb smiled eagerly, her eyes lighting up. "Well, take a seat right here." She placed a hand on the white leather chair she'd just vacated. "I'll go out back and grab us each a wine cooler while you get yourself nice and comfortable."

Taking a seat, Maggie released another heavy breath, looking at herself in the reflection of the big mirror in front of her while Barb disappeared through a hot pink curtain that separated the salon from the back. Chewing her bottom lip, she considered everything for a moment while trying to reason with her self-doubt. It was time for a change. She was ready for a change. This was the beginning of the rest of her life.

Chapter 29

"So, how are you liking Jewel Harbor so far, honey?"

Maggie sipped her glass of sweet bubbles, wincing a little as the sparkling wine fizzed on her tongue. It was horrible, but she managed a smile when she saw Barb's curious gaze in the reflection of the mirror. "Oh, I like it here. It's so different to Boston." Nodding, she continued, as if more to herself than to Barb, "I think I made the right decision coming here, especially for my boys. Boston held too many memories . . ."

Barb continued painting bleach onto the ends of Maggie's hair, wrapping each section in aluminum foil, meticulous with her work. "How are the boys coping?" She added quickly, "I hope it's okay that I know, but news travels fast in this town."

Maggie's eyes widened at Barb's question. Jewel Harbor was a small town, and she knew news traveled fast. Of course, the locals would have heard her tragic backstory by now. Clearing her throat, she said, "Yeah. I think it'll take some time, but things are slowly starting to get back to normal."

"And are you okay?" Barb looked at her closely, pausing what she was doing to place a gentle hand upon Maggie's shoulder.

"I'm okay," Maggie answered truthfully. Because she was. The truth of Tom's affair and the fact that he had been planning on leaving her before his death would die with her. She couldn't let it get out for her boys' sakes. And it was okay. Because of Evan. She had him to confide in, and that was enough. "In fact, Evan Boyd has helped a lot." She smiled at the thought of Evan, her heart jumping at the thought of seeing him so soon, just the two of them.

"Evan, huh?" Barb lifted a brow, the hint of a smile pulling at the corner of her mouth.

Feeling her cheeks flush with heat, Maggie looked down at her hands. "Yeah. Actually . . . he's coming over tonight," she confessed. "I'm cooking him dinner. My way of thanking him for being there for me these last few weeks. Without him—" She shook her head, sighing heavily. "Without him, I don't know where I'd be, right now."

"Ah, so that's the reason for the makeover," Barb teased with a wink.

Maggie's cheeks heated. "No . . . I just . . ." She paused to consider her words, taking a big breath and releasing it slowly. "It's time for a change, is all."

Barb hummed, continuing with Maggie's hair. "He's a good man, our Evan." With that, she gave Maggie a furtive glance, her tone changing when she added, "Just . . . be careful with him."

Maggie stiffened a little, the anticipation that had been roiling in her belly suddenly balling into a heavy lump as she remembered Jane's warning in the same tone. "W-what do you mean? Be careful with him?"

She watched Barb obviously struggle to come up with the right words, a small crease etching between her overplucked brows. For a long moment nothing but silence sat heavily between them, accompanied by the generic pop song playing through the small salon.

"Barb?" Maggie pressed, wanting to hear her take on the elusive Evan Boyd.

With an exasperated sigh, Barb's shoulders sagged. "Look. I love

Evan. He's a good man. But . . . he's been to hell and back. I don't know the ins and outs. I know it has to do with a woman. But he's not the boy he was when he left. He came back a changed man. He drinks a lot, and he enjoys the company of women," she said hurriedly. "This is a small town, and people talk. I don't much care for gossip, but you seem like a nice gal and I know you've been hurt. So just be careful. That's all. A friendly warning." She shrugged and, with a sympathetic smile, she changed the topic of conversation.

Maggie was no longer paying attention to what Barb was saying. Her mind was elsewhere. She sagged in her chair, suddenly feeling very deflated. She knew Evan was appreciated by the women in town; she'd seen it herself every Saturday morning at little league. She'd even witnessed one of his not-dates with one of his many admirers. But was there more to it? Did Evan's past and what happened to him while he was away affect who he is now? Was this what Jane was warning her against? Was she destined to get hurt if she let him in?

Watching while Barb continued talking about the latest episode of some *Real Housewives* television show, Maggie stared blankly at her reflection, hoping like hell tonight was the right thing to do. Her heart had been broken—it was still broken—in the worst way. Sure, tonight was just dinner between friends, her way of saying thanks, a not-date. But what if it was more? What if she was just fooling herself? What if Evan was a risk she couldn't afford to take?

*

"There's two twenties in my wallet. You take them," Maggie said as she drove through the darkening dusk toward the center of town. "I want you to pay for the tickets and the popcorn. And then for ice cream after, okay?"

"Mom, things have changed since the olden days," Jack scoffed from the passenger seat. "Girls are more *self-sufficient* now than they were back when you were my age."

"Oh, of course!" She mock gasped in exasperation, slapping a hand to the side of her head. "Must be my old age brain forgetting again. It was *so* long ago." She shot him an indulgent eye roll which caused Jack to chuckle quietly to himself.

A companionable silence fell between them as some pop princess sang through the radio. Maggie smiled as she thought back to her first date. All the way back to when she was fifteen and Mitchell Holmes had asked her to the movies. He was the older, popular jock, captain of the basketball team. She was the quiet yet slightly rebellious girl from the questionable side of town. The whole school had been talking about their impending date all week, to the point where Maggie had wondered if it was some sick joke. A bet. À la *She's All That*, one of her favorite movies when she was a teen. But it hadn't been a bet. Mitchell had met her at the multiplex. He'd paid for the tickets, and the overpriced concessions. About twenty minutes into the movie, he'd done the sneaky scratch-of-the-head maneuver, his arm snaking around her shoulders, and Maggie had nestled in closer, smiling to herself as she chewed on a Red Vine. After the movie, Mitchell had taken her for a drive in his slightly souped-up Honda. They listened to their favorite songs on the radio until they made it to the beach where they sat on the sand and talked for hours while watching the water. It had been the most romantic night of her life. As romantic as a date could be for a fifteen-year-old on her first real one-on-one with a boy. Like *Dawson's Creek* and *One Tree Hill* all rolled into one; everything her teenage dreams had been made of. After that date, she and Mitchell went steady for three months—an entire lifetime in high school terms—but they slowly drifted apart, their romance short-lived. It was still a nice memory, though.

"Okay. Here we are." Maggie pulled up to the curb outside

the movie theater, glancing up to the marquee shining brightly over the box office.

There were only two movies showing. Only two cinemas. But there was a long line that trailed the sidewalk. Young and old, teenagers on first dates and married couples on date nights. She smiled before glancing at Jack, feeling emotional.

"Oh God, Mom. You're not gonna take a photo or anything, are you?" Jack grimaced.

"No." She rolled her eyes, managing a smile. "My baby is growing up, is all." She flashed him a knowing look as she added, "It's customary for a parent to become emotional during these milestones."

Jack shook his head, laughing under his breath, but then he stiffened, whisper-yelling, "There she is!"

Maggie followed his wide-eyed gaze, spotting the beautiful blonde standing by the lamppost outside the theater. She was dressed in a cute yellow sundress with flowers all over it, and a little white cardigan thrown over the top, her long hair left out, flowing in the gentle night breeze. Maggie glanced briefly at Jack to witness a look of awe in his eyes, and something inside caused her heart to constrict. But she forced herself to pull it together. He wasn't her little boy anymore.

"Okay. Call me if you need anything," she said, causing him to look at her. "I'll be here at eleven to pick you up. If Katie needs a ride home, let her know I can drop her off." She smiled, knowing that if all went well with their first date, she would absolutely be driving Katie home. Anything to squeeze in a few extra minutes out of their night together.

"Thanks, Mom." Jack smiled before moving to open his door. With a fortifying breath, he flashed her one last nervous grin before getting out of the car.

Maggie watched from the opposite side of the street as Jack jogged over to Katie. She waved, nervously tucking her hair behind her ear. He placed a hand on her shoulder, saying something. The two shared a shy smile before walking together toward the end of the long box office line, laughing and giggling together about something no one else would ever be privy to.

With a deep breath, Maggie pulled away from the curb and continued to the pub. She had intended on cooking Evan dinner, but she'd ran out of time, getting caught up with Barb at the salon. So, she'd called the pub and ordered a few dishes from their menu to take away. She was sure Evan would understand. She couldn't even understand why she was nervous. It was just dinner between friends. So what if Evan was the playboy Barb made him out to be? What on earth was there to be nervous about? She reminded herself, yet again, that this wasn't a date.

She repeated the words over and over again in her head. *This isn't a date. This isn't a date. This isn't a date.* But who was she trying to fool? This was totally a date. She just hoped she didn't end up getting hurt like everyone seemed to think she might.

The pub was busy as Maggie snaked her way through the dining room. She waited at the restaurant counter for her pick-up order, and her gaze landed on the bar, more specifically on Liam, the cocky, self-assured bartender she'd met the first night she'd come to the pub.

Moving swiftly back the way she came, she made her way to the bar and waited while Liam openly flirted with a pretty young girl while pouring her a vodka cocktail. Maggie couldn't help but laugh to herself; he sure did have a gift with the ladies.

"Miss Maggie!" Liam exclaimed when he turned, his eyes lighting up as he sauntered toward her. "To what do I owe this delight of a pleasure?"

Taken aback by his greeting, Maggie felt her cheeks blush when he winked at her, leaning closer over the bar; she was only human, after all. Snapping herself out of her daze, she shook her head, collecting herself. "Hey, Liam."

Resting one of his hands on the counter, Liam offered a lascivious smirk. "What can I get you, sweetheart?"

Trying so hard not to roll her eyes or swoon like a teenager, Maggie squared her shoulders. "I need a six-pack of beer."

"O-kay . . ." Liam raised a dubious brow. "Any certain kind of beer?"

Biting her lip, Maggie looked up in thought. What kind of beer did Evan like? She'd only seen him with a nondescript pint glass and the beer Travis had bought after the work they'd all done at her house a few Sundays ago. She couldn't remember the name on the label.

"Maggie?"

Coming back from her thoughts, Maggie met Liam's smiling eyes. Again, her cheeks betrayed her and she tried to remind herself that she was a grown woman. Clearing her throat, she asked, "Do you know what kind of beer Evan likes to drink?"

Liam stared at her for a long beat, his lips slowly curling upwards to match the gleaming look in his eyes. Without saying anything, he turned to the small fridge that sat tucked under the back counter, returning with a six-pack of beer and placing it in front of Maggie.

"Stone and Wood Pacific Ale," Liam said. "All the way from Byron Bay, Australia."

"I'll take it." Maggie handed her credit card across the bar, ignoring the questioning look on his face.

"So, what are the two of you up to tonight? Is this a hot date, or something?" he asked as he processed the transaction.

"No," she guffawed. "It's a not-date."

He arched a brow.

She went on to explain, "I invited him over for dinner. Just a little something to say thank you for helping me at my house. Evan doesn't date. You know that."

"No. He doesn't date . . ." Liam handed her credit card back, placing the beer into a brown paper bag and though he wouldn't meet her eyes, she couldn't miss the knowing smirk on his lips. "But he did come in here all frantic a little earlier, asking me if

I remembered what kinda wine you ordered that first night you were in here." He lifted his face, a glint flashing in his eyes as he indicated the beer. "Now this . . ."

"He *what*?" Maggie's brows climbed high in surprise.

"Yeah." He nodded. "He ran in here in a huff, asked me if I remembered what wine you ordered . . . which I did, might I add, because I'm the world's *greatest* bartender," he said with a smug smile before continuing, "He had a beer, bought the wine, then he ran outta here yelling something about going to buy a new shirt."

Maggie stared at him, trying to make sense of his words. Was he being serious? He looked serious, if a little annoying, like a little brother who knew a secret he wouldn't tell.

"Seems like a date to me." Liam shrugged, smiling to himself as he wiped down the oak countertop with his rag.

Looking down at the brown paper bag containing the beer, Maggie considered what Liam was telling her, a million confusing thoughts swirling around in her brain. But just when she was going to ask more, they were interrupted by another customer at the bar.

"Have a good night, Miss Maggie," Liam said with a wink before turning to the elderly gentleman waiting to be served.

Giving him a tight smile, Maggie grabbed her beer and, with a curt nod, she turned and headed back to the restaurant counter to collect her take away, her heart suddenly racing a lot faster at the realization that tonight was a hell of a lot more than just dinner between friends.

Chapter 30

Evan did one final check of himself as he hopped out of his truck. Glancing at the house, he made sure he was out of sight before looking at his reflection in the side mirror and smoothing back his wayward hair. He blew out a hard breath. He was more nervous than he would ever admit out loud, self-doubt flooding his mind.

Grabbing the flowers he'd picked up in town, and the bottle of wine he'd grabbed from Liam at the pub, he couldn't help but wonder. What if he'd given Maggie the wrong impression? He'd been so quick to emphasize that this wasn't a date. Was it really *not* a date? A date was usually dinner out at a nice restaurant. This was a meal at Maggie's house. Maybe it *was* just a thank-you dinner. Maybe he should have stopped at the wine; the flowers might give off the wrong impression. Evan Boyd didn't *date*. Or . . . did he?

Looking down at himself, he'd even dressed the part of a date in his good pair of blue jeans and the crisp white button-down he'd frantically picked up from Millers at the last minute. He'd sprinted into the department store right as they were closing when he'd realized his only other button-down was still in the laundry hamper from a week ago. God, he really needed to get his shit together.

231

Shaking his head, he sighed heavily in defeat. This was totally a date. Hell, he'd even trimmed his beard. *Not a date?* He scoffed to himself and almost laughed out loud. He needed a drink. That'd help calm his thundering heart. He'd had a beer at the pub when he picked up the wine for tonight. He'd gone there specifically to ask Liam if he remembered what kind of wine Maggie'd ordered that night at the pub. Of course, the cocky bartender had remembered. He'd smugly confessed that he remembered everything about Maggie. Then he'd winked. Evan had almost reached over the bar and grabbed the kid by the scruff of his shirt until he realized he was just trying to rile him up.

"Are you just going to stand out here all night?"

Evan almost jumped a foot in the air. He turned toward the sound of Maggie's angelic voice, but he couldn't see her. Sure, it was dark, the moonlight wasn't bright tonight like it was most nights, but as he scanned the area, he couldn't see her anywhere.

"Over here . . ."

Turning again, he found her standing in the open window smirking knowingly at him from inside the house.

Shit. He'd been busted in his moment of hesitation.

Holy shit . . . He was forced to do a double take.

Of course Maggie looked beautiful. She always did. But tonight she looked different. Her normally long brown hair was now sitting just shy of her shoulders, the ends a little lighter than the rest which brought out the green in her eyes.

Evan shook his head in an attempt to snap himself out of his daze. Clearing the sudden bubble from the back of his throat, he managed to mutter, "Oh, hey."

"You coming in?" Maggie asked with a giggle, waving him in.

"Yeah. Sure . . ." Evan clutched his bottle of wine and those damn flowers like his life depended on it, turning and walking around the house to the porch.

He paused at the first step, taking in the space. It had been transformed. Sparkling fairy lights had been strung up illuminating the porch along with glowing lanterns and a few strategically placed citronella candles. A small table was neatly set with a tiny glass vase of wildflowers and delicate dinnerware.

He was forced to bite back his own shit-eating grin; this was totally a date. He mentally high-fived himself for buying the flowers.

Inside, the house smelled like a dream. Vanilla with floral undertones and so Maggie-like, but also delicious with the hint of something that made his stomach rumble with anticipation. Evan almost floated through to the kitchen. As he continued through the door, he stopped to take in the scene.

Maggie looked good. Better than good. Tight jeans and a delicate white strappy top that made her olive skin pop. Her feet were bare, and he couldn't help but notice the pale pink polish on her toes. Her feet were a bigger turn-on than he'd ever imagined feet could be; he forced himself to look away.

"I hope you don't mind," Maggie began, turning to him, which was when he noticed the sheepish smile on her face. "I got held up at the salon talking to Barb, and I ran out of time to cook anything. So, I just picked up a few things from the pub."

Evan's gaze settled over her shoulder to where there were a few aluminum trays set up on the countertop.

"I didn't know what you'd like, so I just ordered a few different things. Mac and cheese. Clam chowder. Crab stuffed haddock. Cobb salad."

"It all looks great." Evan smiled, moving forward. Remembering the flowers and wine in his hands, he looked down at the items, shifting awkwardly from foot to foot. Looking back up, he met her kind eyes with a nervous smile as he handed her the gifts. "For you."

Maggie's cheeks flushed as she looked from the wine to the flowers, back to the wine, a small smile tugging at her perfect lips. "Oh, my favorite wine. How on earth did you know?"

Evan felt his cheeks heat. Pressing his lips together, he shrugged a shoulder. Sure, he could've told her the truth, that he'd gone to the pub like a goddamn stalker and asked Liam if he remembered what kind of wine she'd ordered the last time she was there. But he already felt way in over his head. And women liked an air of mystery, right?

"Flowers *and* wine . . ." Maggie mused out loud, casting him a wry glance. "Very date-ish. Don't you think?"

His cheeks flamed. *What the hell?* He wasn't the kind of guy to blush; suddenly his cheeks were turning pink every few minutes like a sixteen-year-old schoolgirl. He hoped like hell she didn't notice.

"Would you like a beer?"

"Um, yeah. Sure. Thanks."

"Help yourself. There's a six-pack in the fridge. I grabbed it from the pub when I picked up dinner. Liam helped me pick out your favorite . . ."

Evan paused on his way to the refrigerator, picking up on her playful tone. "Wait . . ." He turned, looking at her. "That cocky little shit told you about the wine, didn't he?"

Maggie glanced at him with an innocent flutter of her lashes despite the smile she was trying to conceal. "Nice shirt, by the way," she said knowingly, running her eyes over the white button-down he was wearing.

Evan shook his head, chuckling under his breath. "I swear, I'm gonna kill him."

Maggie giggled. "I'm going to put these in some water."

He watched as she made quick work of pulling a big glass vase from one of the overhead cabinets, humming to herself as she filled it with water and began arranging the flowers. He couldn't help but grin to himself as he turned and took a Stone and Wood—his all-time favorite beer—from the fridge. He may have been caught out, but he no longer cared; this was totally a date.

*

234

Maggie groaned somewhat shamelessly, her eyes rolling back in her head. "Oh! This is *so* good," she murmured as she popped another forkful of stuffed haddock into her mouth.

"Those noises should be illegal," Evan finally said, shifting in his seat while clearing his throat.

She couldn't help but flush at his words, butterflies fluttering low in her belly when she realized what he was saying and why. "Sorry."

He flashed her a mischievous smirk before mopping some of the garlic butter off his plate with half of his bread roll.

With a sip of wine, Maggie took the opportunity to study Evan while he was busy finishing his meal. He looked handsome tonight. More handsome than usual, if that was even possible. But more than handsome, he looked carefree and happy. He was always happy, or maybe cocky was a better term to use, but with that facade he put on there was a heaviness about him. Not tonight. Tonight he seemed genuinely happy. Tonight his eyes crinkled at the corners with his boisterous laughter, and it made Maggie smile, wondering if maybe, just maybe, it was because of her.

"Can I ask you something?"

Evan looked up from his now clean dinner plate. His eyes met Maggie's with a curious regard. Nodding, he picked up his beer bottle and took a long pull, relaxing back in his chair.

Maggie hesitated for a moment. She didn't want to cross any lines, but she also wanted to know more about him. Where he went all those years ago, and why he came back. So, throwing caution to the wind she did ask, "Why did you come back here?"

A slight furrow appeared between Evan's brows as he stared at her for a few long beats. "What do you mean?"

Maggie shifted, averting her eyes and toying with the stem of her wineglass as a distraction from his weighty stare. She contemplated herself a moment, before looking up at him again. "I was just wondering what made you come back."

He nodded slowly. With a resigned sigh, he rested his elbows on the table, clutching his beer bottle a little tighter, his carefree happiness fading by the second.

Maggie offered a casual shrug. "Why would you give up on what you loved, what you were obviously so good at, to come back here to fix boats?" Realizing how harsh that sounded, she cowered, shrinking a little in her chair. "Sorry. That sounded really rude. There's nothing wrong with fixing boats. I just . . . Oh God. You don't have to answer . . . I didn't mean to—"

"It's okay." Evan chuckled, interjecting her ramblings.

She gave him an apologetic look, hating herself at that moment.

"The truth is I came back here because I lost my shit." Evan's gruff words caused her to stiffen a little. He avoided her eyes, focusing on the beer in his hands, his fingernail picking at the label as he continued, "I was engaged. I told you that. My fiancée left me."

When he met her eyes, she nodded, remembering him admitting that after she'd told him about Tom. But there was more to it. She knew it then, and she knew it now. She could see it in his eyes.

"Well, she left me because things got too difficult . . . shit happened. It caused me to lose my way. I was drinking a lot. Partying. I quit baseball. I just . . . I gave up." He shrugged his broad shoulders, sighing heavily as he stared at the bottle.

Maggie looked at him for a long moment, taking in the sheer despondency that had come over him like a looming storm cloud. Jane's words echoed in her mind and she folded her hands together, hesitating before finally asking, "What . . . what happened?"

With another heavy sigh, Evan placed his beer onto the table, bowing his head, and she watched his shoulders heave with a deep breath. She suddenly wished she hadn't asked. But when he looked up again, he leaned over to the side, reaching into the pocket of his jeans. Pulling out a slightly worn brown leather wallet, he opened it, looking down at it for a long moment. Then, taking something out from one of the pockets, he slid it across the table toward her, not meeting her eyes when she offered him a questioning glance.

With her brows knotted together, Maggie's eyes narrowed on the photograph in front of her. Picking it up, she flashed Evan a cautious glance before looking closer at the picture. The angelic face of a beautiful little girl stared back at her. Golden blonde curls framed a set of chubby cheeks, cornflower blue eyes, and that smile. She'd seen it before. It was Evan's smile. In fact, the little girl was a miniature version of the brawny man sitting opposite her, and she couldn't suppress a gasp when it suddenly dawned on her.

Evan looked up, his blue eyes glassy, reflecting the dim glow of the lantern sitting on the table between them. He smiled, but it was forced and didn't even come close to meeting his eyes. Maggie looked from him to the little girl in the photograph and back again, and, somehow, she just knew, and her heart tore in two.

"Her name was Hannah," Evan said.

Maggie stared at the little girl, tears pricking her eyes, but she remained strong while he continued. "When I first moved out to Oklahoma to play ball, I met a girl. Hailey. She was like no one I'd ever met before. Not through high school. Not through college. She was different. Beautiful, a little crazy. But me and her, we fell in love, *fast*. I was always off in different cities playing baseball, but Hailey was that girl for me. And I loved going home to her."

Maggie smiled, although she could feel his heaviness, and she knew his words were hurting him. She nodded encouragingly for him to continue.

"We were only together a few months before Hailey found out she was pregnant. Nine months later Hannah came into our lives . . ." Evan paused, swallowing hard, his jaw fixed tight as he stared at the back of the photo Maggie was holding.

"When Hannah was three, she, um, well, she started getting real sick." He looked down at his hands as he continued, "We

237

didn't know what was wrong. She slept all the time. She couldn't walk properly. She hadn't developed. She wasn't like all the other three-year-old kids, you know?" He looked at her then and Maggie nodded, trying so hard not to look as sad as she felt deep down. His words were heartbreaking, and she could only imagine what they were doing to him.

"Hannah was diagnosed with an aggressive brain tumor. She passed away a few weeks before her fourth birthday. She'd be almost ten now. Same age as TJ."

Maggie closed her eyes at that, those infuriating tears of hers burning painfully. She didn't want to cry. He didn't need her tears. But she couldn't help it. Reaching across the table, she grabbed Evan's hand and she held onto it tight, finally opening her eyes and meeting the sadness in his.

"Hailey, she couldn't deal with it." He shook his head. "The loss, it was too much for her to cope with. So, she split. Moved out to California. I ain't ever seen her again. Last I heard, she was married to some guy, living just out of Oakland." Evan sniffled, the only sign that his emotions were getting to be almost too much. "I ended up turning to the bottle. Partying. Doing dumb shit. The coaches tried helping me, but I was beyond help, you know?"

Maggie nodded. She didn't know, but she could imagine how something so terrible like losing a child would break someone, even someone so strong as Evan.

"I ended up quitting, and one night I was . . . I was so close to the edge." A faraway look came over Evan as he stared off into the distance of the night, lost momentarily. Then he shook his head and met Maggie's eyes again as he continued, "Janie flew out to Oklahoma the following morning. She found me at my worst. Then she packed my shit together and brought me right back here with her. She . . . she saved my life."

It suddenly all started to make sense. Evan's jaded sadness that he hid so well. Jane's overprotectiveness of her little brother. Evan's reputation. Maggie remembered something he'd said to her not

238

so long ago; *I know what it's like having to keep secrets . . . It'll drive you crazy.* She hadn't known what he'd meant when he told her that while sitting on this very deck a few weeks back. Now she knew, and the thought that he'd been carrying such a heavy weight around with him while she'd been crying on his shoulder and leaning on his apparent strength to deal with her issues with Tom, well, it tore her up.

"I'm so sorry, Evan," Maggie whispered, carefully handing him back the photograph of his beautiful Hannah.

He took the picture, smiling down at it one last time before tucking it back into the safety of his wallet. Shrugging a shoulder, he picked up his beer and finished what was left before giving Maggie a sad smile. "Wow, I really know how to bring the mood down, huh?" he joked, adding a light chuckle.

Maggie smiled sadly, shaking her head as she reached for his hand again, taking them both in hers. "Thank you for telling me. It means a lot that you'd confide in me about your Hannah. So, thank you."

Evan suddenly perked up, turning to the sound of the music that was playing from inside the house. He smiled, a real, genuine smile, his glassy eyes suddenly lighting up. "I *love* this song."

Maggie listened hard, trying to make out the first few chords of the acoustic song playing from the sound system inside. "Everlong" by the Foo Fighters. She smiled. It was a great song.

"Dance with me?"

Surprised by this unexpected question, Maggie watched Evan get to his feet. Her heart suddenly jumped up into the back of her throat. He moved around the table, holding his hand out for her, and all she could do was stare at it hanging in the air between them.

"I thought this wasn't a date . . ." She smirked, meeting his eyes.

Evan looked over her head a moment, contemplation evident in his blue gaze which highlighted the hint of a smile tugging at his lips. "Can't two friends dance to 'Everlong' in the dark?"

Maggie laughed under her breath, looking down, but then she took his proffered hand, allowing him to pull her to her feet.

Evan guided her away from the table to the corner of the deck. With one hand holding hers, he placed his other hand on her waist, pulling her closer, so close their bodies were almost touching.

With a racing heart and goose bumps erupting all over her skin, Maggie looked up at Evan through her lashes, smiling shyly when his gaze dipped down to her lips like it had before their almost-kiss in the kitchen only days earlier. But this time, she was ready. She was expecting it. She wanted it. She'd never felt herself react to anyone the way she was reacting to Evan.

When his eyes met hers again, he lowered his head, inching closer and closer, and the moment their lips touched it was as if the rest of the world simply slipped away. And there, in the dim light of the lanterns and the citronella candles, with nothing but "Everlong" playing softly in the background, Evan kissed Maggie like she'd never been kissed before. And it was better than perfect; it was how it was always meant to be.

Chapter 31

Maggie was on cloud nine. The kiss. It lingered. As if Evan's lips had burned her, his tongue had marked her, his hands had branded her so for the rest of her life she would forever feel him; with one kiss he had claimed her. She was now ruined for anyone else; she knew that much was true and she didn't care.

She'd never even come close to imagining kissing another man while Tom was alive. Tom had been it for her; he'd been all she'd known and all she had ever wanted. Now, it was almost . . . *Tom who?* She felt a pang of guilt at that thought, but she quickly smothered it. She refused to feel guilty over her happiness; it'd been a long time coming and she wasn't going to apologize. This was a new Maggie. Maggie 2.0.

She didn't know what the kiss with Evan meant; she didn't want to read too much into it. For all she knew, it was just that—a kiss shared in a meaningful moment, which she would remember forever. But it wasn't just the kiss she couldn't shake, it was Evan. Her heart had shifted, and with that shift her feelings had changed, too. He'd confided something in her that no one outside of his immediate family knew; that had to mean something, right?

Pulling up to the curb outside the ice cream parlor where Jack and Katie were standing, Maggie smiled, her joy almost exploding when she noticed the two of them were holding hands. She knew not to make a big deal out of it—the last thing she wanted to do was embarrass her son—but it was difficult. Did this mean Jack had a girlfriend? He looked so happy. It was hard to believe after the state he'd been in only a couple weeks earlier. This was good. Better than good. Things were finally starting to look up, for everyone.

Jack opened the back passenger door for Katie, and she slid across the leather seat, Jack following suit. Maggie caught his eye in the reflection of the rear-view mirror and he tried so obviously to ignore her. When he chose to look out the window instead, she noticed his cheeks flushed pink, and she bit back her smile, pulling out onto the road.

"How was the movie?" she asked after a few silent moments, suddenly feeling like a creepy Uber driver.

"It was good," Katie said dreamily. "Funny . . ."

You barely even watched the film, Maggie wanted to say. Instead, she switched topics. "Did you go for ice cream?"

"We got some ice cream and then went for a walk along the dock," Jack responded, and then something passed between the two teenagers in the back which caused Katie to giggle like, well, like the schoolgirl she was.

Maggie grinned to herself, deciding that instead of the forced small talk she'd turn the radio on, anything to mask the teenage tension hanging in the air. Thankfully, only a few minutes later they were pulling up outside Jane's house.

"I'll walk you to your door," Jack said, glancing at Maggie in the rear-view mirror.

Maggie nodded, proud of her son's gentlemanly offer.

"Thanks for the ride home, Maggie." Katie smiled sweetly at her before getting out of the car, Jack trailing closely behind.

"So cute," Maggie murmured with a contented sigh as she watched them tread the stone path that led through the front yard to the porch. Of course, she didn't want to be a total creep, so when they reached the front door and she saw Jack lean in a little closer, she quickly looked away; watching her son end his first date with a kiss was not something on her list of things to do before she died.

Moments later, the front passenger door opened and Jack slid in, bringing with him a dizzying air of lust-filled happiness. Maggie glanced sideways at him as she started the engine, biting back her smile at the look on his face.

Oh boy, she thought. *He's got it bad for that girl . . .*

"Katie really likes you," Jack said after a few silent moments, flashing her a glance. "She was like, 'I wish my mom was as cool as yours,'" he repeated in a high-pitched timbre.

Maggie raised a defiant fist in the air. "Mission complete. All I ever wanted in life was to be a cool mom."

"You are a cool mom, Mom."

Tucking her now shoulder-length hair behind her ear, Maggie blushed at his compliment, his words tugging at the pained strings of her heart. Her son was well and truly back. "Thanks, honey."

She could feel him looking at her for a moment longer and when she turned toward him briefly, she saw his discerning, inky-blue eyes study her closely. "What is it?"

"I know I'm just your teenage son," he said mockingly, "but if you ever wanna talk, you know, with Dad gone and all? You know you can always talk to me, Mom."

Considering herself, she clutched the steering wheel a little tighter before quietly confessing, "Evan came over for dinner tonight and we kissed."

She turned in time to see Jack gawp at her and she swallowed hard, wondering if she'd made the right decision in telling him. His face was completely unreadable, and her anxiety flared.

"You . . . k-kissed him?" he asked, the words clearly hard for him to say.

She nodded. "I like him."

Silence settled between them as she continued driving. It wasn't heavy or light, it was nondescript and that only fueled the uncertainty roiling in Maggie's belly.

Suddenly, Jack spoke. "I think he's good for you."

Maggie did a double take, staring at her son as he looked straight ahead out the windshield.

He continued, "The way you smile when he's around . . . I haven't seen you smile like that in a long time. Not even before Dad . . ." He glanced at her then, and despite the sadness flashing in his eyes from the mention of his father, his smile was spectacular. "You deserve to be happy, Mom."

Maggie released the breath she'd been holding. She smiled again, but this time her smile faltered from the emotion overwhelming her. Reaching out, she touched his hand, squeezing it tight. She loved him more than the world, and she was so glad she had him back. He wasn't just her teenage son he was one of her two very best friends.

They drove in companionable silence through the dark, tree-lined roads, Maggie humming along to the song playing on the radio while Jack tapped out a text message on his cell, probably to the very same girl he left less than five minutes ago. Maggie smiled, but as they rounded the bend in the road, blue and red lights flashed blindingly from up ahead and she was forced to slow down.

"Is that the cops?" Jack asked, leaning closer to the windshield.

Maggie's heart sank into the pit of her belly as memories from only a few months earlier came flooding back to her, the night they'd returned home from Jack's baseball game to find the police waiting outside their house.

She hadn't realized it until right at that moment, but that night still haunted her. Her heart thundered, her palms went clammy, the skin at the base of her neck pricked as she was forced to come to a complete stop behind the car in front.

"Must be an accident," Jack said, worry evident in his tone. "There's an ambulance, too."

Maggie snapped out of her haunting memories, clearing her throat. "I hope it's nothing serious."

Jack craned his neck to the side. "Wait! Is that Evan's truck?"

"What?" Her voice was raw, broken, as if she had no air in her lungs to get the word out. But before she could even react, her son had unfastened his belt and opened his door quicker than the speed of light, anxiety emitting from him as he exploded out of the car.

"Jack!" Maggie screamed, coming to before hurrying out of the car. "Jack, wait!"

She chased after him as he weaved his way through the chaos of broken glass, a wayward bumper, two police cruisers and a *Do Not Cross* tape. She grabbed him when she got the chance, but it was too late. She gripped Jack's arm, staring at the shocking sight of Evan's shiny Dodge truck wrapped around the thick trunk of a sycamore tree on the side of the road. Smoke billowed up from the caved in hood, the windshield was shattered, the smell of burning rubber and fuel hung heavily in the air. Maggie's wide eyes searched the scene frantically, but there was no sign of Evan anywhere, and she didn't know if that was a good thing or not.

"Excuse me, ma'am, you're gonna have to step back."

Maggie gaped at the burly officer as he appeared out of nowhere, standing in front of her. "W-where is he?" she stammered, staring at the man as tears pricked her eyes. "Where is Evan?"

"You know Evan?"

She nodded quickly. "Yes . . . he was . . . he was just with me at my house. We had dinner together . . . less than half an hour ago . . . I-I don't understand." She shook her head in an attempt to make some semblance of sense of everything.

Evan had crashed his truck on the way home from her house. Had he had too much to drink? Perhaps she shouldn't have let him drive. She could have given him a damn lift back into town on her way to collect Jack.

The officer gently yet forcefully grabbed Maggie by her arm and guided her away from the horrific scene, leading her to the other side of the cruiser so she didn't have to look at Evan's mangled truck. Jack followed closely, not letting go of her, his presence comforting despite the chill coursing through her.

"It looks like he swerved," the officer said, his voice low. "Probably an animal in the road. Deer, likely. That plus this darkness . . . We've been trying to get the city to put a goddamn street light on the bend."

Maggie didn't mention Evan had been drinking. She kept her mouth shut, praying to whatever God was listening that Evan would be okay. He had to be.

"He was in a pretty bad way. They've taken him to Sacred Heart down in Manchester. His sister's been contacted."

"Shit," Maggie hissed under her breath. Turning to Jack, she looked up at him. "We should get back to Jane's, check if they need anything."

Jack nodded, grabbing her hand, and he jogged the way back to the car, pulling Maggie with him. Her legs were like jelly as she tried to keep up with him. She felt hollow, like she had no fight left in her, but she knew she had to do something. Evan was hurt. Jane would need her, need help. This was the best she could think of on the spot and, getting back into the car, she made quick work of starting the engine and performing a three-point turn, heading back toward town, toward Jane's house as fast as she could.

*

Jane was standing outside by her SUV by the time Maggie pulled up to the house. She was obviously crying and beside herself while being consoled by her husband, and Maggie didn't hesitate in getting out of the car with Jack and running down the driveway.

"Is he okay?" Maggie gasped as she reached Jane. "Are you okay?"

Jane turned, her cheeks streaked with tears and, instinctively, Maggie pulled her into her arms, glancing at Brad over her shoulder. He looked frazzled, running his hands through his hair. He shook his head, blowing out a breath, his hand resting on his wife's arm.

"Are you heading to the hospital?"

"I'm going," Jane managed through a sob. "Brad's staying here with the kids." She pulled back, wiping her tears with trembling hands. "I don't want the boys to know what's going on."

"I'll come with you," Maggie said defiantly, and when Jane went to say something, Maggie interjected. "Jane, you're *not* driving like this. I'll drive and Jack can stay here and help Brad and Katie with the boys."

"Maggie, I can't ask you to drive me to Manchester, I—"

"You're not asking me." Maggie grabbed her hand. "I'm insisting. Let's go."

Jane gave Brad another hug. Maggie kissed the top of Jack's head and, holding on to Jane's hand, she pulled her down the driveway to her car, wasting no time.

Chapter 32

Maggie followed the darkened highway toward Manchester, the glow of the car's headlights illuminating the way. Nothing but the gentle hum of the radio filled the void of silence between her and Jane, accompanied by the occasional sound of Jane's worried sighs and emotional sniffles.

"Are you okay?" Maggie asked after a beat, reaching out and touching Jane's arm. "Are you warm enough? Need me to turn the heat on?"

"Oh, I'm fine. Thanks, sweetheart." Jane shifted in her seat, sighing heavily. "I just . . . I don't even know what he was doing driving around at night so late. He's normally at home, or at the pub. He drinks a lot . . . more than he should," she added with a defeated tone. "I'm always worrying about him. I told him he could move into our house. Live in the apartment over the garage. But he refused. I hate that he's all alone in that loft over the boat shed. He *shouldn't* be alone." With another sigh, Jane whispered, "God, I hope he's okay."

Maggie gripped the steering wheel a little tighter. Now that she knew what Jane was referring to, it made her stomach knot and pull. Nerves twisted in her chest, and she knew she had to be honest with Jane. She wanted to be honest with her. "Jane, I need to tell you something."

Feeling Jane's gaze settle on her, Maggie stared at the road ahead as she continued, "Evan was at my house tonight." She flashed her a sideways glance finding Jane's face masked with confusion. She explained further. "I invited him over for dinner. To thank him for all his help with the house and . . . well, with everything. He's really been there for me over the last few weeks."

Jane blinked, releasing a breath.

Maggie turned back to the road. "He told me everything."

"He did?" The shock in Jane's voice was evident.

Maggie nodded, feeling Jane's questioning, slightly incredulous gaze burning into the side of her face. "He told me about Hannah."

"He . . . he's never told anyone about Hannah." Jane's voice was quiet and contemplative. "Wow . . . he really *does* like you."

Maggie felt tears sting her eyes as guilt suddenly settled heavily in her belly. "He had a couple beers tonight, but he seemed fine. He wasn't drunk, or anything." She shook her head, raking her teeth painfully over her bottom lip. "We were too busy talking and laughing to drink too much. We danced . . . It was perfect—"

"Wait. Evan *danced*?"

Maggie glanced at Jane to find a confused smile playing on her lips. "Yeah." She didn't know why, but for some reason she couldn't help but laugh as she admitted, "To 'Everlong.'"

Jane laughed then, and not just a small humorless giggle, but a loud barking laugh that echoed through the quiet car. And suddenly, the two women were laughing together as if it were the funniest thing they'd ever heard. But when the moment was over and the laughter died, reality settled in.

Maggie sighed. "Maybe he wasn't okay. Maybe . . . maybe I shouldn't have let him drive."

"Don't say that." Jane's hand rested on Maggie's arm. "Don't blame yourself. Evan's smart. If he'd had too much to drink, he wouldn't have gotten behind the wheel of his truck. He's responsible. Trust me."

Maggie nodded. Jane was right. Evan was fine when he'd left.

"Look, I know he drinks a little too much, and he's kind of a playboy, but he wouldn't do anything stupid." Jane's voice, although tremulous and full of emotion, was reassuring as she patted Maggie's arm. "He's going to be okay. I know he is."

"I hope you're right." Maggie managed a small smile as she glanced at her. "Because I really like him, too, Jane. And I know you're worried and scared that it may be too soon for me, but trust me when I tell you . . ." She paused, considering her words, knowing she could be about to admit more than she wanted to. But she needed Jane to know her feelings toward Evan were real. "Tom and I were over long before he passed away."

"What do you mean?"

Swallowing the lump at the back of her throat, Maggie continued with reluctance, "Evan is the only other person who knows the truth. I can't risk my boys finding out . . ."

Jane shifted beside her.

Releasing a shaky breath, Maggie continued, "Tom had been cheating on me before he died. He'd been planning on filing for divorce . . . I only found out after the accident. I had no idea."

Silence ensued.

Maggie's heart raced.

"Actually, honey, Evan already told me."

Maggie gasped at Jane's words.

"Please, don't be angry at him. He only told me when I started questioning him about the two of you. I told him I was worried that he was going to fall for you while you were still mourning the loss of your husband. He set me straight."

Glancing at Jane, Maggie met her wide eyes. "Jane, TJ and Jack cannot find out about this. It would kill them. Please, promise me—"

"Sweetheart, I promise, I . . ." Jane shook her head, clearly unable to find the words. But then her cell phone rang, interrupting the moment and, startled, she fumbled in her handbag to find the device.

"Hello!" she answered desperately. "Yes, speaking."

Listening to the one-sided conversation, Maggie stared at the road, praying that whoever it was on the other end was calling with good news.

"Yes . . . Okay . . ." Jane spoke tentatively. "I'm on my way . . . We're about fifteen minutes out . . . Okay . . ."

Maggie chewed nervously on her bottom lip.

"Thank you. Goodbye." Jane ended the call and stared down at her cell phone.

"Was that the hospital?"

"He's being prepped for surgery." Jane's voice was small and vulnerable.

Reaching across the center console, Maggie grabbed Jane's hand, holding it tight as they continued through the night with nothing more being said between them.

*

Maggie followed Jane through the emergency entrance of Sacred Heart Hospital. At this time of night, in the waiting room, there was the occasional child dressed in pajamas being comforted by a concerned parent, and the odd drunk with a suspected broken nose.

The women continued to the desk, to the nurse sitting behind the glass screen.

"Hello," Jane said huffing breathlessly. "I'm here for Evan Boyd. I'm his sister, Jane Hannigan."

Studying her computer a moment, the woman looked up, removing her glasses and offering a sad smile. "He's just gone into surgery, ma'am. I can't give you any more information. But if you'd like to take a seat I can call through to the surgical ward and let them know you're here. They'll come and collect you when he's out."

"Why don't we go find the cafeteria?" Maggie suggested,

snaking her arm around Jane's slight shoulders. "Get some coffee while we wait."

After a few beats, Jane nodded, allowing Maggie to lead her away from the desk and the two continued through to the corridor that was signed with directions to the cafeteria.

*

"I always mothered him. Even when we were kids." Jane's face broke into a wistful smile as she clutched her to-go cup of coffee between both hands. "He used to love it. Then, as he got older he acted like he hated it, but he secretly loved it. Even when he was a whole foot taller than me he'd let me boss him around when our momma was at the café and I was in charge because I was older."

Maggie smiled, sipping her coffee. She knew despite Jane's smile, the tears in her eyes were a clear reflection of how much she was hurting. Sure, she had Brad and the three children who she adored more than life itself, but Evan was also her world, her baby brother. Seeing her so despondent, not knowing whether her brother was okay or not broke Maggie's heart, and she tried so hard to keep Jane's mind off the surgery.

"I was an only child so I don't know what that's like, but I can tell you and Evan are close," she said. "And Sam and Ben obviously love him."

"Ugh!" Jane guffawed. "They *idolize* him. Katie does too. She used to follow him around when she was little like a lost puppy dog. Evan's the cool uncle." She smiled, but then her smile fell. "When he came back from Oklahoma, he was a ghost for a long time and that really hurt the kids. But I knew being around them hurt him. He never talked about it, but the kids reminded him of Hannah and what he'd lost."

Maggie frowned. "And what happened with Hailey? She just left?"

Jane shook her head, anger flaring in her blue eyes. "God, I'm so angry at her."

Jane speaking so candidly about another person, with such obvious disdain was quite surprising and so out of character—the look in her eyes alone was chilling. Maggie nodded, silently encouraging her to continue.

"Evan fell for her hard and fast, and when he told me about her I was a little skeptical to begin with. Don't get me wrong, I believe in love at first sight and falling head over heels for someone you just met. I did with Brad. But there was just something about Hailey. She was a bit of a hang-about, and she'd been with a few of Evan's teammates before getting with him. I mean, I'm not one to shame anyone for living their life, but it was a bit of a red flag. When Evan called me to tell me she was pregnant, I . . ." She shook her head, unable to continue. After a few moments silence she began again. "But when baby Hannah was born, I managed to put my feelings aside. Hailey was a great mother. And Evan . . . he just adored his baby girl. When Hannah started showing signs that something wasn't quite right, I begged him to get her checked out, and he wanted to but Hailey refused to believe there was anything wrong. She refused to take her to the doctor."

Maggie's eyes widened at that.

"Don't get me wrong. I don't doubt that she loved that little girl with everything she had, but if she'd just agreed to see a doctor then maybe . . . just maybe . . . that baby girl would have had a fighting chance." Jane stared down into her near-empty coffee cup with a faraway look, sadness clouding her. She shook her head again. "When Hannah . . . passed, Evan shut me out. He shut everyone out. I wanted to stay a little longer after the funeral to help him, to make sure he was okay, but he pushed me away. So, I came back here. I knew he was losing it. Especially after Hailey packed up and left him without even so much as an explanation. I know it must have been hard, God, I wouldn't wish it upon anyone. No mother deserves to go through that. But it was as if she didn't think it was hard for Evan." Jane sniffled, and it was then Maggie noticed the tears shining on her cheeks. "I had to sit here, on the other side of the country, and listen to all the stories and reports of Evan losing his damn mind, acting reckless and dangerous, and there was *nothing* I could do about it. He wouldn't answer my calls or texts. He ended up blocking my number. It broke my heart. I hated that he was going through something like that all by himself."

"I can't imagine dealing with the death of a child," Maggie said with a heavy sigh. "Just the thought of losing Jack or TJ . . ." She shook her head, unable to continue.

"It destroyed Evan," Jane said with a nod. "He's never been the same."

Maggie looked down at her hands, her heart breaking more and more with every one of Jane's words.

"I got a phone call one day, from one of Evan's coaches. He'd quit the team, but the team hadn't quit him. Thankfully they were still looking out for him, even though he'd tried pushing everyone away. When Phillip called me, I remember seeing his name pop up on my screen and my stomach dropped. I couldn't breathe. It was as if everything around me came to a sudden stop. I thought . . . I thought the worst."

Maggie nodded, imagining exactly what Jane had thought.

"When I answered and he told me Evan was in jail, I was so shocked and angry but so relieved. I'd expected so much worse."

"Why was he in jail?" Maggie gasped. "He didn't tell me this."

Jane gave a somewhat wry smile. "He got picked up for trying to start a drunken brawl in a bar downtown. The cops knew him, knew what had happened, and that he was looking for trouble anywhere he went. They threw his ass in jail for his own safety. And thank God they did. Otherwise, who knows? Evan probably wouldn't be here right now."

Maggie released a shaky breath, so overwhelmed with everything Jane was telling her.

"It's been a long time, and while Evan's my brother whom I love dearly, he's so different to the guy he was when he left for Oklahoma. It's heartbreaking. I lost my brother for a long time. And while he's a lot better now, he still loses himself every now and again. He thinks I don't know, but I'm not an idiot. Jewel Harbor's a small town. I know he goes around drinking the night away, going home with questionable women. But I also know he does it only so he can forget. Because he's been living with the ghost of his little girl for the last five years, and sometimes, he just needs to forget."

Hearing Jane talk about Evan's playboy ways caused a pang of painful jealousy to knot Maggie's stomach, but she ignored it as best as she could. She fully understood why Evan was the way he was, and why he did what he did, but it still hurt, because no one else knew. Locals like Barb, and the women like Cindy who hung out at Field Four every Saturday, might have assumed he was a playboy, but there was so much more to him.

"I need to tell you something."

Jane's words pulled Maggie from her thoughts, and she looked up from her hands to find her friend's blue eyes smiling at her, despite the sadness in them. "What is it?"

"I've been seeing more of the old Evan ever since you've been in town," she said, the unshed tears in her eyes dancing beneath the overhead lights. "The way he looks at you when he thinks no one's watching. The way he smiles at the mere mention of your name. Glimpses of the old Evan shine through when he's with you."

Maggie felt her heart jump, her mouth curling into a smile she couldn't stop.

"At first it scared me because I knew you were mourning a loss. I didn't want him to fall hard and fast like he has in the past . . ." Jane pressed her lips together, meeting Maggie's eyes. "But now I know about what happened between you and your late husband . . . well, it makes sense." She stopped then, spearing Maggie with a serious look. "Maggie, do you have feelings for Evan?"

Maggie contemplated Jane's question, and considered her response. Then without any further hesitation she nodded, glancing up to the ceiling as tears pricked her eyes. "Yes. I do. And it's exciting and terrifying and confusing. But yes. I like him a lot. More than I thought I could ever like another man after Tom." When a hot tear hit her cheek, she quickly wiped it away, smiling when Jane reached across the table to take both Maggie's hands in hers.

"Look, I'm not one for all that fate *mumbo jumbo*, but maybe . . . just maybe . . . the two of you were meant to find each other."

More tears hit Maggie's cheeks despite her smile. "God, I hope he's okay. I need him to be okay, Jane."

Jane nodded. "He will be. He has something to fight for now." She smiled, squeezing Maggie's hands.

"Mrs. Boyd?"

Jane and Maggie startled, turning to find a man dressed in scrubs standing in the doorway to the cafeteria. They both stood so fast their chairs almost toppled backward.

"Oh, I'm Jane Hannigan." Jane stepped forward quickly. "Evan's sister."

"Oh, my apologies." The man smiled, shaking Jane's proffered hand.

Maggie lingered closely behind, waiting anxiously with bated breath.

"I'm Doctor Brannon. Head trauma surgeon on duty tonight." He looked from Jane to Maggie questioningly.

"Oh, this is Maggie." Jane reached for her, grabbing her arm and pulling her closer without even glancing at Maggie as she continued, "Evan's *girlfriend*."

Maggie flinched at Jane's choice of label before quickly composing herself as best as she could.

The doctor smiled at Maggie. "Evan's out of surgery and he's stable. He's going to be transferred to Boston General tomorrow, but for now, he's—"

"Boston?" Jane interrupted. "Why?"

The doctor's brows knitted together in confusion, and it was then he seemed to realize Maggie and Jane hadn't been given any details of Evan's state. With a gentle smile, he pointed to the table the women had just vacated. "Shall we sit?"

Jane and Maggie followed, taking a seat opposite him, watching as he took his time to find the right words.

"Mrs. Hannigan . . . your brother suffered serious injuries tonight. Three broken ribs, a fractured pelvis, a shattered femur. There were multiple internal bleeds we were able to stop. Frankly, he's . . . lucky to be alive. It will be up to the discretion of the head surgeon in Boston, but he'll likely need reconstructive surgery on his femur, maybe a metal pin, followed by potentially months of intensive physiotherapy. He almost lost his right leg."

"Oh my goodness," Jane whispered, clutching a hand to her chest.

Maggie snaked her arm around Jane's shoulders, pulling her close. She steadied the doctor with an imploring look. "But . . . he's okay, right? He's *going* to be okay?"

Doctor Brannon managed a tight-lipped smile. "Yes. He's going to be okay. He's in recovery at the moment but when he wakes you'll be able to see him."

Sniffling, Jane wiped her tears. "Thank you, Doctor."

"From what I heard it was a hell of a crash." He looked between the two women with a small smile as he added, "My guess is he had someone watching out for him."

Maggie glanced at Jane and the two women shared a knowing smile through their tears.

Chapter 33

Maggie had been sitting in the uncomfortable plastic chair out in the hallway for three hours. She was exhausted, but there was no way she would have been able to lie down and sleep; the adrenaline coursing through her, as well as the two coffees she'd consumed in quick succession had her wired.

When the door to Evan's room opened, she looked up from the year-old gossip magazine she'd been flicking through, and saw Jane walk out with a sad smile, tear tracks staining her cheeks.

"Is everything okay?" Maggie asked, suddenly worried.

Jane smiled, stopping to take a seat in the chair beside her. "He's okay. Brad's on his way down. He collected a bag of things from Ev's loft and he'll drive down to Boston with me."

Maggie nodded. "Do you need anything? Want me to stay with the kids? Go check on the café?"

She shook her head. "I've told Joe to keep the café closed. Katie will watch the boys today. Brad and I should be back to Jewel Harbor by tonight. I just want to go down to Boston and make sure Evan is settled and comfortable, and everything's okay."

Maggie nodded again.

Jane smiled, squeezing Maggie's hand. "He wants to see you."

Feeling her heart race, Maggie looked at the door left slightly ajar. Evan was in there. She was suddenly terrified. She didn't know what state to expect to see him in. She knew she looked hideous but she wanted to see him, she wanted to see that he was okay with her own eyes. She just didn't want to upset him in any way.

"Go on." Jane encouraged her with a nudge of her shoulder. "He asked about you, asked if you knew what had happened, and when I told him you were out here in the corridor his eyes positively lit up!"

Inhaling a tremulous breath, Maggie stood, wiping the backs of her hands on her jeans before smoothing down the front of her blouse. She was still dressed in her clothes from last night. She was a mess. But Evan wanted to see her, and she desperately wanted to see him. Continuing across the way, she stopped at the door, knocking once before slowly entering inside.

When she saw him there on the bed, bruised and battered and bandaged, his right leg in a cast from hip to toe, suspended in the air, she came to a sudden stop, unable to move as she froze with shock. It wasn't until she saw Evan's blue eyes smiling at her that she was able to breathe again.

"You just gonna stand there and stare at me like I'm a goddamn piece of meat?" Evan's gruff voice teased. "Come on over here."

Managing a smile despite the emotion overwhelming her, Maggie continued toward the bed, her gaze slowly assessing every wire, every tube coming out of him and the machines they were attached to. She stopped, too scared to go any closer in fear of touching him and hurting him.

"It's okay," Evan assured with a knowing grin. "I'm okay."

Maggie shook her head in disbelief. "I'm so sorry this happened, I . . . I shouldn't have let you drive."

"What?" Evan asked, his brows knitted together. "What are you talking about?"

"You'd been drinking. You shouldn't have driven—"

"It wasn't that, Mags. Sure, I'd had a couple beers, but I was fine, nowhere near the limit." Evan interjected. "I was coming up to the bend in the road and a damn elk the size of a Jetta ran out of the thicket. I swerved. Lost control. Maybe I'd been going a little faster than I should've, but I know those roads like the back of my hand. Tonight was nothing more than an unfortunate accident." He shrugged, and the look in his eyes told her that he was being completely honest.

Suddenly, a wave of emotion Maggie couldn't control hit her hard, and a sob bubbled out from the back of her throat. Covering her face with her hands, she stood there blubbering like a damn baby. She hated herself for it. He didn't need her tears. But she couldn't help herself.

"Hey, hey."

She felt his hand touch her arm, soothing her skin with a gentle sweep of his calloused fingertips. Looking through her fingers, Maggie sniffled, swallowing back her sobs.

"C'mere." He pulled her closer.

"No, I can't." She shook her head. "I don't want to hurt you."

"Babe, I'm so hopped on pain meds right now, you're not gonna hurt me," he said through a chuckle. "Now, come here and sit with me." He patted the space on the mattress beside him.

He'd called her babe. No one had ever called her babe before. She tried so hard not to think too much of the term of endearment. He was, after all, hopped up on painkillers. But it still made her skin tingle.

Biting back her smile, she studied the spot next to him, checking for any potential danger or wayward wires. "Are you sure?"

"Please." Evan nodded. "I want you close."

He wanted her close? His words did something to her that she hadn't been prepared to feel. Her heart tugged hard in her chest and, holding her breath, she pulled herself up to sit on the bed beside him, so tentative, so cautious so as not to hurt him.

"Is that okay?"

Evan placed his hand on her thigh, squeezing tight with a smile. "Perfect."

She covered his hand with hers, her eyes zeroing in on the identification wristband he was wearing.

After a few beats, Evan said so quietly she almost missed it, "Tell me I didn't imagine it."

She looked at him then, finding his eyes full of hope and uncertainty. "What?"

"That kiss," he said, his gaze drifting to her lips.

Her heart felt as if it was thumping in her ears. Her cheeks burned. She smiled, shaking her head. "You didn't imagine it. We kissed. And we danced to 'Everlong' . . ." She tried not to laugh at that last piece of information.

"Smooth . . ." He closed his eyes a moment, smiling, as if he was allowing her words to sink in. But when he looked at her again, trepidation shone in his eyes. "They're schleppin' me down to Boston," he muttered with a forlorn sigh. "I don't even know for how long. The doctor thinks it could be a month, maybe even two."

"I can come visit you." Maggie offered a reassuring squeeze of his hand.

Evan sighed again. "I'd rather you didn't."

"Oh . . ."

"I don't mean I don't wanna see you. It's just . . ." He paused, raking his teeth over his bottom lip, a look of serious contemplation coming over him as he considered something. "I need to use this time to get my shit together. Not just this—" He indicated the cast on his leg. "I mean everything. Jane suggested a therapist . . . to talk through my past."

Maggie knew what he was referring to without him having to say it. She didn't want to go one, maybe two months without seeing him, but she knew he had to do what he had to do.

"I . . . I wanna be good for you, Maggie," Evan said so suddenly he startled her. "After everything you've been through, you deserve the best. And I know I can be good for you, but I just need to deal with my past so I can move on, so I can be happy again."

"You deserve to be happy again, Evan." Maggie stared deep into his eyes, finding nothing but sincerity within them.

"You make me happy." His brows raised in hope as he asked, "Will you wait for me?"

She smiled, leaning in even closer, so gentle so as not to aggravate the cuts and bruises marring his skin. "I'm not going anywhere . . ."

Lifting his hand from her thigh, Evan gently cupped Maggie's cheek, his thumb grazing the curve of her bottom lip, his eyes staring at her mouth. "I ain't gonna kiss you. My mouth tastes like blood," he whispered, his words causing her to flinch.

He smiled, then continued in a hushed voice she could feel all the way through to her soul, "But I need you to know all I want right now is to kiss the hell outta you and never stop."

Fresh tears stung Maggie's eyes as she smiled at him. Slowly, she inched closer and closer until their mouths were a mere hair's breadth apart. She wanted to kiss him, desperately. She'd never wanted anything more. But she didn't. Instead, she craned her neck and placed a whisper-soft kiss onto his forehead, allowing herself to linger a moment longer, to really breathe him in and bask in everything Evan, as the world around them melted into oblivion.

*

It was almost midday by the time Maggie arrived home from Manchester. She was an exhausted, emotional wreck.

Thankfully, Brad had dropped Jack and TJ home on his way to Manchester so she didn't have to bypass Jane's house to collect the boys. But she was scared to see them, scared to see the knowing look of horror in their eyes. This was too fresh. They'd not long ago lost their father, and now Evan, a man who had become somewhat of a male role model to the both of them, had come so close to death in the same way their father had perished.

After she pulled up outside the house, she chose to sit inside the car for a moment, collecting what she could of her emotions, her wits, her composure, before heading inside. She couldn't risk the boys seeing her in such a state. She'd cried the entire way home. The roads had blurred through the glassy haze her tears had made of the morning sun streaming through the trees. She didn't know how she'd even made it back in one piece. But she had.

When she knew she couldn't sit in the car all day, that the boys would have seen her as she pulled up, she forced herself out, wiping her damp cheeks with the back of her hand. By the time she made it up the back steps and in through the mudroom, she realized how quiet and still the house was. With a deep breath, she smoothed down the front of her shirt and lifted her chin in a show of defiance she didn't feel. She continued through the door to the living room, finding Jack and TJ on the sofa watching *Space Jam*.

"Hey, guys," Maggie said softly, touching the back of Jack's head.

Both TJ and Jack jumped up, their faces fraught with the kind of worry and concern kids their age shouldn't feel. She was the parent. They were the kids. They weren't supposed to worry. She was the one who was supposed to worry, and protect them from the horrible realities of life.

"Mom, is Coach okay?" TJ asked in a wavering voice so small it broke her heart.

"Yeah, honey." She smiled, gathering him in her arms. "He's going to be okay."

She felt his tense body relax.

Meeting Jack's eyes while still holding TJ, Maggie continued, "He's going to stay in a hospital in Boston for a while so he can get well. But he'll be back in a month or two, and he'll be better than ever."

TJ pulled out of her embrace, looking at her with tears in his inky-blue eyes. "I was so scared that he was gonna be . . . dead. Like Daddy."

Maggie shook her head. "He's okay. I promise."

He sniffled, wiping his nose with the cuff of his sweater sleeve.

"How about you go get a Kleenex?" Maggie smiled at him.

Nodding, TJ turned and ran through the doorway to the kitchen, and she couldn't help but laugh at the honking sound of him blowing his nose. She offered Jack a wry smile as she got back up to her feet.

Jack pressed his lips together in the semblance of a smile, looking at her closely with an all-consuming gaze, his brow furrowed with concern. "You okay, Mom?"

Her tears managed to get the better of her, as the events of the last twenty-four hours came crashing down on top of her.

She wasn't okay. It had been a lot, and it had managed to reopen the wounds she was still recovering from. But she couldn't tell him that. So, instead, she went against everything she believed in and she broke down, right there in front of her fifteen-year-old son. He pulled her into his arms, holding her tight, stopping her from crumbling completely. Suddenly the child was the adult, and the adult was an inconsolable mess.

Epilogue

Three months later . . .

Summer had settled nicely in Jewel Harbor. The sun was warm as it shone down from its periwinkle sky. The scent of the ocean lingered in the air. It was a magical place to spend the long August days, and an even more magical place to relax on the warm August nights.

Maggie spent her summer days working at the café, or doing the little jobs she had left to do around the house. She spent what time she could with her boys, but Jack had gotten a job at the movie theater, and when he wasn't working he was off with Katie; their teenage romance was going strong. TJ was usually too busy with one of his friends from school, off on their bikes doing God only knows what ten-year-old boys do with their days.

The summer had been one of new beginnings.

Maggie had received a letter from Manchester College, accepting her onto their design course. She was due to start classes after Labor Day. She'd never been so nervous in all her life, but she was also excited. She drove TJ, Jack and Katie into the city to check out the campus, and afterwards they stopped in at the Target Supercenter and bought their stationery supplies for the new school year, Maggie included.

Jack, who had turned sixteen in July, had been learning how to drive, much to Maggie's dismay. He was a great baseball player, a good student, he could even cook. He was what one might call a natural talent at most things he did. But driving? It wasn't one of his strengths. Maggie was seriously starting to worry that he'd spent too much time over the years playing those damn video games. She had to keep reminding him that *The Fast and the Furious* was a movie franchise and *not* real life.

While faced with life on her own, Maggie finally managed to find herself, the Maggie she'd lost all those years ago. And when she found herself, she realized, once and for all, that she was going to be okay.

The hate she'd harbored for Tom had dissipated. And while the memory of what he did still hurt her, and it likely always would, all she had to do now was look at her two beautiful boys. Tom was a huge part of them. Without him she wouldn't have them. And she couldn't go on hating the father of her sons; the man who had given her the greatest gift she could ever have asked for.

Her thoughts often drifted to Evan's poor darling Hannah, and it made her realize just how short life can be, and just how grateful she was that Tom had given her the two boys she cherished more than life itself.

*

"Oh no!" Jane cried from somewhere in the kitchen.

Maggie stopped wiping down the tabletops and hurried back through the swinging doors, finding Jane standing in a puddle of water which looked to have leaked from under the industrial sink.

"That damn pipe's burst again!" She threw her hands in the air in frustration. "I'm going to call Steve," she muttered, pulling her cell phone from the pocket of her skirt and carefully wading through the water so as not slip as she went back out to the front to call Steve, the local plumber.

Maggie continued forward, stepping carefully through the puddle of water. She crouched down, opening one of the cabinet doors underneath the sink and noticed a light trickle of water.

"Steve's gone camping with his kids. He left for White Lake this morning!" Jane huffed, coming back through to the kitchen in a complete tizzy. "Maybe I can call Brad and see if he can duck out of his shift and come—"

"Have you got a wrench?" Maggie asked over her shoulder, effectively silencing Jane's words.

"A *what*?"

Rolling her eyes, Maggie couldn't help but laugh. "A wrench!"

"I have no idea what that is . . ." Jane moved to the big locker on the other side of the kitchen, opening the metal door. "We have this here tool kit. Brad left it behind in case of emergencies. Ha." She snorted. "Like I'd know what do with it."

Maggie flashed her friend a wry glance, opening the metal box. She rifled through its haphazard contents before finally locating a wrench, albeit a very rusted one. With the tool in hand, she kneeled down, cringing as the cold water soaked through her jeans. Leaning in through the slight cabinet opening, she searched the dimly lit space for the shut-off valve. It was there somewhere. She narrowed her eyes and managed to find it, reaching her hand in almost blindly. After a few twists of the compression nut the water stopped seeping out of the join, but she gave it a couple more twists just to be sure.

"Can you turn the faucet? See if the water's still coming out?" she yelled back at Jane, waiting until she heard the movement in the pipes.

"Yeah, there's water," Jane responded.

"This should hold it until you can get the plumber to come in and take a look." Maggie exhaled a breath, carefully maneuvering

267

herself back out of the small space. Pushing her hair back from her face, she smiled victoriously up at Jane who was watching her with wide eyes full of wonder.

"How did you know to do that?" she asked with a gasp.

Maggie chuckled under her breath, remembering back a few months to a moment when she was dressed only in a towel with shampoo stinging her eyes. "Actually, your brother showed me."

A small, wistful smile pulled at Jane's lips and a contemplative silence fell between the two women.

Right then, the bell above the door to the café jingled, making Jane jump. She hurried to serve the new customer, but lost her footing and slipped in the water, falling into a heap right on top of Maggie. The two tangled women, shocked at first, suddenly broke out into a bout of uncontainable, howling laughter, Jane still on top of Maggie who was now drenched from head to toe from the water on the floor.

The small bell that sat next to the cash register chimed three times. Whoever was waiting was most definitely not patient.

"Oh, don't get your damn panties in a wad!" Jane muttered through stifled laughter, trying to heave herself up.

"You go." Maggie sniggered, helping to push her up to her feet. "I'll mop up in here."

Jane fixed herself as best as she could, smoothing down the front of her now soaked skirt before hurrying back through to the front of the café, her cheery customer service voice ringing through the air.

Maggie smiled to herself, looking around at the mess. She managed to make it to her feet, her Keds sliding over the wet tile as she stepped carefully across to the cupboard that held the mop and bucket and all the other cleaning supplies.

After mopping up the water, and straightening down the front of her blouse which was so wet it clung to her skin, Maggie smoothed her hair back from her face and walked out to help Jane with whatever she needed. But just as she exited through

268

the swinging doors, she came to an abrupt standstill at the sight of Jane sobbing quietly in the arms of her brother.

"Why didn't you tell me you were coming back today?" Jane managed as she trembled. "I would have thrown a party!"

"That's precisely why I didn't tell you." Evan rolled his eyes at her, shaking his head before pressing another kiss to the top of her head.

He was back? Maggie couldn't help but blink hard in case it was her imagination playing tricks on her again. But it wasn't her imagination. He was real. Standing right there in the flesh, dressed in a pair of worn jeans and a crisp white T-shirt that hinted at his sun-kissed skin, was Evan, the air around him illuminated like a halo.

"E-Evan?" Maggie whispered under her breath.

At that, Evan looked up from where he had his face buried in his sister's hair. His blue eyes shined so bright and when his gaze met Maggie's from across the way, there was a sparkle within them she'd never seen before. He smiled, and that smile took her breath away. He looked healthy, relaxed, and so, so happy.

"You okay?" he mouthed.

Maggie could feel her own infuriating tears threaten to fall. But she swallowed the lump of emotion and smiled back at him, nodding to let him know that she was okay. She was now better than okay. He nodded back. He was okay, too. And so, she stood back and watched the brother and sister reunite, biding her time before she could go running into his strong arms.

*

Maggie added the finishing touches to the potato salad—parsley sprinkled on top, just like her mom always did. She smiled to herself, placing a serving spoon into the bowl and picking it up with both hands to take outside. When she turned, however, she stopped suddenly. Evan was standing in the doorway.

He had his arms up above his head, his hands gripping the top of the doorframe. His navy Red Sox T-shirt climbed up slightly above the waistband of his jeans, revealing a glimpse of toned muscles.

Averting her eyes, she snapped out of her inappropriate reverie, feeling her cheeks flame.

"Need a hand?" he asked with a cocky smirk.

She raised a brow, biting back her smile as she remembered the first time they'd met at the hardware store. He'd asked her that very question while her ass was in the air as she searched the floor for the wayward nails she'd dropped.

Shaking her head, Maggie looked down at the potato salad in her hands. "No. This is the last of it."

Evan nodded. Looking at the bowl, a slight crease appeared between his brows. He stepped forward, moving toward her, the limp in his gait a painful reminder of the crash that almost killed him, the limp which would likely stay with him for the rest of his life. Taking the bowl from her, he placed it onto the counter before resting his hands on her hips. He looked down at her with all seriousness in his blue eyes.

He'd been back two days, and for those two days he'd barely left Maggie's side. He'd stayed each night . . . on the couch, of course. At least until Maggie knew the boys were sound asleep, at which point she would help him upstairs and into her room where they would sleep in one another's arms.

"Thank you," he said after a few long beats.

Maggie's brows creased at his words. "For what?"

He studied her closely, his eyes flitting between hers, dropping down to her lips and back again, taking in every square inch of her face before whispering, "For letting me in."

Maggie grabbed the hem of his T-shirt, tears burning the backs of her eyes. She swallowed the painful lump of emotion in her throat. "Thank you for putting back together my broken pieces."

"We've both been broken, Maggie," Evan continued. "And I know

it's gonna take a while but when you're ready to . . . to love again . . ."
He smiled hopefully. "I don't have a lot to give, but I know how
to love with all that I have, and I hope you might consider me."

Consider him? She wanted to laugh. There was nothing to
consider. She already knew, without a doubt, that Evan was the
only man she wanted to risk loving again. Hell, he already owned
her heart, and she was just about ready to give him every other
piece of her, too.

Her eyes brimmed with tears. She smiled so wide it hurt her
cheeks. When a tear slipped down, trailing her cheek, he reached
forward and wiped it away with the pad of his thumb. The two
stared at one another until their lips were less than an inch
apart. But their moment was then rudely interrupted by a loud,
thundering explosion from outside, causing them both to jump.

"What the hell was that?" Maggie gasped, placing a hand over
her chest where her heart had just about stopped.

"Brad brought fireworks. Said he wanted to make up for me
missing our annual Fourth of July barbecue," Evan said with a
roll of his eyes.

"Isn't that . . . illegal?" Maggie quirked a brow.

Evan grinned. "Have you met Brad?"

She giggled, and he took her hand in his, leading the way out
of the house.

Outside, the purple sky was illuminated with flashes of bright
colors. Cheers, hollers, and hoots of joy rang through the air as
everyone crowded down by the edge of the water, watching with
awed reverie as fireworks exploded high up in the sky.

Evan limped unsteadily as they continued down the embankment to join everyone, Maggie watching him carefully in case he
lost his footing.

The moment they joined the others, they were forced apart
when Brad pulled Evan into a manly embrace, the two laughing
and joking together like brothers.

Maggie checked her boys. She found Jack and Katie standing

together, his arm around her waist as they smiled up at the sky, Katie's head resting on his shoulder. TJ was jumping up and down in excitement with Ben and Sam, the three boys squealing with delight at the spectacular light show up above.

She moved in next to Jane who was beaming with wonder at the sky. Jane glanced at her with a loving smile, her arm wrapping around Maggie's shoulders. Maggie squeezed in closer resting her head on her friend's shoulder.

Looking up as the sky exploded into a kaleidoscope of colors, Maggie realized just how perfect her life was now. A year ago, she'd been a different person, living a different life which, unbeknownst to her, was hanging by a thread. The last twelve months had been the toughest of her life. Losing her husband so suddenly. Discovering the lies and the betrayal. Raising two boys on her own. Moving away. But everything that had happened, had happened for a reason, and it had only made her stronger. And now, she had a whole new life in front of her, one she couldn't wait to live.

Feeling something graze her hand, Maggie turned to see Evan sidle up beside her. He didn't look at her, his gaze was fixed firmly on the sky above. But when she felt his pinkie brush hers before he hooked her finger with his, the hint of a smile ghosted over his lips before he flashed her a knowing sideways glance. She returned his smile, her heart jolting in her chest. He looked back up at the fireworks and that same trademark cocky smirk lingered, as if he knew a secret he'd never tell. But the thing was, she knew his secret. He loved her. And she knew that because she loved him, too.

Maggie had this way of feeling everything Evan felt. Like he was a part of her. As if he was a piece that had been missing in her life. A piece she hadn't realized had been missing until now. Jane had been right. The two had been destined to find one another, and Maggie was so thankful that they had.

Maggie's gaze trailed up to the sky and she smiled to herself when she realized she had found her happiness again. She may have taken the long way to get there, but she was finally home.

Acknowledgements

Firstly, I would like to thank my OG editor, Abi, for taking on this idea during its very early stages. Women's fiction was a new genre for me, but Abi believed in my idea, and she believed in me. Then she left me to have a baby, but I guess I can't take that personally now, can I? But seriously, thank you, Abi for all you've done, and I hope to work with you again in the future.

When Dushiyanthi took over from Abi, I was cautious at first because I know, at times, I'm not always an easy author to work with. But Dushi championed this book from its very rough first draft, and she helped me turn it into a beautiful story that I adore, so thank you, Dushi, and thank you to all the team at HQ and HarperCollins.

A huge thank you to a few incredibly talented fellow authors who read the first few chapters of this story and gave me some invaluable feedback; Louisa Duvall, Jem McCusker, Annie Bucknall, Carrie Molachino, you ladies rock and I cannot thank you enough for welcoming me into your small circle of excellence.

Thank you, as always, to Jackie and Karryn for always being there to listen to me bitch and moan, and to bounce ideas off at all times of the day or night. I know I'm not always present, but I appreciate you two more than you'll ever know.

To Michael and Niall; the two constants in my life. You make me want to be the best I can possibly be, and I love you both more than you will probably ever even begin to understand.

Lastly, to you, my intrepid reader . . . a million thank yous will never be enough. I write because I love it, and I'd still do it even if no one bothered to read my stories. But just knowing that you're there, reading along, rooting for my characters, getting angry at their decisions, and loving the worlds I create as much I love creating them, it is just so humbling. I spent the best part of my 37 years wishing to one day do exactly this, and my dream has become my reality. I honestly cannot thank you enough for believing in me enough to take the time to read what I write. I love connecting with my readers, so please do join me on social media:

Facebook: @ShannMcPherson
Reader Group: www.facebook.com/groups/shannssquad/
Instagram: @Shann_McPherson
Twitter: @Shann_McPherson
Website: www.shannmcpherson.com

Finally, reviews help lesser-known authors like me gain visibility in an overwhelmingly crowded market. If you enjoyed reading Maggie's story, The Long Way Home, please consider leaving a review; I'd be eternally grateful.

**Keep reading for an excerpt
from *Sweet Home Montana* . . .**

Prologue

Ten years ago . . .

I'm the kind of girl who's been dreaming of her wedding day for most of her life. The dress, the flowers, the groom. When I was a little girl, I used to sneak up into the attic and play dress-up with my mom's wedding gown from the Seventies, twirling around in the beauty of the last light of day shining in through the tiny windows, catching the dust particles floating through the air like glitter. In that moment, as a wide-eyed ten-year-old with my whole life ahead of me, it was almost as if dreams could really come true.

Fast forward ten years, and here I am, staring at my own reflection, trying so hard to rack my brain as to who the woman looking back at me even is. Sure, she looks like me. She has my honey blonde hair, and the same gray eyes with flecks of blue and gold, but I don't know her. Standing there in a white dress, gripping a bouquet of wild flowers as if it's her lifeline, the woman staring back at me is a relative stranger, and for some reason it makes my heart jump up into the back of my throat. I can't breathe. It isn't right. There's something seriously wrong. This is my wedding. I'm marrying my best friend, the love of my life. This is the day I used to dream about. I'm a bride. I'm supposed to be blushing, not barely breathing.

"You ready, sweetheart?"

I jump, pulling myself from the overwhelming thoughts consuming me from the inside. Turning, I find my father standing in the doorway, his imposing frame filling the space. He's dressed in an impeccable black suit, a matching Stetson— the good one he saves for formals and funerals alike—perched upon his head. He looks handsome, and proud, and my uncertainty quells when I meet his eyes to see such adoration within his penetrating gaze.

I manage a nod, swallowing the lump of trepidation that sits in the back of my throat. Bunching up the heavy lace train of my dress, I cross the room, staring at the hardwood floor with every tentative step I take. Dad stops me. Reaching out, he tucks his forefinger beneath my chin, forcing my eyes to his, and for a long moment he regards me closely, and I'm almost certain he can see straight through me.

"You know," he begins, his deep voice hushed as he continues, "you don't have to—" With an imploring gaze, he stops himself, silencing whatever it was he was going to tell me.

"What?" I press, my brows knitting together. I'm almost positive I know what he was about to say, but I just need to hear him say it. If he says it, then I know it can't be wrong.

But he doesn't say it. Instead, he presses his lips together in the semblance of a smile, shaking his head dismissively. "You look beautiful, sweetheart. Just like your mother."

My heart stops at that.

My mother.

I blink a few times as a hazy memory flashes through my mind.

I'm seven years old and I've just had a bath, the scent of my favorite bubblegum bubble wash lingers in the damp air. I'm sitting at the vanity in the bathroom and my mother is standing behind me, combing the tangles from my hair, a wistful smile playing on her lips, illuminating her effortless beauty.

"What do you want to be when you grow up, Quinny?" she asks.

I meet her eyes in the mirror, answering matter-of-factly, "A princess."

She laughs, a musical lilt resonating throughout the space, but then a sudden seriousness comes over her, one that she tries desperately to hide with a forced smile that doesn't reach her eyes. "Will you promise me something, darling girl?"

"What is it, Mommy?"

My mother sits down on the bench seat beside me, smoothing the backs of her delicate fingers over my chubby cheek, a faraway gaze in her eyes. "Promise me, whatever you do, never forget to chase your dreams."

I notice a sadness come over her, one I've never seen before. In her eyes there's a sheen that reflects the soft downlights shining from above the mirror. I blink at her, unsure what she means. And, because I'm only seven, I simply offer a smile, craning up to place a kiss to her cheek. "Okay, Mommy."

I wish I'd known more. Maybe I could have saved her. Maybe, just maybe, less than a year later she wouldn't have taken to her wrists with a razor blade.

"Sweetheart?"

I blink hard, shaking my head free of my memory, finding Dad looking at me, concern evident within his inky eyes. As Mom's haunting words echo throughout my mind, my chest heaves to keep up with my suddenly racing heart. A cold sweat beads at my nape. Tears threaten what little composure I have left. My eyes flit frantically from side to side, for what? I don't even know.

"Quinny?" Dad steps in, his large hands enveloping my upper arms and gently pulling me closer to him.

I find his eyes, the safety and familiarity within them, and just like that my anxiety dissipates enough for me to catch my breath. "I c-can't—" I shake my head. "I can't do this," I cry.

He stares at me a long moment, studying me, and then he simply nods.

*

I've left a bunch of times. I can't even count how many. In the three years I've been away at college, I've stood in this very spot in the center of the bustling departure terminal of Great Falls International so many times before, looking my father in his eyes as we fumble our way through goodbye. But never before have I stood here looking at my father with such a resolute finality. This goodbye feels like it might just be forever, and the more I try desperately to swallow that painful lump of emotion that's seemed to wedge its way into the back of my throat, the more the tears sting my eyes.

Dad clears his throat, glancing away a moment before meeting my gaze. He lifts a large hand, scrubbing his stubbled chin, for lack of anything else to do with his hands. "I'll see you for Thanksgiving."

I hesitate a moment, averting my gaze from his eyes, which have always been able to see straight through me. And, although I'm almost certain he knows, I can't risk him seeing the truth. That he won't be seeing me for Thanksgiving. That I probably won't even be home for Christmas. That I don't know if I can ever come back. Not after what I did yesterday. Call me a coward, but my leaving is what's best for everyone.

I nod once, lifting my chin again, and I force a smile through the overwrought sadness that's clawing at me from the inside. "Thanksgiving," I manage, my voice wavering.

He lifts his faded brown Stetson from his head momentarily, ruffling a hand through his salt and pepper hair, which is far more salt than pepper, nowadays, thanks to me. His dark, penetrating gaze steadies me, and in that moment, he says so much with just one look.

"In life, it doesn't matter where we go, or how long we're gone for. What matters is that we never forget where we come from, so no matter what, we can always go home." Royal Wagner is a man of few words. A stoic man who stands at six-foot-three. Imposing and intimidating in every sense of the word. And yet, I find myself completely taken aback by what he's just said to me. So much so that I can't possibly stop my infuriating tears from breaking free, trailing down over my cheeks.

Dad closes the distance, his strong arms wrapping around me and pulling me to him. And I go willingly, holding on to him so tight, burying my face into his chest and breathing him in as more tears fall. When the final boarding call for my flight to Newark rings throughout the vast terminal, I find myself instinctively fisting the fleecy material of his vest, gripping it tight as if I can't bear to let him go. And I can't. I don't want to. But I have to.

"I'll call you," I say through a sob, my broken voice muffled by his flannel shirt. "Every day."

Dad presses a kiss to the top of my head, quietly shushing me, and I could stay like this forever in the arms of the man who has always been my hero. But I know I can't. And, reluctantly, I force myself to pull away. I have to. If I don't, I might never leave.

I swipe at the tear tracks staining my cheeks with the cuff of my New York University sweatshirt, unable to meet my father's eyes as I crouch down to collect my backpack from the floor. And with my gaze fixed on the shiny tile, I press my fingers to my lips, blowing him a quick kiss before turning quickly and hurrying toward my gate, unable to chance a single glance over my shoulder in his direction. Seeing him standing there will only break my already shattered heart. And despite the crippling, self-inflicted pain of leaving my father and my whole world behind, I know it's for the best. It has to be.

Chapter 1

I navigate the Monday morning crowds treading the Fifth Avenue sidewalk, balancing a double-shot Americano, my designer handbag and a thirty-page new-build proposal I was supposed to have read over the weekend for today's monthly sales meeting. I didn't read the proposal. In fact, I didn't even take it out of its perfectly bound folder. And as I hurry into the marble lobby of my office building with a throbbing head, I wish I had read it. Especially last night, instead of consuming an entire bottle of pinot noir while watching *Real Housewives* reruns like the sad, single, almost-thirty-year-old that I am.

Once inside the packed elevator car, awkward silence ensues as we ascend, save for a few people obliging in amicable yet obviously forced conversation with others they'd probably rather avoid. My cell phone chimes loudly three times, bringing with it a few eye-rolls from the people surrounding me, but I ignore the new messages, flashing an apologetic smile at those around me when it chimes one more time. There's no way I can manage my phone, coffee, handbag, and documents. Whoever it is can wait.

I stare straight ahead at the mirrored doors, exhaling a defeated sigh of resignation when I'm forced to look directly at my own reflection. The morning rain has caused my honey blonde hair to frizz and my mascara to run. But I shrug a nonchalant shoulder. At least I managed to make it into the office today. My bed was feeling awfully warm and cozy when my alarm went off. I glance up at the floor counter above the doors, watching as it ticks by, mocking me with every floor we pass.

Do I hate my job? No. My job, my life is what most dreams are made of. The perfect apartment on one of the best cobblestone streets in Tribeca. An enviable designer handbag collection, shoes, too. But lately I've found myself trapped within a funk I just can't seem to crawl my way out of. I don't know what it is. I suppose it could be the dreaded three-zero looming right around the corner.

When the elevator car stops with a sudden and unexpected jolt, I'm knocked by the woman beside me, causing me to lose my balance. And, in a flurry so fast I can't possibly prevent it from happening, lukewarm coffee is soaking through the delicate silk of my shirt as the documents I was holding on to fall from my hand and scatter across the elevator floor.

I pan down to take in the state of my shirt, to the mess on the floor, as impatient people push past me on their way out of the doors, paying no mind to me or my obvious dilemma.

I sigh, my shoulders sagging in resignation.

Sadly, this is my life.

Did I mention I hate Mondays?

*

After attempting to clean myself up in the bathroom, I'm so late to the sales meeting, I can't help but feel all eyes on me, looking me up and down with thinly veiled incredulity as I make my way into the boardroom twenty minutes after go-time, slipping into the only available chair right by Mr. Hawkins, the chairman of one of the most prestigious brokerage firms on the East Coast.

My cell chimes twice, interrupting Keith from our marketing department, as he talks to a detailed presentation on the year-to-date advertising spend. When his eyes flit in my direction, I offer him an apologetic nod as I take out my diary, scribbling some important points. But then I catch my assistant, Oliver, watching me with wide eyes and an obvious smirk pulling at the corners of his mouth as he assesses the glaringly obvious coffee stain on my shirt, accompanied by my frizzy, unruly hair. And it takes all I have not to throw my pen at his head from the opposite side of the glossy teak table.

*

"What on earth happened to you?" Oliver asks with a chuckle as he hurries behind me on my way out of the meeting.

I flash him a warning glare over my shoulder. "Don't even ask," I mutter through gritted teeth, trying my best to cover the brown stain on my silk shirt with my leather-bound diary. My phone vibrates, and I look down at the screen to see a blocked number calling. It's the sixth time so far this morning and they haven't even bothered to leave one message. *Take a damn hint, buddy.* I decline the call, noticing another three new text messages only adding to the myriad other messages already waiting for my attention.

"Is this Versace?" Oliver gasps incredulously, pulling my attention away from my phone as he tugs gently on my blouse.

"Yes," I answer sharply, stopping momentarily to collect a stack of copies from one of the interns' desks. "Can you please send for a new shirt from Saks. Black." I bark my order slightly more abruptly than I had intended before softening the blow with a wavering smile. "I'm sorry. I'm meeting Shareeq at eleven o'clock, and I can't show up like this."

With Oliver hot on my heels, I continue through the length of the bustling sales floor, toward my corner office. The office I've worked my butt off to secure. The office that means that I've made it. Glass walls, glass doors, floor-to-ceiling windows that look out over the concrete jungle that is Manhattan, providing an awe-inspiring view of the Chrysler Building reaching high up into the drab gray October sky. It feels like only yesterday I was tucked away in a cubicle by the fire escape doors, head buried in client cold-calling sheets. Now, here I am, in a glass box with a nice view, my name branded across the door in three-inch gold lettering.

"Someone's a little testy this morning," Oliver says from behind me, a teasing lilt to his voice.

"Yes. *Someone* is a little testy." I turn offering a droll look. "In case you haven't noticed"—I point to the stain on my shirt. "*Someone* didn't get to enjoy her morning coffee . . ."

Oliver chuckles.

My phone chimes again with another new text message and I hold it up in the air between us. "Is there a new listing I'm not aware of?"

He shakes his head with a shrug, taking my diary from me and placing it onto the console table beside the white leather chaise in the corner of the room.

"My phone is going nuts," I murmur under my breath, shaking my head to myself as I take my seat at my desk. I power up my computer, but when I click on my inbox, reading the subject line of my most recent email received less than an hour ago, an involuntary gasp escapes me, and suddenly it's as if I can't even breathe.

Dear Miss Wagner,

I ran into Adam Delaney of CRTJ on Friday evening while I was dining with some associates at the Morrisey Club. We got talking about Prince Street. He raised some valid points about your suitability to take on the project. CRTJ specialize in the new-build market, and they have a dedicated project team for this type of listing.

Mr. Delaney also mentioned that he has firsthand experience with similar developments, particularly in the Tribeca area. He was also the sole listing agent for Broadway Towers, and sold more than 65% of all units at full ask or above within three weeks of the listing date.

Unfortunately, after much deliberation with my team, we feel it is in our best interest to go with Mr. Delaney and his team at CRTJ. I do hope there are no hard feelings. While I believe you're a tremendous agent, and I can't wait to work with you on future projects, we just feel Adam and his team will take better care of our needs during this time.

Please feel free to contact my assistant, Leilani, if you require anything further from me.

Kind regards,

Mihir Shareeq, Head of Operations, BSG

"Son of a *bitch*!"

"What?" Oliver turns quickly, his face fraught with concern as he leans in closely, gawping over my shoulder.

"Adam Delaney . . ." I say his name in some sort of a daze as I scan the length of the email again and again, going through a plethora of emotions with each and every word. "He just– He just *stole* Prince Street."

I'm just about ready to grab my computer monitor and throw it straight through the damn plate glass window, down onto Madison Avenue. My heart races as panic begins to claim me from the inside out, and I look around for something, anything, I don't even know what.

"He can't do that!" Oliver shrieks indignantly, his voice pitchy and piercing. "BSG signed with *you*!"

"No." I shake my head as the weight of the world comes crashing down upon me. Burying my face in my hands, I could just about cry, and I probably would be crying right now if I wasn't so pissed off. "They *didn't* sign. That was my eleven o'clock with Shareeq."

Oliver says nothing as a tense and heavy silence rings through the air.

"Can you please go out and get me a coffee from the café downstairs?" I say, smoothing my hair back from my face as I take a deep, fortifying breath, hoping like hell it helps to provide some semblance of clarity so that I can deal with this situation effectively and rationally. "I need to figure out what the *hell* I'm going to do."

"I'll get Shareeq on the phone for you." Oliver moves quick smart, grabbing me a bottle of Fiji Water from the small refrigerator built into my closet. And that's what I love about him. He just knows what to do and when to do it. I don't even have to ask half the time. He's good in a crisis. Me? Not so much. In fact, I often have no idea what I'm doing. I'm just good at faking it.

I started at Hawkins Group fresh out of grad school with a drive like no other. And in that time, I've managed to work my way up the corporate ladder. From intern to assistant, to junior broker, to broker, to senior broker where I'm now in the top ten in all of Manhattan. I've fought hard over the years to make it to the top. I've sacrificed so much. Almost everything. And I'm damn good at my job. Ruthless at times, or so I've been told, but real estate is still very much a man's world in this city, and sometimes only the strong survive, which is why it is imperative that I keep my cool right now. I can't allow my emotion to show, despite my internal panic. I won't let Adam win.

Adam Delaney has had it in for me ever since a client chose me to list his thirty-million-dollar Columbus Circle penthouse, because my pitch was better. Adam went on social media and not so subtly insinuated that I wear low-cut tops and tight skirts just to get what I want. Misogynistic jerk. I began proceedings to sue him for defamation. Our lawyers settled out of court. I won, of course. And ever since then, he's been vying to take me down one client at a time.

And with this latest stunt, stalking the likes of Mihir Shareeq, coincidentally crossing paths with him at a members' only gentlemen's club in the Upper East Side and casually bringing the luxury fourteen-unit new-build development he knew I was signing into conversation, well, he may have just succeeded.

"I have Shareeq's assistant on the line," Oliver's voice rings through the silence of my office.

"Thanks." I press the flashing button on my handset and wait, ignoring my ringing cell phone as it vibrates loudly on the desk with that same blocked number. I turn it over. Face down, so it doesn't keep distracting me.

"Miss Wagner?" Leilani, Shareeq's assistant, comes through the line, her voice deep and sultry.

"Is he in?" I ask briskly, wishing my racing heart would calm to a more manageable thrum. The sheer inconvenience of a heart attack right now would be all I need.

"I'm sorry, Miss Wagner, he's out of the office all morning."

"Well do you know where he is? It is *vital* that I speak with him." I stand, waving for Oliver through the glass wall to stop him on his way out. He notices my flailing hand and pauses, his brow furrowed as he waits.

"He's meeting with Mr. Delaney for brunch at Illusions. I don't know the address but I believe it is in SoHo."

"It's okay. I know where it is. Thank you so much," I say, signaling to Oliver to forget about fetching me my coffee and to get me a car and a driver immediately before quickly ending the call.

My cell rings again as I collect my things, but I shove it and everything else into my purse. I hurry to the closet and pull out the blazer I keep in there for emergency situations such as this. After I shrug it on, it does little to conceal the coffee stain, but it's all I have right now.

"Hawkins wants to see you in his office," Oliver says as he opens the door for me, his hands held up in the air in surrender.

"Now?" I gape at him from the threshold.

He nods, and I can tell by the way he's biting down on his bottom lip that this can't be good. Mr. Hawkins knows. I just know it. I've just lost the biggest deal of my career. It'd be stupid to think it would be anything *but* bad. I release an almighty sigh and begin toward the glass stairs that connect the sales floor to the executive level.

"Quinn, I heard about the Prince Street deal . . ." someone says from deep within the bowels of the sales floor.

"It's nothing," I yell back over my shoulder, waving a nonchalant hand in the air, my quavering voice doing little to help dispel the obvious doubts of my colleagues. But I ignore everyone and everything, my jaw clenching hard as I proceed up the stairs and into the sleek lobby of the executive floor.

Mr. Hawkins' glamorous executive assistant glances up from her computer, and I almost expect her to stop me, to ask me what I'm doing, but she doesn't. In fact, all she offers is a look of condolence complemented by a pitiful smile as I continue past her. God, even she knows I'm about to have my ass handed to me. My clammy hands ball into trembling fists at my sides as I try to count to ten. I stop momentarily at the imposing double doors, knocking just once.

"Enter!" a booming voice from the other side demands, and I'm literally quaking in my pumps as I reluctantly step inside.

Edward Hawkins is an institution. A force to be reckoned with. At seventy-eight years old and standing at only five-feet-two-inches, with thick wireframe glasses and sheet-white hair, he's the most unexpectedly intimidating person I've ever come across in this cut-throat industry, and that's saying a lot in a city like New York. He meets my eyes with a threatening glower, turning in his chair and reclining ever so slightly, his stubby fingers steepled beneath his white-bearded chin. But I remain defiant, my chin raised slightly higher in a show of confidence I sure as hell don't feel on the inside.

"Sit."

Now, let me get one thing straight. I'm definitely not a "yes, sir; no, sir" kind of gal. I'm a self-respecting, confident woman who just so happened to grow up in a house full of men and thus can take care of myself in almost any and every situation. But when Edward Hawkins fixes you with that all-penetrating and intimidating look in his steely eyes, and tells you to sit, then you better damn well sit your ass down.

"What is this I'm hearing about Prince Street?" he asks in his native New Yorker-accent.

I clear my throat, forcing a smile as I take a tentative seat in the chair across from his sprawling mahogany desk. "It's nothing more than a misunderstanding, sir."

My cell rings again from deep inside my purse and I do all I can to pretend as if I don't even notice it. But I do notice it. So does he. He glances at my purse, his bushy brows drawing together. I blink once, my face impassive as the loud vibration continues through the heavy silence.

"You told me on Friday night that the deal was done," he says finally, regarding me with a hard look over the top of his spectacles. "So, were you lying then or are you lying *now*?"

I swallow hard, carefully considering my words. He's got me there. When he called me, late Friday evening, I was so happy to be able to give him the good news, and of course I told him the deal was done. Because, as far as I was concerned, the deal was done. Shareeq and I shook hands, and where I come from that means something; all a man has is his word and his handshake. Clearly, I was wrong.

"I'm on my way to meet with Shareeq right now to get everything sorted."

Mr. Hawkins narrows one of his eyes, looking at me long and hard. "Do I need to remind you that this is a one-hundred-million-dollar deal?"

"No, sir." I shake my head.

He quirks a dubious brow. "And do I need to remind you what *losing* a deal like this can do to a person's career?"

I shake my head again, vehemently this time, not trusting myself to speak.

With one last lingering look of disappointment, he dismisses me without so much as another word, turning back to his computer, and I take that as my cue to leave, jumping up quickly and hurrying to the door.

"Wagner?"

I stop, my hand on the door handle, and I glance over my shoulder to find him still staring at his illuminated monitor. "Y-yes, sir?"

"Don't bother coming back to the office without that signed listing contract." He flashes me a hard yet fleeting once-over. "Do I make myself clear?"

With one swift nod I slip out of the office as seamlessly as I can, fully aware of that same relentless vibration coming from the depths of my purse yet again. I hurry across the shiny floor, cursing out loud when I make it out into the silent foyer, and I frantically press that elevator call button over and over again, as if my life depends on it.

*

Illusions is a pretentious bistro in the thick of SoHo, and with the morning traffic against me, it takes more than thirty-five minutes to get here. It's quicker on the damn subway. By the time my town car pulls up to the curb out front, I'm a clammy, breathless mess as I cut across the sidewalk, bursting into the restaurant with such gusto, all heads turn to see what the commotion is about.

"Can I help you, miss?" The hostess glances up from her lectern, eyeing me cautiously.

I ignore her, scanning the dining room until I find a familiar head of perfectly highlighted hair, Mihir Shareeq's face falling in stark shock when he catches sight of me, causing Adam Delaney to turn and do an almost hilarious double take.

"You!" I yell, pointing a finger at Adam from across the room, because now is not the time for manners. "Outside. *Now*!" I storm back out to the bustling downtown sidewalk, taking my first real breath in what feels like forever.

"Quinn?"

I turn, finding Adam stepping out of the restaurant, buttoning his blazer, his brow raised in piqued interest as he looks me up and down. He pinches his bottom lip between his thumb and forefinger in an attempt to hide his growing smirk, and my anger increases exponentially.

"Don't give me that look, *Delaney*. You know full well what I'm doing here," I hiss between gritted teeth, stepping right up against him.

He barely bothers to conceal his smugness, leveling me with a single look. And I swear, it takes every last ounce of self-control I have left in me not to clock him with my surprisingly strong left hook. "What the *hell* are you playing at?"

He scoffs, innocently holding his arms out at his sides. "Hey, babe, it's just *business*." He glances up toward the sky, scratching his chin in mock-consideration. "Isn't that what you told me when you *stole* Columbus Circle?"

"First of all, *don't* call me babe!" I warn him. "Secondly, I didn't *steal* anything." I poke him in his chest. "I won that listing fair and square. I can't help it if you can't pitch to save your damn life."

He rolls his eyes indulgently before grinning down at me with that condescending smile I just want to slap right off his pretty-boy face. "Look, why don't you just come inside, we'll chat with Shareeq and maybe we can do a co-listing?"

I fold my arms over my chest, glowering at him.

"I don't know why you don't take me up on my offer to partner up. The two of us together could *kill* it in this city. Number-one agent—" He points to himself, pausing as he looks to me. "And what? Number . . . twelve?"

"Eight!" I seethe. "And I wouldn't partner up with you if my life depended on it."

He scoffs, quirking a brow. "That's not what you were saying a few months ago when you were sleeping in my bed."

I swallow back a string of profanities.

Yes. Call me a masochist, but Adam and I dated. I'm a sucker for punishment. I refer to our two-month tryst as an unfortunate lapse in judgment, a moment of insanity, something I've wished I could take back every day since.

"I swear to God, Adam—" My hand balls into a fist, but before I can do anything, my phone rings yet again, only this time I choose to answer it in the hope it will stop me from killing this impossible asshole in broad daylight where there are far too many witnesses.

"What?" I snap abruptly as I hit the answer-call button.

"Quinn?"

My brows knit together in confusion at the sound of the familiar voice coming through from the other end of the line, crackly and muffled, nearly inaudible. I turn away from Adam, shoving a finger into my other ear in the hope of hearing over the excessive sound of New York City going about its usual business around me. "Hello?"

"Quinn, it's me, Cash."

I can't help but balk. I don't even remember the last time my big brother called me. "Cash? W-what's—"

"You need to come home, Quinny," Cash says with a heavy sigh of despondency.

"What? Cash! What are you talking about?" I shake my head in exasperation, glancing furtively over my shoulder to find Adam watching on like the nosy prick he is. He probably thinks I'm speaking to another client he can steal from me. I get back to my brother's confusing, cryptic phone call. "What is it? What's wrong, Cash?"

"Quinn, it's Dad," Cash's deep voice continues. "H-he's dead."

Dear Reader,

We hope you enjoyed reading this book. If you did, we'd be so appreciative if you left a review. It really helps us and the author to bring more books like this to you.

Here at HQ Digital we are dedicated to publishing fiction that will keep you turning the pages into the early hours. Don't want to miss a thing? To find out more about our books, promotions, discover exclusive content and enter competitions you can keep in touch in the following ways:

JOIN OUR COMMUNITY:

Sign up to our new email newsletter:
http://smarturl.it/SignUpHQ

Read our new blog www.hqstories.co.uk

🐦 https://twitter.com/HQStories

f www.facebook.com/HQStories

BUDDING WRITER?

We're also looking for authors to join the HQ Digital family!
Find out more here:

https://www.hqstories.co.uk/want-to-write-for-us/

Thanks for reading, from the HQ Digital team

If you enjoyed *The Long Way Home*, then why not try another sweeping romance from HQ Digital?